The Kennedy Boys

Keeping Kyler

The Third Novel

SIOBHAN DAVIS

www.siobhandavis.com

Printed by Createspace, an Amazon.com Company
Paperback edition © June 2017

ISBN-13: 978-1546748137
ISBN-10: 154674813x

Editor: Kelly Hartigan (XterraWeb) editing.xterraweb.com
Cover design by Fiona Jayde www.fionajaydemedia.com
Image © istockphoto.com
Formatting by The Deliberate Page www.deliberatepage.com

The Kennedy Boys

Kaden
The Mastermind

Keven
The Hacker

Kyler
The Thrill Seeker

Kalvin
The Player

Keanu
The Poser

Kent
The Delinquent

Keaton
The Joker

A Glossary of Irish words, phrases, and meanings can be found at the back of this book.

Chapter One

Faye

James and Alex are screaming at one another as I ascend the stairs toward her bedroom with a heavy heart. What I'm here to tell them is only going to heighten emotions further. The door is ajar, and I push it the rest of the way open. I know things have sunk to a new low when they don't even attempt to stop arguing for my sake.

"Stop!" I yell, projecting myself in between them. James is glaring at his wife with unrestrained hatred.

I understand it.

I would be furious, too, if my spouse had lied to me for years and I'd only just discovered the son I love with all my heart is not my biological child. Alex's tear-stained face showcases her distress, but she's not blameless.

She knew what she was doing when she deliberately lied to her husband.

I can empathize, to a point. She predicted James would make a far better father for Kyler, and she lied to give her child the best possible start in life. She was thinking selflessly on the one hand but so selfishly on the other.

She didn't properly consider James in all this.

How devastating it would be for him to discover she'd deceived him for years. Now, he's questioning everything, and I don't think their marriage can survive this.

"Ky overheard you. He knows," I admit bluntly, because there's no way to sugarcoat something like this. "And he's gone. He left me this." I thrust the crumpled note at Alex.

With trembling hands, she smooths it out and starts reading. She whimpers, and more tears leak out of her eyes. "Oh, no!"

"Let me see that." James snatches the letter from her hands, frowning as he reads. A muscle pops in and out of his jaw. "Do you see what you've done?!" He crushes the letter in his fist, shaking it at his wife. "You have driven him away. *You* did this." A ferocious glint shines in his eyes. "If he feels anything like I do, then he's in the worst pain imaginable. I hope you're ashamed of yourself, Alexandra. You certainly should be." His chest rises and a strangled sound travels up his throat. "I will never forgive you for this, and there is no coming back from it. We. Are. Done."

She nods in sad resignation. "I understand, but that's not important right now. Finding our son is."

James massages his temples before turning grief-stricken eyes on me. "Do you have any ideas where he might go?"

I've spoken to Kal about this already. The latest sordid family secret has knocked him for six, and he was in a bit of a daze when we talked, but he agrees with me. While I know Ky likes going to the lake to think, he won't go there now. It's too obvious. He wants to be left alone, and I doubt if he even knows where he's headed. "I honestly don't know. But, at some point, he's going to want to talk to his older brothers about his, um, bio dad, so I'd start by contacting Kaden and Keven."

I pull my phone out of the back pocket of my jeans and check it for the umpteenth time. Ky still hasn't responded to the multitude of messages I've sent. Sighing, I put my phone away again. I know he's hurting, but I can't believe he left without talking to me.

I thought we'd moved beyond that.

And if anyone understands what he's going through, it's me. I've only just discovered that I have a different dad, too.

Ky held me in his arms while I read my mum's letter. Comforted me as I struggled to come to terms with every disturbing revelation, but he hasn't afforded me the same opportunity, and one part of me is seething that he's shutting me out like this. Throwing the "I'm not worthy" card at me.

As if.

I hate the thought of him dealing with all this by himself which is why I'm determined to find him. To support him as he's supported me. James is lifting the phone to his ear when I start backtracking. "I'm going to see if Brad has any suggestions." I walk toward the door.

James bobs his head, while Alex sits on the chaise longue with her head in her hands. "Let me know what he says."

I run down the stairs and all the way to Kal's room. I don't bother announcing my presence before I barge inside.

"Whatever happened to your insistence on knocking?" Kal says, glancing over his shoulder at me as he stuffs some garments into a large, black duffel bag. "Could've been naked in here."

"I'm sure I'd have survived the assault on my eyes." I flick my gaze to Brad, lounging against the wall in the corner. "You ready?"

"Yeah." He tightens his grip on the bag slung over his left shoulder. "I still think this is pointless, though."

"Well, stay behind then," I snap, retrieving my bag from the side of Kal's bed where I stashed it a few minutes ago. "No one is forcing you to come look with us."

"I want to help, but driving around the streets in the dark looking for him is a lot like searching for a needle in a haystack."

I dump my bag on the ground at my feet. Planting my hands on my hips, I glare at him. "If you've got a better idea, I'm all ears. And let's not forget who let him leave." That's a low blow and I know it, but I'm too wound up and worried to care.

Brad stalks toward me, anger reflected in his eyes. "And how the fuck was I supposed to stop him?" His boot nudges the tip of my shoe.

"You could've come and told us straightaway. Given us a chance to stop him!"

"Why, Faye? Why would you try and stop him when you know as well as I do what this type of revelation is doing to him?"

"And that's exactly why he shouldn't be alone right now!" I yell.

Brad shakes his head. "This is what he does, Faye. He retreats into his shell and hides away to lick his wounds. This is no different. You've got to let him fix this shit on his own."

"No." My voice booms around the room. "He's been left to deal with too much on his own in the past. It's up to the people who love him to show him there's a different way. *I love him*, and I'm going to be there for him. I'm going to put my arms around him and hold him while he's processing everything, and when he's ready to talk I'll be right beside him prepared to listen."

Kal rests his chin on my shoulder. "And that is why you are so perfect for him."

Brad's face has fallen, and he looks away. "Fine," he says a couple of seconds later in a quiet voice. "Let's split up and see if we can locate him. He hasn't had too much of a head start."

"Did you speak to Keven?" I twist around to face Kal. My eldest cousins had only left a couple of hours ago to return to Harvard.

"Yes, but it won't help. It looks like Ky's ditched his cell."

"Aw, dammit!" I was hoping Keven could use the tracking device on his phone to pinpoint his exact location. The only other option we have right now is to drive around in the hope that we might find him somewhere. He can't have gone too far this time of night, and my best guess is that he's found a hotel to crash in. "Did he contact him or Kaden?"

"Nope." Kal effortlessly lifts my bag as well as his own. "But Keven said he'd call us the second he does."

"Okay. Let's do this." I stride toward the door with the boys trailing behind me. We tiptoe along the corridor, trying to minimize noise so we can sneak past the mezzanine stairs to the kitchen and out to the garage. I doubt Alex and James would approve of our plan, and I don't intend to let anyone stand in our way. The longer Ky is out there alone, the less likely we are to find him. Time is of the essence.

We are just creeping across the lobby when James's deep voice bellows out. "And where do you think you're going?"

I bite out a curse as I slowly turn around, prepared to put up the mother of all fights. "We're going out to look for him, and don't try to stop us because there's nothing you can say that'll keep us here."

"I know where he is."

My mouth is already open in protest before his words register in my brain. "Wait. What? What do you know? Tell me." I race up the stairs, meeting him on the small landing outside his study.

James looks at Kalvin and then back at me. His mouth pulls into a grim line. "You told him?"

"I had to. I needed his help." I look my uncle square in the eye, refusing to apologize for something I don't regret.

"I specifically asked you not to tell anyone. I'm not happy about this, Faye."

"Dad," Kal pipes up from the foot of the stairs. His tone is uncharacteristically soft. "You can't expect to keep something like this quiet. We have a right to know—this impacts everyone."

James exhales, and raw emotion is etched across his face. He's hurting too badly to even attempt to disguise it. "I know that, son, but I was hoping to speak to Kyler first."

Kal comes up the stairs, stopping alongside me. His hand moves to my lower back. "He'll be okay, Dad. He's strong, and he's not stupid. It's obviously a massive shock. He'll come back."

James gulps, and his tormented expression doesn't waver. "I've just spoken with Kaden. He's in Harvard with them."

My eyes narrow suspiciously as I turn around and eyeball Kal. One of my cousins is lying but I'm not sure which one. Kal's eyes dart wide in genuine surprise, and I have my answer. "I'm going over there." I have only taken one step when James tugs on my elbow.

"Not tonight, sweetheart."

"I need to see him."

He kisses the top of my head. "It's late. You can see him in the morning. I think he needs to talk to his brothers."

I know I'm being irrational, that it's completely natural for Ky to want to speak to Kaden and Keven, but I can't help feeling dejected because he hasn't sought to confide in me. *Is that why Keven lied to Kal just now? Because Ky asked him to?* "Okay," I answer meekly, shucking out of his hold. "I'm going to head to bed."

I take my bag from Kal and walk toward my bedroom. "Are you okay?" Brad asks, as my fingers curl around the door handle.

"I'm fine." I give him my best effort of a smile. "Just worried."

He scrubs a hand over his jaw. "I know. Me, too. Try to get some sleep and I'll drive you over there first thing."

"Thanks." I open the door to my room and throw my bag on the floor. "Goodnight, Brad." Looking over his shoulder, I pin Kal with a knowing look. He waits for Brad to enter his own room before stepping into mine. I quietly close the door. "This is totally fishy."

"Agreed." He deposits his duffel on the floor by his sneakers. "Either Keven lied to me or Kaden lied to Dad."

"My money's on it being both of them." It's the only scenario that makes sense. Ky doesn't want his parents knowing where he is so why would Kaden say he was there if he really *was* there? But if I know Ky at all, he would've called his brothers, which means that Keven lied to us too.

"Mine too. They'd never take our parents side over Ky's. Especially not now. I still can't believe it." He shakes his head. "And I can't help wondering ..."

He doesn't need to continue that sentence for me to understand. "If it helps, I fully believe James is your dad. There are subtle differences in your looks and it's one of the ways in which I figured this out. You and the triplets have lighter hair and darker eyes and I believe your mum when she told me about Ky."

"It's difficult to take her at her word when she's told so many lies."

"I get that. James said he was going to organize tests for all of you so you'll know conclusively." I step toward him, patting his arm. "But I wouldn't lose sleep over it. I'm pretty confident he's your dad."

"Easier said than done." He locks his hands behind his head. "What're we going to do about Ky?"

I straighten my spine. "We're not waiting until morning. If we go to Harvard and confront Kaden and Keven *now*, we'll know if they're lying. And, if they *are*, we can make them tell us why."

"Are we bringing Brad?"

"Nope. I think he made his feelings perfectly clear. Let's do this on our own." Grabbing my bag—we may be heading out on a road trip after all—I move toward my window. "Let's sneak out this way."

"A woman after my own heart." Kal swaggers toward the window with a smirk.

Rolling my eyes, I toss my bag out first. Once we are both outside, we creep along the side of the house, ducking down under the bedrooms to avoid detection, and enter the garage from the front of the property. Kal stows our bags in the boot, and I slip in the passenger seat while he gets behind the wheel. His fingers caress the steering wheel as he quietly starts the engine up. "It feels so good to be able to come and go as I please," he murmurs, more to himself than me. "I was going insane cooped up inside."

Kal had been on house arrest in the run up to his trial, and I know the lack of freedom killed him. "I'll bet. I'm just glad it's all behind you now."

He eases the SUV slowly and quietly out of the garage. "Yeah, but I still miss her. Has she been in contact with you?"

"No." Although we had promised to keep in touch, I haven't heard a word from Lana since our conversation outside the courtroom.

"I can't believe I'm never going to see her again. It feels like I've lost a part of myself."

I twist around in my seat. "That's understandable. She's been a part of your life since you were a kid." I stare out the window, angling my head so I can study the smattering of twinkling stars in the nighttime sky. "If she's your other half, your paths will cross again."

He takes his eyes off the road for a split second. We've just reached the end of the driveway. "You believe in all that superstitious nonsense?"

"I believe in true love. The kind of soul-deep love that can only be experienced when two people meet who are destined to be together." A small frown creases my brow. "Or I used to. Now I'm not so sure what I believe in."

The gates slowly part. "Because of my brother?" Kal inquires, edging the car forward.

I shake my head. "Because of my mum and dad." Based on what I read in my mum's letter, my bio dad was her one true love. But then she met my dad, the one who raised me, the only dad I've ever known, and they shared a different kind of love. A love built from friendship, on the foundation of honesty, and they were a real partnership. They adored each other, and me, so now I'm thinking my dad-*dad*, was her one true love. Not Adam. Not the guy she created me with. Which debunks every theory I've ever had about love.

Kal glides the car out of the drive, turning left, and I gawp at the man staring back at me through the lowered window of the silver car parked outside our house. "Stop!" I beseech Kal. "Pull over a sec."

I have the door open before Kal has even brought the car to a complete stop. I fly across the road, slamming to a halt in front of his car. His startled expression no doubt matches my own. I've asked my uncle about him on several occasions, but he always gives me the brush-off. And now Mark's here. Right on my doorstep. "Are you okay?" I ask as my eyes roam over him. I detect no injuries of any kind. No permanent markers from his fight with David.

"I'm fine, Faye." His voice wobbles a little. "And I think that's my line. Are *you* okay?"

I nod. "I'm good. All healed." On the outside at least. "Thanks to you."

"Thank God." He smiles up at me, a relieved, warm, genuine smile that touches his eyes.

Kal places his hand on my lower back the second he reaches my side. My gaze bounces from him to Mark. "Mark, this is my cousin Kalvin. Kal, this is the man who saved me the night of the attack."

"What are you doing here?" he asks in a clipped, suspicious tone of voice.

"Kal!" I hiss, my cheeks flushing with embarrassment. "You're being rude."

His eyes blink excessively as he stares at me in bewilderment. "He's parked outside our house like a creeper and *I'm* being rude?"

Okay, he's got a point, but still. "He. Saved. Me."

"And I'm very grateful to you for that," Kal says, focusing his attention on Mark who has since climbed out of his car. "But it doesn't explain what you're doing outside our house in the pitch dark."

"Nor why you two are going somewhere in the dead of night," Mark throws back.

Kal and I trade glances. "Don't try to deflect," Kal replies. "Answer me or I'm calling my dad." He takes his phone out, his finger hovering over the keypad.

Mark rubs the side of his face, looking conflicted.

"Mark?" My eyes pin him in place, asking an unspoken question.

His eyes shutter momentarily. He takes a step toward me, but Kal holds up a hand to halt him. "Stay right there, buddy."

"I didn't want to do it like this. I wasn't expecting you to come out and see me. I ..." He trails off, looking away.

"He's a freak," Kal mouths at me, and I scowl, shaking my head, denying it. No one who wades in to help a stranger fight off an attacker is a freak.

A freaking saint more like.

Mark lifts his head up, and I'm shocked to see the gleam of unshed tears in his eyes. There is something so familiar about the look that it raises all the tiny hairs on the back of my neck. I lean in, studying his face, examining his wide blue eyes as if I'm properly seeing them for the first time. He runs a shaky hand through his thick, dark hair, and all the puzzle pieces slot into place. A manic fluttery feeling starts building in my chest, and I sway on my feet a little.

"My name isn't Mark," he admits, not taking his eyes off my face. "It's—"

"Adam!" I blurt out, mentally kicking myself for not figuring it out sooner.

His eyes fill with tears, and I grab a handful of Kal's shirt, clinging to him for dear life.

"Yes," he says, nodding as he takes a step closer. "I'm Adam. I'm your father."

Chapter Two

Faye

Blood thrums through my veins as I stare at Mark—Adam.

My dad.

My chest inflates and deflates in perfect sequence, and I can scarcely breathe over the messy lump of emotion in my throat. I can't find any words, and even if I could, I doubt I could articulate them. I can only stare, dumbfounded, at the man I thought was snooping around because he was a reporter. But he was asking for me, taking my picture, because he is my father. Kal is tugging on my arm, whispering frantically in my ear, but the words don't penetrate. I think I've gone into shock or something.

Adam's face softens as he closes the small gap between us. "Faye." His voice is full of concern. "Are you okay? Do you need to sit down?"

"I ..." I don't know what to say. What to think.

"I didn't want to just spring this on you. I'll go if you think it's best."

"No!" The word flies out of my mouth with urgency as the gate opens behind us. A wide beam of luminous light throws us into focus, and we squint as one. A car door opens and closes with a heavy thud. Then James appears in front of us, advancing in long strides with a look of thunder on his face.

"Fuckitty fuck," Kal murmurs.

"What the hell is going on here?" James roars, glaring at Adam. "You two"—he jabs his finger at Kal and me—"get in the house now. I'll deal with this."

"No." I cross my arms over my chest. "I want to speak to my ..." I peek up at Adam, and his tender gaze almost undoes me. "I want to speak to Adam," I add quietly.

James gently takes my elbow, pulling me off to the side. "Are you sure, sweetheart? You don't have to do this, or even do this now. We can arrange a proper time for you two to meet."

I hold my chin up. "I'm sure." I nod. "Could we ... I mean, would it be okay to talk in the house?"

He reels me into a hug. "Of course, sweetheart. Whatever you need."

I step out of his embrace. "Thank you." I turn to Adam. "We can talk in the house, if you like?"

"Great. Would you like to ride with me?" Adam asks.

I shuffle anxiously on my feet. "I'll go with Kal and meet you up there."

"I'm only allowing this because it's what Faye wants," James remarks, in a cold, harsh tone I've rarely heard him use. "But if you put one foot out of line, if you do anything to hurt her, I'll have you on your ass and out in the cold in a heartbeat."

"She's my daughter. The last thing I want to do is hurt her. I just want the chance to get to know her." Sincerity underlines his tone, and I assume that's why James lets it drop.

The three cars maneuver up the driveway, one after the other. Kal keeps a grip on my hand the whole way. He parks the car alongside Adam's and kills the engine. "You want me with you?"

"Yeah. That okay?" I chew on the inside of my cheek.

"Of course. I'm always here for you. You know that."

I twist in my seat, the leather squelching with the movement. "What about Ky? Maybe you should go to Harvard and find out the score."

"That can wait. I'm not leaving you, and that's what Ky would want. Besides, I doubt I'll get past Dad a second time tonight."

Alex opens the front door with a startled expression. She's dressed in pajamas and a dressing gown, and she's clutching an obligatory glass of wine in one hand. Adam frowns. "What's going on?" she asks. "James?"

"Get back in the house, Alex," he snaps. "I've got this."

"Don't tell me what to do in my own house!" she hisses.

"I guess the divorce is definitely back on," Kal mumbles unhappily.

Alex walks out, greeting Adam with an outstretched hand. "Alexandra Kennedy."

"Adam Ryan." My father shakes her hand, offering her a small smile.

"You're Faye's father." Alex gives him the once-over. "She has your smile."

My legs have turned to jelly, and I lean against Kal.

"Let's take this inside," James suggests from the open doorway, ushering us indoors.

We retreat to the main living room, and Alex goes to the kitchen to make Adam some coffee. James fixes himself a whiskey while the rest of us take seats. "Would you like one, Faye?" he asks.

"She's seventeen," Adam pipes up before I've had time to reply. "You shouldn't be offering her whiskey."

"Don't." My gaze vaults between both of them. "Let's not turn this into an argument. God knows I've had enough of them to last a lifetime lately."

Adam's disapproving frown deepens, but he doesn't say anything.

James plants a gentle hand on my shoulder. "How about a coffee then? I'll ask Alex to fix another one for you."

I clasp his hand as I smile gratefully at him. "That'd be great, thank you."

Tension is palpable in the room as he walks toward the kitchen. I fidget with my hands in my lap, sitting stiffly on the couch beside my cousin. I lift my head and eyeball Adam. "When did you find out about me?"

"Seven weeks ago." He cricks his neck from side to side. "I received a letter from your mother, completely out of the blue." His eyes soften. "I'm sorry for your loss, and I can't imagine how difficult these last few months must have been. You must miss home."

"I do, but I'm doing okay, all things considered. I like it here, and my cousins and my aunt and uncle have made me feel very much at home."

Alex appears in the room, holding two coffees. "She's like the daughter I never had," she admits, handing Adam his coffee. "And she's been such a good influence on our sons."

James perches on the edge of the sofa, by my side. "This is her home. She won't be leaving it," he growls, and I'm sensing he's been holding out on me.

Adam takes a sip of his coffee before responding. "There's no need to get ahead of ourselves, and I would never ask Faye to do anything she didn't want to do. All I'm asking is a chance to get to know the daughter I never knew I had." His voice cracks at the end, and his eyes turn glassy.

I stand up, facing James. "I'd like to speak to Adam alone. Could you give us a few minutes?"

"That's no problem, honey," Alex rushes to reassure me, cautioning James with a sharp look.

James isn't happy about this, I can tell, but he acquiesces with a nod. "Fine. I'll be in my office if you need me." He shoots one final glare at Adam before exiting behind Alex.

Kal gets up but I shake my head. "Can you stay?" My entire body is wrung tight, and I'm trembling all over. I need his presence to ground me. I only asked Alex and James to leave because it isn't fair to Adam to have such a hostile audience, and with relations between the two of them right now, I can't guarantee it won't descend into a screaming match.

"What did my mum tell you in her letter," I ask, sitting back down. I curl both hands around the coffee cup, welcoming the heat as it warms my numb fingers.

"She told me the truth about her and—"

I spit coffee all over myself and the floor. Kal jumps up, dabbing at a couple of wet patches on his jeans. He frowns in confusion. "What the hell?"

"Went down the wrong way," I lie. "Would you mind getting me a towel from my room and grab me some pajama bottoms?"

"Sure thing."

Adam waits until he leaves the room. "He doesn't know about his father and your mother," he correctly surmises.

"No, and I don't want him to know either. He's been through enough lately."

"I understand. I was following coverage of his arrest and trial." A layer of unhappiness washes over his features, but he quickly disguises it. "It must have been a stressful time for everyone."

"It was." I nibble on my lower lip. "So, what else did she say in the letter?" I deliberately refocus the conversation where I need it to go.

"She told me what happened with James"—a look of utter distaste is etched across his handsome face—"and how worried she was when she discovered she was pregnant and she'd didn't know who the father was." He sighs, smoothing a hand over his clean-shaven chin. "I understand why she didn't come to me back then, although I wish she had. I'd like to think I would've understood and found a way to help her. I most definitely wouldn't have let her deal with it by herself."

Getting up, he asks, "May I?" pointing at the space on the couch that Kal just vacated.

Butterflies lurch from my chest into my throat as I bob my head. Adam sits down beside me, angling his body so we're face to face. "I understand her reaction at the time, and I can forgive her. She was a little younger than you are now, and it was a lot to deal with on her own. But, I'm not going to lie to you, Faye, I'm struggling to accept the fact she was sleeping with her own brother the same time she was sleeping with me." His face turns a sickly green color.

"I know," I whisper, knotting my hands in my lap. "It was a shock to me, too, and it's something I'm trying very hard not to think about. If I could erase that knowledge from my brain, I would." I lift my chin, staring directly into his face. "But I can't, so what's the point in dwelling on it? It happened, and no matter what you or I or anyone else thinks, it's in the past. There isn't anything we can do about it except accept it and move on."

"That's a very mature way of looking at it." His broad smile is genuine. I shrug. It's not like I'm looking for brownie points or a gold medal or something. I just want to find a way of moving forward with my life.

"I think I need to take a leaf out of your book, but I'm not sure I can." His smile fades a little. "I want to be honest with you, Faye."

"I'd prefer that."

He nods. "Having you under James's roof makes me dreadfully uncomfortable."

My eyes spread wide. "What?" I splutter. "You don't think ..." I can't even articulate the thought.

He shrugs unapologetically. "His moral compass is clearly lacking. Surely you can't fault me for worrying about that?"

My spine stiffens. "James would never hurt me, and if I'm not concerned about that, then you shouldn't be either. Besides, it's not like you can do anything about it. *He's* my guardian, not you." My tone is deliberately harsh. If he's suggesting he plans to uproot me again, he has another thing coming. I dig my nails into my thighs as anger and frustration threaten to burst to the surface.

He opens his mouth and then promptly closes it again. A couple seconds later he speaks. "Okay. That's gone some way toward reassuring me."

A layer of tension flitters away, although I'm still on edge. I don't really know what Adam wants, and until his agenda is clear, I suppose I should remain on guard. He's still a complete stranger to me.

"What about Mum?" I ask. "How do you feel about her now?"

He ponders my question a minute. "I'm finding it difficult to accept she's known I was your father for years and she chose not to tell me. I'm very angry with her over that."

"Me, too. Although, I know she thought she was doing the best thing."

"Yeah." He sighs deeply. "I don't doubt that. Saoirse had a big heart." He scans my face. "You look so much like she did back then. You're every bit as beautiful as she was." He grins as I blush, and his hands twitch at his sides. I can tell he wants to reach out, but he's afraid of startling me. "I couldn't understand how she just disappeared for no apparent reason. I asked all her friends, but they didn't have a clue where she was or what happened. I would've found James too, but her best friend told me he didn't know where she was either. She broke my heart."

"It broke her heart too," I admit in a whisper, recalling Mum's words.

"I never got over her. It seems disrespectful to my ex-wife to admit it, and I don't mean it to come across like that, but your mum was the love of my life. The minute I met her I knew she was the one for me."

Something strange occurs to me as I listen to him speaking. "Why don't you sound Irish?"

His lips curve into another smile. "I've lived in the States since I was twenty-one. My wife is American, and I moved over here after I graduated from Trinity to work for her father's company. I rose through the ranks quite quickly and had a senior management role within a couple of years. It was thought, by the powers that be, that I would fit in better and present more professionally in front of our clients if I didn't sound so Irish. I had a personal voice coach for years. My mother hates my accent now, and I always make an extra effort to sound 'Irish' when I visit the folks back home."

I gulp. "Your ... your parents are still alive? I have grandparents?" My dad's parents—Michael's parents—both died within a year of each other when I was three. My memories of them are fleeting. And Mum's parents died in a house fire when she was a teenager, so I've never known what it's like to have grandparents.

"Yes. My parents had children at a relatively young age, and they are both only in their mid-sixties now. They are dying to meet you."

Air knocks out of my lungs. "They know about me?"

His eyes crinkle with his smile. "Yes, they do. I phoned and told them after I met you that first time. I had to see you with my own eyes. To know it was the truth before I broke the news to them."

"You didn't say anything." I wet my dry lips, thinking back to our first conversation in the diner. "Why?"

"Your mother asked me to let you make that call, and I was trying to respect her wishes, but it was so bloody hard, especially after what happened in the diner that night."

An intense shiver slivers over my body, and I shudder uncontrollably. Any thought of David's attempt on my life has the same effect on me, and I'm still getting nightmares at night.

He takes my hands in his. "I'm sorry. I shouldn't have brought that up, but I've been so worried about you since it happened. I tried to see you in the hospital, but James wouldn't let me. Then he explained that you didn't know yet, and I knew I had to bide my time. But it was damn hard, Faye." Tears well in his eyes, and I can't stop my own from falling. "I nearly lost you just as i found you. He's lucky I didn't kill him with my bare hands, but I was more concerned about getting you the help you needed, so I had to let him get away."

Tears clog my throat, and I'm struggling to hold my shit together.

"Can I hold you? Please?" he pleads. Although he's still a stranger to me, in this moment, I need to be comforted. I need someone to help chase those horrific memories away. Slowly, I inch toward him, and he carefully wraps his arms around me. I keep my hands at my sides, face pressed against his chest, with my pulse racing wildly. We stay locked in our weird embrace for a few minutes until my sniffles have subsided and the moment passes. I ease back first. "Thank you for saving me," I whisper, wiping the moisture under my eyes with the sleeve of my sweater. "I thought I was going to die."

He brushes a lock of my hair back off my face, and I'm a mass of conflicted emotions. This is all too much to take in. "I'll make sure nothing like that ever happens to you again. I don't want to come the heavy, because I know you need time to adjust to all this, but I want you in my life, Faye. We've missed so much time already. You're my daughter, and I want to be a father to you." He pauses briefly. "You're part of my family now, and the others can't wait to meet their new sister."

My breath hitches in my throat. "What?" I croak.

"You have a sister and two brothers in New York, and they are very excited to meet you."

Chapter Three

Kyler

"Here are the keys. We'll keep your bike in storage until you return. Thank you for your business, Mr. Kennedy." The clerk hands me the keys to the rental, and I thank him with a terse jerk of my head.

I'm in no mood for conversation.

With anyone.

I fling my jacket on the backseat and get behind the wheel. My cell pings again. Removing it from my pocket, I stare at the latest message from Faye. She's worried about me, and I'm an ass for not responding, but I know if I acknowledge her, it'll start a conversation I'm not ready to have.

I can't drag her into my shit.

She's dealt with so much the last few months, and she's only just come out the other side. She doesn't need this.

I don't need this. But I've got no choice. This is my new reality, and I can't un-hear what I overheard. Can't undo what's been done.

My cell rings and I hesitate a couple of seconds before answering Kaden's call. "Hey, man. You on the road yet?" he asks.

"Just got a rental." I collapse in the seat as a wave of stress-induced exhaustion waylays me.

"Heads up. I spoke with Dad and bought you some time like we agreed, but he's worried."

"He's not my dad." The statement flows from my mouth almost independently.

"I know how you're feeling. Kev and I went through the exact same stuff. This shit isn't easy to deal with, but your dad is still your dad, Ky. James *is* your dad."

I sigh. This is like déjà vu. When I spoke to him and Keven earlier, I ended up more confused than ever. Kaden approves of my plan to go visit my bio dad, but Kev is dead set against it. He thinks I'm much better off not knowing him, but Kade understands me better. He knows I'll always be wondering if I don't meet him. They both were at pains to point out that James is my dad, *our* dad, irrespective of who the sperm donor was. But my muddled brain can't make sense of it all.

The irony of the situation is that I've spent years arguing and fighting with James, but I always felt like I could count on him. Except for that one time, James has been there for me. Yet I spent years pushing him away. Picking stupid fights with him purely because he was an easy target.

And now?

Now, I wish he was my dad in every conceivable way.

Now, I wish I hadn't wasted years bickering with him.

I wish I'd appreciated him more because nothing is ever going to be the same.

He may have raised me, but it isn't his blood that flows through my veins. His DNA that has me wired in such a fucked-up way. It's almost laughable. All this explosive anger inside me has to have come from somewhere, and I couldn't figure it out before, but now, it's making much more sense. I know I'm not going to like this man I'm traveling to meet, yet I need to meet him. To see him with my own eyes even if I'm terrified of what I'll see. Terrified I'll recognize myself in him and everything that that entails. But I need to do this—to motivate myself to work harder against the dark forces inside me that would happily drag me to the gutter.

I want this man to be a monster.

I want him to be everything my mother and my brothers have said about him.

I need to see that.

I need to finally have an explanation for why I am what I am.

A reason to rise above it.

Otherwise, I fear I'll end up exactly like him.

"Ky?" Kaden's alarmed tone interrupts my thoughts. "You still there, bro?"

"Yeah." I grind down hard on my teeth.

"I wish you could've waited a week so we could come with you. I don't like the thoughts of you meeting him alone. At least Kev and I had each other."

Kade and Kev have stuff for college this week or else they would've come with me. They didn't have to specify that. It's a given. But I'm glad they're preoccupied because I need to do this alone.

"I'll be fine. Just stick with the plan. Don't tell anyone where I'm going. I skipped out during the night, and you have no clue where I went." That's what we'd agreed earlier.

Kaden sighs. "I won't. *We* won't. But it won't take much for them to figure it out. It's the logical next step."

I push the ignition button, and the engine purrs to life. "I know but it'll take a while to find him, and that'll give me all the time I need. It's why I have to take off now. If I don't, I'm afraid Mom will find some way of stopping me. She seems determined to keep us away from him."

"For good reason, Ky." Kade sighs down the phone. "Okay, but promise me you'll stop when you start to feel tired. Find some crappy motel, and get at least a few hours' sleep. You can't drive all night."

"I won't. I promise." I reverse the truck out of the space. "I'll let you know when I arrive."

"One last thing." Kaden pauses, and I put the truck in park. "You should call Faye. Or at least message her. I'm sure she's worried—don't shut her out."

"I'll think about it. Later, bro." I kill the call before he can lay any more guilt trips on me.

A couple of hours later, I'm struggling to keep my eyes open. Pulling into a sleazy roadside motel with a flashing neon sign that indicates vacancies, I park and head into the reception area to bag a room.

The lady behind the desk must be pushing fifty, at least, but that doesn't stop her ogling me like I'm her next meal. She's all skin and bone under a frayed denim mini and tight red tank top which dips into a low V-shape, showing oodles of leathered, wrinkled skin and virtually non-existent boobs. Jeesus. I almost bring up the contents of my stomach.

"You be needing any of these, darlin'?" she says, shoving a basket with a pile of condoms up under my nose. Her accent is a weird mish-mash of dialects suggesting she's moved about a lot.

I slip my wallet in the back pocket of my jeans as my lips narrow in distaste. "No thanks."

"You in need of some company, sugar?" She comes out from behind the counter, resting one bony hand on my chest.

You have got to be fucking kidding me?! I've been hit on by some cougars in my time but not by someone old enough to be my granny.

My eyes narrow and my head lowers as I send her one of my special death glares. The type that usually sends everyone running for the hills. Not this broad. She smiles—legit, smiles—and her hand moves higher up my chest. Although I want to touch her skin about as much as I want to touch a piranha, I take her wrist and remove it from my person, taking a couple steps back as I do. "Definitely not. I just want to be left alone."

"Well, ain't that a darn shame." She winks. "Can't help a gal for trying."

I'm still shaking my head as I turn the key to my room. It's pretty much what I expected. Worn furniture and drab furnishings dating back to a bygone era, but it smells fresh and it looks spotlessly clean. Bonus points for that.

The shower works, much to my amazement. I stand under the water until it turns cold and my body resembles a block of ice. When I crawl under the covers, I'm exhausted, but I still can't fall asleep. Everything Mom said to James is churning around my head, and I still can't quite believe it. It's like I'm having an out of body experience. As if everything I heard, everything I feel, isn't really happening to me. As if I'm trapped in another world with some other version of me.

"When I was in his room, by his cot, singing him to sleep every night when he was a baby, did you feel any guilt? Any remorse? Did you ever consider telling me?"

I never knew he did that. Thoughts of James singing me to sleep as a baby are doing really weird things to my insides and tears prick my eyes but I swipe them away. I'm not going to cry. Crying is for pussies.

"Kyler is such a natural at motocross. I never even stopped to think about that fact."

I laugh into the silent, ominous air, slapping an arm over my forehead. Fate sure loves to fuck with me. How Kaden and Keven believed Mom when they questioned her a few weeks ago about this very thing beggars belief. All it would've taken was being told their bio dad was a motocross champ, and I would've known instantly. I even met the dude once. When I was ten. When all that other shit had just gone down. I was so lost and frightened that day I don't even remember what he said to me.

Doug Grant.

Motocross Legend.

My biological father.

I wonder if he knew who I was. If that's why he approached me that day at the Uxbridge track. It was one of the standard annual events, and the owners always lined up a couple of pros to attend, to help draw in the big crowds. He was already past his prime but a living legend in local circles. Ordinarily, I would've been freaking out after chatting with him, but I was too scared to be awed.

I turn my face into the pillow, wanting to force those memories aside.

Not now. I can't deal with this now.

My cell pings at that exact moment, and I snatch it up like it's oxygen. Another message from Faye.

I LOVE YOU.

My heart soars. I never thought my heart would beat so strongly for a girl. That I had the capacity to *feel* so much. She couldn't know how timely her message is or how much I need to keep hearing those words. To know she understands and supports me even though I left without saying a word. I could live a thousand lifetimes and never be good enough for her.

She deserves better.

Brad is perfect for her. He isn't messed up in the head like I am, and I know he'd treat her right.

I should let her go.

That's the right thing to do, but I'm way too selfish to follow through.

I want her for myself, and I need to make myself worthy of her love.

Which is why I need to do this.

I need to confront the past in order to have a future worth sharing. I only hope I'm strong enough to do this. For me. For her.

My hand moves over the flat expanse of my stomach, rubbing back and forth, but the knots in my gut won't go away. Man, I miss her so much. Not for the first time, I wish she was here. Wish I could wrap myself around her, cocoon us away from the world, and lose myself in her and the way she makes me feel.

But I'm not *that* Goddamned selfish.

She doesn't need that kind of grief now. Not after everything.

I owe it to myself and her to get my shit together. To deal with my demons. So I can come back and offer her something concrete. Something she'll want to hold fast to forever. Because that's what I want with her.

Forever.

That thought should scare the hell out of me, but it doesn't.

It doesn't scare me at all.

"I love you too, babe," I whisper to the empty room, hoping she knows. That I've told her enough. I glance at her message again, and a soothing warmth spreads over me like a heavy blanket.

I fall asleep with the words imprinted on my heart.

Chapter Four

Faye

"Oh, God!" My breathing is ragged as I stare at Adam through the newly formed hazy mist clouding my eyes. *I have siblings?* "I didn't ... I can't ... I ..."

"I think that's enough for one night," James commands, appearing in the doorframe with a concerned expression. "You need to give Faye time to process all this."

"Sure." Adam tilts his head, peering into my eyes. "I'd really like to see you again. I have to return to New York for business, but I can come back here next weekend if you like?"

Somehow, I force my vocal cords to work. "I'd like that. I have other questions and stuff."

"Yeah, me too." He takes out his phone. "Would it be okay to swap numbers? I'd like to have a way of contacting you if I need to."

I gulp, extracting my own phone. "Sure." We input our numbers, and I walk out to the lobby with him. James has the front door open already, as if he can't wait to get rid of him.

Adam stops, turning to face me. Gently, he takes my hands. "It was so good to speak with you. If you need anything—anything at all—before we see each other again, just text me. I may not have been there for you the last seventeen years, but I'm going to do my best to make up for that." For the first time he looks unsure of himself, and I realize this is equally as nerve-racking for him. "If you want that."

I clear my throat as James opens his mouth to speak for me. I nuke his comment with one stern look, and he clamps his mouth shut. "I don't really know what I want, Adam. The man I knew as my dad only died a few months ago and I ..." I smack a hand over my mouth as more tears pool in my eyes. *Gawd. When did I become such a head case?* Adam seems nice, and if Mum loved him, I'm sure he is, but it's all so overwhelming—talk of grandparents and siblings and him wanting to be my dad. I've recently lost the only dad I've ever known, and it's awful to be contemplating replacing him. Guilt and confusion mix with grief and longing, and my head is not in a good place right now. I can't decipher any of it. It's one big jumbled mess.

"I would never try to replace him or ask you to forget who he was to you. I'm just hoping you have some room left in your heart for me." The look of longing and anguish on Adam's face sends me into a downward spiral. Tears pour down my cheeks like a waterfall, and I shatter into pieces. Kal is beside me in a heartbeat, securing me in his arms.

"This is why I asked you to wait," James says in a barely controlled voice. "It's too much too soon. She's stressed enough as it is. If you want to form a relationship with her you need to start by backing off and giving her some space."

In my head, I'm begging James to stop talking. To soften his tone. To understand how traumatic and stressful this must be for Adam too. In my head, I'm explaining it all to Adam. Pleading with him to understand that I'm not pushing him away or putting any of the blame on him. I just can't deal with this emotional whirlwind right now.

Adam reluctantly nods, and his shoulders droop in defeat. The wretched look on his face guts me, but I can't make my legs move. I want to go to him, but I'm like a statue, stiff and immovable. Instead, I cling to Kal, sobbing freely as I watch my father get in his car and drive off.

I don't recall how I got to my bedroom, let alone landed in bed, but I'm figuring Kal had something to do with it. He slides under the duvet alongside me, dressed in gym shorts and a tank top. Gently, he pulls me into his side, and surprisingly I fall into a deep sleep.

I wake with a jolt early the next morning, thoughts of Adam battling renewed concern for Ky. Yanking my jeans off the floor, I search the pockets, removing my phone as I offer up a silent prayer. My heart drops when I check my messages. Ky still hasn't responded to a single one, and I'm getting so worried. *What if he's done something stupid? Please let him be okay.*

Kal is snoring softly, his hair matted on one side, and there's a dribble of drool leaking out of his mouth. He looks so young and cute when he's asleep, so peaceful that it kills me to wake him, but I need to find Ky, and I can't wait any longer—I need to know he's okay. More than that, I need him.

I need him now more than ever.

I shake Kal gently and he barely stirs, so I shake him more vigorously. "Kalvin! Wake up!"

Turning on his side, he groans, "Ugh. Go away." He swats at me with a limp arm. "Need more sleep." I chuckle as he buries his head in the pillow. My cousin is *so* not a morning person.

"Harvard? Remember?"

He groans again. "It's too early. Go back to sleep," he slurs in a sleep-drenched voice.

I glance up at the gossamer curtains. "It's not too early, day is already breaking." I grip his shoulders firmly. "Come on. Get your lazy ass up. Ky needs us, and we need to get to campus early so we don't miss your brothers before classes start." He emits a volley of colorful expletives while hauling himself upright, rubbing his eyes. "Go shower and change and meet me in the kitchen. I'll cook breakfast."

After we've both showered and eaten and I've left a note for Brad under his door, we make our way to the garage. Kal throws our bags in the boot, and I've a mad case of déjà vu. I'm hoping we make it farther than the end of the driveway this time.

Kal is quiet the entire trip to Harvard, but I don't bug him. I wasn't messing when I said he isn't a morning person. He's definitely more of a night owl.

The contrast on campus is marked. Last time, Brad and I arrived at around the same time on a Saturday, and the place was like a ghost town. Today is the start of a new week, and it's a hive of activity. Students with heavy book bags and determined faces brush past us in a hurry. "I hope we're not too late." I quicken my pace, tugging on Kal's jacket to move him the fuck along until we're basically jogging toward my cousin's dorm.

"Slow down," he pleads, a few minutes later, bending at the waist. "I've got a stitch."

A good-looking guy with dark blond hair jogs past us, turning around to give me a brief once-over. I narrow my eyes, and he blows me a kiss. My cheeks inflame, and I quickly look away. Kal snorts, and I glare at him. "You need to do something about that, buddy," I say, deliberately ignoring what just happened. "Your lack of fitness is pathetic. I've seen geriatrics run more energetically than you." He growls at me, and I chuckle. "Man up and move it." I've no time for excuses today. Grumbling derogatory comments under his breath, he limps after me while I try to get a handle on my anxiety, which is currently ricocheting off the charts.

Kal is red in the face by the time we make it to Kaden and Keven's door, and I've pretty much chewed my nails to the bone. I rap firmly on the door, and when I don't get an immediate reply, I rap again, even louder this time. "Open up!" I yell, pounding on the door. "We're not leaving until you let us in."

The creaking of a door opening has me glancing over my shoulder. A tall girl with shocking blue eyes and a mass of red corkscrew curls steps out of the room across the way, eyeing me warily. A guy who looks like her male equivalent lounges against the doorframe with amusement in his eyes.

"Mind your own business!" I hiss at them as my cousin's door finally swings open, and I almost tumble into Kaden's arms.

He sighs, dragging a hand through his messy hair. "I don't need to ask why you're here, but I'd rather not air our business in the corridor." He shoos us into the room, deliberately eyeballing the girl across the way. "Nothing to see here, Tiff." He wiggles his fingers at her as he slams the door shut.

Keven saunters out of his bedroom, yawning. He's in his bare feet, with low-hanging pajama bottoms on and nothing else.

And, oh em gee.

Wow.

I knew Kev was hiding some rocking muscles and interesting tattoos underneath his shirt but nothing like this.

Kev is shredded. Like seriously shredded. There isn't an ounce of fat on his torso, and he has, like, an eight-pack and defined indents at the point where his hips snake into his pants. Ky is totally ripped, and completely lick-worthy, but Kev makes him look like a lazy prick.

Kev clearly works out.

A lot.

I'm suddenly very intrigued by my elusive cousin. I know next to nothing about him, only that he's an enigma wrapped up in an enigma.

I know I'm ogling him in a way that's definitely not socially acceptable, but I've never seen such a carved specimen of a man. I'm struggling to focus on anything else in the room.

"Throw a shirt on before Faye's eyes bug out of her head," Kaden drolls with a smirk, and Kal chuckles.

Planting my hands on my hips, I blush furiously as I send Kaden the evil eye. "Funny, ha, ha. Where's Ky?" I look around the room for any evidence of my boyfriend. Kaden and Keven exchange a look, and I lose whatever sliver of patience I possess. Brushing past Keven, I quickly check all the other rooms, immediately confirming our initial suspicions. "He's not here," I tell Kal. "Was he ever here?" I alternate my accusatory expression between Kaden and Keven. They share another loaded look, and I'm getting more and more pissed by the second. "Where is he?" I shriek. "I'm really worried about him, so if you know anything, you need to tell us." Kaden rubs his taut jaw, and I step forward until we're toe to toe. "Please."

"Crap." He sighs. "He won't be pleased about this."

"I don't care," Keven says, materializing alongside me. "I don't like the idea of him going there on his own. If we can't go, at least let them follow him. I know he thinks he needs to do this alone, but he needs someone with him."

"So, you do know where he is. You lied to me." Kal sulks unhappily.

Keven at least has the decency to look ashamed. "I'm sorry about that, but our loyalties were torn."

"Tell us everything you know. Right. Now," I demand.

"Bossy much, Faye?" Kaden's lips twitch, fighting a smile.

"Screw you, Kaden. I love him, and every second we're wasting is another second he's by himself dealing with all this shit. And I haven't heard a word from him despite the millions of texts and messages I've sent, and I'm totally freaking out here. So, just tell us before I lose my Goddamned mind," I shriek, worrying my lip between my teeth.

Kaden's warm hand lands on my shoulder. "I'm sorry, Faye. I didn't realize he hadn't been in touch at all. He's been keeping in contact with me. He's okay." I try, and fail, to hide my hurt. My cousins trade knowing looks.

"He's an idiot, Faye," Kal says, "but this is his way of trying to protect you. Don't read into it. He's crazy about you and just not thinking straight right now."

"I know, but I hate that he's cut me out. I hate that he's out there wrestling with this on his own. It's not right." I move my shoulders from side to side, trying to loosen the tight kink.

"He's gone to Wisconsin to find our father," Keven confirms. "Give me your cell and I'll plug in the coordinates. The house is a nightmare to find." Kal hands his phone over and Keven leaves the room with it.

"How was he when you saw him?" I examine Kaden's troubled eyes.

"Hurting. Angry. All emotions Kev and I are familiar with. We tried to talk him out of going, at least until he'd properly thought it through, but you know how impulsive and stubborn he is."

"Here," Keven says, giving the phone back to Kal. "I've added the coordinates to the GPS app, and I've also installed the cell tracker app so you can pinpoint his exact location once you get into town."

"He stopped in a motel for a few hours last night, but he's still got a good five or six hours' head start on you," Kaden says. "Hopefully you'll catch up to him before he visits the jerk."

"Is he really all that bad?" Kal asks.

Keven rubs his thumb idly over his bottom lip. "It's virtually impossible to describe him in a way that will fully prepare you. He's a foul-mouthed drunk with an addiction to cheap whores and cheap booze. His house is a cesspit, and he had nothing nice to say to us. Nothing."

"I don't think Ky has any huge expectations," Kaden adds, "but he needs to meet him. It might help."

"I spent so long thoroughly pissed at Mom and Dad, but once I met that man, it was easier for me to understand and accept their decision. I don't agree that meeting him is what's best for Ky, but he's old enough to make his own decisions," Keven admits with a troubled frown. "Ky may be furious with Mom right now, but she did us a solid keeping us away from that A-hole. He'll see that too," he adds.

"Okay, thanks. We better head." I stride purposefully toward the door.

"Will you tell Mom and Dad?" Kal asks, and I turn back around.

"Not unless we absolutely have to. We'll tell them we know where you are, that you're in contact with us, and you'll be home as soon as you can. They'll just have to accept that," Kaden confirms.

"Thanks, bro." Kal slaps him on the back.

"Mind your cousin," Kaden says, pinning him with a serious look. "And don't let her go anywhere by herself. You never know what weirdos you might meet in some of these places."

I look up at the ceiling, summoning patience I don't have. "I'm not twelve, and I know how to take care of myself. I took self-defense classes at home for years."

"If anything happens to you, we're all in the firing line. Dad would never forgive us, neither would Ky, so just stay by Kal's side. Please." He batters his forearms.

I thrust my hands in the air, annoyed over such a flippant waste of time. "Fine, fine. I promise. Happy?" I send him my best fake smile.

"Ecstatic," he drawls, and my bad mood flitters away. Kaden's got a lethal sense of humor that I enjoy.

Keven sees us to the door. "Good luck." He high-fives his brother. "You're going to need it."

Chapter Five

Kyler

I skip breakfast the next morning—no point in risking food poisoning—and get back on the road nice and early. Dawn is transforming to daylight as I speed up the motorway, blasting the stereo to the max, desperately hoping it'll drown out the thoughts in my head.

At lunchtime, I pull off into a small dirt town, find a local diner, and load up before returning to the truck.

I make good time, reaching my destination a couple hours after nightfall. Bayfield is a small quaint town in North Wisconsin, famous for being the gateway to the Apostle Islands National Lakeshore, or at least that's what the sign entering town tells me. Picturesque and charming, it's hard to imagine famed motocross legend Doug Grant living somewhere like this. The main thoroughfare consists of a variety of standard stores, eclectic retail shops, and a few bars and restaurants facing either side of a wide street. I pull my truck into a space in front of one of the restaurants and make my way inside.

I'm still staring at a full plate of food a half hour later. My appetite has vanished along with my resolve. But thoughts of turning around and running back home with my head tucked between my legs are less appealing.

"You want me to heat that up, honey?" The waitress with the strawberry-blonde hair asks, jutting her hip out to the side as she levels an inquisitive glance at me. While she's heavily made up, I doubt she's more than a couple years older than me.

"It's okay," I say, pushing the plate toward the edge of the table. "I'm done." I throw a twenty down and rise.

"You okay, honey? You look a little green in the face." She flicks her hair over her shoulder, before leaning forward to give me a flash of her full cleavage. Her eyes examine mine with open curiosity.

"I'm fine." I force a smile on my face, hoping she'll move out of my way now.

"Was there something wrong with the food?" She frowns, looking down at my untouched plate.

"Nope. Just lost my appetite." My forced smile is even less plausible this time.

"You sure, 'cause I can have a word with the chef. Get him to cook ya som—"

I rudely cut her off. "Is there something wrong with your ears? I said I'm not hungry. It's hardly a crime." My tone is purposely harsh. I'm in no mood to waste time small-talking with some hick waitress in some two-bit town. I want to go meet the sperm donor, get a few things off my chest, and then leave this Godforsaken place.

"That's some mighty big chip you got on your shoulder." She moves sideways, scowling at me as I ease out of the booth past her.

"Whatever." I shrug. Not like I'll be seeing her again anytime soon.

"Suit yourself, asshole." Her mouth pulls up in a sneer as she grabs my plate and the twenty and turns on her heel.

I *was* an asshole to her, but that's my prerogative. She's supposed to be nice to the clientele, no matter what. It's little wonder the place is empty if that's how she speaks to most of her customers.

It takes twenty minutes to get to the sperm donor's place. Kev programmed the exact location into the GPS app on my phone, and now I know why. This place is miles out of town, in the middle of nowhere. I passed the last house about ten miles back, and I can see jack-shit in the pitch dark. There are no street lamps or signs this far out of town. The roads are narrow and bumpy, and I'm grateful I had the foresight to rent a truck. I park at the end of the lane that leads to his house and try to calm my beating heart. I don't know how long I sit there, but it's at least a half hour before a small red car swings into the lane and disappears out of sight. It was too dark to see the occupant, so either it's him or he has company. Great. I wasn't planning on having a showdown with witnesses.

I pull out my cell and send a quick message to Kaden letting him know I'm here. He wishes me luck, but I know it's a futile sentiment. No amount of luck is going to make this visit any less nauseating.

I wait another hour before deciding to close the distance. If it was a visitor, I'd presume they'd be gone by now, so it's must've been him. The sperm donor. My father.

Swallowing the bitter lump in my throat, I crank the truck into gear and turn into the lane. A small, dilapidated building looms before me. The grubby whitewashed walls are in dire need of painting, and overgrown weeds cling to the sides of the house, looking like they've had free rein to reproduce for years. The two-story property has a small veranda out front that is well worn and in ill-repair. An old wooden love seat, missing a few panels, swings gently in the late-night breeze. A light is on in one of the upstairs windows and in one of the ground-level rooms. I get out of the truck on shaky legs, wiping my sweaty palms down the front of my jeans as I approach the house.

I hop up the steps, faltering in front of the door with my hand raised.

It's now or never.

Nausea swims up my throat, and the urge to hurl is riding me hard. Before I can chicken out, I rap firmly on the door.

My heart is thumping against my ribcage as the door swings open. My gaze widens for a fraction of a second before I regain control.

"Well, well. Look what the cat dragged in." The waitress from the diner lounges against the doorframe, eyeing me from head to toe. She's wearing a thin negligee with no underwear, and judging by the tangled state of her hair and her swollen lips, I'd say she's just been royally screwed.

Her sharp eyes miss nothing. "Like what you see?" She puts a hand on her hips, thrusting her chest out as she licks her lips provocatively.

"Who is it?" A gritty, slurred voice rings out from somewhere inside the house.

"Some asshole with your eyes," she yells back over her shoulder.

There's a loud scraping sound, followed by heavy footfall, and then a tall, broad-shouldered man appears behind her. Planting a meaty hand on her waist, he eyeballs me with vacant curiosity. His tan face is craggy, with deep lines, and there's at least a few day's growth of gray-tinged stubble on his chin. His dark hair is littered with generous strips of gray, and it's on the longish side, curling around his ears and his neck. Eerily familiar pale blue eyes meet mine. His gaze rakes over me slowly. Then he guffaws, throwing back his head and laughing. "Well, I'll be damned."

My spine stiffens as I glare at him.

"Was wondering when you'd make an appearance. Figured you had more gumption than those other two idiots who showed up here a few months back."

A muscle clenches in my jaw, and he laughs again.

"Care to enlighten me, Dougie?" his young fuck buddy asks.

Doug's fingers slither into the front of her nightdress, and his large hand cups one of her bare breasts. She arches into him with a whimper, and bile swims up my throat.

"Meet Kyler Kennedy, sweetheart." He pinches her nipple, grinning at me the whole time. "My son."

Chapter Six

Kyler

That out of body experience thing is happening again. Doug Grant, a.k.a. sperm donor, is sprawled in a worn leather reclining chair in his squalid living room, wearing a filthy wife-beater with his beer gut spilling over the band of his low-hanging jeans, eyeing me like it's physically paining him to look at me. He's still a good-looking dude—age notwithstanding—but he looks like a lazy motherfucker. I cannot believe my mother went out with this skeeze.

"You got a sexy fuck buddy, son?"

My ears transmit the words; I just can't believe them. This entire conversation is getting weirder by the second. "What?" I sit up straighter on a springy couch that's plainly seen better days. It's obvious from the state of the place that my father doesn't take pride in his home. Cluttered ashtrays adorn most of the hard surfaces in the room along with a myriad of unwashed plates, bowls, empty pizza boxes, and a multitude of empty beer cans. A half-full whiskey bottle rests in a convenient spot at his feet.

Bending down, he snatches the bottle up and twists the top off with his teeth. He fills up his glass. "Sure you don't want some?"

"I'm sure."

"So, you got a piece of ass?"

"I have a girlfriend," I stupidly admit. *Leave Faye out of this.* This isn't going the way I'd expected it to go at all. Based on what my brothers said, I thought he'd kick my ass to the curb straightaway. Maybe shout at me a bit. Tell me to get lost and never come back.

Not invite me in, offer me a drink, and throw one disgusting question after another at me. It's knocked me off my A-game.

Thoughts of sitting down with James and having a similar type of conversation raise a small smile to my lips. Dad would pitch a fit if he was here for this conversation. Doug misinterprets my expression. Leaning over, he slaps me on the back. "That's my boy. You got a picture?"

As if on auto pilot, I remove my cell, and pull up a picture of Faye. Without thinking, I hand it to him, and he whistles low on his breath. "She's a beauty." His eyes scrunch up as he squints closer at the screen. "Perfect tits, too."

He rubs a hand over his crotch, and I puke a little in my mouth. Snatching my cell out of his hands, I growl, gnashing my teeth at him. "She's my girlfriend and I love her. I won't have you saying shit like that about her. What's your problem?"

He raises his palms in a conciliatory gesture. "Just admiring the little lady. No need to blow a gasket. Indulge an old man his fantasies."

He winks, and the urge to hurl is stronger. I know I made the right decision to leave Faye behind. If she'd traveled with me, she would've insisted on coming here, and there's no way I want her anywhere near this sleazy asshole.

It isn't long before he unleashes his next piece of wisdom. "I hope you're not restricting yourself, son. She's a sexy piece of ass, and you should totally tap that, but, take it from me, there comes a time when the pussy well dries up. You hear what I'm saying? You need to partake in as much pussy as you can while you've still got it going on." He waves his bottle around my persona. "If I looked like you I'd be fucking as much pussy as I could get my hands on." He takes a swig from his bottle, while I make zero attempts to hide my distaste. "Letisha!" he roars, and the blonde saunters into the room a minute later. "You wanna bang my son?"

I jump up, almost choking on my disbelief. "What the fuck? I never said that!"

Letisha strolls toward me, brazenly cupping my junk. I quickly remove her hand and step back to put some distance between us. "I'll fuck ya.

Always wanted to do a daddy and son." She licks her lips, looking over her shoulder at Doug. "What about a three-way?"

His eyes light up as I stumble back. "You have got to be the most fucked-up people I've ever met in my life, and believe me when I say I know some messed-up individuals. But, this is sick." I pin angry eyes on Doug. "You're my dad. Doesn't that mean anything to you?" I don't know why I'm going there. This wasn't what I came here to say, but the words just spew out of my mouth unfiltered.

"That's merely a technicality." He swigs directly from the bottle while his eyes drill into mine.

"Thank fuck." I glare at him, wondering why I'm wasting any more time on this douche.

He chuckles. "I like you." He points the bottle at me. "You've got more spunk than your brothers." Reaching out, he yanks Letisha down onto his lap, smashing his lips against hers as his free hand squeezes her ass.

I stand up. To hell with this shit show. I'm outta here. I've only taken two steps when he calls out. "Hold up, son. Letisha here's leaving so we can have a proper talk. Man to man."

"I am?" I can hear the pout in Letisha's voice as I turn around.

"Call over after your shift tomorrow, sexy, and we'll go another few rounds."

She protests a bit, and he gets up, pushing her out into the corridor. "Stay put," he mouths, walking past me and out of the room.

I rest my head against the wall wondering what the hell I'm doing. I should cut my losses and run. Something sticky adheres to my forehead, and I jerk back, rubbing my brow with the back of my hand. Ugh. Who knows what kind of icky shit is crawling the walls. This place looks disease-ridden and like it hasn't been cleaned in decades.

Doug reappears about ten minutes later, just as I've decided to abscond. Chuckling, he plops down into the reclining chair. "That woman—"

"Is way too young for you," I supply.

"She doesn't discriminate when it comes to cock, and she likes a man with a bit of experience under his belt. It's one of the reasons I like her."

"Can we cut the crap?" I drag a hand through my hair, vastly losing whatever semblance of patience I had. "I didn't come here to listen to you bragging about banging chicks."

He eyes me warily, taking another gulp from the bottle. "What did you come here for?"

Good fucking question. I can't actually remember any of the reasons why I thought it was a good idea to come here.

"I can't see you with my mom. I just don't get it." I shake my head.

He places the bottle down on the ground and pulls the chair into an upright position. "How is *Alexandra* these days?" I hate the way her name rolls off his tongue. I can't decide if it's respect or derision.

"She's good." If you ignore the drinking issue, the fact that she can't tell the truth for shit, and her impending divorce.

"Your mother is a fine lady. A mighty fine lady. Great rack, and a fantastic lay, too. She definitely knows how to please a man."

My insides tie into knots. He has no filter. Zero. Zilch. If he makes one more crude comment about Mom, I'll punch him so hard he'll be eating his teeth for a week.

"She was always too good for me, but she wanted to stick it to her daddy. He was a stuck-up cunt." He leans forward, resting his elbows on his knees. "There was a time when I thought I could change for her." He stares off into space. "She'd just had the first baby, and things were going well for me on the circuit. I tried to clean up my act. Gave up the whoring and the drinking. Looked forward to coming home to her bed."

"But?"

"Her daddy offered me money to stay away. I told him to fuck off at first, but when he came back a second time, I agreed. Because I knew I couldn't do it long term. I loved your mom, as much as I'm capable of loving any woman, but I was never meant to be a family man. I'm just not made that way." He pins me with an introspective lens, and I know what he's thinking. That I'm just like him. "You're not like me," he says, and I fail to hide my surprise.

"I know I'm not," I lie, and he smirks.

"You love your girl, and you're protective as hell. Good for you." He rubs a hand over his protruding belly. "But I see your demons. Bet you got some dark shit in your head, right?" I plaster my impassive face on. No way I'm giving him anything to go on. "Takes one to know one, and I bet I know where it began too."

An icy chill creeps up my spine. "Quit that shit!" I spring up. "Don't pretend like you know me. You don't know me, and you never will."

"I didn't know she'd had a third child by me. Alexandra never told me. Did you know that?"

I'm torn between wanting to leave and wanting to stay. The latter wins out. I drop back down onto the flea-infested couch, shaking my head.

"That day at the Uxbridge track, I took one look at you and I suspected you were mine. Like looking in a fucking mirror, it was. Took all of two seconds to confirm you were a Kennedy, and then I knew for sure." He lights up a cigarette. "I could see how scared you were. Boy, you were quaking in your boots."

My hands clench into fists at my side, the skin blanching with the effort. "I didn't come here to talk about that."

"Didn't you?"

I rest my head in my hands. "I don't know why I came here." I spout the honest truth.

"I'd heard the rumors doing the rounds of the motocross circuit, and I suspected they were true, but that day I knew. I knew only one thing could instill fear in a child like that."

My head jerks up. "Shut. Up."

He ignores me. "And when he stepped in the room and he looked at you? Hell no."

I jump up, lunging at him. "I said. Shut. Up," I roar. My hands fist in his shirt. "Shut. Up. Shut. Up. Shut the fuck up."

He shoves me off him, and I lose my balance, falling to the floor.

He stands up, hovering over me. "You asked me earlier if I cared that I was your dad. God's honest truth is I barely think about any of my kids. Told ya—not cut from that cloth. But that day at the track? That day I cared." He points his finger in my face. "I did you a solid, kid. I took care of that problem. Beat that perv to a bloody pulp and scared him enough that he'd leave you alone. Then I told the owners and made sure they did something about it." He straightens up, and his jaw tenses. "That's the extent of my fatherly duties. I'm absolved." Roughly grabbing my arm, he hauls me up. "Now get the fuck out of my house, and don't ever come here again."

He manhandles me toward the front door, and I manage to extract myself from his grip. "Fuck you." I fix my shirt, slanting him with a hateful look.

"Maybe you are more like me than I realized. You poor bastard."

He moves to close the door in my face and I see red. All the pent-up rage and anger from the last twenty-four hours—hella, the last seven years—bolts to the surface. I can't see or hear or think over the fury surging through my veins. My hand thrusts out before I consciously react. The sound of crunching bone is like music to my ears. The sight of that man, stumbling backward onto the ground, cradling his swollen jaw and cursing like a sailor is the most unbelievably rewarding sight ever.

I'm still pumped full of anger, and it's tempting to go another few rounds, but I'm terrified that once I start I won't stop. I pound my fist into the wall instead, a good couple of times, relishing the stinging pain.

While he's struggling to his feet, I turn to leave. I flip him the bird with a mad grin on my face. That was enormously satisfying, and it's made the trip totally worthwhile. I glance briefly over my shoulder, watching him watching me, taking my last look at his face.

I won't ever be back here.

Mom was right. My brothers were right. No good would come from forming a relationship with that piece of shit.

I open the truck door with the sound of his cursing and yelling still reverberating in my ears. I thrust the truck into gear with a loud roar and get the fuck out of there.

My heart is still beating so fast and blood is thrumming in my ears when I pull up in front of one of the bars back in town about a half hour later. Strobe lights and pumping music assault my senses as I step out of the truck. Adrenaline courses through my system, and I'm a bundle of restless energy. I hold out my hand, laughing manically as it shakes uncontrollably, matching how I feel on the inside. I desperately need something to take the edge off. I yank the door open, almost ripping it from the hinges, and walk into the tavern.

The dive is hopping as I step inside. The room is large and completely open like a giant barnyard with scuffed wooden boards, sawdust on the floor, plain furnishings, and a long counter off to the right-hand side. A set of double doors leads to what I assume are the restrooms. The main space consists of rows of small tables and chairs with a large open area for dancing at the top positioned in front of a small raised dais. A DJ is currently spinning the tunes, and I can barely hear over the thumping music. A lively crowd is dancing energetically, occupying most of the floor space. Rocking crowd for a Monday night, I think.

I shunt onto one of the empty stools at the bar and nod at the pretty bartender. She saunters toward me with a glint in her eye. "What can I get you, handsome?"

"Whiskey on the rocks." I hand her my fake ID and a twenty.

"Coming right up."

My fingers drum off the counter, and I notice my torn, bloody fist for the first time, wincing at the sudden throbbing pain.

She places the drink and my change in front of me. "Keep it." I slide the cash in her direction.

"Thanks." She makes a deliberate show of tucking the cash into her bra, flashing a generous amount of cleavage. "You want something for that hand?"

"Nope." I avoid looking at her, draining my drink in one go. "But I'll have another one of those."

She eyes me curiously but says nothing, stepping away from the bar. Two minutes later, she's back with an icepack and another whiskey. She places the drink in front of me and presses the ice to my hand without invitation. I wince, and the corners of her mouth turn up. She leans over the counter, giving me another eyeful of her rack. "Do I even want to know how you got this?"

"None of your business." I take a healthy glug of whiskey. "And I've got a girlfriend I'm madly in love with, so if you're expecting something in return, you can forget it."

"Well, that's a shame. It's not often we get visitors around these parts, least of all one that looks like you do. Although ..." She taps a slender finger off her lips. "We had a couple of guys in here a few months back that looked a lot like you. You wouldn't happen to be related to them, would you?"

I shrug, wanting to kill this convo dead. I only came in here to drink myself into oblivion, not to make friends with the locals or hook up with any girls. I finish the dregs of my drink just as she slides another one over the counter to me. "Have you checked into the hotel yet? I don't think you're going to be up for traveling any place tonight." Dammit if she doesn't have a point. I shake my head. She pulls out her cell and punches a few buttons before pressing it to her ear. "Hey, Luce. I've got a customer here who needs a bed for the night. Goes by the name Kyler Kennedy. Awesome, Thanks."

She pockets her cell as I arch a brow in question. "Your name was on your ID. And your accommodation for the night is organized." She wipes the counter down with a damp cloth. "You're welcome."

"Thanks," I offer gruffly, returning to my drink.

I lose count of how many whiskeys I drink or how many girls proposition me. I send them all on their merry way with barely a look. My heart is racing in my chest, and images I've long since buried keep flashing in front of me. I knock back another whiskey, but nothing is dulling the pain. Nothing is erasing the memories. I rub the sore spot over my chest as I close my eyes, silently begging the torturous images to screw off. Another drink slides across the counter, and I drain it in one go. Gradually, my mind becomes a tangled mishmash of nonsensicality, and the ache in my chest loosens a little.

I'm swaying on my stool and my vision is blurry when the bartender appears at my side. I think there's a concerned look on her face, but it's hard to tell when I'm seeing three and four of her. "I think you've have enough, Kyler. Is there someone I can call to help you to the hotel?"

I shake my head. "I left her," I slur, completely out of it. "My Faye. 'Cause she's too good for me. She doesn't need my shit, even though I love her more than anyone or anything in this world. I'm alone. I'm all alone."

I don't feel the first tear fall, but before I know it, there's a whole fucking ton of them, and I can't see at all over the blurry mess blanketing my eyes. A crushing weight bears down on my chest and I'm struggling to breathe. Desperately clawing for air, I stumble off the stool, arms thrust out, aimless and terrified. Sobs mingle with labored breathing, and I'm vaguely aware of arms going around me. Someone propping me up. Then I pass out.

Chapter Seven

Faye

It's dark and the streets are virtually empty when we enter the town of Bayfield, Wisconsin. Kal and I took turns driving, and we only made necessary pit stops to refuel the car and ourselves. A puncture cost us an hour when we were only forty miles out of town. I've always thought boys were born with the instinctive knowledge on how to do all manner of manly stuff, but I guess Kal's brain is wired differently because he was every bit as clueless as me. We had to call AAA and wait until someone came to change the tire for us.

Loud music and even louder voices carry outside from the only sign of life in the town. Although it's almost two a.m., the bar across the road looks lively. A couple is outside on the footpath arguing furiously. The girl is wearing ridiculously high heels, an uber-tight, uber-short mini, and a strappy lace vest top that barely contains her ample cleavage. Her long blonde hair hangs in tousled waves down her back. Mascara streaks down her tear-sodden face. "Welcome to Hicksville, USA," Kal drawls, pulling the car to a stop in front of the only hotel in town.

Yawning, I stretch my arms over my head before stumbling out of the car. My limbs are aching and stiff. I peer up at the hotel, clocking the old-fashioned fascia, fresh lick of cream paint, and the clean, shiny windows. Although it looks like it's been around forever, someone is looking after the place. Still, it's hard to picture any Kennedy

staying somewhere so down market. Beggars can't be choosers, though.
"I thought places like this only existed on TV," Kal says, retrieving both our bags from the boot. "This should be an experience."

"You're sure he's definitely here?"

Kal locks the car, shouldering both bags and taking my hand in his free one. "Yep. The app doesn't lie."

We hurry into the lobby and approach the empty reception desk. I'm just about to push the bell for assistance when a thunderous rumbling sound emits from behind the desk. Kal and I peer over the counter as one. All I can see of the receptionist is a mass of curly jet-black hair. She's asleep on her hands, snoring loudly. Kal presses the bell repeatedly, and she jerks awake with a little shriek. Pushing hair out of her face and wiping the drool off her mouth, she attempts to fix hazy, bloodshot eyes on us. Kal's finger is glued to the bell, and she reaches out, wrenching it away. Smoothing down the front of her wrinkled maroon shirt, she pins us with a more professional look. "I apologize. I must've dozed off. We don't get many visitors this hour of night."

"Or at all," Kal murmurs under his breath, glancing around in disgust. The lobby could definitely use a makeover. Drab brown carpet is underfoot, and the circular mahogany reception desk is scratched and stained although spotlessly clean. A large canvas with a mad splash of vibrant color on the wall behind the desk looks out of place. The gray speckled sectional sofas grouped around small oak-stained coffee tables look like a relic from the nineteen sixties, unless they were going for an authentic vintage vibe on purpose.

After booking a room for Kal and using none-too-subtle persuasion to ascertain Ky's room number and a duplicate key card, we are on our way. The lift isn't working so we haul ass on foot to the second floor.

I can't wait a second longer to see my boyfriend so we head straight to his room.

The instant I set foot in Ky's room, my insides lock up and nausea swims up my throat. Ky is spread-eagled on the bed, face down, wearing only his boxers. A pretty girl with wavy dark hair and shell-shocked wide green eyes is sitting up on the bed beside him. At least she's fully dressed, but it's small consolation.

"Who the fuck are you?" Kal demands, dropping both our bags on the ground as everything inside me starts shutting down.

She quickly gets up off the bed, striding toward us. "This is not what it seems, I promise." She stands in front of me. "Faye, nothing happened. I swear."

"How do you know who I am?" I ask, noting her stained jeans and T-shirt combo. She certainly wasn't pulling out all the stops to nab my man.

"Kyler showed me your picture, and he hasn't shut up talking about you all night. This isn't what it looks like."

Kal folds his arms across his chest, narrowing his eyes. "Start talking. Who are you and how do you know my brother?"

She rubs the back of her head. "I work the bar at Randy's Tavern across the road," she starts explaining. "Your brother came in earlier, and he sat at the counter so we started chatting." I send her my best death glare as a bitter taste swirls in my mouth. She looks a little sheepish. "I might've had ideas of hitting on him at first, but he shot me down before I got a chance. Same with the dozens of girls who approached him. He told them all the same thing—that he was crazy in love with his girlfriend and not interested."

That goes some way toward thawing out my heart, but I'm still suspicious. "That doesn't explain how you ended up here," I say.

"He drank way too much so I rang my friend Luce—this is her family's motel—and booked him in for the night. When it was time to call it a night, he could barely stand, and he was really sad, you know?" She looks over her shoulder at him. "He, ah, he started crying, and he wasn't really making any sense, but I could tell he wasn't doing so hot, so I helped him over the road. He threw up all over himself so I got him up here, and helped him into bed. I was rinsing his clothes in the tub, and when I came back out, he was already snoring. I was going to leave, but I was worried he'd puke in his sleep and choke or something. I tried to call you, but his cell is password protected, so I couldn't get your number. My shift is over, so I stayed to make sure he was okay. That's it. The God's honest truth."

I purse my lips as I mull it over. Ky wouldn't cheat on me, irrespective of how drunk he was. It's one of the things he truly despises. He still hates himself for what happened with Addison, even though he was only faking in order to protect me. I know he loves me, and he wouldn't risk what we have no matter how messed up he is right now. It's other girls I have to worry about, *but* I don't think this girl is one of them. I believe her. Maybe if she hadn't admitted to wanting to hit on him, I mightn't, but she was honest, so I'm inclined to believe she's told me the whole truth. Besides, even if she's omitting part of the story, it's obvious Ky is in a bad way and he needs us. Needs me. That's all that's important right now.

I exhale loudly. "Thank you for looking out for him, but we've got it from here."

She nods and the tense look leaves her face. "Sure thing." She stops at the door, turning around. "He'll be glad you're here. He was calling out for you in his sleep."

I walk to the side of the bed and crouch down. Ky looks so young and vulnerable when he's asleep. His skin is lightly flushed, his mouth slightly parted, and he's snoring. His hair is all messy, and my fingers twitch with restless need. I long to touch him, but I don't want to risk waking him up. That would be selfish. His chest heaves and a tiny whimper flees his mouth. I'm so glad we found him. That we're here for him. That he won't have to deal with stuff on his own. Judging from what the bartender said, and the torn skin on his knuckle, I think it's safe to assume he's already met his dad and that it didn't go well.

I want to envelop him in my arms and never let go, but it'll have to wait until morning.

His breath oozes out, fanning my face, and eau de puke mixed with alcoholic fumes has me pinching the bridge of my nose. I stand up, pulling the covers up over him. I scan the room and poke my head in the bathroom. Ky's jeans and shirt are soaking in the bath and a wave of gratitude washes over me. Although I'm still suspicious over the bartender's motives, I'm grateful she was here to keep an eye on him. I hate the thought that he was planning on doing this all alone, and I have a few choice words for him when the time is right.

I open a window in the room to let in some fresh air. "Could you go back down to the receptionist and see if you can get some water and paracetamol?" I ask Kal.

"Of course. I'll be right back."

I get changed into my sleep shorts and top while Kal is gone. Removing my Kindle from my bag, I settle on the bed beside my boyfriend. There's no way I'm sleeping when Ky is so inebriated. I'll watch over him until he wakes. Kal protests when he returns, and I reluctantly agree to take babysitting in shifts. He goes to his room to get a few hours' sleep while I place the water and tablets on the bedside locker on Ky's side. Kissing the top of his head, I open my Kindle and start reading.

I'm on an exciting part of my book when a warm arm drapes over my stomach. "Faye," Ky mumbles, and I look over at him. He's turned on his side facing me, still fast asleep. "Love you," he murmurs, and my heart does a little jump. His hand glides down my stomach, provoking a flurry of tingles inside me. He shunts sideways, eliminating the gap between us, burying his head on my chest. I'm scarcely breathing as I place my Kindle on the bedside locker. "Must be dreaming," he says, snuggling in farther. His hand creeps lower and then his entire body stiffens. He bolts upright, lurching over to the other side of the bed like he's been electrocuted. His eyes blink furiously as he stares at me. Shaking his head, he rubs his eyes hard.

I twist around, sitting up on my knees. "Ky," I say softly. "It's me. I'm here. Kal's in the next room."

He clears his throat. "Faye?"

His voice plugs with emotion, and I reach out, cupping his face. "Hi, baby."

His eyes flood with tears as he stares at me. "Is this real? Are you really here?"

The stark vulnerability in his gaze and in his voice is heartbreaking. "It's real. I'm real. Here." I take his hand and place it over my chest, right where my heart is pounding.

Just for him.

Always for him.

He crawls over to me, and tears leak out of his eyes. *What the hell did meeting his dad do to him?* I reel him into my arms, hugging him to death. "It's okay, baby. I'm here now. I'm gonna take care of you." I smooth my hand up and down his back as he clings to me. He breaks down in my arms, sobbing uncontrollably, and I can't halt the tears that spill out of my eyes or the anguish that spears my heart. Every sob that escapes his mouth pummels my heart until it feels like a hunk of shredded mincemeat in my chest. His body shakes and trembles against mine, and I'd do *anything* to take his pain away. Readily sign my soul over to the devil so I could take his place. I hate seeing him hurting like this, and holding him while he lets it all out doesn't feel like nearly enough, but it's all he needs right now. There are no words in the English language adequate to soothe his torment.

I clasp him tighter to me as silent tears roll down my cheeks.

I maneuver us so we're lying down, and I eventually fall asleep like that—with the boy I love with all my heart, fragile and vulnerable and broken, in my arms.

The smell of coffee wakes me up, and my eyes struggle open. A blurry image of Kal appears in my line of sight. "Morning, sleepyhead."

I look down at Ky, snuggled around me like an octopus, still fast asleep. "How long have you been here?" I whisper.

"Came in a couple of hours ago to relieve you, but you were both asleep. Went back to bed for a while, and I just went out to get some coffee. I think it's time to wake him." He nods at his brother.

I shake my head. "No, let him sleep. He was really upset in the middle of the night, Kal. It was awful." Tears pool in my eyes again. "He's hurting so bad. Let him sleep. Let him put reality off for as long as he can."

"I can hear you," Ky mutters, shifting in my arms.

I scowl at Kal, and he drops into an arm chair, shrugging. "Can't stave off reality indefinitely. Trust me, I'm speaking from recent experience." He takes a sip of his coffee, looking pensive.

"Hey." I run the tips of my fingers across Ky's face. "How are you feeling?"

"Terrible." He sits up slowly, supporting his back against the headrest. "It feels like something died in my mouth." I lean across him, snatching the bottle of water and tablets. Wordlessly, I place them in his hands, and he quickly pops two tablets and drinks half the water in one go. Kal and I exchange concerned looks.

Ky screws the cap on the bottle and tosses it off to the side. Scrubbing a hand over his prickly jaw, he frowns as he scans the room. "Where the hell am I? And how are you two here?"

I fill him in quickly, watching as all the blood drains from his face when I mention finding him unconscious with the pretty bartender beside him. Butterflies are panicking in my chest, and it takes considerable control to downplay this. To focus on his needs rather than my own. "She said nothing happened."

He takes my hand in his, gulping. "The latter part of the night is a blank, I'm not going to lie, but I wouldn't have done anything, Faye. I swear it. When I woke that time, I thought I was dreaming at first, but then I felt your skin under my hand, and I freaked out because I didn't know it was you. That's why I pulled away. There's no part of me that would do that to you, to us, no matter how incoherent I was. I will never cheat on you." He pulls my hand to his lips, kissing it tenderly. "Promise."

"I know." And I do. It's one of those inherent truths. Something you just know deep down inside to be true without any proof or any need for proof.

"You met him?" Kal asks, sitting forward in his chair. "I'm assuming that's the reason for the state you're in."

A dark look crosses over Ky's face as he nods. He holds up his injured hand. "I hit him before I left. Was satisfying at the time."

"Do you want to talk about it?" I unravel his clenched fists and thread my hand in his.

"Nothing much to tell, really. He's a total skid. Was wasted when I got to his house, openly groping this young girl, and giving me advice about banging as many girls as I can while I've still got my looks." Kal looks incredulous while I feel sick to my stomach. "Then he calls her back in the room and tells her to fuck me."

"What?" I screech.

He pulls me into his side, kissing my temple. "That's exactly how I reacted. Then she suggests a threesome, and I tried to leave, but he booted her out instead and ..." His face turns an even paler shade of white.

"And?" Kal prompts.

His body starts trembling, and a light layer of sweat dots his forehead. I turn in his arms, reaching out to touch him, and he flinches. I share a troubled look with Kal. "What happened, Ky? Did he start the fight? Did he hurt you?"

He barks out a laugh as an errant tear sneaks out. I'm horrified. I don't know what's happened but I hate seeing him so cut up, and I feel so helpless. "He knew," Ky whispers, shaking his head. "He was the one who stopped it. How messed up is that?" He's looking off into space, like he's almost forgotten we are here. More tears roll down his face, and Kal's anguished expression mirrors my own.

Tentatively, I reach up and cup Ky's face. He doesn't flinch this time. "He knew what, babe?" I ask in a soft tone of voice.

Ky pierces me with those beautiful blue eyes of his. His mask is down and he's letting me see everything. Opening up that dark, corroded part of his heart to me. I feel his pain as acutely as if it's my own. These hidden depths are what connect us. What drew us to one another in the first place. Well, that and the electric chemistry we share. Ky understands where my demons originated because I've shared my history with him, but he's only ever alluded to his.

Now, he wants me to know. It's written across his face.

It's time.

He curls one hand around my neck and pulls my face to his.

"Your scars, your flaws, your fears, your pain—they're mine too," I whisper. "You hurt, I hurt." I stare deep into his eyes. "I'm here for you. Let me help."

Pressing his mouth to my ear, he says, "I can't say this in front of my brother. I'm not ready for that yet."

I nod, understanding what he's asking and what I need to do. I kiss his forehead before I swing my legs off the bed. "Kal, can I speak to you outside, please?"

Kal glances at Ky uncertainly. He has pulled his legs up to his chest, and his head is buried in his knees. He's seconds away from losing it, and I need to do this quick. I tug on Kal's elbow, dragging him from the room under protest.

"Faye, what is going on?"

I close the door over, keeping it open a fraction, talking in a low tone. "He needs to get something off his chest, but he can't say it in front of you yet."

"Why the hell not?" His voice betrays his hurt.

"Don't take it personally. Remember how you felt when all that stuff happened with Lana? How you didn't want to talk about it until you'd processed it? He's going through something similar."

"I get that, but he's willing to talk to you."

"And that's a good thing, right?" I touch his cheek, forcing his gaze on mine. "It's good that he wants to talk to one of us. It's good that he's not locking it all up inside."

"I'm worried about him, Faye. I've never seen him cry. Like ever."

"I'm worried about him, too, and this isn't about you. He loves you. Look at the lengths he went to in order to protect you, to stop that recording from coming out? This isn't about you. It's about him and how he needs to deal with this, so don't hurt. Do what you can to help. Call Kaden and update him, and sort out the rooms. I don't think we'll be going anywhere for a while. Organize some food. Do what you can to help."

He nods. "You're right, and I'm glad he has you. Lana was that person for me. It was one of the hardest things about all that crap she put me through— my instinct was to run to her, to lean on her, but she wasn't there for me anymore. So, go." He gives me a gentle shove. "Go help my brother."

I shut the door quietly as I reenter the room. Ky emerges from the bathroom, looking at me through wounded, grief-stricken eyes. He flops down on the bed, and the devastation and helplessness in his expression is heartbreaking. I want to kill whoever put it there—wipe them from existence so they can't hurt him anymore. I climb onto the bed beside him, sliding my hand around his back. His head lands on my shoulder and we don't talk for several minutes. I'm letting him control this, and I won't force him to speak. He'll talk to me when he's ready. I run my fingers through the top of his hair and along the shorn, velvety sides, pressing tiny kisses to his face. His body is a solid block of tension against me, and he's holding himself rigidly still.

After an indeterminable period of time, he lifts his head, angling his body around so he's facing me. Tears pour down his cheeks, and I cup his face, kissing the tears away. "I love you." I penetrate his eyes. "I'll always love you. You're my everything."

He presses his forehead to mine, and his breathing is ragged. "I love you, too, and I've never needed anyone as much as I need you right now. Thank you. For ignoring me. For coming here. For not judging."

I hug him. "You're a good person, Ky. You protect and support those you love, and it's our turn to do that for you. There's nothing you can tell me that'll change how I feel about you. *Nothing.* If you want to tell me, I'll listen, but if you don't, that's fine too." I ease back, wiping my thumbs under his moist eyes. "I'm not going anywhere. We're in this together."

"This is the first time in my life where I feel it's okay to lean on someone else. I've never had this before, not with anyone. I want to tell you but I'm scared."

"Why?" I push his hair back off his forehead.

"It's not that I'm scared to tell you or scared how you'll react. That's not it at all." He gives me a smile and his eyes shine with love. Pressing my lips to his forehead, I close my eyes, and we stay like that for a bit. When he pulls back, he looks more assured. "I'm scared because telling you is only the first step, and I don't know if I'm strong enough to take the rest."

I circle my arms around his neck, pinning him with a determined look. "You are one of the strongest people I know. I know you can do this. And you're not alone, because I will be with you every step of the way. If that's what you want."

He nods, and more tears well in his eyes. "God, I love you so much, and I'm still falling for you. Every day, I fall a little more." My heart swells at his words and the earnest look in his eyes. "I will never want anyone else by my side. Only you, Faye. Only ever you." He kisses the tip of my nose and my cheeks, before delicately brushing his lips against mine. "And that's a promise."

My heart thrills at his words, amplifying until I fear it might burst out of my chest. Despite the circumstances, I can't keep the goofy grin off my face. "I love you to the moon and back." Mum used to say that to me all the time, and it never failed to perk me up.

"You're mine. Now and forever." He pulls me onto his lap, winding his arms around me. "This isn't going to be easy to say, so bear with me."

I kiss the top of his head, nodding. "Take your time. I'm not going anywhere."

He clears his throat, looking me directly in the eye. There is so much pain and hurt reflected in his gaze, and it's difficult to stay strong, to not collapse, but I do, because he needs me to be strong for the both of us.

"I was abused when I was ten," he blurts out, and the bottom drops out of my world.

Chapter Eight

Faye

I'm not sure what I was expecting him to say, but it most definitely wasn't that. Fighting back tears, I caress his face and wait for him to continue. His head drops back, and he looks up at the ceiling. "I used to attend a different motocross facility before I started going to Rick and May's. It's not around anymore. It closed down after the scandal." He pins his eyes on me again. "That track produced a lot of pro bikers, and they often returned for special events or turned up on free weekends to help out with the kids. There was this one guy who started showing up when I was ten."

He shivers profusely, and I wrap my arms more tightly around him. "I didn't like him from the minute I met him. You know when you get a gut instinct, bad vibes?" I nod. "I knew he wasn't a good guy, so I did my best to steer clear, and it worked at first. He didn't pay me any attention, and as the weeks turned to months, I kinda forgot about him, but then I started to hear things, rumors that he was doing stuff to some of the other boys. A few boys dropped out, switched tracks, and I was feeling uncomfortable, but I tried to shake it. Then this one Saturday, Julia, the owner, had a family emergency, and she had to leave early. She asked him to lock up. We were the last session of the day, and I was waiting by the door for Dad to pick me up, watching as one by one the other boys were picked up." He pauses to draw a concentrated breath, and my body is wired tight with apprehension. "He was tidying up in the main area where we were waiting, messing about with boxes by the door, when I felt his hand brush my leg. At first I thought I was imagining it, but after the second or third time, I knew it wasn't my imagination, especially when his hand inched higher up my leg."

He buries his head in my chest, his body quaking and trembling. I run my hand up and down his back, kissing the top of his head continuously. I don't speak because I don't have any words. Even if I did, I doubt I could verbalize them. Ky doesn't need that anyway. He needs the opportunity to explain things in his own way. So, I just hold him, touch him, and wait for him to gather the strength to continue.

After a couple minutes, he lifts his head, and the agony in his gaze punches a hole straight through my heart. His voice is strained when he resumes talking. "Dad was never late, and I mean never. He was usually one of the first to arrive but not this day. I watched in absolute panic as the last boy was picked up. I wanted to run to Drew's dad and beg him to take me with him, but I couldn't move. Couldn't speak. I was terrified, Faye."

His chest heaves up and down. "I can still remember how I felt. My heart was beating so hard in my chest, and I didn't know what to do. I was so scared." He closes his eyes briefly, and I use the opportunity to wipe a stray tear away.

"He locked the door and turned to me. 'Come 'ere boy' he said, and I swear I can still hear those words as clearly as if it was yesterday. Finally managing to get my feet working, I lunged for the door and tried to open the lock, but he was fast. Grabbed me up, kicking and screaming, and took me into the locker room. He pinned me against the locker and grabbed me by the throat. Told me if I spoke about this to anyone that he'd kill me. Said no one would believe me either. That it would be my word against a local motocross hero."

Tears cascade down my face, and I can't do a damned thing to stop them. Ky's eyes look dead as he stares ahead. "He ... he made me touch him, and when he was done, he did the same thing to me." A strangled sob rips free of his mouth, and he pulls me into his body, hugging me fiercely as he cries into my shoulder.

I'm crying with him.

Crying for the terrified ten-year-old boy who was subjected to such abuse and for the seventeen-year-old boy in my arms who has tried so hard to bury this pain but who has finally realized he can't keep pretending it didn't happen.

"I'm sorry, Ky. I'm sorry that happened to you," I whisper, holding him so tight I'm probably constricting his blood flow. "I want to kill him stone dead for subjecting you to that." Rage is the new blood flowing through my veins.

He looks up at me, eyes brimming with tears. "I've never told anyone that."

That admission increases my agony one-hundred-fold. He's kept that inside for so long. "Thank you for telling me."

He studies my face, and we stare at one another, searing emotion silently filling the space around us. I cup his face and kiss his cheek. He gulps. "Dad turned up a few minutes later, full of apology. He'd gotten a flat on the way and had to stop to change the tire. Of all the fucking days to get a flat." He shakes his head sadly. "He didn't even notice how quiet I was on the trip back because the triplets were fighting in the back of the car, and he was too busy to notice. I didn't know what to do, Faye. I wanted to tell my dad, but I was embarrassed, ashamed. Felt like it was my fault somehow. Maybe if Mom had been there, but she was away working that week."

He stares off into space. "I didn't want to go back the next Saturday, and I tried making up all kinds of excuses but Dad was having none of it. There was a race on I'd been excited about for weeks. Dad presumed I was nervous and he was boosting me up and telling me I'd be fine when I got there. Except I wasn't. I threw up in the bathroom, and my whole body was soaked in sweat. We were waiting in the back area, getting ready to go out and race, and I kept looking over my shoulder, waiting for him to arrive. Sure enough, as soon as Dad went out to the bleachers, he showed his face. But this time he wasn't alone. There was another motocross legend with him that day."

He starts rubbing circles on the back of my neck with his thumb. "I started shaking, couldn't help it. Almost pissed my pants I was that terrified. I saw the other biker looking at me strangely, and I was scared he was planning on doing the same thing. I thought about running out to Dad and begging him to take me away, but we were lining up for the start of the race, and I was afraid Dad would get mad if I bailed." He pulls my head down and kisses me hard. When we break apart, we are both breathing heavily.

"Then everything turned crazy. The two bikers started fighting while we all looked on in astonishment. The owners rushed in along with some of the parents, and there was lots of shouting, but I couldn't hear, because *he* was glaring at me. He made a sliding gesture with his hand across his neck, and I ran out, headed straight for Dad. Of course, he thought I was panicked over the adults fighting, and even later, when it all came out—how he'd been abusing several boys at this track and a few others—he never stopped to think it might've happened to me."

"What?" My tone is dubious. "They never even asked you?"

"Oh, they did. When Mom came back from her latest foreign trip, they both sat me down and explained what had happened to some of the boys and how the track was closing down. Apparently, the owners were fielding a ton of lawsuits and members were leaving in their droves, so they informed me they'd enrolled me in the Middleborough program, alongside Brad. At the end of the conversation, they asked me if he had touched me or upset me in any way."

He holds my face in his large, warm palms. "At the end, Faye. They asked me *at the end*. As a passing remark. Why didn't they ask me that first? Why wasn't that the most important thing to discover from the outset? Why didn't they see how much I was hurting? Why did Dad get a flat that day? Why did that man pick on me? Why didn't I tell my parents? Why did I lie when they asked and said no, he hadn't hurt me. Why, why, why?"

He sighs, weaving his fingers through my hair. "That's all I've thought of over the years. All the whys. I read the trial reports a few years back, and it was pretty gruesome reading. I got off relatively light. Others weren't so lucky." He shakes his head, clamping a hand over his mouth. "He legit destroyed their lives, their futures. I feel sick at the thought of what was going on around me and I didn't notice a thing."

"You were only a little boy, Ky. How would you have known?" I press a kiss to his cheek.

Slowly, he nods. "He was sent to prison for what he did to the others, and I read a few years back that he was knifed in jail and didn't survive the attack. That made me feel tons better. I even got drunk that night and cursed him in my head. Hoped he was in hell and that every sick thing he'd done to others was being done to him."

He rests his head on my shoulder. "I thought it would make me feel better, knowing he was dead, but it didn't help. I still had this big gaping hole in my chest. I was still full of so much anger and rage. I was still taking it out on Da ... on James." His Adam's apple jumps in his throat. "But I don't want to do that anymore because I realize what's wrong now. I'm angry at myself. You know what that's like."

"Yeah, yeah, I do, because I did the same. Internalized everything. Beat myself up for being so stupid in the first place."

"Exactly. I should've walked out to Drew's dad that night and asked him to take me home, but I was too fucking petrified. I failed to protect myself, and I swore after it all went down that I'd never appear so weak and vulnerable again and that I wouldn't fail the people I loved."

God, so much of this adds up now. Who he is, and why he is the way he is—that glaring protective streak that borders on possessiveness at times.

I understand it now.

There are so many things I want to say to him. So many things I learned from my own therapy. Things I know will help him. But I don't say any of that because I know from experience that he has to want those things for himself. He can't do it for anyone else. He has got to make that decision. "What are you going to do?"

"I'm not one hundred percent sure yet, but telling you was the first step. Getting that off my chest has been a long time overdue."

"I'm glad you told me, Ky, because keeping that locked up inside would've eaten you alive. Destroyed *your* life, *your* future. You don't need me to tell you that or tell you why I'm saying that. You know why, but I'm curious, why did you tell me now? I thought this was going to be about your bio dad."

He harrumphs. "Fate is one fucked-up bitch." He drags a hand through his hair. "I've spent years being mad at Dad for failing to protect me that day. For failing to spot what was under his nose, but the irony is that my dad *did* save me. I just didn't know it at the time."

I frown, completely confused.

"That other man, the other motocross champ that came to the track that Saturday? *He* protected me."

I'm still trying to figure it out.

"That other man was Doug Grant, Faye."

A light bulb goes off in my head as he says, "Doug Grant is my biological father. He's the one who saved me."

Chapter Nine

Faye

"Oh, em, gee. *He knew*? He knew who you were and what happened?" I ask.

Ky nods. "Apparently—if he's to be believed—he never knew Mom had a third child by him until he came to the track by chance that day. He says he knew I was his the minute he saw me, and he could also tell I was scared. He said he'd heard the rumors going around about his colleague, and it didn't take much to work out what was going down. He fought him and told the owners. My bio dad forced the scandal to come out and saved me from further abuse."

"And you punched him?" I scratch the top of my head, perplexed.

"He told me that was the extent of his fatherly duties and to get the fuck out of his house and never come back. I saw red. Hit him once. Did the rest of the damage pounding the wall." He flexes his injured hand.

"Ho. Lee. Shit."

"I know. What the hell am I expected to do with that?"

"Fecked if I know," I admit. Silence descends. "What do you want to do now? You can't avoid Alex and James forever."

Sliding me off his lap, he stretches his arms out over his head as he sighs. "I know, but I'm not ready to face them yet." He gets out of bed, pulling me up with him. "But I don't want to run into that asshole either, and I'd like to put as much distance between me and this town as possible. How about we get some breakfast and then start the trip back but find some place to stop off and lay low for a few days."

"Okay, if that's what you need. I'm down with that."

He grins, already seeming a little lighter. I know from experience how cathartic it can be to get stuff like that off your chest, to free your soul of some of the dark matter weighing it down. "You should call Dad and ask him to smooth things over for you at school. I don't want you getting into trouble on my account," he says.

I don't think he's realized that he just called James "Dad," but I'm not going to point that out. James *is* still his dad even if they don't share the same flesh and blood. Just like Michael will always be my dad too. "I'll ring him. You go shower first, unless you want to speak to James?" I keep my voice steady, devoid of the tendrils of hope building inside me.

He shakes his head and his smile fades. "Not ready to face that yet."

"He's hurting, too. I was in the room when he found out, and he was devastated, Ky. He loves you so much."

"I know, but it's too soon. My head is such a mess." He hauls me into his chest. "I just want to lock myself away with you for a few days and chew things over. Then I'll go back and talk to them."

I wait until I hear the shower turn on before I phone James. "How is he? Are you all okay?" he says by way of greeting.

"He's hurting, but we're okay. He's not ready to come home, so I'm going to hang around here for a few days with him. I haven't spoken to Kal yet, so I'm not sure what he'll want to do. Can you square things off with Principal Carter for me, please?" I figure it's best to tell him, not ask him and give him a chance to say no. Not that it would matter. Wild horses wouldn't drag me away from Ky.

I'm met by silence and heavy breathing. "I'm not happy about this, but I'll agree because there are extenuating circumstances. I'll give you a few days, but he needs to come home, Faye. We need to speak to him. I need to speak to him. This is equally upsetting for me."

"I get that, and he does too, but don't force him to confront this until he's ready."

"Has he met him?"

"Yeah. It wasn't a good meeting, and I don't think he'll be going back there."

"I'm sorry he's hurting. Tell him ... tell him I love him, and this changes nothing. He's my son, and this will always be his home."

After a quick chat to update Kal, we all meet in the lobby a half hour later and check out of the hotel. Kal has deets of an all-day breakfast place on the outskirts of town. I drive with Ky in his rented truck, and we follow Kal to the restaurant.

After we finish eating, we discuss plans over coffee. "I may as well head home," Kal suggests.

"It's up to you." Ky shrugs.

"It feels like I'm in the way," he admits, holding out his cup for a coffee refill when the waitress appears.

Ky leans over the table. "You could never be in the way, and if I've given you that impression, I'm sorry. You're my brother, and I'm really grateful you came with Faye. That means a lot."

Kal takes a slurp of his coffee, carefully choosing his next words. "I can't pretend to imagine what you're going through. I know it's some bad shit, and I wish you could tell me, but I get it. You need Faye, and I'm cool with that. I can wait until you're ready to confide in me."

Ky puts his cup down. "Kal, it's not like that ... it's just incredibly difficult to talk about." He reaches under the table, lacing his fingers through mine. "Faye is the first person I've told in almost eight years, and it took enormous courage to even tell her. I want to tell you, honestly, I do."

Kal frowns. "I thought this was about your bio dad?"

"It is, but it's bigger than that."

Kal's concerned gaze bounces between us. I give Ky's hand a reassuring squeeze, and he turns to look into my eyes. Despite his hangover, they appear clearer, brighter than they have in a long while. His eyes seek my advice, and I nod in encouragement. Leaning in, he kisses me sweetly and my lips tingle blissfully.

Kal gets up to leave. "Look, I'll give you both some space. You need this time alone. It's no sweat."

Ky rises, slapping a hand on his brother's shoulder. "No, don't leave. Let's go for a walk."

I insisted they talk alone, so I head to a small beauty salon across the road and get a mani-pedi on a whim. My phone chimes with a message from Adam. *"It was wonderful to finally meet you, and I'm looking forward to spending time together. You set the pace. I'm still prepared to visit you this weekend, but if you need more time that's no problem. Let me know."*

I lean my head back and close my eyes. I'm not sure what I want, but I don't want to say no in case I decide I *do* want to talk to him. I still have so many questions. I tap out a quick reply. *"Can I think about it and get back to you in the next couple of days?"*

His reply is immediate. *"Of course. Talk to you then."*

Kal and Ky are lounging against the wall outside, talking in hushed tones, when I step outside the salon. "Hey." I walk into Ky's welcoming arms. "You okay?"

He nods, offering me a small smile. "Kal knows." I flip my head in his direction.

"I can't believe he hid that for so long. It puts a lot of things in perspective." Kal kicks at the dirt under his boot. "I'm glad that bastard is dead." His fists clench at his sides. "Otherwise I'd probably be finding myself back in a courtroom."

"You and me both." I rest my head on Ky's chest, listening to the steady beat of his heart.

"You're going to be okay." Kal places his hand on Ky's shoulder. "And I think you two need some time alone. You've both had the mother of all bombs dropped, and you need each other. I'm going to head back. I don't want to miss any more of school."

"When did you become so conscientious?" Ky half teases.

"Since I had to contemplate the very real possibility of a life behind bars. It's changed my outlook on certain things."

Reaching out, I give him a brief hug. "I'm so proud of the person you're becoming. Drive safely."

He hugs me tight, leaning in to whisper in my ear. "Please help my brother heal."

We both set out on the road at the same time. Ky has already called ahead and made hotel reservations in Cleveland, Ohio. It's a city about halfway between here and home. We're planning on spending the next few days there, and although it's hardly a vacation, the prospect of spending so much alone time with Ky has me pumped full of nervous excitement.

While I have plenty to update him on, we don't talk much on the journey, preferring to listen to music instead. We trail Kal for a few hundred miles before turning off and heading for Cleveland.

Ky locates the hotel easily, and in next to no time, we are checked in and making our way in the lift to the penthouse suite. I still can't get over how flippant all my cousins are in relation to money. While I never felt deprived growing up, my parents had to budget for everything, and they would never have had the money to splurge on the best suite in the hotel. Ky just whipped out some black credit card and casually handed it over, like it was no big deal.

"Wow!" I gasp the instant we step into the suite. It's almost as big as an apartment with two separate bedrooms, two bathrooms, and a massive living space resplendent with plush leather sofas and the largest wall-mounted TV screen I've ever seen. Marble, mirror, and glass reflect the clean lines of the interior decoration, emitting a contrasting sense of minimalism and decadence. On the top floor of the hotel, the tall, wide glass windows offer a breathtaking view of the city below.

Opening the sliding doors, I step out onto the expansive terrace and soak up the view.

Ky's warm arms slither around my waist. "Is it really selfish of me to be extremely happy you are here?" He rests his chin on my shoulder as I lean back into him.

"It's not selfish at all. Which reminds me ..." I spin around in his embrace. "I have a bone to pick with you for running off like you did." I rest my hands on his chest, tilting my head up to look him straight in the eye. "We're a team and you took off without me. That is not going to happen again." I send him my best stinky-eyed look.

His expression softens. "You're too good for this, Faye. And you've had your fair share of crap to deal with. I didn't want to add to that."

My arms creep around his neck. "What if I had run off without you when I discovered the man who raised me wasn't my father? How would that have made you feel?"

He tightens his arms around me. "Mad and worried," he immediately replies.

"Exactly. I could barely sleep Sunday night because I was so worried you'd wrap your bike around a tree."

"But I was in the truck."

I prod him in the chest with a finger. "And how was I to know that when you wouldn't even respond to my texts? You freaked me out, Ky. You can't do that to me again. And you have got to stop pushing me away. Either we're a team or we're not. You can't keep saying it and then not following through. That's not how this works."

He runs his hand up and down my spine. "You're right. I'm sorry. I was only trying to protect you."

I sigh, trying to put a leash on my anger and frustration. "You've shown me you're the protective type time and time again, and I understand more clearly where that's coming from now, but you've got to let *me* protect *you* sometimes. I"—I press a kiss to his right cheek—"want"—I press another kiss to the tip of his nose—"to protect"—I kiss his left cheek—"you." I join my lips to his in a sweet, soft kiss. "And you're going to let me." My tone brokers no argument.

"I'll try. I promise."

I smile up at him as I frame the next question carefully. "Have you ever considered talking to anyone about what happened? A professional?"

His muscles bunch up. "You mean a shrink?" I nod. "Not really."

"I think you should. Consider it, I mean."

He purses his lips. "I thought you were anti-psychiatrist."

I vehemently shake my head. "No, I never said that. I said I hoped I never had to see one again because it feels like I've spent a lifetime in therapy already, but I didn't mean to imply that it wasn't beneficial or that

I wouldn't go to therapy again in future. I just meant I hoped I'd never need to. That I'd gotten through the difficult phase of my life."

"Do you think I should?"

I cup his cheek. "Yes. Therapy helped me, and it was actually a relief to speak to someone who didn't know me. I could speak my mind without fear. I could tell her every horrible dark thought in my head, and she didn't judge me. What I liked most about therapy was how she guided me to a better path. Fiona didn't *tell* me what to do. She helped me identify what *I* wanted to do. She helped me put it behind me and move on. She empowered me to make my own decisions, and I think you need that too."

He drags his lower lip between his teeth. "I'll think about it."

"Good." I kiss him again. "Now, how about we explore the town and find somewhere romantic to eat?"

Chapter Ten

Faye

We wander around the town holding hands and window shopping for a few hours. Ky disappears on his own for a half hour while I peruse the shelves in the bookstore. Finding a quaint little Italian restaurant up a side street, we head inside and secure a private table in a secluded corner of the room. The overhead lighting is dim, and the small tabletop candle casts magical shadows on the walls behind us. We order pasta and drinks, and Ky maneuvers his chair over beside mine, taking my hand in his. "I can't believe we haven't been on any real dates before now," he says, bringing my fingers to his lips.

I shrug. "I don't need dates. I just need you."

He kisses me sweetly, easing back as the waitress places our drinks down. She smiles knowingly at me, and I can't help smiling back. It's contagious, and nothing could impair my good mood. Irrespective of all the heavy stuff we've got going on, I'm in my element right now. I know I just told Ky I don't need dates, but what girl doesn't love to spend cozy romantic nights with her boyfriend? And this is exactly what we need. A night to just be young and in love. A night to forget the pressures hanging over us. We keep our talk casual and teasing at the table, and the only time Ky lets go of my hand is when we eat.

Nighttime has fallen when we emerge from the restaurant, and the air is distinctly cooler. Ky drapes his arm around my shoulders, and we stroll back to the hotel in quiet contemplation. Once we are back in our suite, Ky grabs a bottle of wine he had chilling in the fridge and two glasses and takes my hand, leading me out to the terrace.

We snuggle up under a thick plaid blanket, sipping our wine and surveying the bustling nightlife below us. "I could get used to this, you know," he says a few minutes later. I twist my head around to look inquiringly at him. "Us, together like this. You're the other piece of my heart, Faye. I can't ever imagine my life without you in it."

My eyes light up. "Nor me." I put my glass down on the coffee table and lean into him. "I've never felt this way about anyone before, Ky. It's never felt so right with anyone else. We are meant for each other. You're mine. I'm yours."

His lips crash onto mine, and he cups the back of my head, holding me close. His kiss is urgent and needy, and it works me into a frenzy in no time. We devour each other without apology, and I just can't get enough of him. My hands are everywhere—winding in his hair, gripping his strong, broad shoulders, and exploring the ripped planes of his chest and abs. It's as if God plucked all the thoughts of my dream boy straight from my head and created Ky especially for me.

"There is one positive to come out of this mess," he rasps against my lips, and I open my eyes. Raw desire glimmers in his eyes. "We're not blood related. There is nothing to stop us being together now."

"I know. I was thinking the same thing on the journey here. We can be a normal couple." Although, he'd have to come clean about his real dad for that to truly be the case, and I'm not sure he'll want to go there. But, for now, I'm going to enjoy the fact there is no impediment to our relationship.

His fingers drift in and out of my hair. "That's what I've always dreamed of. It's killed me knowing you and Brad were together in public, even if it was fake." His brows knit together. "Well, on your side, at least."

"Ky." I silently beg him not to go there. Not tonight.

He palms my face. "We can't ignore reality forever."

"I know, but we can have this one night. Tomorrow we can talk about my dad and yours and Brad and what we're going to do, but right now, being with you like this is everything I've wished for. I just want to enjoy us. I want to hold you and kiss you knowing that we belong together and there's no one or nothing to keep us apart anymore."

His answering kiss melts me into a puddle of goo. His lips worship mine with so much adoration that I can almost feel my heart swelling to bursting point. I will never get enough of this all-consuming feeling when I'm with him. Soon, I'm straddling him as we pump and grind against one another. His hands sneak under my sweater, roaming my curves, and I don't care that I'm whimpering like a puppy in heat. My skin is on fire from his touch, and I want to shed my clothes, strip him of his, and do all kinds of naughty stuff.

When his hand creeps into my bra and he runs his thumb over the hard peak of my nipple, I arch my back and cry out. I rock into his hips, and he groans as his lips crush mine with intense need. He pulls his mouth away a minute later, yanking my sweater up over my head and tugging my bra down. A welcome cool breeze coasts over my bare skin. I moan loudly when he sucks the sensitive tip of one nipple into his mouth while his hand plays with my other breast. I'm panting and writhing on top of him now, and he's bucking his hips against mine, his arousal straining against his jeans.

He stands up suddenly, holding me to him, and I wrap my legs around his waist as he starts walking back inside. I pepper his face with hot kisses as he walks toward the bedroom. We fall back on the bed, kissing feverishly as we pull at our clothes until we are flesh to flesh with no barrier between us. My hands wander greedily over his bare skin, gliding over the defined muscles of his back and down to his ass. I pull him against me, and we both groan.

He repositions us on the bed so I'm underneath him with my head on the pillows. Holding my hands stretched over my head, he hovers over me, his impressive naked body brushing against mine as his eyes roam over every inch of me. I'm burning up from his gaze and the promise of what's to come.

Dipping his head, he worships my mouth, kissing along my jawline and down my neck. He presses the lightest of kisses to that delicate spot on my collarbone, and I shudder all over. My fingers tangle in his hair as he glides down my body, licking, nipping, sucking, and kissing as he goes. I'm gasping and moaning and squirming in need as his lips leave scorching imprints all over my body. Spreading my legs wide, he eases one finger inside me, and I almost come on the spot. When he adds a second finger, I scream, and he chuckles. "Oh, God, don't stop. Just don't stop."

He replaces his fingers with his mouth, and I nearly buck off the bed. My hands grip his head, holding him in place as blissful tremors start building inside me. I shatter, falling apart in exquisite waves of pleasure as he continues to worship me, wresting every last drop from my body. My skin is hot and sensitive as he crawls over me. Clasping my hands over my head again, he stares intensely into my eyes. My tongue darts out and I trace a line around his lush lips. His eyes burn with hunger, asking a silent question, and I convey my agreement with my lusty gaze and a determined nod.

There will never be a more perfect moment, and I'm done waiting.

I want him.

I want him inside me right now.

He grabs a condom from the pocket of his jeans and rolls it on. "Are you sure, Faye? Because it's okay if you're not." My answering yes is breathy and needy, and the biggest smile spreads across his mouth.

His eyes never leave mine as he aligns our bodies. My heart beats wildly in my chest, and I can't believe the moment is upon us. I've wanted this so badly for months now, and, finally, he will truly be mine. Releasing my hands, his mouth caresses mine as he slowly inches inside me. I gasp as he fills me up, whimpering with my eyes closed. "Are you okay?" he asks, halting all movement.

"Perfect," I whisper, opening my eyes and latching onto his. "You feel so good. Don't stop."

He moves gently. Our eyes are locked on one another, and I reach out, palming his face. "I love you."

"I love you, too." He starts thrusting, slowly at first and then with more urgency as his movements grow harder, stronger, more intense. My legs go around his waist, and I lift my hips up to meet him, building a steady rhythm as liquid fire ignites every part of my body. My fingers dig into his back, and he moans into my mouth, capturing my lips in a searing kiss. His lips trail down my neck and over my collarbone before worshipping my breasts. My hands knead his ass, pulling him even closer to me, and our ragged breathing is growing more and more frantic.

Heavenly tremors start building inside me again, and I'm floating on a sea of sensation. I'm writhing and moaning as Ky whips my body into a frenzy.

My first time was absolutely nothing like this. There was no insatiable need. No unquenchable thirst. No waves of continuous pleasure. No sensual looks and caresses. No touching of souls. This is all that and more. Ky is all that and more, and I don't think I'll ever get enough of him.

When he shatters, his body trembling and pulsing over me, I quickly follow him over the ledge, never once removing my eyes from his, and it's *everything*.

Everything I've dreamed of.

Everything my first time wasn't.

Everything I want for the rest of my life.

He gets up to dispose of the condom, returning with a warm cloth to clean me. Then he encloses me in his arms, and I snuggle into his chest. "You okay?" He kisses my forehead tenderly.

"More than okay," I reply. "That was amazing." My hand glides over his stomach and lower. "I'm thinking we might have to do it again, just to make sure it wasn't a fluke." He chuckles, and I brace on one elbow, twisting to face him. "Was it ... good for you?"

He kisses the tips of my fingers. "It was incredible, Faye." His eyes grow glassy. "Sometimes intimacy has been uncomfortable for me, but not with you. Never with you. With you, it's always felt right, and all I'm thinking in the moment is how good it feels. How natural it feels." He pulls me down on top of him, circling his arms around me. "We fit together perfectly in every conceivable way."

I press a slew of drugging kisses to his chest, grazing the column of his neck, and I'm thrilled when he hardens underneath me.

Round two is even better than round one, and when we finally collapse atop one another, sweaty and sated, we grin at each other like lovesick fools.

I fall asleep enveloped in his sturdy arms, and no place has ever felt more comfortable or more like home.

I wake up first the next morning with Ky's arm draped across my stomach and one of his legs covering mine. Warmth and happiness suffuses every inch of my body, and I nestle into him, inhaling the scent that is all male. My limbs feel deliciously sore, and I ache in places I never knew I could ache.

"Morning, gorgeous," he says before opening his eyes. He pulls me in flush to his body, and every part of me sparks to life. "Last night was amazing." He buries his head in my shoulder, nuzzling my neck with his nose. "Waking up beside you is amazing as well, and something I plan to do for a very long time."

"Don't I get a say?" I tease, running the tip of one finger up and down his arm.

"And what exactly is your objection?" He sucks on my neck in the exact spot where my pulse throbs uncontrollably.

"None," I gasp in a breathy voice. "I could never complain about falling asleep and waking up in your arms. Never."

"Good answer," he agrees, flipping me on my back and covering my body with his. His mouth meets mine in a hungry kiss, and I yank him down on top of me, wrapping my legs around his waist as I guide him closer. Expertly rolling on a condom, he situates himself exactly where I need him. His hands stroll up and down my body, caressing my curves as he thrusts into me in one fluid move. He makes love to me slowly and sweetly, and we rock gently against one another, kissing languorously, and I have no desire to ever get out of this bed.

We eventually get up an hour later, when the need for food temporarily overrides our hunger for one another. Ky orders room service while I take a quick shower. We eat breakfast at the dining table, in our toweled dressing gowns, sharing secretive glances every couple of minutes. "It feels different now," I say, pushing my plate away and rubbing one hand across my satisfied stomach. "Does it feel like that to you?"

He stretches across the table, taking my hand. "Yes. Now that I know what it feels like to be inside you, I'm on a permanent boner."

I fling my napkin at him. "That's not what I meant and you know it."

"I'm only teasing, babe, although that's no word of a lie. But, yeah, I've got all the feels too."

I smile at his statement. "I won't ever want to leave here."

He shrugs. "Then we won't."

I roll my eyes. "We can only avoid the outside world for so long." And Adam is waiting on an answer from me, and it's not fair to keep him hanging. I still don't know what to do, and my head is a horribly confused place in that regard.

"Hey." Ky moves over beside me. "Where'd you go?"

"I haven't had a chance to tell you this yet, but I met my bio dad. I met Adam."

His eyes pop wide. "You did? How was it?"

I proceed to fill him in on how it went down, and he listens attentively. "I'm glad your meet and greet with pops went better than mine," he half-jokes when I've finished talking. I send him a sympathetic look. "If you want to meet him this weekend, we can head back. I was only joking before. I know we can't hide away forever. I know I have to confront my parents at some point."

I rub a hand behind my neck. "I don't know what I want. He seems nice, and he's trying to make the best of this, like me. And I have questions. Lots of them. But I'm not sure I'm ready to hear about his other kids, about my siblings. What if they want to meet me?" A fluttery sensation takes up residence in my chest.

"He said you could set the pace, right? So tell him you need to go slow. Get to know him first before you even start thinking about that. Unless you don't want to get to know him at all?" Ky tilts my chin up.

I fidget with the belt on my dressing gown as emotions churn in my mind. "Is it disrespectful to my dad, my real dad, to want to get to know Adam? Because guilt is a huge part of what I'm feeling."

"Your mom said in her letter that your dad had wanted to tell your bio dad when they first found out. If that's the kind of man he was, then, I think he'd want you to do whatever *you* feel comfortable doing. And your mom said this was your decision."

I tip my head up to the ceiling, sighing. "What would you have done? If your dad had been different. Had been decent?"

He blows air out of his mouth. "Honestly, I don't know. I'm still processing."

I nod in agreement. Ky called it. I'm still trying to figure all this out, and I think I need more time to consider it. I'll text Adam later and ask him if we can meet the following weekend instead. At least I'll have had more time to structure my thoughts by then. I peck Ky on the lips. "Thank you."

"For what?" He gives me a funny smile as someone raps loudly on the suite door.

Ky frowns, getting up to check it out before I can answer him. I pull my knees up to my chest and start making tentative plans in my head for today.

"What the hell?" Ky yells, and I hop up, racing to the other room.

My mouth hangs open as I reach the front door. Two policemen wearing blue shirts and navy trousers are standing in front of Ky with fierce expressions. The short, stouter man is holding Ky's hand, inspecting his injured knuckle. He nods at the second man, as he simultaneously twists Ky's hands behind his back.

"Kyler James Kennedy. You are under arrest for the murder of Douglas Brian Grant."

Chapter Eleven

Kyler

"He's *dead*?" My eyes dart between the two police officers but neither of them is giving anything away. I glance over my shoulder at Faye. Her eyes are wide and panicked. "Call Dad." The officer who cuffed me starts nudging me out the door.

"At least let him get dressed," Faye demands, hurriedly composing herself. "You are not bringing him out there like that." She glares at the cops, and they exchange looks.

"Fine," the taller, older man says. "But I'll be in the room with you."

Faye harrumphs. "What, you think he's going to jump off the roof like he's Spiderman or something?"

"Watch your tone, young lady, or I'll detain you for obstructing an arrest."

"Fine." She shrugs. "See if I care."

"Faye." I shake my head. There's no way I want her tied up in this mess. "Just call Dad and tell him to get Dan on the case."

I get dressed with the cop facing the door, and he insists on re-cuffing me before we leave the room. I hope there's no press around. Mom will have a conniption if this gets out. Not that I care what she thinks anymore. It'd serve her right. Let her be blindsided and see what that feels like.

Faye flings her arms around me before I'm removed from the suite. "I've spoken to James and he's on it. I'll follow you to the station. Don't say a word until your attorney arrives."

I nod. "The keys to my truck are in the pocket of my other jeans," I tell her before I'm steered out of the room.

I do the walk of shame across the crowded hotel lobby, staring straight ahead and not making eye contact with anyone. A couple of flashes go off in my face out on the street, and any hope of keeping this on the down low is fading. Once they figure out who I am and what I've been arrested for, it'll be all over the net.

The cruiser pulls away from the sidewalk, and I stare out the window as the magnitude of what's happening starts to hit home.

The sperm donor is *dead*?

And they think *I* did it?

Which must mean I was one of the last people to see him alive. Panic presses down on my chest, but I plaster a blank expression on my face. I'm not showing shit, saying shit, until I speak to an attorney.

The journey back to Bayfield drags by, and it does nothing to stem my nerves. I go over and over Monday night in my head, wondering if I hit Doug harder than I thought. He was still on his ass when I left, but he was coherent enough to scream obscenities at me while I walked away. I can't believe that one punch was enough to kill a man, but I'm terrified it did.

I'm brought into the station and processed quickly. Before I know it, I'm in a lineup, facing a glass window, along with four other guys. I show no reaction as I'm called forward, stepping out and then falling back as instructed. When it's over, I'm escorted into an interview room and left there with only my thoughts for company.

The longer they leave me in isolation, the more freaked out I'm becoming. Thoughts of what Kal recently went through are at the forefront of my mind. It didn't take much to frame him for a crime he didn't commit. Sweat coasts down my spine, and my foot taps nervously off the floor.

The door slams open, and I jerk a little in my chair. Two plainclothes detectives enter the room and sit down across from me. The dude with the buzz cut slaps a paper folder down on the desk and pins me with a grim look. The other guy slouches in his chair, yawning and feigning disinterest.

They turn on the camera and read me my rights. "Where were you Monday night between the hours of eight p.m. and two a.m.?" Buzzcut asks.

"I want an attorney."

"I understand someone is on their way." He puts his elbows on the table, straining toward me. "But this doesn't look good for you, kid, and the sooner you start talking, the sooner we can eliminate you from our investigation."

Does he think I was born yesterday? "I'm not saying a word until my attorney gets here."

The two detectives share a look while I fold my arms across my chest and lean back in my chair.

They stand up, chairs screeching in the process. "Fine. Your funeral."

I release the breath I'd been holding the second they exit the room. I crick my head from side to side, attempting to loosen up. Every muscle in my body is corded into knots.

About a half hour passes before a distinguished-looking guy steps into the room. He sits down beside me, extracting some papers from a well-worn brown leather briefcase. "My name is Fitzgerald Manning, and I'm an attorney with Manning, Tanner, and Hawthorne. My services have been retained by Dan Evans, acting on behalf of your parents. I'll be representing you in this matter." He opens a pad and removes a slim, silver Montblanc pen from his jacket pocket. Setting both items down on the table, he clasps his hands in his lap and swivels in his chair, facing me. "I can't do my job unless you are completely honest with me."

I'm not an idiot. I know it must look bad or they wouldn't have arrested me. And I'm not naïve enough to believe this will go away because I actually am innocent. Look what happened to my brother. "I didn't kill him," I admit truthfully.

He scrutinizes my eyes, and my focus doesn't waver. "Okay."

"I didn't. My girlfriend and my brother will confirm I was drunk and passed out in my hotel room when they arrived."

"I have already spoken with Ms. Donovan, and she has given a statement to that effect. The police are interviewing the bartender in Randy's Tavern as we speak, but that only accounts for the latter part of the night. It doesn't exonerate you for the hours leading up to your arrival in the bar."

"Is Faye okay?"

"She is fine. She's waiting outside for your parents to arrive. My understanding is they are traveling by private plane and they are expected shortly." He takes the tip off the pen, holding it poised over the pad. "We need to go over this before the detectives return, so let's take this step by step. Where were you Monday night?"

I fill him in on everything from the time I stepped foot in the town, leaving nothing of relevance out. I don't mention the part of the conversation surrounding past events at Uxbridge because it has no bearing on this, and I don't want any whiff of that getting back to my parents until I'm ready to tell them about it.

"Do you own a gun, Mr. Kennedy?" He scrutinizes me over the edge of his black-rimmed spectacles.

I shake my head. "No." My eyes narrow as I come to the obvious conclusion. "He was shot? That's why they took swabs of my hands earlier?" I wait with bated breath for his reply.

He nods, and a layer of stress releases knowing I definitely didn't kill him. "Yes. The good news for you is that no gunshot residue was found on your hands, no gun was uncovered at the crime scene, and forensics didn't discover any incriminating evidence in either of the hotel rooms you occupied or in your truck."

"But?" I know there's one coming.

"A witness identified you from the lineup, and she has confirmed that she left you with Mr. Grant in his house on the night of his murder. In her statement, she has referred to you as, and I quote, 'an asshole with a major chip on his shoulder.'"

"I know who she is. She was waitressing at a diner in town, and she was fucking Doug Grant when I arrived at his house. She doesn't know me, and it's not like I'm denying I was there that night."

Manning takes off his glasses, rubbing the bridge of his nose. "It is most likely you were the last person to see him alive."

I stiffen. "No, I wasn't. The killer was." I grind down on my teeth.

"Let me rephrase. You were the last person *seen* with the victim and that's not looking so good for you, even if all they have is circumstantial evidence right now."

I drag a hand through my hair. "I told you he was alive when I left. I punched him once, knocked him on his ass, but he was most definitely alive. I didn't do this. Are the cops even looking for anyone else or have they already deemed I'm guilty?"

"It's an open investigation, Mr. Kennedy, and the police will pursue all leads. However, at this time, you look good for this. Ms. McKenna, the waitress, has already told them you were his son, and they are keen to pursue that line of questioning. Look at it from their perspective—you have motive, a witness has placed you at the scene, you agree you fought with the victim, and most likely there is DNA evidence that will corroborate same."

"I know how it looks," I roar, losing the battle with my self-control, "but I'm telling you, I didn't do this. Someone else killed him. He's well known, and given what I saw of him, I'd say he's made his fair share of enemies over the years. God only knows how many kids he's fathered with various women, so I can't be the only one who'd have motive to kill him. And do they even know he was murdered? What if he shot himself?"

"They can tell from the bullet trajectory that it wasn't a suicide, but we won't have conclusive results until the autopsy report is issued." He looks at his watch. "The detectives will be here any minute now. Do not blow up like that in their presence. Tell them what you've told me, and only answer questions where I nod my agreement. I'll intervene if they ask you something I don't want you to answer."

The detectives reenter the room and waste no time getting stuck in. The interrogation goes on for hours, and they keep asking me the same questions over and over, trying to trip me up. Eventually, they call a halt to the interview, rising along with my attorney. "Unless you are charging my client, I expect he is free to go?"

"That will be all for now. Mr. Kennedy is free to leave, but we ask that he remains in the vicinity for the time being. We will need to question him again in due course."

Manning nods his agreement, keeping a hand on my shoulder to hold me in place while the detectives exit the room. "They don't have enough to charge you, and let's hope it stays that way. I expect your parents are here by now, but, I must warn you, news of your arrest is already in the public domain, and a few reporters had gathered outside when I first arrived. I'd imagine their numbers have swollen by now. Prepare yourself."

I get up, arching my stiff back. "I'm well accustomed to dealing with the media. It's part and parcel of growing up in the family I did."

He ushers me from the room and out into the front reception area. Faye races toward me the second she sees me, enfolding me in a mammoth hug, almost squeezing the life out of me. Mom and Dad are standing behind her with worried expressions on their faces. I'm surprised to see Kal, although I guess he may have been required to give a statement, too. Manning goes to talk to them. I hold Faye close, smoothing a hand over her hair and allowing her body heat to soothe me.

"Stupid question," she says, peering up at me. "But are you okay?"

Air escapes my lungs in a mad rush. "I will be as soon as we get out of here. Are there many reporters out front?"

Her mouth narrows in distaste as she nods. "I'm sorry, Ky. It's all over the news already."

I peck her on the lips. "I figured as much when people started taking photos of me as they led me out of the hotel."

"If they're letting you go that must be a good thing, right? They know you didn't do this?"

"It's not that straightforward. The girl who was with him at the house picked me out of a lineup, and they're going to find my DNA on him, and my injured hands confirm I fought with him, but it was a gunshot wound that killed him and they haven't found the gun so that stands in my favor."

Faye scratches the side of her head. "I saw a girl leave here a while back with blonde hair, pretty, if a bit rough around the edges. Kal and I saw her the night we arrived. She was outside the bar arguing with some guy. Was that the girl your dad was with?"

"Sounds like it."

"Well, maybe she killed him? Lovers tiff gone wrong? She was pretty smashed when we saw her, and she was crying. She could've gone back there and fought with him?" Her eyes fill with hope.

"It's a possibility." I take her hand. "Come tell the attorney what you just told me." I walk her over to where my parents are speaking with Manning. I avoid looking at either Mom or Dad as Faye tells the attorney what she saw. Kal confirms he saw the waitress too. Manning agrees to update the police, advising both Faye and Kal that they may be called back to revise their statements.

Dad steps in front of me when the attorney leaves to update the detectives. "It's going to be okay. We'll fix this." Looking at my feet, I nod. I can't face him, even though this isn't his fault. For once, I'm on his side, and it's Mom I'm furious with. "Let's get out of here," he adds. "We have reserved rooms in a hotel in the next town over. We didn't think it was a good idea to return to the scene of the crime."

I have a quiet word with Kal before we leave. I'm not sure I'll get the alone time to make the call and rearrange our plans, so he'll have to do it on my behalf. He agrees without argument, and I send her number to his cell.

Faye grips my hand tight as we vacate the station. Swarms of reporters crowd the pavement outside and Dad has to wrestle his way through the masses to get us to the rental. Mercifully, he had the forethought to organize a vehicle with blacked-out windows, and I only start breathing again once we are safely tucked away inside.

No one speaks the entire ride to the hotel, but that suits me just fine. Faye never lets go of my hand, and I'm so grateful for her support. Her unquestioning loyalty. Mom checks us in, and I'm beyond pissed when I discover she's booked separate rooms for Faye and me. Before I can raise any objection, Faye takes matters into her own hands. "I'm staying with Ky, so you can return this key and get your money back."

"Honey," Mom starts to say, but Faye stalls her with one of her special, deadly looks.

"I'm not leaving him by himself. Period." She stubbornly holds the key out to Mom.

My eyes meet Dad's for the first time, and a flare of pride glimmers in his gaze. Mom pouts, frowning. "For God's sake, Alexandra," Dad says, not attempting to hide the disdain in his tone. "Let them be. They need each other."

Mom takes the keycard from Faye without another word, returning to the reception desk. Kal is the only one to wait for her. Dad takes the elevator with us, and we ride to the top floor in awkward silence. We reach our door first.

"Kyler." Dad sounds nervous. "I'd really like to speak with you."

I rest my forehead on the door, squeezing my eyes shut. It's not that I want to shut him out. I know he's hurting as much as me, and that's the whole point. *I can barely handle my own pain, so how the hell am I expected to deal with his too?*

"Please, son. I need you to hear me out." His voice is choked with emotion, and that decides it for me. For years, I've harbored anger at his failure to protect me the one time I really needed him to. For years, I've enjoyed taking Mom's side in arguments purely to punish him. For years, I've picked fights with him, knowing it stressed him out and relishing that fact. These last few months have inflamed my anger—his affair with Courtney, his handling of the situation with Kent, his collusion with Mom in hiding the truth about Keven and Kaden, the sick revelation of his relationship with his sister, all adding fuel to the fire—and I've taken pleasure from watching him struggle.

But I don't take pleasure in this.

I wouldn't wish this on my worst enemy.

For the first time, all my rage is reserved for my mother, and my full sympathy is with Dad.

It won't kill me to do this for him.

And I think I need it as much as he does.

I pick my head up, turning to face him. "Okay."

Chapter Twelve

Kyler

The look of blatant relief on his face has me feeling all kinds of guilty for running away without giving any consideration to his feelings. Faye opens the door to our room and dumps our bags quickly. "I'm going to scout out the hotel. I'll leave you two to chat in private."

"You don't have to leave."

"I won't be far. Text me when you're done, and I'll come back up." She hugs me, and my arms automatically wind around her waist—I love holding her close. "Open up to him," she whispers in my ear. "Tell him how you're feeling. I promise you'll feel better for it."

I cup her face in both hands, and kiss her briefly. "I love you." I don't care that Dad hears. "Thank you for standing by me."

"I love you too." Her whole face lights up like a glow worm. She pecks Dad on the cheek, squeezing his arm as she passes.

Silence descends when the door closes after her. I shuffle anxiously on my feet, looking everywhere but at him.

"I'm glad you have her by your side."

"Me, too."

"I'm going to make a coffee. Would you like one?"

I look up. "Um, sure."

Dad fixes coffees while I take a seat at the small circular glass dining table. My eyes scan the room flippantly. It's not as plush as the suite we had back in the last hotel, but it's a decent size, and it has a nice balcony too. It'll suffice for however long we're forced to remain here.

Dad hands a cup to me, and I accept it gratefully. "Thank you."

He claims the seat across from me, clasping the cup between his large hands, as he stares at me. I stare back, seeing the same hurt and confusion in his eyes. "How are you coping?" he asks finally.

I shrug.

"Your mother and I have made our fair share of mistakes, I know that, and I'm no saint, but this ..." He clamps a hand over his mouth, and I'm horrified when tears flood his eyes. "This is the worst betrayal. I can't believe she lied to me all these years. Now, I understand why she was so insistent on keeping the news from Kaden and Keven in the first place. She knew this would come out eventually, and she was doing everything she could to avoid facing facts."

"You never suspected?" I take a tentative sip of my coffee.

He vigorously shakes his head. "No. Never. You're a lot like me in so many ways, Ky, and I always thought our relationship was strained because we were so similar. This has ... this has destroyed me."

"How do you think I've felt?" I put my coffee down, unable to swallow over the tears clogging my throat.

Silence engulfs us again. There's so much I want to say but can't get out. I'm generally not good with heavy emotional stuff.

He leans back in his chair, sighing. "I'm upset because it's made a mockery of my memories, made a mockery of my marriage, and everything I thought I knew, but, it wouldn't be killing me in here"—he slams a hand over his heart—"if I didn't love you so much." His eyes pool with tears, and I'm struggling to keep a grip on my own composure.

I'm not going to cry again.

Especially not in front of him or Mom.

"That will never change, and you will always be my son. That awful man may have played a part in your creation, but he will never replace me as your father."

My chest tightens. Dad's words hang in the air, and the anguished look on his face makes him appear more vulnerable than I've ever seen him. I remember how distraught he was the day he found out that Faye's mom had been killed, but that pales in comparison with how he looks now. "I'm sorry," I blurt out, and he frowns. "For running off without speaking to you. For fighting with you all these years. It seems so pointless now."

And it does. I think back to all the arguments we've had and how I used to wish he wasn't my dad. Now, I'd do anything to take those wishes back. To know he was my dad in every meaning of the word. To undo all knowledge of the sperm donor and of Mom's betrayal. I don't feel any grief or pity he's dead. My only feelings where he's concerned are selfish ones—I don't want to end up being wrongly accused of his murder—and that's the extent of it.

"That doesn't matter now," Dad says, stretching across the table to pat my hand. "All that matters is not losing you. I couldn't bear to lose any more than I already have."

My throat constricts, and speaking is becoming difficult. "I don't want to lose you either."

Dad stands up, tears freely flowing down his face. "I know you're a grown man, but I really need to hug you right now." He walks around the table, pulling me up and into his arms.

A sob rips from my throat, startling me. I lean into the hug, needing this more than I realized. "What do you say we use this as a fresh start?" He shifts a little so he can look me dead in the eye.

I nod, surprised at how genuine my response is. A do-over sounds pretty perfect. While it won't change the facts, I'm so relieved that he still wants me in his life. That the mistakes of my past haven't pushed him away. That calling me his son means so much to him.

I never realized before how much I need him.

How much I love him.

Why does it take the threat of losing someone to make you appreciate them in the way you should?

Faye and I spend the remainder of the evening half-heartedly watching old movies on the TV in our room. Later, we meet Dad and Kal for a late dinner in a private section of the dining room. Mom tried to talk to me earlier, but I made it clear I'm not ready for that showdown yet. I appreciate that she declined to join us for dinner, knowing full and well that if she attended I would have stayed in my room.

I don't miss the surreptitious looks leveled my way as I walk hand in hand with Faye through the room after dinner. She glares at every person who dares look sideways at me, and it's the first thing to bring a smile to my lips all day. She has no idea how much her loyalty and support means to me.

I'm lying flat on my back in our bed, staring blankly at the ceiling when Faye emerges from the bathroom bathed in a cloud of steam. Her hair is pinned in a messy bun on top of her head, her face is flushed red and scrubbed clean of makeup, and she has her candy-colored pajama shorts and tank top on. She looks so adorable, and I love that she doesn't try to impress me. There's nothing more attractive than a girl who's confident in her own skin.

Addison was so tiring in that regard. While she was always groomed to perfection, she constantly sought out compliments. I was so naïve back then. I used to think she needed reassurance. Now, I know it was all down to vanity and her need to be the center of attention. Faye is her polar opposite and I couldn't be happier about that. She doesn't need praise or the adoration of her peers to feel comfortable in her own skin. She owns it effortlessly, and I love her so much for it. My eyes drink their fill, and my heart swells with everything I feel for her. She looks good enough to eat, and all the blood rushes to a certain part of my anatomy.

She leaps onto the bed, holding a glass bottle with a fancy label on it in her hand. She scoots to my side. "Roll over." I quirk a brow. "Don't ask. Just do." I love her bossy side, and I do as I'm told, flipping over onto my stomach. She straddles me, pressing that soft part of her body against my ass and I'm rock hard in a split second. She rubs her hands together, before tossing the bottle on the bed beside her. "Now blank your mind and just relax."

Her oily hands land on my bare back, instantly heating me all over. She kneads the knots in my shoulders before maneuvering her way along all the stiff muscles of my back. A moan flies out of my mouth as I sink lower into the mattress. Next, she runs her thumbs outward from my spine in strong, bold moves that penetrate bone deep. She keeps up a similar pattern, firmly kneading my back, loosening my muscles, and releasing some tension. My hard-on is digging into the bed almost painfully, and my skin is on fire from her skillful ministrations. When her fingertips flit lightly up and down my back, like a feather-soft brush sweeping across my skin, a heady moan slips out of my lips. "Where'd you learn to do this?" I murmur in an intoxicated voice.

"Mum did a course in massage and reflexology a few years ago," she explains, continuing to sweep her fingers over my back. "I was her guinea pig, and she practiced on me every day for a month. It was great." She laughs and it's so wonderful to hear her speaking about her mother without the usual grief and hurt undercutting her tone. "I liked it so much I got her to show me some of her techniques."

"Your hands are magic," I rasp, and I know I sound like I'm high.

She chuckles. "So are yours."

I take that as my cue, bumping her off and flipping around mega fast. I pull her down on top of me, angling my hips so she can tell how much I want her. Shuttering her eyes, she throws back her head and emits a throaty, breathy sound that supercharges my lust. "Now it's my turn to make you feel good," I murmur before my mouth claims hers in a scorching hot kiss.

My hands are all over her, greedily caressing the creamy skin and generous cleavage hiding under her shirt. Her nipples are already hard, and she grinds her hips against me as I tweak her nipples playfully. Sitting up, she whips her top off, gyrating against me with wild abandon. We strip off the rest of our clothes, and when I thrust inside her, everything else is forgotten. In this moment, all that matters is how much I love the girl exploding on top of me and how amazing it feels to be moving with her like this.

We are lying flat on our backs, bodies slick with sweat and chests visibly heaving, exhausted from our lengthy lovemaking. With the tip of my finger, I make circular swirls on her stomach. Bending my head, I gently kiss the jagged scar running horizontally over her belly button.

When I think of everything we've been through, it's amazing that we've gotten to this place. I couldn't be any happier with this aspect of my life. "Being confined to this hotel for the next few days is looking more and more appealing," I tease, grazing my nose up the column of her neck.

She giggles, squirming underneath me. "I agree completely." Her hair is fanned out behind her head, and her entire face is flushed and glowing. She looks like a fucking goddess—all ethereal and shit.

"I love when you look at me like that," she whispers, running the tip of her finger along my bottom lip.

I prop up on an elbow, pressing a delicate kiss to that sensitive spot just behind her ear. She shivers, and my chest puffs out with pride. "Like what?"

"Like you see right into me. Into all the hidden parts, and I'm exposed but I don't feel afraid because I see the understanding and love shining in your eyes. And your eyes. God, Ky. They're so dark and smoldering, and you consume me with such an intense look. It sets my body on fire." Her eyes glaze over, and she emits a breathy gasp that reignites my desire. "But it's more than lust. It's completeness. I see your devotion and the accompanying emotion—it's like you can't get enough of me."

"I do, and I can't." I plant a flurry of tiny kisses up and down her neck, and my body starts stirring to life again.

She palms the back of my head, forcing my gaze to hers. "I'm loving being here with you like this, but I'm worried about you too."

I rub my thumb along the crease in her forehead, smoothing out the line. "I'm not gonna lie, I'm worried as well, but I didn't kill him and I've got to hope that's enough. And maybe you were right about that girl. Perhaps she did it." I drop down on the pillow beside her, entwining my hand in hers. "Hell, it could be any number of suspects. A man like that has to have had a bucket load of enemies, and it's not like I'm the only kid he fathered."

She sits bolt upright, her hair tumbling in waves over her bare shoulders. "What do you mean by that?"

"He made some flippant comment about not caring for any of his kids. I got the sense he wasn't just talking about me, Kaden, and Kev."

She bites down on her lower lip, and a primal growl erupts from the back of my throat. I'm hard as a rock and ready for the next round. She glances down my body, and a lusty grin appears on her face. All conversation ends when she straddles me, lowering herself steadily on top of me, inch by slow inch.

A loud pounding on the door wakes us both up the next morning. "What the heck?" Faye asks in a sleep-drenched tone. I grab my jeans off the floor, hastily pulling them on as I head across the room. The last time we were in a hotel and there was a knock on the door it was the cops. I'm hoping I'm not in for a repeat experience.

I check the peephole, and a huge grin spreads over my face. I yank the door open and my brothers bail into the room without apology. Faye yelps, dragging the covers up under her chin. One by one, my brothers greet me, and I'm touched they came all the way here. Brad is the last to step inside, and his eyes lock on Faye's before he's even met mine. Although he plants an appropriate expression on his face as he turns to me, he isn't quick enough to hide his blatant unhappiness, or his longing. That's another situation that needs to be dealt with, but I'm leaving it for another day.

"Hey, man." He punches me in the arm. "Good to see you."

"You too."

"How come you're all here?" I ask Kaden.

"Dude, it's Thanksgiving, and even though we've all this shit to wade through, family is family."

"And Kennedys stick together," Keven adds.

"Stop it!" Faye screeches, and I jump to her rescue.

Kal and Keaton are on either side of her on the bed, tugging playfully on the comforter and teasing her about her obvious nakedness. "Off. Now," I demand. "As much as I love that you're all here, you need to get out and let Faye get dressed. How about we meet downstairs for breakfast?" I suggest. "See if you can get that private section again, Kal."

I shoo them all out, and then Faye and I take a shower together that turns into a steamy session in more ways than one. When we eventually make our entrance in the restaurant, my brothers clap loudly, adding a few catcalls into the mix. Faye buries her head in my neck, and I laugh. I'm so glad they're here. This kind of distraction is exactly what I need.

Kade and Kev take me aside after breakfast, informing me that all my brothers know about my real dad. Apparently, Mom informed everyone before she left. I'm glad I don't have to break that news. I tell them everything about my meeting with Doug on Monday night. Keven laughs. "I can't believe you punched him. Wish I'd been a fly on the wall for that."

"I can't believe you *didn't* punch him," I retort, knowing Kev's penchant for getting into trouble.

"I wanted to, but he had us out of his house so fast I never got the chance. At least he seemed to want to talk to you. Why was that?"

My stomach lurches to my toes as I lie. "Who knows?" I shrug, averting my eyes so I'm not lying to their faces. I want to tell my brothers about that, but I can't face up to it yet.

"Perhaps he felt closer to you because of the motocross connection," Kaden muses.

"Don't say that," I snap. "I hate that." And I do. My ambition in relation to motocross seems tarnished now. I don't want any connection to that man. While the media hasn't reported on the fact he was my biological father, focusing instead on his murder and my arrest for questioning in relation to same, I know it's only a matter of time before they discover the facts. Before they draw inevitable comparisons. Suddenly, motocross seems like a dirty word to me. I'm not sure how I'm going to deal with that.

Kaden and Keven scowl at something or someone behind me, and all the tiny hairs on the back of my neck stand to attention. I know she's there before I've even seen her, and I know I can't avoid her forever.

"Kyler," Mom says, materializing at my side. "I need to talk to you, and I'm not taking no for an answer today."

Chapter Thirteen

Kyler

We're in Mom's suite, and I'm seated across from her on one of the couches waiting for her to speak.

She wanted to do this.

She can kick it off.

"I'm very, very sorry, Kyler," she says in a quiet voice, knotting and unknotting her hands in her lap. "There isn't really anything I can say that is going to excuse what I did or make it better."

That majorly pisses me off. I stand up. "I guess that about covers it." I stalk toward the door, every step infusing my cells with raw anger.

"Stop," she calls out in a firm voice. "Sit back down. I'm not done."

I spin around, glaring at her. "Why should I?! It'll only be more lies." Crossing my arms, I stand my ground.

She gets up and walks toward me. "I deserve that. I deserve your anger and your frustration. I've lied to you about something important, and you have a right to hate me. I don't blame you for that, for anything. It was unforgivable. It *is* unforgivable. I know that."

"So why did you do it, Mom? Why?"

"You know why, Kyler. I chose the best dad for you. My motivation was pure even if the way I went about it wasn't."

My anger bubbles up again. "You don't get to choose something like that! You're not God!" I start pacing the room, trying to put myself in her shoes, to fathom why she did the things she did. "Were you so unsure of James that you presumed he'd walk out on you? Is that it?"

"That was part of it. I know now I was wrong. James would have stood by me, and I didn't give him the chance to do that. I got pregnant before I met him, and he wouldn't have held that against me. He took Kaden and Keven on as if they were his own, and I know he would've done the same with you." Her eyes well up. "I wish I could go back. I wish I did so many things differently. I wish he had adopted you three and you'd known from the start that he was your stepdad. That's what I *should've* done, but I was too young, too naïve, too scared, to even realize I had options back then."

She gently takes my arm. "Tell me what I can to do fix things between us and I'll do it." A lone tear rolls down her cheek. "I love you, honey, and I don't want to lose you."

My mind is a quagmire and I'm sinking, fast. I can't make any sense of the crap in my head. "I can't tell you how to fix this when I don't even know *if* it's fixable, Mom. Maybe, I could accept what you've just said if you didn't lie about it a few weeks ago. When Faye figured out the truth about Kaden and Keven, you should have told me then that he was my dad too. But you didn't. Not only that, when my brothers asked you outright if he was my dad too, *you lied*. To. Their. Faces."

I shuck her hand off, scrunching fistfuls of my hair. "You just kept piling on the lies. Instead of facing the truth, instead of *owning* it, you dug bigger holes. How am I expected to have any respect for you when you conduct yourself like that? You are supposed to be our role models in life, and both you and Dad are acting appallingly. I don't know what's going on in your marriage, what's going on with Courtney, but you have both behaved completely selfishly, and I don't know that I can forgive you for that."

She wraps her arms around herself, and her bottom lip trembles.

"At this point, it feels like I'm better off on my own, because all my pain stems from irresponsible adults. The only people I can truly rely on are my brothers and Faye. They are the only ones without an agenda."

"Kyler. Your father and I don't have an agenda except to love and provide for you and your brothers. I cannot deny anything you've said. You're right. I've been taking a long hard look at myself, at my life, confronting the mistakes I've made, and the ones I'm still making, and I'm going to make changes." Her chin lifts defiantly. "I don't think it's too late to fix certain things, is it?"

I throw my hands up in the air, shaking my head. "I don't know, Mom. It's too soon to say. I need time, and I can't think straight when I'm so angry with you. It's hard to find any love in my heart for you right now."

The look of naked grief on her face is hard to stomach, especially knowing my words put that look there, but I'm done lying. I'm done hiding. I'm done pretending. If things are going to change in our family, we need to start speaking more openly and honestly. I can't control how my parents or my brothers act, but I can control how I act. And I'm done hiding behind a wall, disguising my feelings in some misguided attempt at protection. Faye is right about that. I need to protect myself, first and foremost. Dad spoke about a do-over, and I'm going to embrace that fully.

Mom organized for caterers to serve our Thanksgiving dinner in her suite, but it's the most sober, most low-key celebration in the history of Kennedy family celebrations. Mom and Dad are sitting at opposite ends of the table failing to hide the animosity between them. Kaden and Keven won't even look at Mom, and Keaton is on the verge of tears the entire time. Kent is sullen and withdrawn—not that that's anything new—and Keanu is staying out of it as usual. Brad is sneaking glances at Faye when he thinks I'm not looking, and I'm growing more and more frustrated with him by the second. Kal and Faye are the only ones acting normally, keeping the conversation flowing, but it's strained and rather one-sided.

When the buzzer sounds and my attorney walks into our suite, you can almost hear the collective sigh of relief at the welcome interruption.

"I'm sorry to interrupt," he says.

Mom smiles. "Not at all, Fitzgerald. And thank you for interrupting your day to update us."

"I have some good news." He looks directly at me. "You're off the hook for now, and you're free to return home, but don't leave the country."

"Does this mean my son is no longer a suspect?" Dad asks.

"Unfortunately, no. He is still being looked into, but for now, they don't have enough to hold him or charge him. There was no gunshot residue on his hands, and without the weapon, all they have is circumstantial, but that doesn't mean they have ruled him out completely. Their investigation will be ongoing, and Kyler must be prepared to return for further questioning if required."

Dad places his napkin on the table, standing up. "Of course, and thank you." They shake hands.

"What about that girl?" Faye asks. "The waitress. Is she a suspect?"

"I don't believe so. It seems she has an alibi from the time she left Mr. Grant's property earlier on that night until the next morning. It wasn't her."

Faye sighs. "Do they have any other suspects?"

"I believe they are exploring several lines of inquiry" is the vague reply. It doesn't give me a warm and fuzzy feeling. Neither does the prospect of going home. The tension here today is almost unbearable, and I'm not sure I can take much more of it.

We pack up pretty much immediately and make our way to the airport where Dad's private jet awaits. He had too much wine at dinner, so Michael, Dad's standby pilot, is flying us home. We have only just taken off when Mom hands me a sheet of paper. "I'm issuing this press release the minute we land. If you have any problem with it, now is the time to tell me."

She returns to her seat while Faye and I read over the official statement she's planning on making. My stomach churns anxiously as I read. "Wow," Faye whispers. "She's really going to come clean about that?"

"This is damage control, pure and simple." I can't keep the disgust from my tone. Her statement confirms that her three eldest children were Doug Grant's biological children and her husband has always known. Dad has signed off on this lie, which surprises me. I unbuckle my seat belt and walk over to him. "Why are you agreeing to this?" I thrust the press release in front of his face. Kade and Kev materialize at my side, also clutching a copy of the statement.

"Sit down," he gestures, and I slink into the seat beside him while my brothers take the pair of seats facing us across the glossy walnut-topped table. Dad swirls the whiskey in his glass. "I'm only agreeing to this for you three. I'm certainly not doing this for your mother," he adds bitterly. "This family has had enough press intrusion recently, and I'd like to make this go away as fast as I can. Putting an end to speculation up front is the best strategy." His gaze skates between us. "For your sakes."

"The press release also confirms the divorce is going ahead," Kaden remarks.

Dad makes a disgruntled sound. "You hardly expect me to stay with your mother after this." He knocks back his drink. "We can barely tolerate each other at this stage."

Kev looks away, and Kaden rubs a hand along the back of his neck. "I'm not trying to tell you what to do, Dad, but you're upset right now. Perhaps it isn't the best time to be making such a big decision. You may feel differently in a few weeks after you've had time to think about it." Kade's suggestion is pragmatic.

"The trust is gone, son. On both sides, and I have to shoulder my fair share of the blame. Once the trust is gone, it's very difficult to continue a marriage."

"If you're going to speak about me behind my back, you could at least keep your voice down," Mom hollers, attracting everyone's attention.

"You're releasing a statement to the press the second we get off this plane. It's going to become common knowledge. Stop trying to pick another fight. I'm done arguing with you," he shouts back.

"What statement?" Keaton asks from behind me, leaning over his chair with a perplexed expression. I hand him my copy, watching as all the blood leaches from his face while he reads. Keanu, Kal, and Kent all read over his shoulder.

"What does this mean?" Keaton asks with tears in his eyes. "Please don't leave again, Dad."

"I'm not going anywhere," Dad confirms, nudging me in the side. I step out, allowing him to go to Keaton. He pulls him into a hug, kissing the top of his head. "Your mother and I are divorcing and there's lots to be decided, but for now, we will continue to live in the same house. Your mother will bury her head in work, and you'll hardly see her. It won't feel any different," he snipes.

Faye glances at me with saddened eyes, and I'm so over all this drama. If my parents are going to continue acting like juvenile brats, I'm damned if I'm going to stick around to watch the next episode.

It's late by the time we get back to the house. Everyone goes their separate ways, and I pull Faye into my room. "Are you planning on returning to school tomorrow?"

"Yeah. I've missed enough time, and it's better to show my face and deal with the latest crap than hide away here."

I kiss her hard. "I love that about you."

"I love everything about you," she murmurs, and my heart does a funny flip in my chest.

"I'm going to face the music too, and I've been thinking about something on the flight back. Everyone is going to know we're not related now, and I want to make our relationship status official. Are you okay with that?"

Her hands creep up my chest. "I'm more than okay with that." She gives me a big grin, and I kiss her again. "But are you sure you want to do this now? There's going to be enough gossip tomorrow as it is."

"My new motto is it's best to get everything out in the open."

She tweaks my nose. "Okay. I'm in."

"Then we need to talk to Brad. Agree how we deal with the ending of your 'fake relationship.'"

She grimaces. "Aw, crap. I'm so not looking forward to that conversation."

"I know, but I can't say I'm sorry." I don't voice my suspicions, because I don't think she has quite figured it out, and there's no harm in sparing her the additional guilt. "I'll talk to him. You go to bed, but make sure to leave your window open." I smooth a hand up and down her back, squeezing her ass playfully.

"Nice try, mister." She extracts my hand from her ass. "As much as it's tempting to chicken out, there's no way I'm not sitting in on this convo."

Faye waits in the games room while I go to get Brad. He drops down onto the couch across from us, crossing his leg over his knee while he leans back casually. "'Sup?"

"The fake relationship ends now," I blurt, and Faye prods me in the ribs, rolling her eyes and shaking her head.

"What Ky means," she says, pinning me with a formidable look, "is that we're really grateful for your support with stuff at school and all you've done to help us, but we're going public so we need to discuss how we end our pretend relationship."

I drape my arm around Faye's shoulder, eyeballing my bud. "Yeah, that."

Brad shrugs, trying to downplay it, even though he looks like he just swallowed something nasty. "You haven't been at school all week, so we can say we broke up last weekend, and no one will be any the wiser," he suggests.

"How will we get the word out?" Faye asks.

"Tell Rose and Zoe first thing, and ask them to start spreading it around. I won't sit with you at lunch anymore—I'll sit with the guys and find some opportunity to slide it into conversation. It's no biggie."

Except I suspect it is.

Faye's brows crinkle. "The lunch thing is only temporary though, right? I like sitting with you for lunch."

I smother the possessive growl lurking at the base of my throat. I know she doesn't mean it like that.

Brad shrugs, feigning indifference again, and he's really starting to piss me off now. "We'll see how it plays out."

He stands up, making a show of stretching his arms out over his head. His shirt lifts, exposing a strip of his toned abs, and I know he's done that on purpose. Only this isn't like the time with Addison, because I didn't love her like I love Faye. If Brad is fixing to mess this up for me, he can think again. My throat constricts.

If it comes down to it, I'll choose Faye.

It will always only ever be her.

He should know better than to test me a second time.

"I'll see you in the morning. Night." He ambles out of the room, whistling under his breath like he hasn't a care in the world.

"Huh," Faye says, flopping down beside me. "That went easier than I expected."

I'm not buying that she's buying this for a second. She's way too smart to fall for that load of bull, but I don't want to get into it with her. She's my only link to sanity and the one person I don't want to pick a fight with right now. "At least it's one less thing to worry about. You sure you're okay with this?"

She twists around to face me. "Yes. I want people to know I'm yours. We should go out this weekend, somewhere really public, so people see us together."

"Good idea." I kiss her forehead, before pulling her up on her feet. Sweeping my arms around her, I lift her fully off the ground. She laughs, and I swat her butt. "I have a couple things to do before bed. Why don't you go get ready, and I'll join you in a bit?"

"I'll do that, but don't be long." She plants a quick kiss on my lips. "I'll be waiting under the covers for you as naked as the day I was born." Fire simmers in her eyes, and it's like a shot of liquid lust straight to my dick. Before I can take advantage, she steals away from me, blowing me a cheeky kiss as she sprints to her room.

Little tease.

I head to my room, quickly stripping and changing into sweats. I check the time and then make the call I need to. "Hey. It's Kyler. Sorry about today. Couldn't be helped, but I can reschedule it for tomorrow it that works?" Excited chatter meets my ears, and I grin. I can't wait to see her face. "It's cool. No sweat. Great. See you then."

I end the call with a smug smile on my face.

I stop by Brad's room on my way to Faye. "We need to talk." I shut the door behind me as Brad pulls his earphones off.

"About what?"

I lean against the wall. "You know what." His brows lift, and sudden darkness rushes me. "Knock that shit off, bro. I know you've got feelings for her, and I'm not doing this with you again."

"Doing what, Ky?" Brad's snarky tone surprises me. "You're the one with the girl, as usual, so don't come in here all pissed and try to rile me up. I haven't done anything wrong this time, and I'm not going to either."

I sigh, walking over to his bed and dropping down beside him. "You can't have feelings for her. She's it for me, Brad. She's the one."

His expression turns solemn. "Are you on the level?"

I nod. "I'll never want anyone but her. I've never felt more sure of anything."

His shoulders drop, and he loses the mask of indifference. Staring at me, he looks utterly miserable. "I want to be happy for you, man, I do, but it's hard because I'm in love with her too."

I cringe. This is much worse than I thought. "What are you planning to do about it?"

He looks startled. "What the hell?!" Now *he* looks pissed. "I'm not planning on doing anything! She's yours. I get that, and I'm under no illusion. She loves you, not me. I'll get over it."

"What about us?" I ask. He shrugs, and I lock my hands behind my head. "Your friendship matters to me, but she means everything. Maybe we all just need a little distance."

"You want me to move out?" he asks.

"What?" I level a disbelieving look his way. "No! Of course not." I know he doesn't really have anywhere to go, and I don't want to make him feel unwelcome here. "You're family, and you're welcome to stay here as long as you need to. No matter what transpires between us going forward, don't ever doubt that."

He nods. "Thanks."

"I know it's like living in a lunatic asylum, but it's got to be better than sleeping in your car."

Marginally.

He smirks. "Dude, you're not wrong, but it's weirdly comforting. Makes my problems seem like a walk in the park."

"You still haven't heard anything?" He shakes his head. "That sucks," I admit, even if a part of me wishes my parents had to exile themselves to a different continent. I feel guilty the instant that thought surfaces in my mind. Brad's missing his family like crazy, and I know he'd do anything to be with them, and here I am wishing to offload mine. Other people's issues always have a way of putting things into perspective.

"Will you be around tomorrow night?" I ask.

"Can be."

"That thing that was supposed to happen today is happening tomorrow now. I'd like you to hang with us, if you're okay with that? I think I'll need some masculine moral support."

"I'll be there."

I rise. "Thanks." I stop at the door, turning to face him. "Keep looking out for her in school, okay?" He nods slowly. "Even though Addison has been cautioned to keep her distance, I wouldn't put it past her to get Peyton to do her dirty work."

"I agree, and don't worry, I'll make sure she's safe. I don't want to see anything else happen to her."

"Are we going to be okay?"

"I hope so," he says, but the look on his face tells me he's every bit as worried as I am.

Chapter Fourteen

Faye

Brad is uncharacteristically quiet the next morning on the journey to school. Things have never been more awkward between us, and I want to mend that, but I don't know how. Right now, I have more pressing concerns, like the fact that Adam is arriving tomorrow to speak to me. *I've no doubt it's a reaction to the current media reports because why else would he go back on his word?* He told me to set the pace, and I requested another week to think things over, but his text told me this was not up for debate.

He'll be in town tomorrow morning, and he asked me to meet him at the diner. I informed him of the need to change the venue, due to the diner's closure, so we're meeting at a small café on the other side of town instead. The coffee is pretty dire, but the muffins are to die for.

"You okay to do this today?" I ask Brad as we walk into the school building.

"What choice do I have?" His tone is biting, and a flash of hurt flickers over his face. I knew he was totally spoofing last night. That look just confirmed it.

My stomach drops. "I knew it would end badly," I mutter, half to myself. I yank my locker open with more force than necessary.

His warm hand lands over mine. "I'm sorry, that was unfair of me. I'm happy things have worked out with Ky and that you're able to have a normal relationship."

I grab the books I need and drop them in my bag. "You really mean that?"

He pauses before answering. "I want to mean it. Does that count?"

His words further confirm my suspicions, and I don't know what to do with that. *Is this my fault? Have I led him on?* "I'm sorry." My eyes penetrate his, and I hate seeing the hurt there, knowing I'm responsible.

"You have nothing to be sorry for." He smiles but it doesn't quite meet his eyes. "Don't mind me. I'm just having a bad day."

"You sure?" He falls into step beside me as I walk toward my first class.

"Yeah." He leans in to kiss my cheek and stops. "Sorry." His skin flushes ever so subtly, and he takes a step back. "It's become too comfortable with you. I'll get the word out during first period, and if you do the same, I'm sure it's all anyone will be talking about at lunch."

I flatten my back to the wall, noting the snide glances being leveled my way as students pass by. "Yeah, that and the latest Kennedy scandal." At least there were no reporters outside our school this time, but judging by the crowd outside the house this morning, I'm sure my cousins are fighting the vultures over at O.C. Not for the first time, I wish Ky went here with me. My protective instincts are flying at full mast, and I hate that I can't be there to deflect some of the heat. Kal assured me he'd watch out for him, but it's not the same. *I* want to be there for him.

I wave goodbye to Brad and step into the classroom, ignoring the hushed whispers as I tap out a quick message to my boyfriend. *"Miss you already. Don't let the haters get you down."*

I manage to fill Zoe and Rose in during the break between classes, telling them that Brad and I broke up at the weekend and I'm dating Ky now. While it isn't news to Rose, this is the first time Zoe is hearing about it. Her nose wrinkles in distaste. I slam to a halt in the corridor, and the girl behind plows into me, cursing. I mumble an apology over my shoulder, and she quickly backs off. "What?" I whip around to Zoe. "You don't like Kyler either?"

"It's not that. He's your cousin."

"Only by marriage. Haven't you seen the news? He has a different dad, and there's no blood ties."

"I heard that, but you've been living as cousins up to this point, so were you, like, getting it on while you thought you were? 'Cause that's kinda sick."

"We weren't," I say, and it's not really a lie. We didn't sleep together until after we found out. "And none of that matters now. He's my boyfriend, and there's no law that says he can't be."

I storm off leaving those parting words ringing in her ears.

Every pair of eyes follows my movement the instant I set foot in the cafeteria, but I don't care. I've been expecting this, and the benefits of coming clean far outweigh the negatives. By next week, this will all blow over, and Ky and I will be free to date and be together with nothing in our way.

I'm walking toward our usual table when Peyton steps in front of me, startling me. My glass of juice spills onto the tray. "Move," I demand.

"No." She plants her hands on her hips, glaring at me. The football team hasn't arrived yet so it's little wonder she's pulling this stunt now.

"Move or I'll make you." I glare back at her.

She laughs, and her eyes narrow to slits. "You are in no position to make demands." She starts circling me, her eyes flashing with glee. "You're a sick bitch, but you know that, right." Her voice raises a notch. "What kind of twisted inbred fucks her own cousin?" Her insult projects around the room. She prods me in the shoulder, and I grind my teeth down to the molars.

"He's not my cousin, and you know that. Your pathetic attempts to reassert control are just that. *Pa*-thetic. Now get out of my way before I fucking make you."

She violently slams her hand up underneath my tray, dislodging the contents. Particles of food cover me, and rivulets of juice sluice down my front. The tray crashes to the floor, sending spatters of food flying in all directions. A few girls shriek, lurching out of their seats to avoid getting sprayed. If anyone wasn't looking at us before, they sure as hell are now.

All eyes are glued to this spot.

I pull a string of spaghetti off my face and flick it at her. She doesn't react fast enough and it lands squarely across her forehead. I smirk, flexing my fist before it juts out and hits her firmly in the face. She staggers back, clutching her nose. "You bitch!" she roars before hurling herself at me.

We tumble to the ground, and my head whacks off the hard, tiled floor. We roll around, kicking and punching one another. She grabs tufts of my hair and yanks painfully. My head is tugged back as she rams her fist in my stomach. I lash out, scraping my nails across her cheek, and her ear-piercing scream almost deafens me. "Oh my God, I'm bleeding," she shrieks, letting go of my head. "I'm fucking bleeding!" I scramble to my feet, swaying on shaky limbs as she grabs hold of my legs, pulling me back down. My knee stabs her in the chest as I sprawl awkwardly on top of her.

Her nails dig into the flesh of my stomach, right at the place of my recent scar, and I scream out in agony. Darts of pain ricochet all over my stomach, and my head explodes with a burst of blinding white spots. Biting down hard on my lip, I taste blood but it's secondary to the anger-fueled adrenaline coursing through me, taking control. I lash out, swinging wildly as her fingers continue to inflict pain. My fist impacts her nose with a satisfying bone-crunching sound.

Pounding footsteps barely register until I'm ripped away from her. Someone is holding me up as my legs and arms flail about. Murderous rage still lingers in my tissues, and I'm thrashing about like a crazy person.

"Faye, stop. Calm down," Brad whispers urgently in my ear. "The principal is coming."

"You two," Principal Carter shouts, pointing between Peyton and me. Steam is practically billowing out of her ears. "In my office. Now!" Lance is holding Peyton firmly across the waist, but she's bucking and writhing as much as me.

"You're dead, bitch," she threatens, spitting at me, and I bite out a laugh.

"Yeah, I don't think so." I flip her the bird, and she goes crazy, fighting and screaming at Lance to let her go.

Principal Carter looms in my line of sight again. "Did I not make myself perfectly clear? Get into my office now or I'll expel you both!"

Brad escorts me to the principal's office. I glance down at myself and my ruined clothes, pulling up the hem of my sweater to inspect my stomach. A trickle of blood seeps out of the corner of my scar, and the skin above it is marred with a line of jagged nail marks, also oozing blood.

"What the fuck?" Brad gestures at Lance, pointing to my stomach. "You're going down for this." He sneers at Peyton, and my heart warms at his loyalty.

"If I'm going down, then so is she. Look what she did to my nose!" she hollers, pointing at the swollen, bloody mess in the middle of her face.

I'd say we're pretty much even-stevens.

The principal opens the door to her office and shoos us in with an impatient wave of her hands. "Sit there." She points at a line of chairs against the wall in front of her secretary's desk. "You as well," she tells Brad and Lance as they make a move to leave. "I don't trust these two to be left on their own."

The boys sit down.

"Given the seriousness of this situation, I have already called your parents. We'll wait for their arrival." She stomps into her private office, slamming the door shut behind her. I've never seen her lose her cool, so I know I'm in a shitload of trouble. I'd like to say I care, but honestly, I don't. Peyton doesn't get to call me an inbred and get away with it.

Peyton and I spend the next twenty minutes in a silent face-off while the boys trade hushed insults every few minutes. I glare at her, putting every ounce of hatred for her and Addison behind it. I think her nose might be broken, and it would serve her right. It would almost be worth getting expelled for.

"Honey, are you okay?" Alex gushes, rushing into the room, exuding concern. James sends me a disappointed look, and my bluster starts to wobble. Alex's eyes widen in horror when she sees the blood trickling over my stomach. "Faye needs medical attention, and this is unacceptable," she protests, scowling at the principal's secretary.

"I'm only following orders, ma'am," the mousy-haired secretary replies, squirming in her seat.

Principal Carter opens her door, alerted by the raised voices. "Mr. and Mrs. Kennedy, thank you for arriving so promptly." They shake hands.

"My niece needs to see the nurse," James grits out.

"Our nurse is on standby. Ms. Moore is on her way, and once we have discussed this matter and dealt with it by mutual agreement, the girls can go to the nurse's station."

Alex opens her mouth to protest, but the principal stalls her with a no-crap look. "Their injuries are not life threatening, and they can wait. Perhaps, next time they won't be so quick to assault one another." She turns to Brad and Lance. "Boys, you are excused. Get to class." Brad shoots me a sympathetic look before he walks out.

James and Alex sit down on either side of me. "What happened?" James whispers, as Alex's gaze roams over Peyton, skimming the tight, cheap vest top and hot pink mini that is barely school appropriate. She doesn't do anything to disguise her aversion. Peyton folds her arms over her chest, shooting a filthy look at Alex.

"She called me an inbred and then upended my tray all over me so I hit her." No point in lying.

"That's not very ladylike, Faye," Alex murmurs under her breath.

"Screw being ladylike when someone is insulting Ky and me. I'm not going to take that crap from anyone, least of all her," I hiss.

The door opens and a rake-thin bleached blonde runs into the room, breathless and clutching her chest. "What the fuck have ya done now?" she says by way of greeting to her daughter. Her coarse voice raises all the tiny hairs on the back of my neck. "I'm sick of being called to this office." She swats Peyton across the back of the head. "I had to cut my shift short to come here. You'll pay for that." Peyton's sulk turns unhappy.

Peyton's mum whips around, staring me out of it. She takes one look at Alex, and her entire demeanor changes. Her back stiffens and her eyes narrow as she looks my aunt over from head to toe. A look of sheer contempt washes over her pinched features. "Well, well. If it isn't Miss High and Mighty." Her grating laugh brings the memory to the forefront of my mind, and I freeze.

Peyton's mum extracts a crumpled paper from her bag, thrusting it in Alex's face. "Guess you're not so high and mighty after all. Slut."

My jaw hangs open. James, surprisingly, stands up to defend his wife. "I think that's enough."

It's almost comical how quickly her expression changes as she rakes her eyes over my uncle. "I hear you've taken to slumming it these days." She presses into him, running a finger up and down his arm. Peyton leans forward, placing her elbows on her knees as she stares unhappily at her mum. "Good for you." James removes her hands as the principal steps out of her office, summoning us all in.

I shuffle into the office, drop into a chair, and zone out of the conversation except where I'm needed to explain my version of what happened. Outside of that, my brain is churning, computing scenarios and trying to figure it out. Excitement replaces the blood flowing through my veins. I need to speak to Rose. To confirm what I'm thinking.

"One week's suspension for both of you," Principal Carter says as I refocus on the meeting. Alex and James are protesting, but Peyton's mum already has her jacket buttoned and she's standing, ready to go.

She drags Peyton up by the arm. "Get your stuff so we can get out of here."

"This is your final warning, Peyton," Principal Carter calls out before she leaves. "One more infraction. One more write up, and your time at Wellesley Memorial will be at an end."

"I understand," Peyton says. "I'm sorry, it won't happen again." I'd think she was almost genuine but for the scathing look she flings my way before she exits the room.

I jump up, anxious to hunt down Rose before I leave.

"Ms. Donovan, sit back down for a moment." The principal rustles some papers on her desk while I drop into the seat again. "I don't know what issue there is between you and Ms. Moore, but I suggest you learn to take the moral high ground. Your grades are excellent, and apart from your run-ins with Peyton, and your absence this week, your behavior is exemplary. I'd hate to have to expel a student as promising as you, but I can't be seen to take sides, you understand, and fighting of any kind is not permitted."

Yeah, yeah, blah, blah, just get it over and done with. "I understand. Can I go now?"

"Yes. I'll have your teachers email your coursework for the next week, and I'd suggest you do additional study at home so you don't fall behind."

"I will. Thanks."

It's the middle of class and I won't be able to talk to Rose yet, so I let James bring me to the nurse's office, where she cleans and dresses the wounds on my stomach. The bell is booming just as we leave. "I need to talk to Rose super-quick, and then I have to grab my books from my locker. How about I meet you out the front in ten minutes?"

James checks his watch. "Fine, but get a move on."

I nab Rose at her locker and drag her into the bathroom, checking the cubicles are empty and locking the door behind us.

"What happened with the principal?" she asks.

"I got suspended for a week." She opens her mouth, but I shake my head. "Forget about that. I've something more urgent to ask you."

She tilts her head. "Okay, I'll bite."

"Remember that conversation we overheard at Addison's house that night?" Rose nods. "Can you remember exactly what was said?" I think I can but I need to hear Rose confirm it too.

Her eyes scrunch up as she racks her brain, trawling through the memory. "They were talking about how what they did was best for Addison, and she told them both to stop ambushing her, that she didn't want to hear it anymore. Then Addison's mom gave out to the other woman for forcing her to tell her, saying you reneged on our deal."

I'm almost bursting with excitement. I jump up and down, and Rose looks at me like I've lost the plot. "That's how I remembered it too."

Rose frowns. "Am I missing something here?"

"Think about that conversation now in the light of what Keven discovered. Now that we know Addison was adopted."

Awareness spreads across her features. "That other woman was her birth mother!"

"That's my conclusion. It stacks up, right?"

Rose bobs her head vigorously. "Definitely, but I still don't see where you're going with this."

She looks totally confused so I decide to let her out of her misery.

"I know who the other woman was, Rose. It was Peyton's mum. I'll never forget that rough voice." Adrenaline courses through my body. "Peyton's mum isn't Addison's aunt. She's Addison's *mother*!"

Chapter Fifteen

Faye

"Okay, let's say you're right," Rose supplies, "because I can see how that adds up, but how exactly is it helpful?"

"It's what sent Addison off the rails a year ago. She found out she was adopted and that her aunt was really her mum, her cousin really her half-sister."

"I'm still not getting it."

I roll my eyes. "Addison has a major hard-on for the Kennedys, and it started when she changed. She *changed* when she discovered who her mum was, so I'm betting that whatever motive she has for ruining my family is connected. Now we have something concrete to start digging with."

"Why does it really matter anymore?" She shrugs. "Addison's credibility and standing is at an all-time low. She's been cautioned to stay away from all of you, and now you and Ky have gone public, so she knows there isn't a hope in hell of ever getting him back. It's over. Let it go."

I shake my head, staring off into space. "She tried to frame my cousin for rape. You don't do something like that 'cause you're pissed when you discover you're really trailer trash after all." Rose snorts. "No." I shake my head repeatedly. "Addison has an agenda, and until I find out what it is, I won't rest easy. Maybe I'm crazy. Or maybe my gut is off-kilter, but there's more to this than meets the eye, and I intend to find out why."

My phone pings and I groan when I see James's text. "I gotta run before my uncle throws a hissy fit. I'll call you," I shout over my shoulder, wiggling my fingers at her.

Racing to my locker, I shove everything in my bag and dart out the front door. I'm breathless by the time I land in the passenger seat of James's car. He sends me a grave look. "Sorry. I just had to talk to Rose about something important."

He thrusts the car in gear, and we glide smoothly out onto the road. I'm expecting a lecture, but after a few minutes of stony silence, I can't take it anymore. "Look, I'm sorry. I shouldn't have hit her, but she's had it in for me from day one." I lean back against the headrest.

"Alex tells me Peyton is Addison's cousin?" James says, his eyes never straying from the road.

"Yeah." Or half-sister if I'm right.

"Alex says gossip was rife around town when Peyton's mom was a teen. She was wild, and if Peyton is anything like her mom or her cousin, then you need to stay well away."

"Oh, don't worry, that won't be a problem. Where is Alex anyway?"

He harrumphs. "Where do you think?" He looks at me fleetingly. "She had to get back to work."

I prop my feet up on the dash. "I appreciate that she came. You too, and I'm sorry. I know you don't need any more grief."

James turns into the drive, blaring his horn and forcing the huddle of reporters at the gate to disperse. "I honestly don't care about that, but I do care about you. I worry that we're corrupting you. I'm beginning to think Adam may be right."

All the blood leaches from my face as I swivel in my seat. "What does that mean?"

He grips the steering wheel tightly. "Nothing. Forget I said anything."

I stew for a bit. When he's parked the car and killed the engine, I reach over, tugging on his sleeve. "I know it was nothing. Tell me."

He rests his forehead on the steering wheel, emitting a tired sigh. "He thinks we're a bad influence on you. That it would be better if I let you go. Let you live with him."

"No way!" The words burst out of my mouth. "Mum assigned you as my guardian for a reason, and I love my cousins, and Ky, and—"

He cuts me off. "You're not going anywhere, Faye." He pats my cheek. "That slipped out without thinking. I imagine that's what Adam wants to talk to you about this weekend."

"I don't even know him! I don't want to live with him! He can't make me, right?" I'm struggling to keep the rising panic from my voice.

James opens and closes his mouth, and that horrible fluttery sensation is back in my chest. My mouth has gone dry.

"Dan is looking into everything. Your mother assigned me as your legal guardian until you are eighteen which is only a couple of months away. I doubt Adam can enforce anything before then, so don't worry. No one is making you do anything you don't want to do. I give you my word."

"I don't want to see him tomorrow." My jaw tautens with determination. "I thought he wanted to get to know me, not try and ... and force me into living with him. I like living here."

"I think you should meet him tomorrow and tell him all that. I've been having some humdinger arguments with him these last few weeks, but I can tell he cares about you, and I'm not going to criticize him for that. If you tell him you're happy here and why you want to stay, I believe that'll go a long way toward reassuring him."

I sniff. "I'll think about it."

I get changed into fresh, clean clothes and make myself something to eat. I'm starving. I check my phone, noticing a recent message from Brad. He's wondering where I am, so I message him back with the news of my suspension. No doubt the gossip mill is already in overdrive.

I waste a couple of hours flicking through some trashy American TV shows before I hear the front door open. I toss the remote on the bed and pad out to the lobby. Kal, Kent, Keaton, and Keanu are just arriving home from school. "Where's Ky?" I ask, eyes darting about.

"He had to go into the city. He said to tell you he won't be long." Kal throws his bag on the floor and pulls me into his side, smacking a sloppy kiss on my cheek. "How come you're back early?"

Usually, I'm home after my cousins. "I, um, might've gotten suspended today," I admit, somewhat sheepishly.

"Get out!" Keaton says, staring at me like I've grown a pair of horns.

"Bad ass!" Kent predictably replies, reaching out to high-five me.

Keanu just shrugs like it's no biggie.

Kal slings his arm around my shoulders, pulling me into the kitchen with him. "If I guess the reason, what do I get?"

"A slap in the head," I retort, shoving him. Keaton chuckles as he walks into the kitchen alongside us.

Kal winks. "I'm betting it was a chick fight. Am I right?" I stick out my tongue, and he laughs. "Knew it! Was it hot? Did you grab some boob?"

I shove him again. "Ugh, dude, that's just ... wrong, so wrong."

Keaton's cheeks are flushed, and I give him a funny look which he pretends not to see. I fill my cousins in quickly, and Kal's good mood evaporates. "She called you an inbred?" he growls.

"Forget it." I shrug. "She isn't worth it, and I can handle her."

"I knew that bitch Addison was too quiet today," Keaton supplies. "Even if she was purposely laying low on her first day back."

"You think she put Peyton up to it?" I ask doubtfully.

"Most likely," Kal responds, unwrapping the cling film from the plate of sandwiches left out for us.

"Peyton's a right cow. She doesn't need Addison to supply the ammo, she's more than capable of doing that on her own." I sit on the bench alongside Keaton. Kal sits across from us, sliding the plate into the middle of the table. As they eat, I tell them about my meeting in the principal's office and my assertion about Addison's birth mum. "What do you think?"

Kal waves his spoon in the air. "I think that makes a lot of sense. I also think you're right not to let this go, but you shouldn't involve Ky. Don't drag him into this." He sends me a cautionary look.

"I'm not keeping secrets from him."

Kal leans over the table. "I'm not saying you should. Maybe investigate it yourself first, and if there's something there, then share it with Ky."

I chew on my lower lip, mulling it over. Ky *is* dealing with a lot of heavy stuff, and maybe I should do some searching on my own before jumping the gun. While I'm pretty certain I've called it correctly, it's just a hunch at the moment. Best to get some concrete proof before I open up the whole Addison drama again. "Let's call Keven."

Keaton heads off to his room to get ready for a date with his girlfriend, Melissa, while Kal and I go to my room to call Keven. He answers on the first ring, and I let him know what I've discovered. "I haven't had time to do much research this week," Keven advises, "but it's very helpful to have her birth mother's name. I've got a couple of free hours on Sunday, and I'll see if I can dig up anything."

I hang up and flop down on my bed. Kal throws himself on the bed beside me. "What was it like in your school today?" I ask. "Were there reporters outside?"

"Yep." He stretches out, leaning his head back on his hands. "But only a handful so it wasn't too bad."

"Did Ky get flack?"

He crosses his feet at the ankles. "A bit, but most were too afraid to call him on it. Sounds like you've drawn the short straw in that regard."

"I wasn't expecting the issue to be my relationship with Ky, but I guess I was naïve. People still think it's gross."

My door swings open and I look up. Ky is lounging against the doorframe looking awfully chuffed with himself. "Hey, babe."

I climb off the bed and go to him, throwing my arms around his neck and pressing my body into his. His eyes darken with lust, and the usual spark of electricity charges the air between us. My chest pumps up and down as he rubs his thumb along my lower lip. Raw need pulses between my legs, and my knees turn weak. Gripping the back of my head, Ky lowers his face, capturing my lips in a passionate kiss. I melt into him, moaning into his mouth as his tongue lashes against mine. He rubs up against me, and the feel of his arousal grinding right where I need him is like a shot of liquid lust straight to my core. I'm only short of crawling up his body like a love-addicted spider monkey.

"That was disturbingly gross," Kal says directly into my ear, and I shriek, caught off guard.

Ky loosens his hold on me, looking back into the corridor and mouthing something. I frown in confusion, trying to step around him, but his arms are like solid metal restraints around my waist. "I have a surprise for you." My eyes expand, and he smiles broadly, showcasing his exquisite smile and those cute dimples I love. "Close your eyes." I do as I'm told without question, allowing him to spin me around and guide me out into the corridor. “Open them.”

I blink my eyes open and scream.

Chapter Sixteen

Faye

Racing forward, I throw myself at Jill and Rachel, tears flowing freely down my face. We indulge in a group hug, jumping up and down and squealing like we're toddlers. "Oh my God, you guys, what are you doing here?" I ease back, looking at both their excited faces. "How are you here?"

"Ask the ride behind you," Rach teases, winking at Ky.

I pivot around. "You did this?"

He saunters toward me slowly, nodding. "I knew you missed your friends." He tucks a few stray strands of hair behind my ear. "They were supposed to be here for Thanksgiving, but I had to adjust our plans last minute."

I launch myself at him, and he almost loses his balance. "I love you." I dot kisses all over his face. "I love you so much." I claim his mouth in a soul-altering kiss.

"Totally gross," Kal says from somewhere behind me, making a gagging sound.

"Wow," Ky says when I eventually let him break away. "Remind me to surprise you more often." His eyes sparkle with desire and love.

I grab his hands and pull him over to my friends. Kal is already there, introducing himself in his usual inimitable style. Jill is flushed and giggling while Rach is studying him like he's some strange creature. "How long are you here for?" I ask.

"Until Sunday evening," Rach confirms.

Ky drags Kal aside. "I know you girls want to catch up, so why don't you show them to a couple of the guest rooms, Faye, and when you're ready, meet us in the games room?"

"Sure thing. Come on." I bend down to pick up one of their bags. "This way."

"This place is lethal," Rach says, walking around the purple guest room in a daze.

"Wait 'til I show you my wardrobe," I tease, fingering her new red locks. "When did you do this?"

"Just last week. You were my inspiration," she admits. "Although the red does look better on me." She winks, nudging me with her hip.

"I'm not going to disagree. You look gorgeous. It really suits your skin tone."

"And Ky is *gorgeous*, Faye. No wonder you couldn't resist him." She waggles her brows. "I didn't realize he was so tall and so built. When we got off the plane, he was out on the tarmac leaning against his car looking sexier than any boy should. He's seriously fit, and please tell me you're doing him, because it's a damned waste of male hotness if you aren't."

My lips curve up at the corners. "I am."

Rach high-fives me. "Nice one, girlfriend."

"I'm totally jealous," Jill admits with a grin.

I bump her shoulder. "You've got Sam now. How's that going?"

A dreamy expression coasts over her face. "He's great, and I'm so in love. I was going to bring him this weekend, but Rach persuaded me to leave him behind."

"I'm sick of watching you eating the face off each other," Rach deadpans. "And, besides, we're here for Faye." She loops her arm in mine, and her eyes light up in transparent mischief. "But that doesn't mean I'm shying away from any action. On the contrary, I'm definitely game for sampling some American hotness. Ky mentioned a party tonight, and I'm already drooling."

I lift an eyebrow. "He did? That's the first I've heard of it."

She licks her lips. "Let's go ask him about it."

Kal, Kent, and Keaton are waiting with Ky in the games room. I make another round of quick introductions as the new housekeeper arrives with some platters of finger food. The girls tuck in, ravenous after their flight. We chat casually as we eat. "Where's the party tonight?" I ask Ky.

"Trent's house. You don't know him, he goes to O.C., but he's cool. Most of the usual gang will be there." I frown a little, and he moves closer. "I won't leave your side, promise."

"I was thinking more of you. You'll be the focus of attention after today's media reports. You sure you're up for that?"

"I'm not hiding from this." Lifting my hand, he kisses the tips of my fingers. "And if you still want to do a grand public gesture, this is the perfect place to do it."

"Do you?"

He bobs his head. "But only if you're one hundred percent cool with it." He lowers his voice. "Brad told me what happened today. Are you okay?"

I flap my hands, dismissing the incident. "I'm fine. Don't think Adam's going to be too pleased when he hears the news though."

Ky jerks back a little, slanting me with an inquisitive look. "I'll tell you later," I whisper, placing my hand on his knee. My friends are absorbed in conversation with my cousins. "Thought you had a date?" I say to Keaton.

"I do, but I don't need to go yet."

"Are you gonna join us at the party?"

"Hell to the yes." He grins, leaning over to high-five me. A wave of happiness consumes me, and it's like a welcome breath of fresh air. I'm giddy with excitement for the weekend ahead, and it's the first time in ages I've felt so ecstatic.

"Why are you pinching yourself?" Rachel asks.

"Because I still can't believe you're here," I squeal, clapping my hands like a moron. Reaching out, I pull her into a bear hug. "I have missed you guys, soooooo much."

Ky is smiling at us, and I snake my arm around his back, pressing a quick, hard kiss on his lips. "I can't believe you set all this up. You're amazing."

"Next he'll be climbing into your room with a rose between his teeth spouting Shakespeare," Kent derides.

"Dude, her bedroom's on ground level," Keaton reminds him.

"Dude, who cares? The point is, Ky has turned into a fucking pansy. It's pathetic."

Rachel and Jill shoot inquisitive looks at me. "Don't ask," I plead. They'll get the makings of Kent this weekend without the need for any advance explanation.

I'm expecting Ky to tear him a new one, but he surprises me. Enfolding his arms around me, he presses a delicate kiss to my forehead. "I'm betting you go to greater extremes when you find your dream girl."

Kent snorts. "That will never be me. Girls are good for one thing and one thing only." He turns a sleazy look in the direction of my friends, slowly perusing both of them from head to toe. There's a naughty glint in his eye. "Bedroom door is always open, ladies. Feel free to stop by any time." He runs a finger up a shell-shocked Jill's arm. "And I do mean *any time*." He hops up and saunters off, laughing.

"Wow. I can't believe he's only turned sixteen. He's definitely a wannabe bad boy in the making," Jill comments astutely. "And that was mild compared to some of the stuff he was saying."

"Ignore him," Ky says, "he's going through his asshole phase."

"Takes one to know one." Brad steps into the room with that enlightening comment filtering from his lips. Swigging from a bottle of beer, he is barefoot, bare chested, and wearing jeans that are hanging indecently low on his hips. "You don't even know the half of it, but no doubt Faye can fill you in," he adds. Jill's mouth hangs open in obvious admiration as she peruses Brad in all his shirtless glory. He extends his hand. "I'm Brad. Nice to meet you." A slow blush creeps up her neck when he plants a kiss on the back of her hand.

Rachel's eyes narrow curiously. "So, *you're* Brad."

He turns the full extent of his dazzling smile on her. "The one and only." He drops Jill's hand like it's on fire, taking a step in Rachel's direction. His eyes take their fill as he lazily caresses every curve on her body. "Who are you, and where have you been my whole life?" His gaze turns leery as he sinks onto the couch alongside her. She folds her arms over her chest, eying him warily.

What the hell?

Ky chuckles, while I try to hide my confusion. "Brad, this is Rachel and that's Jill. My two besties from home. Ky arranged a surprise visit for me."

"How awesome. Isn't he just the perfect boyfriend," he drawls sarcastically. He takes a long hard slug from his beer as I squirm uncomfortably in my seat. Before anyone can take him to task over his blatant derision, he turns his full attention to Rachel. "What about you, beautiful?" I flinch at his use of that word. "Do you have a boyfriend I should worry about?"

"She's single," Jill pipes up, trying to be helpful.

"Sweet." Brad leans into Rach's face, until there's barely a millimeter between them. Rachel gulps, and I don't think I've ever seen her so lost for words. "Fancy hooking up later?"

"Brad!" *What on earth has gotten into him?* While I can guess where this new animosity is stemming from, I don't know what happened between leaving school and now to make him act so abnormally.

"Bro, you're kinda being an asshole," Ky tells him.

"Maybe I like being an asshole," he retorts. "Maybe I've always been an asshole and I've been hiding behind my nice guy image. *Maybe* I'm tired of that shit. Or maybe I just want to hook up with a girl who's *available* for a change?"

I can't believe he just went there. *Is he drunk or high or something?*

"Aw, poor little rich boy," Rach teases, finally finding her voice. "All sore 'cause he didn't win the girl." She stabs her finger in his bare chest. "Grow up, and get a life. And put a damned shirt on. It's the middle of winter, dickhead."

Brad throws back his head, laughing hysterically. Ky and I exchange more worried glances. *How much has he had to drink?*

Rachel scowls, narrowing her eyes at him. Then she turns to me. "He is not at all what I expected. I thought you said he was cool?"

Brad stops laughing. "What were you expecting exactly?" He sizes her up.

"Faye has had nothing but nice things to say about you, so I wasn't expecting the half-drunk half-naked look or the arrogant personality or the massive chip on your shoulder. Need I continue?"

He laughs but it lacks humor. Leaning in with a transparent sneer on his face, he says, "You don't know shit, honey. You think you have the measure of me after two minutes? You don't know me. You know nothing, so do us all a favor and fuck off."

I gasp, completely appalled.

Ky shucks out of my embrace, ready to tear strips off Brad, but I hold him back. I stand up, taking a minute to get a handle on my anger. Grabbing Brad's arm, I pull him aside. "What the hell has gotten into you? How dare you speak to my friend like that!" I face Rach. "He isn't usually like this, I promise."

"Quit apologizing for me. I'm not sorry I spoke my mind." He turns the full extent of his anger on me now. "Red is hardly in any position to throw stones unless that prissy, stuck-up, better-than-you attitude is actually who she is, and then I'm even less sorry. At least I'm speaking my mind, not hiding behind my anger."

Rach's nostrils flare, and I shoot Jill a worried look. Rach is like the most vicious tiger when challenged, and she ain't afraid to use claws. "You self-righteous pompous prick!" Rachel's face is puce with rage. "Who da fuck do yo—"

"Ohmigawd," Jill shrieks, deliberately butting in. "I almost forgot about this!" She pulls a slim white envelope out of her bag. "Luke gave this to me to give to you." I take the envelope, with my name scrawled in messy black pen on the front, with a slight frown. "Actually, he turned up at Dublin airport and tried to come with."

I rub the back of my neck. "Really? Why would he do that?" I've heard nothing from my ex since I left Irish shores, and I haven't given him a second thought either.

"Why'd ya think? He's still got the hots for you." She smirks, pleased to have diverted World War III in the making. Not that it's completely smoothed things over. I haven't missed how Brad and Rach are facing off, scowling at one another with blatant hostility.

A warm arm encircles my waist. "Should I be worried?" Ky peers at me with a slight frown. "Who is this guy, and why haven't I heard of him before?"

"What guy?" James asks as he enters the room.

"No one," I say, the same time Ky says, "Luke. Some jerk who's still in love with Faye."

I roll my eyes. "Hardly. He's the other side of the world, and you have nothing to worry about, trust me. He's *so* not in your league."

"That's the guy I met back at your house?" James asks. "Your ex?"

"Yep." I nibble on my lip hoping he'll let it go. As distraction techniques go, I'm not sure Jill has the skill down pat yet.

"Don't worry." He slaps Ky on the back. "The guy is harmless, and he seemed decent enough." I can't help my natural gobsmacked reaction, and James laughs. "I know, I know. I was a bit of an ass when we met." He chuckles at the memory. "But, in my defense, he was in bed with my niece and he had his hand somewhere he shouldn't have."

I slam my palm into my forehead as I groan. Jill and Rach both shriek "What?!" and Ky growls. Brad leans back against the table with a smug grin on his face.

"Seriously, can we drop this? It's giving me a headache."

"I don't like the thought of any other guy with his hands on you," Ky whispers in my ear.

"It was before I knew you even existed," I whisper back.

"Doesn't stop the visual."

"At least it's only in your imagination." The words are out of my mouth before I can stop them.

Ky winces, pulling me in tighter to his chest. "You're right. I'm sorry." He rubs his hands up and down my arms, but it's too late now. Recollections of him and Addison swarm my mind, extinguishing my good mood in a nanosecond.

James clears his throat loudly, gesturing at my friends, and I wriggle out of Ky's grasp and set about introducing him to Jill and Rach.

"I think I've died and gone to heaven," Rach admits in an awestruck tone of voice as she swoons and cries over practically every item in my walk-in-wardrobe.

"Borrow whatever you want. Knock yourself out." I pull out a pair of black skinny jeans.

Rach whips the jeans out of my hands, throwing them on the ground. "Not a chance, sister. We are going all out tonight. Let's show these Yanks what they've been missing."

I drag Jill over to my side. "A little help here?"

"I'm with Rach," she says, holding a short black and red baby doll dress against her body. "It's my first American party, and we are dressing to impress!" She screams in delight, a shrill ear-piercing sound that almost deafens me. Planting my hands over my ears, I relent.

Rach nudges me in the ribs, glowering. "Ow! What was that for?" I ask, rubbing the sore spot under my boob.

"Most of these clothes still have tags on." She looks at me like I'm an alien being in a human body. "I would die for this wardrobe. *Die*, I tell you."

"Well that would be stupid. Then you wouldn't be alive to wear any of them."

"What do you think?" Jill asks, giving us a twirl in the dress.

"It's stunning, but a little too big around the waist," I answer truthfully.

"Here," Rach says, thrusting a silky black cumber band at Jill. "Let me see if this works." She crisscrosses it around Jill's waist before tying it into a bow in front. It works perfectly.

"Amazing. You should be working in fashion, Rach. I'll introduce you to Alex tomorrow and you can ask her all about career options if you like."

Rachel grips my arms. "I would love that! I'm so excited to meet her."

I'm actually a little pissed that she didn't come out of her home office to say hi to my friends, but there must be something up as I've noticed her work colleagues coming and going all evening, so I try not to take the snub personally.

An hour later and we are finally ready to rock and roll. Rach chose a vibrant purple skater-style dress that stops just above her knee. Stylish black sandals with a wedge heel complete the look.

I take one last look at myself in the mirror, marveling at the professional hair and makeup job the girls did on me while I fuss with the hem on my ridiculously short dress. "Stop that!" Rach slaps my hand away. "That dress was made for you. You look totally fuckable. He won't be able to keep his hands off you."

The black silk mini dress hugs my curves in all the right places, and although it looks like it's welded on, it feels soft and comfortable against my skin. There is a wide ruffle detail over one shoulder and that's the only embellishment. I'm wearing black and red open-toed stilettos that elongate my legs, making them look like they go on forever. Although I'm feeling exposed, there's no denying it's a classy dress. I've just never been all that comfortable highlighting my body in such a transparent way.

"You should wear dresses more often, Faye. They really suit you. I would kill for your long legs," Jill says, knowing I need an injection of confidence. My heart inflates. I doubt I'll ever meet more supportive friends.

"You two are the best. You know that, right?" My eyes well up.

Jill wraps her arms around me. "We know, and you mean that to us too. We have really missed you. Missed this."

Rachel leans in and we indulge in a group hug. My phone pings with another message from Ky. "We need to go before Ky goes all Neanderthal Man and storms in here to claim me."

"Wait a sec," Rach says, shuffling nervously on her feet. "I have something I need to tell you. I wanted to wait until you were both here to say it."

"Ohmigawd, you're pregnant?" Jill roars, and I clamp a hand over her mouth.

"What? No!" Rach shakes her head in consternation. "I don't even have a boyfriend."

"You always have a different boy draped over you at parties, and you have a habit of disappearing with them," Jill replies, with a knowing smirk.

"So what?" Rach retorts, her skin turning puce. "It doesn't mean I sleep with all of them. Give me some credit."

I wade in before they start bickering. "You're not pregnant. Got it. So what's your news?"

"My family won the Euromillions."

Okay. So wasn't expecting that.

"Was it that win that was all over the news recently?" Jill asks. "Like eighty million?" Her eyes blaze with excitement.

"Eighty-three million seven hundred thousand and five to be exact," Rach confirms.

"Ho. Lee. Shit. That's an epic amount of money."

"I know. You'd want to see Mum and Dad since the win. I don't think they've slept, and there's champagne on tap at our house, but they are keeping it contained until they decide what to do. We were all sworn to secrecy, but I got them to agree I could tell you this weekend." She snatches her purse. "So now you know and drinks are on me!"

Chapter Seventeen

Faye

We walk toward the lobby like three wannabe Kim K's in the making—flinging our hair over our shoulders, wiggling our hips, and pouting provocatively as the noise of our heels taps off the polished floors announcing our arrival. The boys instantly mute, standing there with their mouths hanging open. *Mission accomplished*. Ha. I grin at my friends. Tonight is going to be so fun.

Kal whistles under his breath. "You look absolutely stunning, ladies. You are all anyone is going to be talking about at this party."

"We hope so," Rach says, sending him a saucy wink as she loops her arms in his. "Lead the way."

Ky stalks toward me with a possessive glint in his eye. The usual electrical current sizzles between us as he advances. He's wearing my favorite dark denim jeans and a fitted black shirt that is rolled up at the sleeves, showcasing his strong, muscular arms. His hair is styled to perfection, and his designer stubble is intact. He is sex on legs, and the urge to jump his bones is strong. It's as if some switch has been flicked inside me. Like the instant we had sex, I've turned into some sex-crazed maniac, because all I can think about when I see him is peeling the clothes off his back and riding him like a horse.

I fan my face with my hands, but it does nothing to quench the flames overtaking my body.

Reeling me slowly into his chest, he roams his hands over my back and my ass, his fingers lingering on my bare thigh. I run my fingers back and forth across his prickly jawline. "You should be locked up," he whispers, grazing his nose along my neck. "You are far too tempting to be let out in public."

"Does that mean you like it?"

A primal growl gurgles up from the base of his throat. "Like it? I *love* it. You look sexy, and you're all mine." Burying his head in my bare shoulder, he presses a lingering kiss to that sensitive place on my collarbone as his sneaky hand creeps up under the back of my dress. The ache between my legs intensifies, and I shiver all over. "And don't think I missed the dirty look on your face, either. I want to know all the naughty things you're thinking," he whispers in my ear, sending another round of tingles zinging through my body. If he wasn't holding me so tightly, I don't think I'd be able to keep myself upright.

"Fuck and be done with it," Kent suggests, brushing past us. "You're like two wild animals who've just been let out of a cage."

We break apart, and I scowl at my younger cousin. "Do you have to be so crude all the time?" I take hold of Ky's hand as we walk en masse out the front door. Kent shrugs, smirking. He likes saying things for the "shock" factor, but I'm not sure how much of it is real and how much is for show.

Jill and Rach shriek in excitement when they spot the waiting limo. I turn to Ky, and he smiles. Throwing my arms around his neck, I fuse my mouth with his, sliding my tongue inside and pouring everything into the kiss. "You just wait 'til later," he purrs into my ear, before pulling me inside the car.

"You must want in her pants real bad," Brad says, popping the cork on the champagne.

"Shut the fuck up," Ky snaps. "There doesn't always have to be an ulterior motive. This is Jill and Rachel's first time here, and I wanted to make it special for them."

"I want him when you're done with him," Rach pipes up, sending me a teasing grin.

"You'll be waiting a while," I reply, accepting a glass of champagne from Ky. "Like eternity."

Ky leans in, grinning again as he plants a hot kiss on my mouth. I grab his waist and pull him to me, not bothered about the audience or the champagne which I'm most likely spilling all over the floor. My core pulses with need, and I don't know how I'm expected to wait until later tonight to have my wicked way with him. I want him inside me now. I whimper at the thought.

"Can't you two keep your hands to yourselves for even five seconds?" Brad hisses, and we break apart with a sigh. We haven't set out to intentionally make things difficult for Brad, but this is the first time Ky and I can be ourselves in public, and it's hard to ignore our natural instincts. I just want to weld myself to his side and never let go.

"They're hot for one another," Kal says, instantly coming to our defense. "And this is the first time they can publicly be together. Give them a break."

"Bro. Chill," Kent says, slapping Brad on the knee. "Trent's parties are legendary. There'll be tons of pussy. You can fuck that girl right out of your hair." He snatches a bottle of beer from the cooler, smirking.

I slap a palm to my forehead. *Did he have to tag that on the end?* My shoulders are corded into knots now.

"Words fail me," Rach says, knocking back her champagne in one go. Jill and I exchange the usual look. I make a mental note to ask Kal to keep an eye on her tonight. Rach has a tendency to overdo it on the alcohol front, and once she's lost her inhibitions, she gets all kinds of messy. We've tried talking to her on several occasions, but she always brushes our concerns aside.

"Sounds like a plan, dude." Brad taps his beer bottle against Kent's like they're partners in crime.

"Brad is getting on my last nerve," Ky whispers, sliding his arm around my back.

"He's your friend and he's hurting. Cut him some slack," I whisper back.

"I'm trying to, but it's not easy. If anyone even looks sideways at you, I want to rip their intestines from their body."

"Ew, Ky." I slap his arm. "That's gross, and totally uncalled for."

He shrugs. "Just being honest. I'm a jealous motherfucker. Don't say I haven't warned you."

"You have nothing to be jealous of." I kiss the tip of his nose. "No one else exists for me but you. The instant I laid eyes on you I knew it."

"God, I fucking love you." He slams his mouth to mine all too briefly, but I know that's for Brad's benefit, and I'm not going to fault him for caring about protecting his friend's feelings. "You have a big heart, Faye." He caresses my cheek, his eyes simmering with pride. "It's one of the things I love most about you."

I swoon at his words, grinning at him as I bask in a happy bubble that is all Ky-induced.

♥♥♥♥♥♥♥

The party is in full swing by the time we arrive. The limo deposits us out front and we walk around to the back of the house. Trent's parent's property sits on a vast plot that appears to rival the Kennedys for sheer size and impressiveness. The house is huge. It's three stories high with a mix of red brick and cream stone façade, wide, extensive windows, and copious balconies. Steps lead from the rear of the house down to the biggest pool I've ever seen, set in front of a well-manicured lawn. Two large hot tubs off the side of the pool are full to the brim with half-naked boys and girls. Jill clutches my free hand, literally frothing with excitement.

We make our way inside, and a good-looking guy with a blond buzz cut approaches us. He's wearing dark jeans and a navy and red polo shirt that stretches in sinful yumminess across his broad chest. Rachel's eyes light up, and I attempt to smother my giggle.

"Dude. Glad you could make it," the unfamiliar boy says to Ky.

"Thanks for inviting us." Ky gestures with his hand. "Girls, this is Trent." We smile at him as Ky continues the introductions. "This is Faye, Jill, and Rachel. You know my brothers, and Brad."

Trent high-fives the guys before kissing each of our hands in turn. He pins his stunning ocher-colored eyes on me, not even attempting to disguise his slow perusal of my body. Ky encircles my waist from behind, brushing my hair to one side and planting a territorial kiss to my neck. "You're every bit as beautiful as Ky said," Trent tells me.

"Thank you," I coolly reply.

"Now I get it," he says to Ky. "Good for you." Someone catches his attention from the other side of the room. "I've got to make rounds. Have a good time. Help yourself to drinks. We've a full selection in the kitchen, and there's beer and shit in buckets around the place."

"What was all that about?" I ask Ky as we venture into the main living area that's been cleared to accommodate a makeshift dance floor. A DJ pumps out beats from his station in the corner of the room.

"Some of the guys can't understand why I let Addison go."

"After what she did? Are they idiots?"

"They think with their dicks half the time."

"You've just proven my point."

We locate Keaton and Melissa in a corner of the room, joining them, while Ky, Brad, and Kal wander to the kitchen to get us drinks. "I have never seen so much male hotness in one place in my entire life," Rach rasps. "I fucking love America."

Melissa giggles, and Kent sends her a scathing look that has her almost withering on the spot. Keaton pulls her into his protective chest, glaring at his brother.

"What about Trent?" Jill asks. "I'd do him if I was single."

"I'm happy to offer my studly services," Kent interjects, sending Rach an overtly suggestive look.

"Sorry," she says, not sounding in the least bit apologetic. "But I'm not into kids."

Kent's pride looks wounded.

"Bro, your game needs serious work," Kal supplies, distributing wine coolers to my friends.

Ky gives me my drink before circling his arm around my shoulders. "What'd I miss?"

"Rachel is crushing on that sleaze Trent," Kent huffs.

"I said no such thing," Rach replies tartly. "With this much hotness in the room, I'd be a fool to limit my options so early in the night."

"Spoken like a true lady," Brad snarls before downing his beer.

"Oh, whatever." Rach sighs, showing him her middle finger. "Come on, girls. Let's dance."

I press a quick kiss to Ky's mouth, but he has other plans. Wrapping his arms firmly around my waist, he hauls me into his body as his lips claim my mouth. His tongue swirls around mine, and I'm dizzy with lust. Leaning me right back, my spine arches as he kisses the heck out of me. I dig my fingers into his shoulders, pulling him even closer. His arms hold me firmly around the waist, ensuring I don't lose my balance. Heat from his body mingles with the spicy masculine scent that is pure Ky, and I'm lost in an alternate realm. One where it's only him and me, and the way he's holding me, kissing me, is the entire center of my world. When we finally come up for air, I'm struggling to breathe.

Kal slaps him on the back. "Marking your territory?" he quizzes with a grin.

"You forget I know most of these horn dogs. Just protecting my girl." His dark stare is shamelessly domineering, and I stare back at him through dazed eyes. I'm still trying to return to earth after that incredible make-out session.

Rach loops her arm in mine while she peers up at Ky. "Which of those horn dogs would know how to kiss a girl like that?"

"I'm one of a kind," he quips, with a smirk.

Her face drops. "Was afraid you were going to say that."

I finally snap out of it. "Come on. Let's get out there before he does that again and sends me into a coma."

"You love it!" he calls out after me.

"I do," I shout over my shoulder, smiling like the biggest idiot on the planet. Ordinarily, if a guy blatantly branded me in the way Ky just did, I'd be hopping mad but not on this occasion. I love that he was bold enough to put an end to the speculation. Brave enough to stick the proverbial fingers up to those would-be detractors. This is all I've dreamed of for months, and now that it's finally happening, I couldn't be more delighted. I want everyone to know I'm his. That he's mine, and if he has to kiss me like that to make a statement, I'm certainly not going to complain.

Rach is tugging me toward the dance floor when a flash of red catches the corner of my eye. Jerking my head around, I stare Addison directly in the eye. She's standing off to the side, wearing a bum-skimming hot red mini, with Jeremy her only companion. From the unhappy pout on her face, I can tell she saw us kissing, and it gives me an inordinate amount of pleasure. She makes a gagging gesture with her fingers and her mouth, and I just smile.

A whopper smile.

The kind that almost hurts.

It'd be easy to flip her off or make an equally repulsive gesture in return, but why bother? Even though half the community incorrectly thinks I'm an inbred, I got my guy, and that's all that matters. Nothing can take the sheen off my happiness in this moment. Especially not that conniving biatch.

Rach plows into the crowd, moshing on the dance floor, and we quickly work up a sweat. If feels unreal to be dancing with my besties again, and I quickly lose track of time. Soon, we're surrounded by a sea of hot guys, and Rach is on the verge of self-combustion, her eyes lighting up in obvious delight. We sway to the beat, and I feel footloose and carefree, and it feels *incredible*. A laugh bubbles up my throat as I check out my friends. Rach is dancing raunchily with a tall, dark-haired guy I've seen around, while Jill is doing her best to fend attacks from all angles. It's almost comical to watch her. Ky's demonstration has worked its magic, and though I feel plenty of admiring eyes on me, no one dares approach or come anywhere near me.

Sturdy arms encircle my waist, and I lean back, stretching one arm up to cup the back of Ky's head. "How did you know it was me?" he murmurs, his lips brushing against my neck.

"I'd know your touch anywhere." I shimmy my body up and down, grinding against him. He grips my hips, swaying with me as we start dancing in time to the beat. I lose track of our surroundings again as we dance like we're the only two people on the floor. Ky's hands are everywhere and I love it. Angling my head, I claim his lips in an open-mouthed kiss, writhing against him as we continue to dance to the rhythmic music. Flipping me around in his arms, he teases my legs apart, places his knee in between, and I shimmy my leg around his, allowing him to set the pace. Sliding my hands up and down his impressive chest, I rock against him as the throbbing between my legs pulses achingly. From the hungry look in his eyes, I can tell he's as turned on as me. Arching my back, I let my hair tumble over my shoulders, granting him greater access to my neck. His tongue darts out, and he runs a line up and down my neck, sending waves of fiery tingles all over me. I smash my hips against his, emitting a needy moan as I pull his lips to mine and plunder his mouth. Our lips move urgently, frantically, our tongues crashing and tasting, our bodies fitting together like we were carved from the same mold. This feels so good, and I'm primed to explode, like I could practically orgasm on the spot.

"You make me sick!" someone says beside us, voice dripping in venom. Ky stiffens against me, straightening us up and keeping his arm firmly around my waist. We turn and face Addison and Jeremy, noting others have formed a loose circle around us. Everyone watches with bated breath and anticipation is almost palpable in the air. "You are making all of us sick," Addison sneers, looking me up and down.

"I can't imagine why," Ky calmly replies. "We aren't related." He shrugs. "There's no reason why we can't be together. You're just pissed because your little plan to ruin my life failed. Because I would rather hump a dead body than hook up with you. Because Faye is worth ten million of you and I couldn't be any happier. Look around, Addy. No one here even likes you. You're a pathetic clinger, and we all know it."

"This isn't over." She jabs a finger in his chest.

I thrust her hand away. "Keep your disease-ridden paws to yourself."

"Make me." She plants her hands on her hips, deliberately taunting me.

If she thinks I'm going to lower myself to her level, she can think again. I've already gone a couple rounds with Peyton this week and I'm determined to play it smarter from now on. I make a show of removing my phone from my bag in slo-mo. She pins me with a derisory look. "You've been officially cautioned to stay away from us. You too." I jerk my head in Jeremy's direction. "I wonder what the cops will say when I tell them you're already violating the terms of the agreement and deliberately trying to provoke a fight." I tap in a few numbers, and she attempts to snatch the phone from my hand, but I preempt the move, extending my arm up over my head, well out of her petite reach.

She stomps her foot in frustration—a move I've seen her exercise before—and Jill and Rach burst out laughing. That sets the crowd off, and soon everyone is laughing and mimicking her. Her skin flares up and her body is trembling with rage.

"Get lost, Addison," Ky says, resting his chin on my shoulder. "No one wants you here." The crowd starts up a chant, "Out, out, out," and her lower lip wobbles.

Sweeping past us like a tornado, she leaves the house, dragging Jeremy with her. "Fuck you, Kennedy," Jeremy snipes, flipping his middle finger up as he passes.

"What a bitch!" Rach exclaims, clasping her bottle of beer to her chest and slurring her words a little. She staggers against the guy propping her up.

The crowd disperses now that the thrill of a potential fight has evaporated, and as they do, I spy Brad heading farther into the house, towing a cute brunette by his side.

We decide to take a break from dancing, finding a semi-private spot in the front room to make out in peace. After a while, we wander back into the main room. Rach is kissing the face off some unsuspecting guy on the dance floor while Jill is chatting with Kal in the space where we left them. Melissa is snuggled into Keaton's chest, and his arms are loose around her waist. Kent is M.I.A., as per usual, and there's no sign of Brad.

"How much longer do you want to stay?" Ky asks.

I shrug. "Depends when Rach and Jill want to leave. Why?" I peer up into his gorgeous blue eyes. "You in a hurry or something?"

"Or something." He grins, pulling me in for another kiss. "I can't wait to get you home," he whispers in my ear, and I shudder uncontrollably at the seductive tone in his voice.

Kal and Jill meander over. "I think we should check on Kent," he suggests, and Ky nods.

"Are you having a good time?" I ask Jill after the boys have headed out in search of their brother.

"Yeah. This place is unreal." She leans into my ear. "I'm so happy things have worked out with you and Ky. He's very attentive, and you seem really happy. I'm glad because I was so worried about you after what happened in the diner. I even spoke to my parents to see if they'd agree to let you move in with us."

"You did?" I can't disguise the surprise in my tone.

"Of course! You're my best friend, and you know my parents love you, but we just don't have the room." Jill comes from a traditionally large Irish family, and she's telling no word of a lie. Their house is already crammed to the rafters.

I give her a quick hug. "I know that and I'm chuffed you asked. That was really sweet of you, but you don't need to worry about me. I'm happy here. I can't say it's been a walk in the park, but I've been made to feel like a part of the family, and while Ky and I still have stuff to work through, I know he's a keeper. I've never felt this way about anyone before. He makes me feel so alive. So cherished."

"Good. You deserve it." Her eyes wander out to the dance floor. "At least I only have one bestie to worry about now."

My eyes follow hers. Rachel is kissing a different guy now, and she's staggering all over the place. The dude has major grabby hands, but she's too out of it to notice. "We need to stage an intervention."

Jill sighs. "Story of my life." We walk toward the dance floor, but before we can reach Rachel, Brad does. He hauls her back against his chest as words let loose on his tongue. I can't hear what he's saying to the guy from here, but he's unmistakably ripping him a new one. The guy mouths off at him before storming away. Rachel slumps against Brad, clawing at his shirt.

"I think that's our cue to leave."

"Agreed," Jill says, while we watch Brad supporting Rachel.

They walk toward us. "She's smashed," he says. Rachel mumbles incoherently.

"Brad?" The brunette he was with tugs on his arm.

"Not now." He scoops a wobbly Rach up into his arms, before shooting a fleeting glance at the other girl. "I have to leave. I'll see you around." He brushes past me, and the girl's mouth curls into a sneer. "I'll wait in the limo while you round up the others," he tells me.

The brunette watches as he leaves with Rachel. "He didn't mean to run out on you," I supply, feeling the need to explain his actions.

She snorts. "Please, get real." She flicks her hair over her shoulder and smooths her hands down the front of her dress. "We fucked. It's no biggie. I couldn't care less." I spot Kal entering the far side of the room as she saunters up to another guy, running her hands over his ass and smiling provocatively. Well, then.

"Ky'll be out in a minute," Kal says, reaching my side. "He said to wait for him in the car."

"You go. I'll wait here for him." Jill stays with me while Keaton, Kal, and Melissa head outside.

Ky marches toward me, half-dragging Kent with him. Kent is cursing at the top of his voice.

"Oh, boy," Jill exclaims. "What is his problem?"

"He's angry all the time, and so closed off."

"Out." Ky gently pushes Kent ahead of him, before reaching out to take my hand. We are nearing the corner of the house when Ky's name is called from behind.

Ky sighs. "What now?"

We turn around as Addison throws herself out the side of the hot tub almost tripping over the edge. She runs toward us, water dripping down her bikini-clad body, wobbling on her wet feet. Pushing damp strands of her blonde hair back off her face, she reaches for Ky. He steps in front of me, keeping one arm around my waist while he holds up the other in warning. "Don't come any closer."

"I'm surry," she slurs, looking up at him with pleading eyes. She sways on her feet, almost losing her balance.

"You're drunk, and I'm done with you." He moves to turn around, but she grabs his elbow. He shucks her hand away. "Get your hands off me. I want nothing more to do with you. What part of that don't you understand?"

"You donzt mean it," she slurs. "I only did it for you. Fur uzz."

She reaches for him again, and I slide out of his hold, positioning myself in between them. "What do you mean by that?"

She growls at me. "I hate you."

"The feeling is mutual."

She moves to go around me but stumbles awkwardly on her ankle. Crying out, she crashes to the ground on her knees. I bend over to help her up, but she pushes me away. "Don't tush me!" She glares at me before looking over my shoulder at Ky. "I love you. Please, baby." She's whimpering now, trying to climb to her feet. Her knees are gashed and bloody, and I reach out again to help her up. "Screw off!" she screams, lunging at me. I step back, and Ky circles his arm around my waist. "This is all your fault, you whore! I hate you." A loud sob rips from her throat, and she sags dejectedly to one side. Ky starts backtracking, putting more distance between us as Jeremy stalks toward us in his swim shorts, nostrils flaring. "She ... she said—"

Jeremy clamps his hand over her mouth, muffling her words. Lifting her up, he cradles her against his chest. "Get lost, asshole," he sneers at Ky.

Instead of responding, Ky takes my hand and spins us around, nudging Jill forward with a soft hand on her back. Kent is shaking his head, laughing. "Man, your ex is a fucking crazy bitch. You sure know how to pick 'em!"

"Shut. Up. Kent." Ky's jaw is tense as he steers us to the car.

We scramble inside, and Brad is holding Rachel's hair back while she pukes into the ice bucket. Melissa has a hand over her mouth, looking like she might spew herself. Keaton moves her head to his chest, running his hand up and down her back. Kal is watching Rach with a faraway look on his face.

"I'll do that." I get up to move to Rach's side as the limo glides out of the driveway.

Brad waves me away with his hand. "I've got it." After she's finished puking, she accepts the tissue and bottle of water Brad holds out. Mascara is smudged under her eyes, and tendrils of hair are plastered to her forehead. Dropping her head, she rests it on Brad's lap and promptly conks out.

Ky asks the driver to stop, and he gets out of the car, leaving the ice bucket at the side of the road. Hopping back in, he lowers a couple of the windows, and we all breathe a collective sigh of relief as cool, fresh air replaces the previous offensive stench.

Jill sighs beside me. "She's gotten worse," I whisper, and she nods. "Why? Why does she do it to herself?"

Jill shrugs. "I don't know what's going on with her, but it's been awful since you left. She's way out of control, and all we seem to do is argue these days. I was delighted when Ky phoned and asked us to come visit because it's the first time in months I've seen her genuinely happy."

"You should've told me."

"You have enough problems of your own. Besides, what could you do from the other side of the world?" While her words aren't meant to upset me—she's merely stating facts—I can't help the pang of guilt that slices across my heart. Contact with my friends *has* been dwindling. Not on purpose, but we *have* been slowly growing apart. I don't know if it's inevitable when someone moves away, but I make a silent promise to myself to make more of an effort going forward. It also reminds me that I need to start making some concrete plans for my future.

When I first came here, it was a necessary evil—a temporary move necessitated by the guardianship order. My plan had always been to return to Dublin after graduation and to apply to Trinity, but now I don't know what I want to do. This is home now. This is where my family is. It'll be difficult to form a relationship with Adam if I'm back in Ireland, and leaving Ky behind isn't an option, so I'm not sure where that leaves college. I don't even know what Ky plans in that regard, and that's something we need to discuss. And soon.

But more pressing is figuring out what Addison meant just now. Although she was drunk, and being her usual bitchy self, she wasn't so incoherent that I couldn't understand what she was saying.

What I'd like to know is who she was referring to, what *she* said, and why?

Chapter Eighteen

Faye

Rachel is still sleeping off her hangover when I leave the house the next morning. Ky is dropping me into town to meet Adam for breakfast, and then he's promised to head back to the house to keep Jill company for a couple of hours.

"Are you pissed you're missing the re-launch?" I ask, buckling my seat belt. I know he'd been looking forward to today's event at the Middleborough motocross track almost as much as May and Rick—the owners—were.

He cranks the engine into gear, easing the SUV out onto the drive. "Yeah."

"It's so unfair considering you're the one who made it all possible."

"It wasn't just me. You donated most of the funds, and lots of people helped with the renovations." He curses under his breath as we approach the gate. "Keep your head down," he instructs, glaring at the handful of determined reporters still hanging about outside. I want to roll down my window and scream at them to screw off. To leave my boyfriend and my family alone. It's their fault that he's missing out on the re-launch. With the scandal surrounding his bio dad, and news of his being taken in for questioning in his murder, Ky felt it was best to stay away from the track today. He didn't want to do anything to undermine all the hard work May and Rick have put in. They were understandably upset but grateful all the same. This is make-or-break time for their business, so while I know they wish he was there, they don't want anything to jeopardize the re-launch. It still sucks though. I was looking forward to it, too, and it would've been cool to show Rach and Jill around.

I straighten up once we move past the gate. "Let's go into Boston today. Show the girls the harbor, do some other touristy stuff, and, if we have time, we could visit Harvard? Then catch dinner and a movie, maybe?"

"Sounds good." Smiling, he reaches out and takes my hand.

He pulls up in front of the café where I'm meeting Adam and kills the engine. My knees bounce up and down, and my palms are clammy all of a sudden. Ky gets out his side, running around to open my door. "You nervous?" He reels me into his comforting embrace, tucking my hair back behind my ears. I nod. "I can stay with, if you like?" he offers.

I spy Adam by a table at the far side of the window, watching us with a neutral expression. I shake my head as butterflies take up residence in my stomach. "No. I need to do this by myself, but I would like you to meet him, if that's okay."

"Sure." Lowering his head, he gives me a soft, sweet kiss that takes the edge off my apprehension. Easing back, he scrutinizes my face in that intensive, exploratory way of his. Like he can see straight through to my soul. As if all my thoughts and feelings are wide open for him to analyze. "Ready?"

I grip his hand. "Yes. Come on." I lead him into the café and down to Adam's table.

Adam rises, nodding at me. "Faye." He smiles. "I'm glad you could make it."

"Um, sure." I chew on the inside of my mouth. "I wanted you to meet my boyfriend. This is Kyler."

Adam surveys him coolly as Ky extends his hand. He shakes it firmly, eyeballing him the entire time. "It's nice to meet you, sir," Ky says, and I have to smother my chuckle. Look at him being all polite and shit.

"Likewise. Thank you for dropping Faye off. I can drive her home after."

"Actually, we're heading into Boston. Some of my friends are visiting from Ireland, and we have plans, so it'd be better if Ky just collected me from here."

"Okay. No problem." Adam gestures at the empty chair. "I didn't order yet. I was waiting for you."

I give him a tentative smile, turning to Ky. "I'll see you later."

He pecks my lips, and my cheeks flush. "Message me when you're ready." He gives my hand a squeeze before leaving.

I drop down on the chair and—feeling Adam's eyes on me—bury my face in the menu. The waitress arrives and we place our orders. She fills our cups with coffee, and I set my hands on the table in front of me, trying not to fidget.

He clears his throat. "How long have you been dating Kyler?"

"Not long," I say, being evasive on purpose.

"He seems like a nice guy."

I take a sip of my coffee for want of something to do. "He is." My lips curl up involuntarily. "He's great."

"Is he your first boyfriend?"

Is he for real? I'm almost eighteen for cripes sake. "No. I was going out with a guy back home for a couple of years. It was pretty serious, or at least it was at the time."

"Is it serious with Kyler?"

What's with the twenty questions? I feel like I'm being interviewed for a job. "Yes. I'm crazy about him."

The waitress appears with our food, and there's an uncomfortable silence while we wait for her to leave. I tuck in straightaway, hoping to deflect any more embarrassing questions.

Adam watches me quietly, and I force food down my throat, hugely self-conscious. After a couple minutes, I put my knife and fork down and stare at him. "If you have something to say, just say it."

He wipes his hands down the front of his trousers. "I've been reading the media reports these last few weeks, and I've got to be honest, Faye, I'm concerned about you living with the Kennedys."

James was right.

"You shouldn't believe everything you read in the papers," I hiss, stabbing my eggs like they've done some injustice to me.

"I understand that, but when you peel back the layers, the fundamentals of what's being reported are the things that are causing me concern."

I chew my food slowly, counting to ten in my head. "They are not bad people. They've just made some bad mistakes. None of us are perfect."

"I know we don't know each other that well, and it will take time for you to trust me, but if you came and lived with me, even on a trial basis, it would give us the opportunity to get to know one another, and I'd feel more comfortable knowing you were safe."

My fork clatters to the table. "Are you implying that I'm not safe with the Kennedys?"

He holds up his hands in a conciliatory gesture. "You have to see it from my point of view. You were almost killed under your uncle's watch, one of your cousins was recently accused of rape, and your other cousin—your *boyfriend*—is being investigated for murder. I don't want my daughter getting caught up in all that."

I stand up, slamming my chair back with a screech. "None of them have done anything wrong!" I snap, anger getting the better of me. "You've been my dad for all of ten seconds, and that doesn't give you the right to show up here and try to tell me what to do! And how do I even know you are my dad?! All I have is my mother's word, and that doesn't count for much these days." I pull my phone out of my pocket. "This was a mistake. I knew I shouldn't have come. I asked you for time and you ignored my wishes. I'm leaving, and I'd like you to respect that."

I don't even wait for a reply. I just storm out of the place, uncaring that every pair of eyes is glued to my retreating back. I'm shaking as I step out onto the footpath.

"Faye, wait, please. I'm sorry." Adam plants himself in front of me. "Don't leave. I was out of line, and, you're right, I shouldn't be pushing you. I'm just worried about you."

"You haven't earned that right!" I holler.

He shakes his head. "I disagree. I don't need to earn the right to worry about my own daughter. I've only just found out about you, and we've already lost so much time!" His eyes glisten. "I want to get to know you, but I'm scared something is going to happen to you before I even get that chance." He stops, drawing an elongated breath. "Is there a right way to do this? How does one form a relationship from scratch with your almost grownup daughter? A daughter you didn't know existed until recently?"

Ever so gently, he pulls me aside as a couple emerges from the café doing their best to look like they're not listening.

"I just want a chance to get to know you," he says more quietly. "A chance to learn to love you like I love my other children. A chance for you to become a part of my family. Is that so bad?"

A blast of cold air hits me full on, and I shiver without my jacket.

He moves in front of me. "Look, it's freezing out here. Can we go back inside and talk? I promise I'll listen to what you have to say."

His honest eyes are pleading, and my anger is fading. "Okay, on one condition. That you accept I am happy living with the Kennedys and you stop criticizing them. James gave me a home when I had nowhere to go, and I've grown close to him and my cousins. They are far from perfect, but they're *my* far from perfect."

"I don't want to be an overbearing father or the type of man that forces anyone to do anything against their will, so I'll drop it, for now, if *you* can promise me one thing."

"Shoot."

"If you change your mind about living with them that you tell me instantly. That you genuinely reconsider my offer then."

I shove my icy hands in my jeans pockets. "I can agree to that."

He smiles, cautiously placing a hand on my lower back. "Okay, let's go in and eat our breakfast, assuming it's not cold by now."

The waitress brings us fresh plates, and the awkward tension has been eliminated. We chat more casually as we eat this time. When my belly is full, I push my plate away and groan. Adam smiles, summoning the waitress over with a hand gesture and holding his cup out for a refill.

I decline, mulling over a few things in my mind. "I've been thinking about what you said the last time. About my, um, half-brothers and half-sister. Do they know about me?"

He puts his cup down. "Yes. I told them earlier on in the week. My ex-wife too."

"And how did they react to the news?"

"The twins are very excited and dying to meet you. Whitney was ... quite blasé about the whole thing, but I wouldn't take that personally. She's fourteen and going through a difficult stage."

Hhm. Sounds a bit like someone I know. "Do they look like me?"

"You share the same eyes, but they are more fair-haired. They have my ex-wife's coloring." He leans over the table. "I can arrange a time and a neutral place whenever you are ready to meet them. I won't rush you. Just think about it."

"Okay. Thank you." We chat a while longer about his business and the fact that I no longer have a job. The diner remains closed, and now that David is incarcerated in a psychiatric facility it seems unlikely that it will be reopening any time soon. Unless his ex-wife gets control of it, I suppose.

"I want to say something, but don't read too much into this," Adam says. "This is not me pressuring you. It's just a suggestion."

I automatically stiffen, and he notices. "Please, relax. I meant it when I said I won't force you into anything. You're a responsible young adult, and I trust you to make the right choices for you. I just want you to understand you have other choices now too." Gingerly, he takes my hand in his. "I want to be a part of your life, and I want to help in any way I can. You've been through a huge amount these past few months, and I want to protect you from further pain. You're already precious to me, Faye. Your mother was the greatest love of my life and we created you. How could I not already love you to bits?"

Tears sting my eyes. "Everything has changed so much. It's challenging to wrap my head around all that's happened, and some days I don't even feel like me anymore."

He pats my hand. "Anyone would struggle to deal with the things you've dealt with. It's natural to feel like that."

"I do want to get to know you, and my siblings. I just need some time."

"I understand, and that's perfectly fine." He smiles. "I'll try to be patient."

I return his smile, carefully removing my hand and placing it in my lap. "So, what was it you were going to say?"

"Well, you know I have my own business." He has already explained how he moved to New York with his American wife to take up a position in her father's company just after he graduated from Trinity and married her. Her father's company developed software for the aviation industry, and Adam rose quickly through the ranks, becoming CEO before he was thirty. When his marriage fell apart, he thought it best to step down. He set up his own tech company, developing regulatory software systems for the financial services industry, and it has developed rapidly. He now employs over two thousand people, and they've recently branched out globally. "If you need a part-time job, I can employ you. We are always recruiting. Of course, you would have to move to New York."

I open my mouth and he holds up a hand, stalling me. "This is not me pressuring you to move in with me. This is me letting you know you have options."

He seems intent on drilling that point home. "I appreciate that, but I'm going to see if I can find something else locally, unless the diner reopens." Although that's probably just wishful thinking.

He looks contemplative. "Good luck with it, and if you need a reference, just let me know." My brows nudge up, and he laughs. "If I can't use my position and my connections to help my own daughter out, there is something very wrong with the world."

"Okay, thanks." I think.

"Same goes for college. Have you given much thought to what you want to do after graduation?"

How coincidental that he should ask me that when I've only recently begun thinking of my future. "I'm not sure what I want to do. Initially, I thought I'd return to Ireland and do social studies or psychology in Trinity but now I don't want to leave here," I answer truthfully.

His eyes sparkle with hope. "So you definitely want to go to university? You're considering staying in the States and going to school here?"

"Yeah, more than likely. Although ..." I trail off, knowing if I follow through that he'll jump in with the solution.

He cocks his head to one side. "Although?" he prompts, and I know he won't let it go.

"I don't think the money my parents left will be enough to cover the cost of university here. From what I've heard, it's way more expensive than back home." Selling my parents' house in Dublin is an option, but not something I can bear to think about right now. It's the last link I have to them, and even though the thoughts of living there without Mum and

Dad is excruciatingly difficult, so is the idea of selling the property. I'm not ready for that. At least, not yet.

He places his hands palms down on the table, peering intently into my eyes. "If you want to go to college here, I can help with that. I know you know that, and I'm guessing it's not something you want to have to accept, but I'm putting it on the table anyway. Don't let that stop you from making more permanent plans to stay in the States."

He leans back in his seat, studying me earnestly. "My other children all have trust funds, and I've already set one up for you." I gawp at him. "I won't treat you any differently just because you have a different mother, or the fact that you weren't raised by me. You won't want for anything, Faye. And I'm sure your uncle would say the same."

I squirm in my seat, hugely uncomfortable with the direction this conversation has taken.

"That makes you uncomfortable, doesn't it?" His observation is astute.

"We weren't poor, by any means, but I've done a full one-eighty since coming here, and it's hard to grasp sometimes. It feels wrong to be given something I haven't earned, something I haven't worked for."

Unnamed emotion flits across his face. "Saoirse raised you well. I'm already so proud of you." He takes both my hands in his. "I'm really glad you're in my life, and I'm looking forward to getting to know you better."

As I look over the table at him, at the same blue eyes staring back at me, my heart rate accelerates. I think of all the ways this could have gone. Of how awful Ky's experience was when he met his birth father, and I realize I'm lucky. While no one will ever replace Michael as my dad, Adam seems like a decent person, a decent father, and I could do a whole lot worse. He's already putting my own needs before his own and allowing me to call the shots. He's letting me know I have options and that he wants to share in my life, and while I've still got a crap ton of stuff to sort out in my head, it feels good to have someone else in my corner.

I'd be a total fool to push him away.

Mum loved this man for a reason, and I think I'm beginning to see why.

"Me, too," I tell him, and as he beams at me, I realize exactly how much I mean those words.

Chapter Nineteen

Faye

"Aw, crap. Is it much longer?" Rach moans, for like the tenth time, rubbing her belly and resting her pasty face against the window of Ky's SUV.

Kal sends her a sympathetic look, while Ky chuckles. "We're just approaching the exit for Boston now."

I reach around, handing her a bottle. "Drink more water. It'll help flush the alcohol out of your system."

"Or maybe try taping your mouth shut next time," Brad unhelpfully adds.

"I wasn't the only one knocking back the beers," Rach retorts.

"At least I can handle it." He shakes his head. "You have no idea the state you were in. Anyone could've taken advantage of you, and you wouldn't have known. That's not smart, Rachel, and it's the type of behavior that'll only get you in trouble."

"Thanks for the lecture, *Dad*." She swigs forcefully from the bottle.

"Brad is right, Rach," I say. "I've never seen you so drunk." She's always had a tendency to overdo it but never like that. She barely even knew her own name by the end of the night.

"I have," Jill interjects quietly.

"What the feck is this?" Rach asks, looking hurt as her gaze dances between us. "I've got the mother of all hangovers, and the last thing I need is a bunch of know-it-alls trying to tell me what to do. Butt out, the lot of you." Her lips pull into a tight line as she glares out the window.

Ky places his warm hand on my knee. "Let it go," he mouths, and I reluctantly nod. I don't want this weekend to be overshadowed by arguments even if I am worried about my friend.

We spend the afternoon doing some touristy things—visiting Boston Common, Quincy Market, the Bunker Hill Monument, and we even squeeze in a flying visit to the Boston Irish Famine Memorial—before driving over to Harvard to introduce the girls to my older cousins. We have a coffee in one of the campus dining halls with Keven and Kaden before heading back into the main city for dinner. They both cry off, citing previous arrangements, so it's just the six of us who make our way to the quirky little Mexican restaurant Brad booked before we left Wellesley. Apparently, it's one of his favorite places to eat in the city.

Sandwiched between more illustrious restaurants, this place is a little hidden gem. Rustic tables and chairs sit atop an original stone floor. Vibrant orange and red walls are decorated with numerous traditional ornaments and paintings, giving the place a very authentic feel. Lighting is soft and the place is abuzz with chatter. The restaurant is packed to capacity, and I notice several curious heads glancing our way as the waiter brings us to a table tucked unobtrusively into a hidden nook at the back of the room.

Our little tourist trip around the city has done wonders for Rachel's hangover. Color has returned to her cheeks, and she's looking more like herself. "So, Brad," she says, taking a sip of her Coke and eyeing him over the edge of the glass. "Why exactly are you living with the Kennedys?"

"Rach!" I elbow her softly in the ribs.

"What? It's a genuine question." She looks perplexed. "Unless there's some big secret?"

"You didn't tell her?" Brad looks surprised as he leans back in his chair.

I shake my head. "No. It wasn't my story to share." He smiles at me, one of those long, lingering, heartwarming smiles of his. I shift uncomfortably. Ky narrows his eyes in a deliberate glare.

"So, um, what are you going to do about college now, Faye?" Jill asks, doing her best to deflect the burgeoning tension. "Are you still planning on going to Trinity?"

Ky whips his head around to me, his eyes reflecting his surprise. "That was the original plan before I moved here," I tell him quickly, giving his knee a reassuring squeeze. "But plans change." He looks deep into my eyes, seeking the answer, and I decide it's time to put him out of his misery. "I've been mulling it over, and I'm pretty sure I know what I want to do." I twist around in my chair, facing my friend. "My family is here now. My home is here now. Returning to Ireland no longer feels like the right call." As my words settle around the table, the clarity of my decision astounds me. A layer of stress releases, and I know I've made the right choice. "While I haven't made any hard and fast plans yet," I say, looking purposely at Ky, "I think I'll be going to college here now."

"Oh." Jill looks crestfallen, and I understand why. It had been our dream to attend the iconic Trinity College Dublin together.

"I'm sorry, Jill, but everything is different now." Ky threads his fingers in mine, and I can sense his smile without the need to see it. "Will you still go?"

She bobs her head enthusiastically. "Definitely. Sam is thinking of going there, too." I don't feel quite so guilty now.

The waiter arrives then with our food, and group conversation ceases.

"Do you really mean it?" Ky whispers in my ear. "You're going to stay?"

"I think so."

He frowns a little. "You think so?"

"I ... actually, could we talk about this later? We haven't really spoken about college or the future and I'd like to, just not here." I gesture at all the inquisitive eyes and ears around the table.

"Sure thing, babe." Leaning in, he kisses me firmly on the lips, and the sudden unwelcome surge of anxiety retreats.

After dinner, we emerge into the darkness outside to discover a street bustling with activity. Street musicians entertain the crowds wandering in every direction. "Is it always this busy?" I ask Ky as he takes my hand leading the way.

"This area is popular with students, and it's a Saturday night, so it's usually fairly happening."

"I like it. There's a lovely vibe about the place."

"We should come back here by ourselves again. There's a nice Chinese place just over there," he says, gesturing across the road.

Throngs of men and women are hanging around outside a bar adjacent to the restaurant, smoking, drinking, and laughing. Faint sounds of live music trickle out of the open doorway, but it's the heart-wrenching sound of a girl crying that snatches my attention. My eyes hone in on the boy and girl standing at the corner of the bar, facing into a narrow alleyway. "Hey." I tug on Ky's shirt, pulling him back. "Is that Keanu?"

Ky looks to where I'm pointing, nodding. "Come on." We run across the road to him.

"Hey, man," Ky says, cautiously approaching. "Is everything okay?"

The girl stops crying, burying her face in Keanu's shoulder at the sound of my boyfriend's voice. Keanu steadies her at the waist while his other hand smooths down her long, dark, glossy hair. "Everything's fine, Ky." His tone holds a distinct "butt out and mind your own business" edge.

Ky looks at the girl cowering in Keanu's arms. "I'm not here to interfere. I just wanted to see if you needed any help."

"We're okay. Selena was being hassled by a jerk inside, and she got a little upset, but she's okay now. Right, baby?" Keanu shifts position, drawing her around into the shelter of his arm.

This girl looking at us is recognizable purely from the photos I've seen of her modeling for Kennedy Apparel with Keanu. Selena is even more stunning in real life. Apart from mascara and lip gloss, her face is devoid of makeup, and she's absolutely breathtaking. Although her skin is flushed red from crying and her eyes are undeniably tear-stained, her flawless complexion, perfectly proportioned features, and wide brown eyes combine beautifully. Tall and thin, she has curves in all the right places, and I'm not in the least bit surprised she's a model. I'll bet she's in high demand.

Not that any of us would know.

Keanu tells us next to nothing about her. I don't know if they are officially boyfriend and girlfriend, just friends, or work colleagues.

"Hi." I extend my hand in her direction. "I'm Keanu's cousin, Faye."

Her smile is genuine but tinged with sadness, and her handshake is soft and reluctant. "Hi." Her voice is barely louder than a whisper.

"This is my brother Kyler," Keanu says, motioning toward Ky.

"It's nice to finally meet you. You'll have to come up to the house sometime." Ky's tone and voice are deliberately soothing.

Her answering smile seems tentative. "Maybe."

Keanu pulls Selena in tight to him, holding her firmly around her waist. "I see the others approaching across the street. I'd rather they didn't know we are here. Please, Ky."

"No sweat, once you're sure everything is okay."

"I'm sure."

He moves to walk around us, but Ky blocks him. "Does Mom or Dad know you're out here?"

Keanu's cheeks pucker sourly. "I'm sixteen, Ky, not six." He clearly doesn't like to be called out in front of Selena. "And it's a work-related function. Mom is well aware I'm here."

Ky holds up his hands in defeat. "Fine. Just looking out for you, bro."

Keanu rolls his eyes, ushering Selena toward the door. "I'll see you later."

Ky scratches the side of his head. "Is it just me or was that weird?"

I take his hand, pulling him back across the road. "It's not just you. That *was* a little strange, but who are we to judge?"

♥♥♥♥♥♥♥

Back at the house, we watch a couple of movies in the cinema room until the early hours, before everyone scatters to bed. Ky steps into my room as I'm crawling under the duvet. He's not disguising the fact he's staying in here anymore. I can tell Alex is unhappy about it, but she doesn't want to do anything to cause further cracks in their relationship, so she hasn't interfered. I think James is pleased that Ky is leaning on someone, and that's why he's permitting it. Either way, I'm glad we aren't sneaking around anymore.

"What did you make of that earlier?" he asks, stealing into bed beside me. I scoot over, snuggling up against him..

"About what?" I murmur, running my nose along the length of his neck.

"Keanu and Selena." His voice is husky.

I move my hand along the expanse of his naked chest as I haul myself up on one elbow. "I don't know what is going on with those two, but they seemed close and very comfortable with one another. Are they officially a couple or what?" My hand glides lower, and Ky sucks in a breath.

"I'm not sure. I've asked Mom before but she's as tight-lipped as Keanu is. All she'll say is that Selena had a tough upbringing and she's not good in social situations."

My hand palms the bulge in his boxers, and he grabs me by the hips, pulling me up onto his lap. "It's late. Aren't you tired?" I ask with a reckless glint in my eye.

His gaze darkens as his eyes rake over me with obvious desire. Pumping his hips, he grins seductively, and I moan, grinding into him with unabashed need.

"I'm never too tired for you." Our mouths collide in a hungry kiss as our hands roam in mutual urgent need. Soon, we've shed the rest of our clothes, and he's thrusting into me, filling me so completely that I know I'll never be empty again. Never feel alone again. His eyes hold mine as he makes love to me, spearing me with the extent of his devotion, and as he rocks me into a blissful state, all I can think is how I want this—want him—and nothing else for the rest of my life.

The next morning, Jill comes with me for a swim while Rach hangs out with Alex. Ky makes us a late breakfast before taking us all to the motocross track. Rick and May fill Ky in on what was, by all accounts, a very successful re-launch while I show the girls out to the bleachers. The place is virtually empty today, which suits me fine. I was hoping to have a chance to speak to Rach and Jill alone before they have to leave.

"What's going on with you?" I bluntly ask Rachel as we settle onto the bench to wait for the boys to appear on the track.

"What do you mean?" she asks, acting surprised.

"You know what she means," Jill murmurs.

Rach drops her head in her chin, sighing. "There's just some shit I'm dealing with at home, and I'm trying to decide what to do with my life after I leave school in June."

"Surely you have plenty of options now?" I say, thinking of her family's recent lottery win.

"It opens some other doors, but it doesn't mean I automatically know what the right path is."

"What about doing something in fashion?" I suggest, uncapping a bottle of water. I hand one each to my friends. "You've always had a good eye and a genuine interest in clothes. I think you'd be good at it. Did you mention anything to Alex?"

Her eyes spark to life. "I was too awestruck to ask her about that. You should see the stuff she gave me. I about died."

"See that's what I'm talking about." I grin at her. "Your whole demeanor changes when you're talking about clothes. You should research courses in the fashion industry when you go back, and I can always ask Alex for her advice. I'm sure she'd email you about career options and stuff."

"You're lucky, Faye."

I almost fall off the bench. "How do you figure that?"

"You aren't answerable to anyone, and you don't have family holding you back, fucking with your head and messing with your life."

I stand up, a sour taste churning in my mouth and my stomach. "I cannot believe you just said that."

"Nor me," Jill cuts in. "Rach, how can you say that to Faye after everything she's gone through?"

Tears prick her eyes as she rises. "Shit. I'm sorry, Faye. I didn't mean it like that. I was just thinking of my own situation." Huge tears roll down her face. "You know I loved your parents, and your house always felt more like a home to me. I just meant that ..."

"What, Rach? What is troubling you?"

She shakes her head, sniffling. "Nothing. That was terribly insensitive of me. I'm so, so sorry. Can you forgive me?"

One look at the genuine sincerity on her face, and my anger evaporates in a puff of smoke. Rach has been my best friend for over four years and she helped me through some difficult times. I'll never forget how she and Jill took me under their wing when we moved from Waterford to Dublin, how they helped me settle into my new school, and how understanding they were when I told them the reasons why I'd had to leave my old school. Rach's dry sense of humor and mischievous spirit have always endeared her to me, but she's changed. There's a tortured darkness to her personality now that wasn't evident before. She's clearly dealing with something, and I wish she'd open up. Let us help her. But I know from personal experience that it isn't something you can force. Still, it's hard to see her in self-destructive mode and not do anything about it.

I pull her into a hug. "There's nothing to forgive." Jill and I lock eyes, and concern filters between us. There has always been something off about Rach's family life that bothered me. Her parents were polite and welcoming, but we were never invited around much. Rach much preferred to hang out at our houses. I've often wondered what it is she drinks to forget, but trying to get information out of her is like trying to pry The Biebs away from his partying lifestyle.

Brad and Ky appear on the track below, granting a much-needed reprieve. Kitted out in their biking gear, they are both looking hot as hell. We watch attentively as they go head to head, chatting more casually and leaving a lot unsaid.

All too soon, it's time to head to the airport. We say our goodbyes to May and Rick, and Brad heads back to the house while Ky drives the girls to the private hangar of Logan International Airport.

Our goodbye is predictably tearful. I don't know when I'll see them again, and I cling to them with fierce possessiveness as the thought invades my mind. "Thank you so much, Ky. It's been a wonderful trip." Jill hugs my boyfriend. "And you two should visit us soon." She gives me a final hug. "Everyone would love to see you. Will you think about it? Maybe at Christmas or Easter or even the summer holidays." A loud sob escapes her mouth. "Seriously," she whispers in my ear. "Don't lose touch. You're still my best friend, and even though there's an ocean separating, us it's no excuse for not staying in close contact."

My cheeks are damp as I pull away from her. "I know, and I promise to call more."

Rach hugs me fiercely. "If you ever want to talk about it, or you ever need to get away from it, you know where I am," I tell her.

"You're welcome anytime," Ky adds.

"Thanks. That means a lot."

Ky envelops me in his arms as I watch my friends wave one final time before disappearing into the cabin. He kisses the top of my head. "Did you have a good weekend?"

I peer up at him through watery eyes. "The best. Thank you. It means a lot that you'd do that for me with everything you have going on."

He kisses the tip of my nose. "That's what you do when you're in love. Nothing else matters but you, Faye." He rubs his thumbs under my eyes, smoothing the moisture away. "Not now. Not ever."

Chapter Twenty

Faye

Neither of us feels like going back to the house yet, so we grab some takeout and head to Ky's lake. It's not quite evening yet, and there are a few families and couples milling about. Ky spreads a blanket on the ground in front of his favorite tree, and we sit cross-legged with our backs against the tree trunk as we eat.

After, I settle between his legs with my back against his chest. His strong arms wrap around my waist, and I link our fingers together. We stare out at the placid lake, swathed in the second blanket Ky brought from the car, and I figure this is as close to heaven on earth as it gets. I could quite happily stay here like this forever. I sigh contentedly as he plays with my hair, planting delicate kisses along my face and in that tickly place just behind my ear.

Gradually, the other people disperse until we are alone. Day is transforming to night, and slashes of red, orange, and yellow are fading in the purple-blue evening sky. "It's so beautiful here. So peaceful," I say. "It reminds me a little of home. Dad was big into nature, and it wasn't uncommon for us to trek for miles through forests and up mountains during his weekends off." I stare off into the distance as memories flood my mind. "One of his favorite places to visit was Blessington Lakes. It wasn't too far of a drive from our house. It has tons of walks and trails, and the views from the lakes are spectacular. He would've loved it here."

"Do you think, if your parents hadn't died, would we have ever met?" He caresses my cheeks with his fingers.

I turn around in his arms so I can see him. "I'd like to believe we would have," I reply with conviction, smiling.

"Because this feels like fate?"

"Yeah." My smile magnifies.

"What?"

"You're really quite the romantic." I kiss his cheek.

"I have my moments. Just don't tell anyone." Smirking, he leans in and kisses me, slowly and sweetly, and my arms curl around his neck.

"I love you, Kyler Kennedy." I pull back, staring into his eyes. "So, so much."

"I love you, too, and I want a future with you, Faye. If I haven't been clear about that before, I want to make sure there is no confusion now." He palms my face. "We're a team. Wherever you go, I go, and if that means we move to Ireland so you can go to Trinity like you planned, then that's what we'll do."

I sit up straighter, still hanging onto him. "You would do that for me?"

He tweaks my nose. "Yes! I don't really care where we go to college once we're together."

"What about your plans? Where do you want to go?"

His eyes wander, and he stares off into empty air. "It's always been assumed that we'd go to Harvard. That's where Mom went, and her father before, dating all the way back to her great-great-grandfather."

"You don't want to go there?"

He shakes his head. "That's not it. I kinda thought I'd be on the pro circuit. College didn't really factor in my plans."

"And now?" I run my fingers through his silky hair.

"Now I'm not sure whether I want that anymore."

"Because of your father?" I say, remembering his previous comments on the subject.

He kisses my forehead. "Yeah. It's all become interconnected, and not in a good way."

"You might feel differently in time."

He shrugs. "Maybe."

I kneel in front of him, taking his hands in mine. "Can I say something and you promise you won't get mad?"

He pauses before replying. "I'll try."

"I think you should see a therapist and sooner rather than later. You can't make life-altering decisions regarding your future until you've dealt with the ghosts of the past. I did some research, and I found a lady in Boston with great credentials. I think she could help you, and no one else would have to know. I could go with you and"—I place my finger on his lips as he opens his mouth to speak—"this isn't me telling you what to do. This is me letting you know you have options, ways of dealing with everything going through your head, that you aren't alone in it, and I'll support you whatever you decide." I draw a lengthy breath, dipping down to kiss his cheek. "Okay, shutting up now."

He leans his head back against the tree, pulling me in close to his chest. His hands run up and down my arms, heating me on contact. "I'm grateful for your help, and this isn't me saying no, just that I need time for stuff to sink in."

"I get that. Honestly, I do." I rub my hand over his chest.

"I couldn't have gotten through this last week without you, and your support means so much. Thank you. I can't believe I ever thought I could push you away, leave you behind."

"That was idiotic, all right," I joke.

He starts tickling me, and I scream, wriggling around in his lap. Without warning, I'm flat on my back, and he's hovering over me. "You really shouldn't have started something you can't finish." His teasing eyes are inflamed.

"Who said I have any intention of *not* finishing?" I smooth my hand over the growing tent situation in his jeans, and the ache down below multiplies tenfold. I pop the button on his jeans and slip my hand into his boxers. He's rock hard, and I love how much I turn him on.

"Faye, stop. We can't." With a tortured expression, he removes my hand from his boxers.

I pout, reaching for him again. "Why not?" I look around, and the place is desolate. "There's no one here, and no one is likely to arrive at this late hour." I push up and straddle him, forcing him flat on his back. Planting my hands on his chest, I stare earnestly into his eyes. "If there's one thing I've learned these last few months, it's that you don't know what's around the corner. What new curveball is waiting in the wings. Life is for living, Ky. For taking risks. For following your heart. For throwing caution to the wind. Hell, I could throw out a hundred other clichés, but they all mean the same." I run my thumb along his lower lip. "I don't want to have any regrets. My parents are dead. I almost died. There isn't much else I'm afraid of, except something happening to you."

"I don't want you to worry about me." He places his hands over mine. "It's my job to worry about you."

I grin at him, slowly rubbing against his arousal. "That's sweet, but unnecessary. Worry and regret and risk, they are all strong emotions, but I'm done expending so much energy on them. Life *is* for living. I never really got that before, but I do now. Life is too precious to waste a single second worrying about something that may or may not happen, or being too afraid to take a risk. I'm not saying I'm going to be stupid about it, or that me almost dying is something I'm even close to getting over, or that I don't miss my parents, but they would want me to be happy, to move on in my life, to be the person they raised me to be." I pause momentarily, wetting my lips.

"So, I'm going to make decisions that I feel are right for me and *own* them. I'm going to get to know my birth father, and if he's someone I need in my life, then he'll be in my life." I lean down and kiss him. "I'm staying here and going to Harvard with you or I'll go to Harvard and follow you around the circuit in my free time." He opens his mouth to speak, but I shake my head. "I'm not done."

He swats my ass, and I laugh.

"Being with you is the most normal I've felt in a long time. I don't care what anyone says. That we're too young, or it's still gross because we're related by marriage, that we don't know our own minds, blah, blah, blah." I pull up the edge of his sweater, palming the sculpted contours of his ripped stomach. "I know what I want and it's you. Everything else will get figured out along the way. So, mister"—I lean down again, planting a needy, hard kiss on his mouth—"if I want to do you out here in the open, I'm going to do it, and I don't care if someone catches us. Fuck being sensible. Fuck following rules or acceptable social norms. Just, just ... fuck it."

He has me pinned on my back in record time, his mouth crashing against mine as we frantically devour one another. "Awesome speech," he murmurs, pushing my sweater up and planting his hot mouth against my equally hot skin. "Very motivational." His hand creeps into my knickers, and he dips two fingers inside me.

I moan, sliding his jeans and boxers down his legs as his fingers pump frantically inside me. I wrap my hand around him as he whips my jeans off in one smooth move. My knickers follow and then he's rolling on a condom and he's inside me, thrusting hard in one stretching motion as I beg for more. My legs suction around his waist, and I rock my hips up, grabbing his ass and pulling him in closer. Our tongues are tangling violently, and I've never felt such overwhelming all-consuming need before. He's giving me everything, and still I want more.

He stands up, our bodies joined together, and presses me against the tree so he can thrust deeper. I moan and scream as he pounds into me, sucking on his neck and digging my nails into his back. It's raw and rough and needy and I'm loving it. I don't even feel the sting as my back chafes against the bark. There is only toe-curling bliss as Ky rocks my world. We jump off the cliff together, exploding in a fireball of heavenly pleasure.

"You okay?" he asks, when he finally has his breathing under control.

"Never been better," I rasp. "That was hot." I grin manically.

"That was fucking incredible. Jeez, baby." He kisses me passionately. "I don't think I'll ever get enough of you."

"Good." I extract my aching legs from around his waist, and he helps steady me. "I don't want you to get enough of me."

♥♥♥♥♥♥♥

It's completely dark by the time we arrive back at the house. "What the hell?" Ky exclaims, and I follow his line of sight. Courtney is pounding on the front door with a thunderous expression on her face.

"Damn, this can't be good."

Ky brings the car to a halt and hops out just as the door opens and James appears.

I follow him, both of us hanging back a little.

"You can't shut me out!" Courtney shrieks at the top of her lungs. "I won't let you."

She beats on James's chest, and he reaches out to grasp her wrists. "We're over, Court. I will never be with you again, so please just accept that and back off, move on. You got what you wanted, so let the rest go."

"No!" She wrestles against his grip. "Let go of me!" James releases his hold on her. She prods a bony finger in his chest. "You're a part of this, and I won't be happy until I have it all." She stabs him in the chest with the tip of her long, sharp nail. "You. Belong. To. Me."

He bats her hand away. "I don't belong to anyone, least of all you. Consider yourself lucky, Courtney, and cut your losses."

She laughs, shifting slightly on her feet. "You think you get to call the shots? I'm in control here, *babe*, or have you forgotten?"

Panic flares in James's gaze, and his eyes dart briefly to where Ky and I are standing. Courtney notices, swinging her gaze around to us. "Well, well. Look who it is." She smirks, her gaze roaming my jeans and sweater combo in blatant disgust. "Like father, like son, I see." Her eyes pierce Ky. "You are making all the wrong choices too, Kyler. It clearly runs in your DNA." Evidently, she hasn't been reading the news lately. Throwing back her head, she laughs hysterically. "Gosh, the irony!" She sniggers but none of us are in on the joke.

"It's time for you to leave, Courtney. I'd prefer you to show yourself out, but I'm happy to call the station and organize a police escort for you." James folds his arms unsympathetically.

She shakes her head. "What the hell has gotten into you? You're not even with her anymore and you're pushing me away?" She closes the gap between them, running her fingers up and down James's folded arms. "We're good together and you know it. You are letting her cloud your judgment, as usual."

James's eyes narrow to slits as he removes her hands. "Whether I am with Alex or not makes no difference. There is no *us* anymore, Court.

Deal with it and move on. Now, leave and don't come back, or I'll have you forcibly removed."

"Don't threaten me, James." Her voice has turned to ice. "There will be consequences. I'll release it. I'll tell the world and laugh as everything you hold dear crumbles underneath you. Don't test me. I'm warning you."

James grabs her by the arm, hauling her toward her sporty blue car. "You're hurting me!" Courtney screams. "Stop it!" She wrangles her arm free, stumbling and almost losing her balance. "You'll be sorry you did that, James. I'm going to call my publicist right now." She sends him the evil eye, and I half-expect an eerie cackling sound to reverberate across the rolling nighttime sky.

He puts his face in hers, calm anger etched across his features. "No, you won't. Because if you do, then you'll lose everything, too. Now get your skanky ass off my property, and don't come back." He bumps her into the driver seat, slamming the door shut.

Courtney glares at him, before narrowing her eyes. "You were a lousy lay, anyway. It won't take me long to land a new conquest." She turns lust-filled eyes on Kyler. "Anytime you want to sample a real woman, give me a call, sugar." She blows him a kiss, laughing wildly as she cranks the engine and the car jerks forward down the drive.

James scrunches handfuls of his hair, watching until she is out of sight. "I'm sorry you had to hear all that, but she's not going to be a problem anymore. I'll make sure of it."

"What was she talking about?" Ky asks. "What did she mean she has all the control?"

James slaps Ky on the back. "She's delusional. Honestly, I think she needs psychiatric help, but she's not my problem any longer." He musses up my hair playfully, smiling as if the showdown with his ex-mistress hasn't just occurred. "Come on, let's head inside. Ky's got school tomorrow, and I want you up as usual, studying from home. Being suspended is no excuse for falling behind."

Ky and I exchange wary glances as we walk into the house.

Yeah, he's buying that deflection about as much as I am.

Chapter Twenty-One

Faye

"She's never going to leave us alone, is she?" Alex asks from the top of the stairs, and we all look up. Dressed in lacy silk pajamas, she's holding a glass of red wine in her left hand.

"She got what she wanted." James is sullen and avoids looking Alex directly in the eye.

"I know you're still pissed with me," Alex says, setting her glass down and descending the stairs. "But we need to work as a team if we're to defeat her once and for all."

Ky frowns, exchanging another loaded look with me. I wish they'd tell us what's going on with Courtney, and why she seems to have dug her claws in so profoundly. *She is obviously holding something over them, but what?*

"Pissed?" James glares at his wife. "Pissed doesn't even being to describe how much I despise you," he snaps. "Courtney is dealt with. Move on, Alex." He strides down the corridor toward the guest room he's been staying in, leaving us standing awkwardly in the lobby.

"Kyler," Alex says, gulping. "Could we talk, please?"

Ky crosses his arms, scowling at his mother. "I have nothing to say to you." Taking my hand, he moves toward the corridor, but Alex steps in front of him.

"You can't avoid me forever. Hate me forever."

"Wanna bet?"

"I'm sorry, son! I'm so sorry. Please, please forgive me."

"I told you I need space, Mom, so please back off and give me some."

The air is laced with tension, and Alex looks on the verge of tears.

"Okay," she says after a bit, placing her arm on mine. "Faye, could I have a word, please?" Her smile is sad.

Ky looks at me with a perplexed expression, and I hate feeling like piggy in the middle. "It's fine." I kiss him briefly. "I'll be down shortly."

We walk up the stairs and into her suite. Alex gestures for me to sit on the chaise, and I plop down onto it.

"I want to ask for your help again with Courtney," she says, getting straight to the heart of the matter.

"But James just said—"

"I know what he said, but he's wrong. Courtney will not back down until she gets everything she wants," she cuts in, pacing the floor in front of me.

"And what else does she want?"

"Him, among other stuff."

I twirl a lock of hair around my finger. "I don't understand, Alex. Why are you bowing to her? Giving her such a powerful promotion and allowing her to get away with this, whatever *this* is?"

She drops down beside me, taking my hands in hers. "I'd like to be completely upfront with you, but it's better if you don't know. Courtney has something on us, something that could ruin us, and she's resorted to blackmail. That's all I'm at liberty to say."

"Is she really going to become VP?"

Alex sighs, and her lips turn down. "I still have one week until the promotion is official, and I'm working a few angles." She looks down at her hands, folded neatly in her lap. "I want to avoid it, but it involves taking huge risks, and I'm not sure if I'm ready to go there yet." She gulps, staring absently at the wall with an anguished look on her face.

"Why is she doing it?"

She shrugs. "Why does anyone resort to blackmail and fraud? Money, power, and control. I don't know much about Courtney's background, but she didn't come from money. Oftentimes, those who grew up without wealth think it's the solution to everything. Little do they know, it causes worse problems."

"If it's about money and power, then why does she want James? This almost seems personal."

"It is. This is about me," Alex agrees. "She harbors some form of resentment against me, and I don't think she'll be happy until she's taken my husband from me too."

"James doesn't want to be with her. You heard what he said."

"But is it the truth?" Alex muses, tapping a manicured finger against her lips. "That's what I'd like your help with. Could you be my eyes and ears around here when I'm not in the house and let me know if she shows up again or if you know he is going out to meet her?"

I shift uncomfortably. "I'm not altogether comfortable spying on my uncle, Alex."

"It's not spying per se. All I'm asking is if you find out something or come across something that you let me know."

I agree with Alex that Courtney seems like the kind of woman who doesn't take no for an answer, and I'm betting that isn't the last time she'll attempt to reclaim James. She got to him once before, who's to say she won't be successful again? She's poison through and through, and I don't want my uncle anywhere near her, so, really, I'd be doing him a favor by looking out for him. "Okay. I'll do it. But I'm doing it for James."

She smiles. "Of course, and thank you." She gets up.

"Could I ask you something?"

She nods, sitting back down. "What do you know of Peyton's mother?"

"Not much," she admits, pulling her knees up to her chest. "Wendy was a few years older than me, and she attended your school, so our paths didn't cross much. I've heard gossip about her over the years. Apparently, all her children have different fathers, and she's raised them as a single mom for most of that time." She cocks her head to the side. "Why do you ask?"

"Just curious." I shrug, deliberately downplaying it. "I'm still trying to get to know people in town."

Alex yawns. "I strongly suggest you avoid Peyton and her family. Judging by what I've heard around town, and based on how they conducted themselves at that meeting on Friday, it's obvious they're not from good stock." While her assessment on both counts is bang on, her comment still rubs me up the wrong way. I like Alex, and she's been nothing but kind and welcoming to me, but there's no denying the snobbish attitude both Kal and Lana referred to previously. I don't like people who judge others without good reason, and her assumption makes me uneasy. Nevertheless, I let it go. It's late and I want to crawl into bed with Ky and forget about everything fighting for space in my head.

I wander down to breakfast the next morning in leggings and one of Ky's shirts. "Don't you possess any of your own?" Kal teases, fingering the hem of the shirt.

"Sure, I do," I reply, jostling him out of my way as I open the fridge door. "But I *like* wearing Ky's." I bury my nose in the material. "It smells just like him." My eyes glaze over, and I'm sure my smile is goofy.

Strong, familiar arms snake around my waist from behind. "I *love* you wearing my shirt. You look fucking hot." Pressing his mouth to my ear, he whispers, "Although I'd prefer if you were naked underneath it."

"I just puked in my mouth," Kent says, brushing past us. "You two are thoroughly nauseating." He sticks his fingers in his mouth, gagging for show.

Ky swats him across the back of the head. "I think someone's jealous."

Kent snorts. "As if. I'm bathing in a sea of pussy while you're stuck on a life raft with the same girl and no land in sight." He flicks my cheek. "B-or-ing!"

I push him away, rubbing my sore cheek. "You're fooling no one, Kent. Least of all me."

He shrugs. "Whatever, sweetheart." Flipping Ky the bird, he saunters out of the kitchen whistling.

"He won't be so cheery when he realizes Dad's bringing him to the shrink tonight," Kal announces.

"I hope it helps him," I say, extracting myself from Ky's grip to pour some juice.

"Here, I prepared your fruit and yogurt already." He hands me a bowl, and I beam at him.

"You're so sweet." Flinging my arms around his neck, I smack a loud kiss on his lips.

"I'm with Kent on this one," Keanu hollers from his seat at the table. "Some of us are trying to eat here."

I pull back from him, sighing as Brad enters the room. "What's going on?"

"Nothing." The word flies out of my mouth. "Try not to miss me too much today." I grin as I slide onto the bench alongside Keaton. Ky sits down across from me.

"Being suspended is no laughing matter," James says, materializing in the kitchen. "And I fully expect you to maximize study time while you're off. Adam expects no less either."

I drop my spoon, and it clangs noisily off the tabletop. "You told him?" I had deliberately omitted any mention of my suspension at breakfast on Saturday because I don't want him thinking he has some say in how I conduct my life. Not yet, at least. Plus, it would only give him further reason to claim the Kennedys are a bad influence.

"I had no choice." He grabs a cup of coffee before sitting down alongside me. "Your chat with him worked, and he's agreed to hold off on lodging any custodial claim on condition that I keep him fully informed of anything important. That seemed like a fair trade-off."

"Aw, great," I complain, wondering when I'm going to get a call. I'm surprised he hasn't tried to contact me yet.

James sets his mug down. "Faye, sweetheart, you don't have to do anything you don't want to in relation to Adam. I've deliberately not said anything before because I don't want to influence your decision, but it is *your decision*. He isn't listed on your birth cert and you'll officially be a legal adult in a couple of months, so you can decide on what is and isn't acceptable in that relationship, or if you even want one with him."

I mull it over, and James is right. Adam can attempt to lecture me all he likes, but he wasn't the one who raised me. I'm only a couple of months shy of my eighteenth birthday, and I'm responsible for myself. I'll take myself to task over my actions if necessary. He hasn't earned the right to meddle in my life. Maybe someday, I'll want that. Maybe someday, I'll feel like it's right and the way things should be, but we're definitely not in that space yet. I'm sensing that James is struggling to accept Adam's role in Mum's life and the role he may play in mine, and I can understand that, to a point. But we can't change the facts, and I do need to set him straight on one thing. "I agree, and Adam has said he'll let me set the pace, but I do want to get to know him. I owe him that much."

"Honey, you don't owe him anything."

Instinctively, I smooth a hand over my stomach, remembering what Adam did for me. And it's more than him coming to my rescue. It extends beyond that. "He was robbed of my childhood as much as I was deprived of his existence. This isn't his fault, James, and I believe him when he says he would've stood by Mum. That she was his one true love. And he seems like a nice guy." My eyes meet Ky's across the table, and his imperceptible nod encourages me to continue. "I think I'd regret it if I didn't at least take the time to get to know him before I decide if I want him in my life or not."

James looks introspective. "I can tell you've given this much thought."

"I have."

"I'm on your side, Faye. Always. And I'll support you if this is what you want to do."

My cousins trade looks around the table while Brad continues to eat his cereal with his head down, trying his best to look and act inconspicuous.

"Thank you. That means a lot."

He clears his throat. "He mentioned he was hoping to introduce you to his other children once you were ready to meet them, and I thought it might help if we invited them here? We could organize caterers to come in and prepare a causal buffet, keep things light. If you like?"

I think about it. "Actually, that sounds great. Thanks." At least if I'm in my own home with my cousins around, I'll be buffered if it doesn't go well.

My own home.

I shock myself with my thoughts, and tears glisten in my eyes. While this isn't the first time I've felt like this, it's the first time I've properly contemplated what it means. I never thought I'd utter those words again. That anywhere could feel like home with mum and dad gone. The enormity of the moment isn't lost on me.

Ky is around the table and by my side in a heartbeat. "What is it?" He crouches down, holding my hands in his.

"It's nothing really." I smile, trying to deflect the attention. He wipes a tear from my cheek, and I read everything in his eyes. I can't believe he's so concerned for me with all the crap he's dealing with. I don't know what I did to deserve him, but I offer up thanks to whoever set our paths on a collision course. I squeeze his hands and look around the table. "I was just thinking it would be more comfortable to meet Adam and my new siblings in my own home." I look James straight in the eye. "I never thought I'd have that again, but it really, truly feels like home here." I worry my lip between my teeth. "The realization took me by surprise."

Keaton places his chin on my shoulder. "You will always have a home with us, right, Dad?"

"Right, son."

The bench screeches as Brad gets up. "I, ah, better get ready for school." He deposits his dishes in the dishwasher and practically sprints from the room.

"Crap," I exclaim. "That was really insensitive of me." I allow Ky to pull me into a standing position.

"It's like standing on eggshells around here these last few months," Kal supplies. "This family is so due a break."

"I second that," James says.

"I'm going to go talk to him. See if he's okay."

"I'll come with," Ky says, but I shake my head.

"Let me speak to him alone. He's done so much for me at school, and I want him to know he can still talk to me anytime." I kiss him on the cheek. "Besides, you lot need to get to school. I'll catch you later."

I knock timidly on Brad's door. "Brad, it's me. Can I come in?"

The door swings open, and I step into his bedroom. The room is pristine, with barely an item out of place. There are no personal effects of any sort, nothing that brands this as his domain. The room is beautifully decorated in shades of warm brown and cream, and the wooden furniture gives it a definite masculine feel. But it's missing something. It's impersonal and cold, and like stepping into a hotel room—a place that's luxurious and comfortable but temporary.

"Where's all your stuff?" I blurt.

He bends over the bed, placing some books into his bag. "I took what I needed and then stored most of the boxes in the garage when I moved in."

I walk over and plop down on the bed. "Is it because you see this as temporary?"

"It *is* temporary, Faye. They're not my family."

I reach out and touch his arm. "You're more family than I am, Brad. Ky has told me how you and he spent virtually every minute together growing up, either here or at yours."

"That was in the past, and I can't impose forever." He sits down beside me. "Besides, I'll be going to college next year, so there's no point trying to put down roots."

"I'm sorry for what I said in the kitchen. I wasn't thinking."

"I know that, and it's not your fault. I was being stupid."

"It's not stupid, and I'm sorry if I'm making things uncomfortable for you here."

"Like I said, it's not your fault." He stands up, swinging his bag over his shoulder. "And I'd better leave or I'll get another tardy. Need to keep my record clean if I'm to bag a scholarship. I'll see you later."

He walks toward the door with purpose while the seeds of an idea are forming in my mind.

I go to my room, spread my books out over my bed, and settle in for a couple hours of studying. When James pops his head in to let me know he's going out for a bit, I wait about twenty minutes before I set my plan in motion. This may be overstepping the line a little, but if Brad gets mad, I can always put it back the way it was.

I'm carting the last of the boxes I need to Brad's room when the front doorbell chimes. Alex comes speeding around the corner from the direction of her home office like a woman on a mission. She opens the door and ushers a dozen men and women inside. "I'll be having a lot of business discussions this week," she explains, "so you can expect plenty of traffic in and out of the house. They are members of the Kennedy Apparel board, and we have some important things to discuss. We will most likely be sequestered in my office well into the early hours of the morning. I hope that won't interfere with your studies," she says, eyeing the brown cardboard box in my hands.

"Not at all. Don't mind me. Pretend you never saw me."

"I'm sure I don't want to know what you're up to, so I'll happily take you up on that." Her lips tug up as she spins on her heels and follows the members of her board down to her spacious office.

I spend the rest of the afternoon rearranging Brad's room in between peppering Ky with a ton of questions via text. I've just hung the last picture on the wall when a noise at the door startles me. Ky is lounging against the doorjamb, inspecting my handiwork. "Wow, you've been busy." He strolls into the room, looking all around, before reeling me into his arms. "So, studying went well then?"

I swat his butt. "This was more important. We haven't done right by Brad, Ky, and we need to fix that. He doesn't have any family, and he needs to understand he belongs here. Do you think he'll like it?" I try to look at the room objectively, pleased that it's lost that impersonal vibe.

The bookshelves are crammed with Brad's books and model airplanes, trophies, and sporting memorabilia. Photos and posters of motocross champs, bikes, and star football players are hanging on the walls. I placed a few framed photos of his family by his bedside, and I even hung the poster with the scantily clad models in bikinis on the ceiling over his bed.

Ky flops down on the bed, chuckling as he stares up at it. "I definitely think he'll appreciate that."

Lounging lengthways on the bed alongside him, I swat him on the chest this time. "I hope he won't be cross. Won't think I've overstepped the mark."

"Why would I think th—" Brad's voice peters out as he glances around his modified bedroom. He says nothing, just stares, drinking everything in. Ky rubs soothing circles on the back of my hand with his thumb while a fluttery feeling builds in intensity in my chest.

I bite down on my lip, before deciding to grab the bull by the horns. "Say something." I laugh lightly. "Do you like it?"

He runs the tip of his finger along the frame of one of the family photos by his bed. "Get out." His voice is cold, undercut with anger.

"I was only trying to he—"

"I said get out," he yells, not even looking at me.

Ky springs up, eyes blazing. "Don't you dare shout at Faye like that!"

I swing my legs off the bed, tugging on Ky's arm. "Don't," I mouth, shaking my head.

Brad is hunched over his bedside locker, both hands gripping the wooden edge with stiff fingers, his body heaving with some unnamed emotion.

I drag Ky to the door, pleading with him to ignore Brad's emotive outburst. Before I close the door, I say, "I'm sorry, Brad. I thought it would help. I'll put it all back tomorrow."

Ky is furious as he stomps to my room. "That was way out of line," he fumes, kicking his shoes off and collapsing spread-eagled on the bed. He pats the space alongside him, and I duly oblige.

I curl into his side. "I shouldn't have interfered. I thought it would help him feel more at home."

"You were only trying to help. He's an ass."

"He's lonely and upset," I counter. "And I overstepped." I can see that now, even though it seemed like a good idea earlier.

Ky sighs after a couple of minutes. "I know, and you're right. We haven't given enough thought to his feelings."

"I have another idea." I push up onto my knees.

Ky groans. "I had a feeling you were going to say that."

Chapter Twenty-Two

Faye

Brad doesn't emerge from his room for the rest of the night. I ask Keaton to bring him a plate at dinnertime, and I'm glad that at least he accepted it, that he's not starving to death. The following morning, he walks silently into the kitchen, grabs some fruit and a bottle of water from the fridge, and leaves without speaking a word to any of us. "Do you think I should put it back the way it was or just leave it?" I ask Ky as I'm kissing him goodbye in the garage.

He pushes me against the side of his car, caging me in with his powerful arms. He kisses the tip of my nose. "I think you should leave it alone. Give him a bit more time to cool down, and then ask him if he would like you to return it to the way it was."

I cup his cheek. "Okay. You know him best."

Ky plants a soft kiss in that sensitive spot just under my ear, and I shiver all over. "I'm not sure I know him at all anymore," he admits, dotting tiny kisses over my cheeks. "He's saying jack shit about what's going on with him, and he's not acting like himself, so I don't know what he's thinking."

I push on his shoulders, and he lifts his head up. "Is this to do with me?"

"Some of it is, yeah, but he's got other stuff going on too. I wish he'd unburden himself to me, to someone. Has he said anything to Rose?"

I shake my head. "No. He's been closed off with her too. She's worried about him."

Ky scratches his stubbly jawline. "I'll try talk to him tonight."

"Don't. You have enough going on, let me."

A sheepish look crosses over his face. "Babe." He caresses my cheek. "I know you only want to help but—"

"I'm part of the problem," I guess, cutting in.

Ky looks apologetic. "I see the way he still looks at you, Faye. He wants you."

I lean my head back and close my eyes. "I never should have agreed to the fake boyfriend deal." I *adore* Brad and his friendship means a lot to me, so I hate this.

Ky gently grips my chin, pulling my face toward his. I open my eyes. "I don't think it would've made any difference. You're too easy to fall in love with, and we have always gravitated toward the same type of girl. I think it was destined to happen."

"We need to find him a girl," I muse out loud.

Ky swallows hard. "I'd like that a hell of a lot, but he'll find someone in his own time. We can't interfere. He'll go crazy if he thinks we're trying to fix this, fix him."

He's right.

Leaning in, he kisses me long and hard. His body presses against mine, and I clutch him to me, wishing we didn't have to separate for the next several hours. He leans his forehead against mine. "I hate leaving you."

"I hate it too. I miss you when you're not here." I pout, and his answering smile lights a fuse inside me. Sheer happiness invades every nook and cranny of my being. I used to think I was in love with Luke, but it isn't a patch on the strength of my feelings for Ky. My entire world starts and ends with him. When he isn't with me, he's all I think about to the point of obsession.

"I love being in love with you." His fingers dance in and out of my hair, and I lose myself in his pale blue eyes, swimming in the depths of his love and adoration.

"I never imagined I could feel this way. That true love would feel so unbelievably amazing. You make me so happy, Ky." I thread my fingers in his. "I never want to stop feeling this way."

He pulls me into his chest, hugging me tight. "Me either, and we won't. You're my forever girl, Faye. There will never be anyone for me but you."

He kisses the top of my head, and a happy sigh escapes my lips. "Are you doing okay?" I ask when we eventually break apart. He's dead late for school now, so what does another few minutes matter?

"I'm okay," he answers quickly. "Trying not to think about it."

"James says Dan hasn't heard anything more from the cops, so that's got to be a good sign. You didn't kill him, and they must know that by now."

Ky flips his keycard over and over in his hand. "Hopefully, but I won't properly relax until they tell me I'm in the clear." He opens his car door. "I better go and face the music."

I lean in and kiss him on the lips. "Drive safe, and don't forget about tonight." I'm determined to show Brad how much he means to us, so, tonight I'm preparing dinner myself. I've already squared it off with Alex and the housekeeper, and all the ingredients for our Mexican feast are bought and waiting for me in the kitchen. I hope this won't anger him further, but I'm not going to let that stop me from showing him how much he matters. He will never admit it, but he needs to know that. To feel part of the family.

"I won't. Have a good day. Love you." He blows me a kiss before maneuvering the car out of the garage and out of my line of vision. I practically skip back to my room, forgoing study so I can research recipes on the internet.

It's early evening and everyone is home from school. Predictably, Brad came in and went straight to his room, avoiding contact with all of us. Spicy, sweet aromas waft through the air as I navigate the myriad of different pots and dishes I have on the go. "This smells amazing," Ky says, stepping into the kitchen. He's wearing my favorite dark-washed jeans and a form-fitting white T-shirt. Clean, classic, and oh so hot. His hair is still damp from the shower, and tiny beads of water drip slowly down his neck in silent invitation. Fire burns in my eyes.

Reading my horny expression, he chuckles as he saunters toward me. Drawing me into his arms, he presses his mouth close to my ear. "I like where your mind has gone, and if we were alone, I'd take you right here, right now, bent over the counter."

The ache down below intensifies, and I squeeze my legs together. "You're such a tease," I whisper, lifting my head to kiss him as the sing-song chime of the bell rings out.

"I'm only a tease if I have no intention of following through." He starts backing away, winking. "But we'll definitely be taking a rain check later tonight, and that's a promise." I grin like a lovesick fool at him. "Go, get the door." I turn, smiling to myself as I stir the pots and check on the burritos in the oven.

Raised voices from the lobby claim my attention, and my body instantly seizes up. Call it intuition, but I have a sixth sense when it comes to Addison, and I just know it's her at the door. Turning the temp down on the stove, I head toward the lobby, tiptoeing quietly so as not to be heard. I hover just inside the door, listening.

"Please, Ky. I'm sorry I fucked up. I miss you so much. It was never meant to happen like this."

"I don't care." Ky's harsh, impersonal growl pleases me no end. "I despise you and everything you stand for. I'm in love with Faye, and she's the only one for me. Get that through your thick skull, and leave me and my family alone. This is your final warning. If you show up here again, I'll report it to the cops. You know you're not permitted to be here."

Her breath leaks out in exaggerated fashion. "Please, Ky," she pants heavily. "I don't know what I'm doing anymore. I want it to end, but I don't know how to get out of this mess." Her breathing becomes more pronounced. "Please don't shut me out," she gasps, almost like she's struggling for air. "I love you, and I can't bear it."

There's a loud thud, followed by Ky's urgent footsteps. "Addy!" Her strangled breathing causes my feet to move of their own accord. I step around the door and into the lobby. "Where's your inhaler?" Ky asks, crouched down over her prostrate form.

She's lying on her stomach, gasping for breath. "Don't ... have ... it."

"Wait here." He straightens up and turns around, startled to see me. Grabbing my hand as he passes, he pulls me with him back to the kitchen. "Don't say it. This means nothing."

He yanks open a cupboard, pulling a large medical box out. Flipping the lid, he starts pulling items out, tossing them onto the counter.

"Why should you even care?" I ask petulantly. "Can't you just call someone to come get her?"

He stops what he's doing, placing his hands on my shoulders. "This is self-preservation, pure and simple. I don't want her to die on my doorstep and add another suspicious death to the list."

I know it's more than that. Despite the nasty things Addison has done, she was a big part of his life once, and he can't erase their history. Doesn't mean I'm not suspicious of her motives. That girl is capable of everything and anything. I scoff. "Please. Jill has severe asthma, and I've witnessed some asthmatic attacks over the years." I thrust my arms in the air. "That act out there is all for show."

"I'm not taking that risk." Ky begins rummaging in the box again. "Got it!" He snatches the inhaler and legs it out of the kitchen. I race after him, almost colliding with his back in the empty lobby. He throws the inhaler at the wall in a temper, roaring. "Addison! Where the fuck are you?" He storms down the corridor toward his room with me hot on his heels.

Addison saunters toward us like she hasn't a care in the world. "Calm down, Ky. I was just using the bathroom."

His eyes narrow, and his head dips as he stabs her with a venomous look. Icy chills whip up and down my spine, and the air is fraught with tension. Gripping her arm, he starts tugging her back the way we came.

She slaps at his hand. "Stop it! You're hurting me."

He flings her into the lobby, glaring at her. Hostility and rage emanate from him in waves. "What have you done? What are you up to this time?" His lips curl into a snarl, and his body is taut and tense as he stares her down.

Addison plants her hands on her hips, faking confusion and hurt. "What do you mean?" She waves an inhaler in the air. "I had one in my bag after all, and I went to the bathroom to compose myself. There's no big conspiracy theory." She rolls her eyes. "Honestly, Ky. What the hell has gotten into you?"

He stalks toward her with a menacing glint in his eye. I position myself in the gap between them, holding him back. He can't afford to lose his cool around her. I don't trust her an inch. "You happened." I stare her down and her amused smug grin is taunting. I'd love nothing more than to wipe the smirk off her face, but then I'd be giving her exactly what she wants. I keep a cool head and an impassive face. Walking to the door, I open it with a flourish. "Get out and don't come back."

She glances at Ky briefly before walking to the door. Turning piercing eyes on me, she smiles maliciously. "You'll never be enough for him, and he'll never forget his first." Her eyes sparkle with superiority. "Enjoy it while it lasts, Ireland."

I slam the door shut and storm back to the kitchen. Turning up the heat on the cooker, I check the food in the oven, banging the pots down as I try not to let her words affect me.

"She may have been my first, but you'll be my last," Ky says softly, moving stealthily behind me. I bang a few presses, slamming the utensils around as I take my rage out on the kitchen. Warmth seeps bone deep as he clasps my wrist. "Stop, baby. Tell me what's wrong."

I whip around, hair flying in all directions. "Everything's wrong!" I yell, thinking of how perfect everything was this morning and how one manipulation from Addison has everything turned upside down. "Why didn't you tell me she was the first girl you slept with?" I demand.

"Because I knew you'd go apeshit." He sends me a knowing look, and my middle finger twitches impatiently. "But mainly because it doesn't matter. She's my past, babe." He pulls me up against his chest, ignoring my feeble attempts at resistance. "And you're my future. My only future." He presses his forehead to mine as he holds me even tighter.

Stress leaks out of my pores as he runs his hand up and down my spine. "She doesn't matter, Faye. We are all that matters. *You* are all that matters." He presses a kiss to my hair, and I sigh.

"Why won't she leave you alone? Leave us alone? I'm sick of her, Ky."

He tucks my hair behind my ears, sighing. "I know and we won't see her again. I promise."

"How?"

"I don't know but I'll figure it out. Don't worry. I'll take care of it." He kisses me softly, and I melt into the touch and taste of him, but when he pulls away, that undercurrent of worry, of anxiety, resurfaces, attempting to drag me back into a dark mood.

I know Ky believes Addison is behind him, and that we have nothing to fear from her, but my sixth sense is uncanny when it comes to that girl. I very much get the sense that she's going nowhere. That this is far from over.

Chapter Twenty-Three

Faye

I lay everything out on the formal dining table before calling the others to dinner. Standing back, I wipe tiny beads of perspiration from my forehead as I survey the impressive spread, and I have to admit it looks pretty darn good, even if I do say so myself! Delicious aromas punctuate the air, and my mouth waters in anticipation. My cousins bound into the room with Ky and Brad at the rear, trailing behind James.

"Wow, this looks and smells *ah-mazing*," Keaton exclaims with a wide grin.

"You didn't have to go to so much trouble, Faye," James says, taking a seat at the top of the table.

I shrug. "I don't mind. I love to cook, and I thought we could start a regular Tuesday tradition." He quirks a brow. "Each week one of us gets to pick the theme and I'll cook it. I know Mexican food is one of Brad's favorites, so I thought we'd start with that."

I risk a look at him, and the expression on his face is priceless. "You didn't have to do that," he says, his voice a little strangled, "but thank you."

He seems pleased, and if it's helped him to thaw out, then mission accomplished. "Should we wait for Alex?" I ask James, but he shakes his head.

"She's in another meeting."

"I'll save her some. Everyone tuck in."

My cousins waste little time demolishing the meal, and it gives me an inordinate thrill to watch them enjoy it so much. If it wasn't for the crappy hours and the foul-mouthed head chefs, I might actually consider a career in the restaurant business. Conversation is casual around the table, and for once the atmosphere is lighthearted. Ky squeezes my knee under the table, smiling at me.

Brad helps me clear the table while the others stay chatting. In the kitchen, he pulls me aside. "Thank you so much for that, and for my room. I'm sorry for how I reacted yesterday."

I gulp. "It's okay. I should've asked your permission first."

He shakes his head vigorously. "It was a lovely gesture, and I acted like a jerk. It's just ..."

Tentatively, I reach out and take his arm. "What? You can tell me."

His chest heaves as he stares into my eyes. "Planting new roots is scary. Becoming attached to others is far too dangerous." He averts his gaze, and I step closer.

I tilt his head frontward. "Why? It's only us. We're your friends, your family."

"That's the thing, Faye. Friends drift apart and family leaves. It's happened with Ky once already, and, well, you know the score with my fam. I'm not sure my heart could withstand it a second time."

"Oh, Brad." I don't hesitate, moving in for a hug. His arms hang loose at his sides at first, but slowly he circles them around me, hugging me back. "Relationships don't come with guarantees." I look up at him. "That's where trust and respect and loyalty come into play. Things you have here with us. I understand where you're coming from, but you can't live the rest of your life in fear, because you'll miss out on too much of the good stuff."

"You make it sound so simple when the reality is way more complicated." He smooths a hand over my hair, gazing adoringly at me. I take a step back as sirens blare in my head. Out of the corner of my eye, I spot Ky hanging back by the door, a noticeable frown on his face. "And you've just proven my point." Brads sighs, leaning against the counter.

"I'm sorry. I'm trying to help, but I keep making things worse." I shuffle awkwardly on my feet, shoving my hands into my pockets.

"Please stop apologizing. You haven't done anything wrong, and none of this is on you. I really do appreciate what you've done the last couple of days, but you have to stop trying so hard."

I tense up. "I can't do nice things for a friend?"

He puts his head down on the counter, groaning. "God, this is so fucked up." Ky makes a move to step into the room, but I stall him with a shake of my head. Brad straightens up, piercing me with an honest look. "You *should* be able to do things for a friend, but that's the issue. I don't want you as *just* my friend, and the more you do stuff like that, the more I fall in love with you, and then I hate myself because I know you don't feel the same way, and I despise myself for betraying Ky with my thoughts. Honestly, I don't know if I can continue to live here with you both. It's killing me."

My mouth hangs open. I haven't a clue how to respond to that. I knew he had some feelings for me but not like that.

"Get away from her," Ky growls, approaching from behind.

"Shit." Brad swings around to face him. "You heard that?"

Ky's face tenses up. "Yeah. What the fuck do you think you're doing?" He shoves him, and butterflies erupt in my chest.

Brad holds up his hands. "I don't want to fight with you."

Ky rolls his sleeves up to his elbows. "Maybe you should've thought about that before you told my girlfriend you love her."

Brad squares up to him. "Look, man, you're angry. I get that and you've every right to be, but would you rather I lied? I can't help how I feel even if I know it's wrong." He looks Ky directly in the eye. "She loves you, everyone can see that, and you're perfect together. I have no chance. I know that and I would never ever make any move on her. I meant what I said before. I won't do that to you again, and I'm trying so damn hard." He sighs, looking down at his feet. "It's a shitty situation, and I don't know what to do about it."

"Find someone else," Ky grits out, but the murderous look is fading from his face.

"It's hardly fair to bring someone else into this," Brad argues.

"Maybe not but I can't have you looking at her the way you do. Seriously, dude, I can't handle this shit right now." He locks eyes with me. "She's mine, and I'm not ever letting her go."

"I know, Ky. I understand that. I'm sorry. Truly, I am." Brad hangs his head, and a dead weight presses down on my chest. This is unbearable.

Ky holds his head in his hands, exhaling loudly. "I need you to keep your distance from her."

I open my mouth to protest but think better of it and shut it again. Brad has been a great friend to me, to both of us, and he's hurting too. Shutting him out doesn't feel like the right solution. I hate this. I really do, but I won't add to Ky's stress. If this is what he needs, then I'll comply whether I agree or not.

The next morning, after the others leave for school, I spend over an hour in the pool, stretching my limbs until they ache deliciously. My thoughts turn to Brad, but they're futile. There isn't anything I can do to smooth things over, and as much as I hate that there's no point getting depressed over it either. I wanted to help make things better for Brad, but I've only made things worse. I shouldn't have meddled in the first place, but if it's a choice between hurting Brad and protecting Ky, then there's no decision to be made.

Makes me feel like the crappiest friend on the planet, but it is what it is.

Once I'm changed, I start tackling my studies and get stuck in. I'm a couple hours in when my phone rings. I pick it up and stare at the screen, debating whether or not to accept the call from Adam. No point in delaying the inevitable, I suppose. Mentally preparing myself, I press the button. "Hey."

"Hi, Faye. Can you talk?"

I sit up on the bed, crossing my legs. "Sure. I was just studying, but I could use a break."

"How is your week going?" *Here we go.*

"Grand. I've studied, swum, rearranged Brad's room, and cooked up a Mexican feast last night."

He latches on the one part of that conversation I didn't expect him to. "You like to cook?"

"Yeah. Mum used to bake with me from a young age, and Dad always bought me a new cookbook on my birthday every year. I was always experimenting."

"You'll have to cook for me some time," he suggests.

"Sure. Speaking of, James has proposed you could come here with your, ah, children so we could all meet?"

"It's nice of him to offer, and I'm happy to do that if you are." I can tell he's making a huge effort to ease me into this and it goes a long way toward reassuring me.

"Okay. How about this weekend?"

"I think that's workable. Leave it with me and I'll come back to confirm."

"Cool. I'll need to double-check with James also."

"Great." I hear hushed voices in the background. "I need to head out for a client meeting, but I'll message you later."

"'Kay. Bye."

I flop down on my bed, tossing my phone aside. Adam is actually pretty cool, I've got to admit. I thought he would lay into me for getting suspended from school, but it's like we already have this unspoken agreement. He knows he can't start acting all strict, and he isn't even attempting to go there. I respect him so much more for that. But it's still so surreal and that's before I've even met my brothers and new sister. This weekend should be interesting, that's for sure.

I'm in the kitchen fixing a chicken salad for lunch when the bell peals. I'm halfway to the lobby when the sounds of multiple visitors stepping inside distract me. Feet troop inside in droves, and I turn around, heading back to my prep. Alex wasn't joking on Monday. This place has been like Grand Central Station all week. I hope whatever she has up her sleeve is going to stick it to Courtney once and for all. I'm totally rooting for my aunt in this showdown.

I eat my lunch alone in the kitchen, staring absently out the window at the rain sheeting down by the bucket full. I can't wait until the weather turns. Despite the fact I grew up in Ireland—well accustomed to the rain and the cold—I hate winter. Spring is my favorite time of year, when the weather has turned warmer, and the evenings are brighter, and I can leave the house without the need for a thick coat. Plus, my mood is always more upbeat when the weather is perkier.

I clear away my lunch things and head back toward my room. A gust of cold air blasts me the minute I step into the lobby. The front door is wide open, granting full access to the elements. The floor by the door is wet from the pelting rain. Shaking my head and muttering under my breath, I close the door carefully and then retrieve the mop and bucket and soak up the excess water.

I'm responding to a message from Rach when I step into my room. My head is down, and my focus is fixed on the screen when the sounds of heated arguing reach my ears. I tuck my phone in the pocket of my jeans and set out in the direction of the raised voices.

I round the corner and slam to a halt, gasping at the two figures in front of me. The door to Alex's office is wide open, and the men and women around the long table are watching the interactions in the corridor with keen intensity. My heart rate picks up as I stare into familiar grayish-green eyes. Courtney smirks over her shoulder at me.

"I won't ask you again," Alex demands, in a barely contained voice. "What the hell are you doing in my house?"

I've never heard her so rattled, and judging by the shell-shocked expressions on her colleague's faces, neither have they.

Courtney runs a hand down the front of her skirt. "I'm here for the meeting," she retorts coyly.

"Like hell you are. You weren't invited and you aren't welcome here. Leave or I'll call Officer Hanks." Alex straightens up, glaring at her arch nemesis.

Courtney lifts her shoulders and stiffens her spine in a defiant stance. "I'm VP of business operations. I have a right to be here, and I'll have to report you for misconduct. You have no legitimate excuse for excluding me."

"You are not VP yet, and I have every right to exclude you." Alex steps up to her, pinning her with a cold, stubborn gaze. The sounds of murmured whispers echo from the room behind her. "If you wish to command the respect of your colleagues, I suggest you leave voluntarily, although, I'll happily organize a police escort for you if you refuse."

A muscle ticks in Courtney's jaw as her eyes narrow to slits. A look of pure unadulterated hatred fills her eyes, and I get legit chills all over. Lifting her chin, she pierces Alex with a calculating look. "I'll go but things will be different next week, Alex." She brushes past my aunt, jostling her shoulder. "This is the last time you'll tell me what to do." With that parting threat lingering in the air she walks away with her head held high. Alex looks tellingly at me.

"I'll make sure she leaves." I race after her, trailing her all the way to the front door. She sends one last smirk my way before I slam the door shut with force.

Alex is waiting for me outside my bedroom door. "What did she want and how did she get in here?" she ruminates out loud.

"I'm not sure, and someone left the door open."

"I don't like it. She was in this house for a reason." Alex starts pacing the floor. After a couple of minutes, she thrusts her hands in the air. "I don't know! Dammit. Maybe we should search all the rooms."

"She can't have caused any damage. She could've only been inside for a few minutes," I supply, computing the timeline in my head. "Perhaps we caught her in time."

"I hope you're right." She claws her hand through her hair. "And I can't spend any more time worrying about it. I need to get back to my meeting."

I tell Ky what happened when he gets home from school. "What is she up to this time?"

"Who knows? Blonde bitches seem fixated on the men in this family," I part joke.

"Did you let Dad know?"

"Yep. I called him earlier."

Ky soars onto my bed, pulling me down with him, and the mattress shakes underneath us. I rest my head on his chest, listening to the steady beat of his heart. He plays with my hair, and I allow myself a moment to truly appreciate what I have. It's the simple things he does that mean the most. The way he holds my hand. The way he looks at me, into me, seeing right to the very essence of my soul. The way he cradles me to his chest like I'm the most precious cargo. The thoughtful gestures that show how much he cares. Honestly, I could live in a shack with Ky and still be amazingly happy.

"I've been thinking about what you said the other day, about therapy," he admits, as I trace a line with my fingers up his arm. "I'm going to give it a try. I want to tell my parents, but I'm still so angry with them over it, and that's not really fair, so I'd like to work through some of that stuff before I confess. I don't want any more arguments. I want to be able to tell them calmly, and I don't think I'm in that space yet."

I push up on my hands, leaning over him. "I'm glad. I think it will help. Do you want me to come with?"

"Yes, please. I know you can't participate in the session, but even having you waiting outside will help steady my nerves."

I dip my head and kiss him. "I can do that. I'm happy to do that."

"Thank you." His hands wander to my butt, and a devilish glint appears in his eye.

"I'll make the appointment for you tomorrow." I deliberately move his hands off my butt. His mother still has a houseful of guests, and there's no way I'm indulging in sexy times when there's a crap ton of people who might hear.

"I think that deserves a reward." He returns one of his hands to my ass, squeezing firmly. Holding my head in place with his other hand, he pulls me toward him, and I give in to the inevitable.

Trying to resist him is a bit like being offered the most decadent chocolate cake in the world and then being told it's calorie free.

So, I give in. Letting him claim his reward in his own unique fashion.

Chapter Twenty-Four

Kyler

Addison is waiting by my locker *again* when I get to school, and it takes enormous self-control not to smash my fist into the wall. I don't know how I can be any blunter. I'm tired of telling her we're over, but she's not getting the message. They should invent a new word especially for her. Stubborn doesn't even come close to explaining her pigheadedness. "Go away," I snarl, yanking my locker open.

"Where is all this pent-up frustration coming from, I wonder?" she says in that whiny voice she adopts whenever she's trying to get her way. "Ireland mustn't be putting out, huh?" She sends me a faux sympathetic look, and the urge to bash my head against the wall is riding me hard. *Why does she continue to bust my balls?* There's enough crap crammed in my head without Addy's additional bullshit.

"I'm not discussing Faye with you except to tell you, *again*, that she makes me unbelievably happy, way more than you ever did." I pile the last of my books into my bag, grab a carton of almonds, stash it in the front pouch, and bang the door shut. I sweep past Addison without waiting for a reply.

Stubborn isn't a strong enough word for her. The same thought keeps repeating as I shake my head and try to lose her. She appears on my left side, almost running to keep up with my long strides. I slam to a halt in the middle of the corridor, and someone crashes into me from behind. I'm too incensed to care, let alone check if the person is all right. "I. Will. Not. Say. This. Again," I yell. "Leave. Me. The. Fuck. Alone!"

A small crowd is starting to form around us, and Addison goes into full-on performance mode. "Suit yourself, asshole. And don't say I didn't try to warn you."

"Screw off, Addison. I mean it. Stay away or you'll be sorry." My eyes narrow, and my lip curls into a snarl as I send her my most threatening look.

She pivots on her heels, storming off with her hair flying out behind her like it shares her sense of indignation.

"What'd she do this time?" Dylan asks, appearing alongside me. He's our star quarterback and someone I've started hanging out with since Brad transferred. He's actually pretty smart and cool for a jock, and he's been exclusive with Hailey, the head cheerleader, for the last two years. They make a good couple, and it's refreshing to meet people who appear stereotypical but aren't.

"What she always does," I growl, swinging my book bag over my shoulder. "Merely exist." I rub my stubbly jaw. "I swear she was put on this earth just to mess with me." Although it's unfair to blame her entirely for my foul mood. This shit show with Brad has me pretty messed up. We fall into step as we head toward class.

"I heard she hooked up with Grayson last weekend."

"Hallefuckinglujah," I say, entering the room and heading to my usual seat. Curious eyes surround me, and I turn a sweltering glare in several directions. "Maybe now she'll forget about me."

"Doubt it," Dylan says, sliding into the seat behind me. "Grayson isn't exactly Mr. Commitment and she knows it. The way I hear it, she told him she was only doing him to make you jealous. She wanted it to get back to you."

"Ugh." I drop my head to the desk, groaning. "What the hell is wrong with her? She knows Faye is my girlfriend. I'm a total ass to her, yet she still won't fuck off."

"Dude, can't you report her to the cops? I thought she had to stay away from you and your family."

"She does, but they can't enforce that rule strictly at school which is why she has taken it upon herself to stalk me everywhere I go. I know some of the teachers have had a word with her, but she doesn't seem to care. I don't know how much more of this I can take."

"She'll get the message eventually."

I snort, lifting my head up as the teacher enters the room and the lesson starts.

The door swings open five minutes before class is due to end, and three men step inside. My heart plummets to my toes as I recognize the detective from Bayfield. It can't be good if he's come here as opposed to calling me back for further questioning.

Buzz cut talks discreetly in the teacher's ear while his eyes scan the room. His gaze latches on when he finds me and my gut tightens. The two uniformed officers accompanying him stand with their legs slightly open and their hands behind their back, looking like prize douchebags as they scan the room.

I start packing my bag even before the teacher calls my name.

I saunter to the top of the room like I haven't a care in the world. Planting my game face on, I look bored and unconcerned even though my heart is hammering against my ribcage and my palms are sweaty. Nausea hovers at the base of my throat, and my stomach churns unpleasantly. The detective takes my bag, handing it off to one of the officers, while the other cop grabs my hands behind my back. *What the fuck?*

The detective starts spouting a load of bull, but I tune him out. His words blur as my mind whirls in a mad panic. It was only yesterday that Dan called Dad to say it looked like they were pursuing other lines of inquiry. That I might be in the clear. That the bartender had given a statement verifying my version of events from later that night. *What the hell could have happened between last night and this morning to change things?*

I avoid looking at any of my classmates, staring straight ahead with a blank expression as if I don't give a shit. My cuffed hands scrunch into balls of fury behind my back. *The assholes couldn't have arrested me after school?*

The bell clangs just as I'm led out the door. Crowds swarm the corridor, instantly stopping when they see me being led out by a uniformed cop with my hands in cuffs. Kal pales when he sees me. "Call Dad," I mouth, and he nods, whipping out his cell immediately. Addison is chattering away to that annoying redhead she hangs around with—the forgettable one who was always hitting on me behind her back—as she emerges from class. Her mouth hangs open when she spots me, and a brief flash of what looks like concern flits across her face, but it's gone so fast I can't be sure of it. I pretend not to notice her, or any of the inquisitive looks, keeping my focus dead ahead as I'm led off school property.

I'm shoved roughly in the back of the cruiser and taken to the local police station. After telling the police I have nothing to say and requesting my attorney, I'm left in a small, whitewashed room by myself. The obligatory mirror-slash-window mocks me from the back of the room, and I try to limit my fidgeting to the minimum, but it's hard. I'm freaking out like I've never freaked out before.

After an eternity, the door opens and Dan Evans, our family attorney, steps into the room. I've never been happier to see any dude in my life. "What's going on?" I ask before he's even sat down.

Carefully setting his briefcase on top of the table, he claims the seat beside me. "They have found the gun that was used to kill Mr. Grant."

I sit upright in the chair, confusion bunching my forehead into creases. "That's great, but why have I been arrested? Surely that exonerates me?"

He removes his glasses, pinching the bridge of his nose. He sighs. "It would if they hadn't found the murder weapon in your bedroom."

"What?" I yell, vaulting up. My chair knocks to the floor with a bang. "No frigging way! That's impossible. I didn't kill him. I swear to you. He was alive when I left, and I've never owned a gun. Never even handled one."

"Kyler, sit down. Now." Dan's look and tone broker no argument, so I do what I'm told. A heavy weight is pressing down on my chest, making breathing difficult. He wets his lips. "I'm not sure what's going on here, but it seems apparent you're being set up. An anonymous tip was placed in the early hours of this morning, advising the investigating officer to search your room for the weapon. They showed up at the house just after you left for school and found the gun right where they had been told to expect it."

"Holy shit! I have no idea how it got there."

He leans forward in his chair, angling his body toward me. "Think carefully, Kyler. Someone planted that weapon in your bedroom. Who had access to your house this week?"

I throw my hands in the air. "Mom's had work colleagues over all week so there've been people coming and going nonstop. It must've been one of them." All the blood drains from my face as I recall Tuesday night. I clamp a hand over my mouth.

No way.

Yes way, the other voice in my head protests. She was prepared to let Kal go to prison for a rape he didn't commit.

"What is it?" Dan asks, expertly reading my changing expressions.

"My ex turned up at my house Tuesday night." God, Faye was right. *Why didn't I listen to her?* She's always right when it comes to Addison. "She faked an asthma attack, and when I went to the kitchen to find an inhaler, she disappeared in the house. I didn't really think much of it ..." I trail off, so fucking mad at myself for being such an idiot.

Then another awful thought hits me. "Jesus!" I pin worried eyes on Dan. "If she planted the gun, then that means that she killed him. Addison killed Doug Grant."

Chapter Twenty-Five

Kyler

"I have a PI I use regularly. A good guy. I'll get him to look into Addison Sinclair and see if he can find any evidence to back up your claims. But if she's done this to frame you, then I expect she's covered her tracks. Why would a young girl do such a thing?" His eyes crease at the corners as he frowns.

"She's a fucking psycho, that's why." My foot taps nervously off the floor. *How did I not see how deranged Addison was?* Honestly, it's like the sweet girl I fell in love with in ninth grade was a figment of my imagination. *Did she plan this thinking she was doing me a favor or something? Or did she follow me and walk unsuspecting into that cesspool of a house?* I can only imagine how Doug would've reacted if Addy turned up on his doorstep. *Is this some new angle to pull me back to her side?*

I sigh, rubbing the tense spot between my shoulder blades as all manner of other questions assault my mind.

I can't figure it out unless she's holding something back that will prove my innocence and planning on using that to barter with. The more I think of it, the more that scenario seems plausible and like something she'd do. She's already proven she isn't opposed to blackmailing me back into her arms. I break out in a cold sweat at the thought.

Something else occurs to me. "They swabbed me for gunshot residue, and there was none on my hands, and they won't find my fingerprints on that weapon either. Plus, you said the bartender confirmed my story, so why are they so sure I'm the murderer? Surely they can't make this stick?"

"Those are valid points and ones I intend to raise, but this is still an ongoing investigation, and they are exploring all avenues. I will be sure to pass on your intel regarding Ms. Sinclair; however, the bartender's evidence is actually more harmful than helpful."

"In what way?"

"She has told them how you turned up with bloody knuckles, in a clearly emotional state, proceeded to get drunk, and had to be helped to your hotel room where you broke down again. The officers are connecting it to the murder. The way they see it, it's the actions of a guilty man."

"They think it's because I murdered him in some kind of rage?"

"You've got to admit that sounds like a plausible theory."

I snort. "How about the fact it's a normal reaction considering I'd just found out the man I thought was my dad wasn't my biological dad and that my birth dad was an asshole who kicked me out of his house after suggesting a threesome with his girlfriend!" I kick out at the leg of the table in frustration. "Anyone would be messed up after that. Doesn't mean I'm a murderer."

"Please refrain from doing that. It's not helping," Dan chastises. He pauses briefly and I can almost see the inner workings of his mind as he contemplates something. He leans forward on his elbows. "Kyler. Is there anything else you haven't told me? Anything at all that could help explain your behavior that night?"

My chest tightens and nausea builds at the back of my throat. A line of sweat trickles down my spine. I don't want to have to confess to what happened when I was ten and how my birth father stepped in to halt the abuse before shit got real. But things aren't looking good for me, and I can't rely on Addison to come clean because that's still only a hunch, and she's undeniably swinging off the cray-cray tree.

"Anything you tell me is in complete confidence," he adds quietly. "I know your father pays my invoice, but I am representing *you*, Kyler, and I can't help you if I'm not aware of all the facts. I'm sensing you're holding something back, and I need to know if it could help your case or not."

My legs are shaking and my entire body trembles. Turning slowly, I face him, seeing nothing but calm concern in his gaze. I nod my head, and bit by bit tell him the parts of the conversation with Doug that I omitted last time, holding nothing back about the events at the track years ago. He listens patiently, jotting down a few notes, never once interrupting me.

When I stop talking, he puts his pen down and takes his glasses off. "I take it your parents aren't aware of this."

I shake my head. "I hadn't told anyone until last week when I spoke to Faye. She convinced me to see a therapist she found in Boston, and she was going to book the appointment today."

His smile is sad. "You've got yourself a good one there, Kyler."

"I know. She doesn't deserve all this. She deserves someone better."

Like Brad. It's not the first time I've had this thought, and it's like a dagger straight through my heart.

"Take it from an old man who has been around the block a few times," he says, chuckling. "Let the girl decide for herself, and if she wants to remain by your side, let her. Don't push her away. You will need her support in the coming weeks."

"What's going to happen next?"

"I need to go out and update your parents, and I'll let the officer know we're ready for the interview to commence. Then we wait to see if they're going to charge you or not. The M.E.'s report has issued, and the timeline is tight but not inconceivable; however, that plus the forensics report on the gun should be enough to create reasonable doubt." He pats my arm. "I will do my utmost to make this go away. I know you didn't do this, son."

"Thank you." I mean it. I've no doubt Dan is being paid handsomely for his services, but he's a damn good lawyer and has served our family well over the years. He's also an honorable man, and I imagine the same can't be said for all lawyers.

He exits the room, leaving me alone with my frantic thoughts. While the evidence seems blatantly obvious, I'm still struggling to grasp the fact that Addy is a murderer. *What the hell happened to that girl that she's become so warped?* And now I'm worried about Faye. If Addison is this unhinged, who knows what she's got planned for my girl. I need to get my ass out of here, stat.

Dan returns with the detective a little while later, and the interview begins. I tell them about the abuse and what Doug Grant told me, explaining that I kept those details back because I was ashamed and struggling to deal with it being brought to the surface after so long. I tell them my parents don't know and I was afraid of them finding out. I share my suspicions regarding Addison and how the gun was planted in my room. Dan reminds them they found no trace of gunshot residue on my hands, casts doubt on the timeframe given how accurately the waitress pinpointed my arrival at the bar, and states they will not find my fingerprints on the gun. After a bit of back and forth, they agree to release me into the custody of my parents. I have to sign a sworn statement confirming I will not leave town.

I do the walk of shame through the station out into the waiting area. Mom runs toward me, enveloping me in her arms. Her sobs fill the half-empty room. She grabs my face in her hands. "Are you okay?" Her eyes are shiny.

I nod as if in a daze. "Just get me out of here. Please. I need to see Faye. Warn her about Addison. She's not safe."

"Don't worry, Kyler," Dad says, patting me on the back. "I have re-hired security, and they are en route to the house as we speak."

The front doors of the station open, and the roar of a large crowd tickles my eardrums. Media hounds. Awesome. Brad runs into the room, looking flustered. "I came as soon as I heard."

After yesterday, that's kinda surprising, but I'm glad he's making the effort, that our friendship isn't completely in the toilet. "Thanks, bro."

"The mob is getting rowdy out there, and I was just talking to Faye, and she said there are several news crews and a chopper back at the house."

"Is she okay?"

"She's fine. Worried about you but fine." He plants a reassuring hand on my shoulder.

Mom hands me a plain back hoodie. "Put this on and keep your head down. Max will pull up right outside."

"Mom, I'm not going to hide. I haven't done anything wrong."

"Sweetheart, please."

I thrust the hoodie back at her. "What do you care about more? Me or your precious reputation?" I snarl.

"Baby. You know I'm only trying to protect you."

"I'm not wearing it." I grind down on my molars.

Her shoulders hunch in defeat. "Fine. Have it your way."

"I have an idea," Brad says, turning to me. "Why don't you leave here in the Merc but then switch to my SUV before we get to the house. I can drop you off at the old entrance at the back of the property, and you can get in the house without having to face the reporters."

"Sounds like a plan."

Camera flashes almost blind me when I step outside the station, flanked on either side by my parents. Brad slips out unnoticed, hurrying to his car. Reporters shout questions at me, but I block them all out. I only release the breath I'd been holding once I'm safely secured in the back of the car. "Don't they have anything better to do?"

"I'm sick of being gossiped about," Mom complains.

"I'm sorry I make your life so difficult," I retort, unable to keep the hurt and malice from my tone.

"Baby, that's not what I meant." Her voice is soft.

I lean my head back and close my eyes, refusing to speak to her. While I know it's unfair to blame her for this particular situation, I am totally pointing the finger in her direction. If she hadn't lied to me, I wouldn't have taken off half-assed to meet my bio father, and I wouldn't be in this mess.

Wordlessly, I get out of the Merc at the rendezvous point, gratefully sliding into the car beside Brad. He floors it, leaving a cloud of dust behind us. "Want to go somewhere? Take the bikes out?"

"While that sounds tempting, I need to speak to Faye."

"Sure." His voice is terse, and tension bleeds into the air at the mere mention of my girlfriend. My head clutters with fear and jealousy and frustration. Brad is in love with Faye, too. There's no way to avoid the awkwardness, but I don't want to give up on my buddy either. He's been through the wringer as well, and I won't cut him loose, no matter how much it's pissing me off that he's coveting my girl.

He'll get over her in time.

Hopefully.

"I can't believe they found the gun in your room," he admits, and I slant a surprised look his way. "Faye called me and explained. She wanted to go to the station with your parents, but they wouldn't let her. She suspects Addison planted it." I want to be mad that they spoke after I asked him to keep his distance, but I'm not unreasonable either. Given the circumstances, I can cut him some slack.

"That's what I think, too."

"Man, why is she doing this?"

I shrug. "Your guess is as good as mine, but this is different, Brad. If our hunch is correct, she's *killed* someone. And if she did that to try and get me back, then she's got severe mental issues. I'm scared for Faye. Scared she has something awful planned for her." Goose bumps sprout up and down my arms at the thought of anything happening to my baby. I nearly lost her once, and the guilt almost destroyed me. I wasn't there for her that time, so I'm going to make damn sure I'm here for her now.

"Dammit!" Brad growls, slamming his hands against the steering wheel as he looks in his rearview mirror.

"What?" I ask, turning around. A large black official-looking SUV is trailing us.

"I thought I'd seen the last of them."

"Who?" I pin him with a curious look.

"I've noticed that vehicle following me a few times these last few weeks. Always when the media are around."

He curses, slamming his hands against the steering wheel again.

"Don't sweat it," I tell him. "Once I'm through the gate, I'm on private property, and they can't follow me." I tap out a quick message to Faye as Brad floors it, attempting to lose the tail.

He drops me off at the rear gate, and I immediately head to the guest house. Faye is already there, waiting on the steps with a look of concern etched across her beautiful face. Jumping up, she skips down the stairs and flings herself at me, clinging tightly to my chest, while peppering my face with kisses. I wrap my arms around her and inhale the comforting scent of vanilla and lavender. Burying my face in her neck, I squeeze her tightly, relaxing when her hands run up and down my back. "Baby, are you okay?" she asks.

I lift my head. "I am now." I offer her a smile, and she takes my hand, pulling me into the house. She asks me what happened, and I tell her everything that went down at the station. The whole time, she's holding me in her arms, planting soft kisses to my cheek and rubbing soothing circles on my hands, and despite the predicament I'm in, I'm happy. I've never felt so comfortable with any girl or more loved. She's definitely bringing out a softer side of me.

"Okay," she says when I've finished talking. "First things first." Pulling her legs underneath her, she kneels up facing me. "Are you going to tell your parents?"

I massage my temples as a dart of pain penetrates my skull. "I was thinking of this on the way back. I have no choice but to tell them. There's a chance this could come out, and they can't discover it in a media report."

She nods. "I think you're right. I'll go with you, if you want."

I tweak her nose. "Well, duh. That's a given."

Her face contorts, and transparent anger flares behind her eyes. "What are we going to do about Addison?"

I bolt upright, angling my body and our knees brush. "*We* are going to do nothing. For now."

She opens her mouth to protest, but I press my fingers to her lips. "Faye. She's dangerous. Unpredictable. Besides the obvious safety concerns, if either one of us go anywhere near her, she could twist it and use it to her advantage. Dan is right on that point. Let his PI do some snooping and hope that the police won't pursue charges once the forensics come back on the gun. As much as it kills me to say this"—and it does, because I feel like charging over to Addy's house and throttling her until she fesses up—"I can't risk getting into deeper shit." I curl my hand around the nape of her neck. "And that goes for you too."

She scowls, and I know what that means. "You have to promise me. I'm scared she's going to hurt you, and I need you to agree not to do anything because I'll lose my freaking mind worrying otherwise."

Her features soften. "It feels wrong to sit around and do nothing."

I sigh, pulling her face closer. "Believe me, I know, but we've got to let the experts do their thing." All further conversation is halted when I close the gap and fuse her mouth with mine. As distraction techniques go, this is number one on my list. Our kissing escalates and soon her hands are hoisting my shirt up and I'm letting her. We undress quickly, and then I carry her to the furry rug in front of the fireplace.

"Are you sure you want to do this?" She holds her palm against my chest. "I don't want to take advantage."

I throw back my head and laugh. "Babe. There isn't a scenario I can ever imagine where that would happen. Feel free to take advantage whenever you get the urge." I wink, and she narrows her eyes suspiciously. "Sweetheart." I lean in, planting a hungry kiss on her lips. "I need to lose myself in you." I run circles on her stomach with the tip of my finger, mentally fist-pumping the air when she trembles underneath my touch. "This is the best thing you can do to help me right now."

"Well." She grins seductively, reaching down to grab me. "When you put it like that, I can hardly refuse, now can I?" Her lips twitch with mirth, and I graze my tongue along the side of her neck. She shivers all over, and when her desire-laden eyes meet mine, I lose the last shred of my control, crashing my lips on hers and ravishing her mouth like I'm starving.

Chapter Twenty-Six

Faye

Ky is beyond nervous as we sit in James's study, waiting for Alex. His foot taps idly off the floor, and he drums his finger anxiously on the arm of the chair. I reach out and lace my hand in his, giving him a comforting squeeze. James is watching us with keen, troubled eyes.

Alex strides into the room all business-like. She perches on the edge of the desk alongside her estranged husband. "Sorry I'm late. You wanted to talk to us?" Something akin to hope lingers in her eyes. I know the gulf between her and Ky has been traumatic, but if she thinks this is going to mend bridges, she's in for a shock. If anything, this is only going to add to her guilt. "Kyler?" She tilts her head, waiting for a response.

I make an executive decision. Getting up, I curl myself into his lap, winding my arms around his neck. I caress his face. "You can do this. It's okay. Just tell them like you told me."

"Kyler, please," James says. "You're scaring me now."

Ky looks into my eyes and his expression guts me. Right now, I can visualize what he must have looked like at age ten. Vulnerable and petrified and desperately needing protection. I take his hands and plant them firmly around my waist. "Lean on me. You can do this." I nod at him in encouragement.

He clears his throat, twisting his head to face his parents. "I have something to tell you. Something that happened long ago that I never told you about. Something you need to hear now." His chest visibly rises, and I feel his fear as if it's my own. "You remember the scandal at the Uxbridge track when I was ten?"

Alex frowns a little, while instant recognition dawns on James's face. "Oh dear God," he says, slouching against the desk as he clamps a hand over his mouth. Alex's face has turned ashen.

I give Ky a quick shoulder squeeze. He peers up at me, and I reassure him with my eyes. "That man abused me too," he admits quietly.

Tears prick Alex's eyes as she drops to her knees in front of him. "No, sweetheart! Oh no."

"Son, I'm so sorry." James looks like he's aged twenty years in the last twenty seconds.

"Why didn't you say anything when we asked?" Alex cries. Tears are flowing freely down her face.

"Why didn't you notice?!" Ky's voice cracks, and my heart feels like it's splintering in two. Alex and James share anguished expressions. "Because you were too busy with work," Ky cries, piercing his mum with a hurt look. "And you were late!" He levels that comment at James. "You were late, Dad. The one and only time you were late, and it had to be that day." Ky hangs his head, and his entire body is stiff underneath me. I press a kiss into his hair, and he buries his head in my shoulder.

"Fuck!" James almost yells. "I remember that day. I sensed something was off when I picked you up. You were so quiet in the car, but every time I asked you if you were okay, you snapped at me that you were fine."

"Kyler." Alex speaks in a soft voice, cautiously placing her hand on his knee. "How long did it go on for?"

Ky lifts his head, and the tormented look in his eyes is almost my undoing. I hold him even closer, and his arms tighten around my waist again. "It was just that day, and Dad arrived before he could take it any further. He didn't rape me, but I've no doubt he would have if he'd had the chance."

Alex is sobbing quietly at Kyler's feet. "I'm so sorry that happened to you, honey." She pierces him with a loaded look, filled with a lifetime of regret. "I'm so sorry I was too busy to notice." She sits up on her knees, swiping her thumbs under her damp eyes. "That is never going to happen again. I give you my solemn promise. You and your brothers and Faye are my priority now."

Ky raises his eyes to the ceiling, and I know it'll take a lot more than words to prove that to this family. Ky barks out a laugh. "You haven't heard the most fucked-up part of it yet." James and Alex give him their full attention. "My biological father, Doug—he stopped it." James's mouth hangs open while Alex just looks confused. "He was at the track the week after it happened. He told me this when I was in his house. He said he knew I was his son when he saw me that day, and he could also tell I was scared. He'd heard rumors about the other guy, so he took him aside, beat him up, and then reported him to the owners."

"Oh my gosh!" Alex falls back on her butt.

Ky snorts. "How freaking ironic, right? I wanted, no *needed*, you to save me from that, to notice how fucking terrified I was going back there, to see the truth behind my lies, to know I was in trouble"—his gaze oscillates between his parents as his voice elevates a few notches—"but it was my bio dad who protected me. Doug saved me, and I don't know what the fuck to do with that knowledge."

Ky is quiet for the rest of the day, and we spend it sequestered in my room watching movies. He doesn't want to talk, and I get it. He's drained. So I offer the only comfort I can. I'm by his side, holding him, kissing him, and letting him know I'm here for him. He isn't up to facing his brothers, and they respect his privacy even though I'm sure it's killing them. Kennedys stick together in times of crises, so it's hard for them not to rally around Kyler.

When I'm plating up dinner to take back to my room, they all accost me in the kitchen demanding to know how he is. Kal carries the tray for me, and we talk in hushed whispers as we make our way down the corridor. "I'm not sitting back anymore," I tell him. "Addison needs to be shut down and shut down quick. Are you in or out?"

Kal tugs on my elbow. "What do you have in mind?"

"I have a few ideas, and I'm going to do some snooping tomorrow. Are you going to help me or not?"

He pins me with an "Are you for real?" look. "As if you have to ask." He rolls his eyes. "Of course, I'm in. I still owe that bitch for what she did to Lana."

Interesting. Not what she did to *him*. He wants payback for what she did to *Lana*.

We resume walking. "Good. He's not to know."

"Agreed."

I take the tray from him. "How you doing this week?" I've barely spent any time with him since we returned from Wisconsin and now I feel bad.

He shrugs. "Just trying to keep my head down and get on with things."

"I meant what I said before. I'm proud of you, Kal, and I'm hoping that someday, somehow you and Lana will get your happy ever after."

He shrugs again. "I think that's just wishful thinking, Faye. And you're all loved up so you want everyone else to be too."

"And what's wrong with that?"

"I can't entertain hope. Not now. Not ever. She's gone and she's not coming back. I messed it up, and I have to live with the consequences."

"Once you live your life, Kal. She wouldn't want you to throw your whole life away pining for her. If it's meant to be, you will find a way back to each other."

"I think you've been reading too many sappy romance novels. Real life isn't like that, and allowing myself to believe in it will only hurt me more. Lana's gone, and it's my fault, and this is my punishment. Don't feel bad for me. It is what it is." He gives me a gentle nudge. "Now, go. Before that gets cold." Leaning in, he kisses me on the cheek. "And thanks for looking after my brother."

Ky is out for the count beside me, snoring softly. I'm glad he was able to fall asleep after the events of today. He's emotionally exhausted, and I'm so worried about him. All day, I've been mulling over scenarios in my head. *Whoever framed Ky must've killed Doug Grant, but is Addison really capable of pulling off something like that?* Something feels off. Addison wasn't the only one to steam roll herself into the house this week.

Courtney was here too.

Whatever is going on, I'm determined to get to the bottom of it. I am *not* going to stand by and watch while Kyler gets accused of something he didn't do. He can't do anything to bring further attention to himself, but he was wrong earlier because *I* can and *I* will.

Addison is not going to ruin him. I'm going to stop her once and for all, and my gut is telling me this is connected to her parents. I won't rest until I discover the truth.

I creep out of bed quietly so as not to disturb him. I can't sleep with so much troubling me. Snatching my phone from the top of my locker, I tiptoe out of the room. Outside, I tap out a message to Keven asking him to dig up dirt on Courtney. Not that it'll probably do much good, because Keven seems to have feck all time to help, but no harm in asking, I guess.

"Already on that case" is his immediate reply. I guess Alex must have roped her son in to help, too. Another text pops up on the screen. *"I have some intel on A. I'll bring a copy in the morning and we can talk then."* Alex and James have called a family meeting in the morning, but none of us know what it's about. It must be important if they're allowing my cousins to skip school. Ky has asked for a bit more time before he tells the rest of his brothers what went down at the track seven years ago, so I'm trusting they are not about to break that promise. They must have something else to share.

I walk on bare feet to the kitchen to fetch a glass of water. The low drone of hushed conversation greets me as I step into the living room. Alex and James are seated on the long couch, hunched over a bunch of papers spread out on the table before them.

"Hey," I murmur.

Their heads jerk up in unison. "What are you doing up so late?" James asks with a frown.

"I'm having difficulty sleeping."

"I know, sweetheart. We're still reeling," he admits frankly.

"He's going to be okay." Confidence emanates from my words, because I truly believe Ky is strong enough to come through this.

"Thank you for looking after him, honey," Alex says. "We are so grateful he is at least letting you in. Please be there for him until we can convince him we're on his side too."

"Don't worry, I'm not leaving him to deal with this on his own."

Kaden and Keven arrive at the butt crack of dawn the next morning for the family meeting. We have breakfast at the formal dining table first. After the breakfast dishes are cleared away, Alex and James tell us they have something important to say. I hold Ky's hand under the table the entire time.

"Your father and I have made some important decisions in relation to our future," Alex announces, kicking off the conversation. "In different ways, we have failed you all, and for that we are truly sorry. In trying to build a life for this family, we've ignored the most important part of the equation. Being there for you when you needed us." Her gaze flits between her boys, lingering on Kyler a little longer.

"We cannot undo our mistakes," James adds. "But we can make changes so we don't repeat them in future. Your mother and I were up all last night agreeing on what we need to do." He looks to Alex and she nods subtly. "We need to explain certain things first so you have some context. Courtney has been blackmailing your mother and me for the past few months. She discovered a secret we've been keeping, and she's been lording it over our heads. We were trying to extrapolate ourselves from the situation, but it involved taking enormous risks, making enormous decisions, and until yesterday, we weren't sure it was the right path to take."

"What happened yesterday?" Kaden asks, leaning his elbows on the table. Ky tenses, and I squeeze his hand.

"That's not something we can share yet," Alex explains, holding up a hand as a round of groans whips around the table. "Hang on here a sec, boys. Someone confided something in us and asked us to keep it private for the moment, and we have to respect that; however, it's not the *what* that matters. All that matters is it was the final wake-up call we needed." Tears well in her eyes. "I'm so sorry, boys, if I've given you the impression that work was more important to me. The only thing that matters, the only people who matter, are around this table. In trying to build a successful business, I was thinking of your futures. Being able to provide you with the best education and having trust funds set up so none of you needed to worry financially. Somewhere along the way, I lost sight of my personal goals. Kennedy Apparel means nothing to me if I don't have my family. This family is suffocating, and I didn't read the signs or I chose, subconsciously, to ignore them."

She stifles a sob, raising her hand to her chest. "That all changes now." She looks to James, and it's obvious from his facial expression that he's feeling as emotional as she is.

He picks up. "Courtney discovered the Kennedy Apparel brand has been built on a lie. We can only assume she got close to me to gain access to the house so she could uncover the truth. We still don't know exactly how she obtained the information, but that's neither here nor there now."

I'm not sure I buy that. Her obsession with the need to ruin Alex seems to be behind her desire to have James. Almost like she wants to take over her entire life.

"She threatened to expose us to the KA board and to the press," James continues.

"And we couldn't allow her to do that," Alex cuts in. "Not just because we didn't want embarrassment brought on our family, but such an announcement would devalue the company's stock and cost thousands of jobs, and I couldn't do that to the employees. None of them deserve that."

"What's the secret?" Keven asks.

Alex gulps, looking nervously at James. He clears his throat. "My family is not connected in any way to the infamous Kennedys. We had documents forged that verified our claims, and we used that to build important contacts and build the KA brand in the early days. We knew that gave us an edge and it worked. It transformed the business to what it is today."

"So that's the real reason you didn't buy that estate in the Kennedy compound in Hyannis Port a few years back?" Kal asks.

"Yes," Alex confirms. "We have deliberately avoided close contact with the Kennedys because we knew if we tried to ingratiate ourselves they would investigate and probably uncover the truth. While we have alluded to the heritage and used it to build the brand and connections, we haven't imposed on any of them or made any attempts to connect on a personal level. In doing so, they have left us alone, and it suited us perfectly."

"Until Courtney discovered the truth," I say.

"It's definitely time to bring in the hired guns," Kent says, and everyone groans. He holds up his hands. "What?"

Keaton bumps his shoulder. "You can't suggest killing people every time they cross us. You're playing way too much *Assassin's Creed*."

Kent shrugs, but I know it's all for show. He likes to be the center of attention is all.

"What have you decided to do about it?" I ask.

Alex folds her hands on the table. "Last night, I sold the business to our chief competitor." She lets that shock settle before continuing. "They are going to absorb the brand into their overall brand so the impact on share price should only be temporary. I had to take a hit on the sale, but it was still a good deal. All the employees will get a payout and eighty percent of them will keep their jobs."

"What about me and Selena?" Keanu asks.

"You have new modeling contracts. Don't worry, son, I made sure you were both looked after."

Keanu visibly relaxes. "Thanks, Mom. What about you? What are you going to do now?"

"I'm stepping down as CEO this morning with full approval of the board. The new owners have asked me to work in a consultancy capacity during the transition, and after that I'm going to take some time off to be at home with my children. Maybe in future, when you have all left the nest, I might start up something, but I've no immediate plans. We are financially secure, and there is nothing to stop me from prioritizing my family." She leans forward in her seat, and her whole face radiates happiness. "But it's more than that. I want to be here for all of you. No more drinking. No more business trips. I'll just be Mom." She beams at her boys. "And I couldn't be any happier about it."

Chapter Twenty-Seven

Faye

"What are you doing about Courtney?" Ky asks after the initial shock of Alex's confession has sunk in.

"She is being served with papers this morning. We are suing her for personal damages on account of her blackmail," James explains. "We've had an official PI trailing her for weeks, and Keven has gathered some useful intel which has given us enough evidence to take this legal."

"Won't you get in trouble for forging documents?" I ask.

"It's true there are some legal issues to work through, yes, but Dan assures us he can make this go away with payment of a fine," Alex confirms. "Courtney is also being fired this morning in front of the board. Blackmailing the CEO and threatening to bring the company into disrepute gives us enough grounds to terminate her employment contract without compensation," Alex smiles like all her Christmases have come at once. "I can't wait to see that smug look wiped off her face."

Kal high-fives her. "You're bad ass, Mom."

"For the record," James speaks up, squirming a little in his chair. "I made a mistake when I slept with Courtney, and I knew it pretty much immediately, but she's been blackmailing me into staying with her. That's all over now. She is out of our lives."

Alex's lips narrow. "She is ruined, both financially and professionally, and I think it's safe to say that's the last we'll be seeing of her."

"Does that mean the divorce is off?" Keaton asks, his voice tinged with hope.

Alex looks down at the table. James looks sad. "I'm afraid not, son. We have more problems than just Courtney."

"We have hurt each other a lot by keeping so many secrets." Alex levels grave eyes around the table. "I hurt your father by lying about Kyler's biological father, and that doesn't seem to be something we can put behind us. Anger and mistrust are not the foundation of a solid relationship, and the cracks have been forming for years."

A somber mood settles over the table.

"It doesn't mean we won't be a family," James is quick to reassure them. "We are still committed to all of you."

"Just not to one another," Keaton says, and it's clear he's fighting tears.

"We are committed as parents and we'll still do things together, but we won't be married. We are both sorry it has come to this, but we believe that splitting up is genuinely in the best interests of this family. We are trying to right the wrongs of the past, but we don't have all the answers either," James says. "We hope you can bear with us and understand we are trying to do the best for all of you. You are all that matters and we're going to make sure we show you that from now on."

Later that afternoon, I nab Keven for a chat. "What have you discovered?" I ask him as we hide out in James's office. The others are playing Xbox in the games room.

"You were right. Peyton's mother, Wendy, *is* Addison's birth mother, but get this, her dad is still her dad."

I ponder the implications. "So, her dad had an affair with his wife's sister, and then *they* kept the baby?" I surmise, an incredulous note creeping into my tone when really there's no need. Given all the revelations these past few months, there shouldn't be anything that surprises me anymore.

"That's the way it looks."

"Do you have anything else for me?"

"Like what?" He crosses his feet at the ankles.

I shrug. "I don't know. Anything else suspicious in her background?"

He shakes his head. "Not that I've discovered so far."

"Well, damn. I was hoping you might have found out why she has targeted Ky. I thought it was linked to her secret, but maybe I was wrong." Another thought occurs to me. "Did you discover anything interesting about Courtney?"

"Nothing springs to mind. Why do you ask?"

"Call it a gut instinct."

"Anything I had I've turned over to Mom and Dad's guy. I can't think of anything that would be helpful in this situation. I was just looking for evidence of her blackmail."

"What about the stuff the PI uncovered? Can you get your hands on that?"

"Sure. I can hack into his server and pull his files." He shrugs. "But is there much point? You heard what my parents said back there. She's finished after today."

"Let's just say I need it for peace of mind."

He pushes off the desk. "Okay, I'll get the stuff and glance through it this weekend to see if there's anything of interest."

"Thank you."

"How's my brother?"

"As well as can be expected."

"Let me know if I can do anything to help."

Shouts from down below distract us. I open the door, and find Kal at the bottom of the stairs. "The press conference is starting. Come on."

We run down to the games room, and I drop onto the couch beside Ky. All the major news channels are covering Alex's press release. Keaton pulls up the large screen, and everyone quiets to listen as she announces the sale of Kennedy Apparel to the Accardi Company and confirms she has stepped down from the board and from her position as CEO. Shocked gasps emerge from the media crowd when she announces that the brand was built on a lie, and after explaining, she apologizes for any offense.

She speaks eloquently and passionately about why she made that decision and how much the business has meant to her. In stepping down, she acknowledges the error of her ways. She ends her statement on a more personal note.

"I would like to thank all the Kennedy Apparel employees for their dedication to the company over the years, and I can assure them they are in great hands with Accardi. They have ambitious plans to develop the business, and I have no doubt they will grow from strength to strength. I would also like to thank my colleagues on the board who have worked tirelessly this past week to sign off on this deal. Lastly, I would like to thank my husband and my children. They have sacrificed a lot so I could pursue my business ambitions, and I couldn't have achieved what I achieved without their support."

She pauses briefly, scanning the large crowd in front of her. "There have been a lot of reports and speculation in the media recently about my family, and that has, in part, contributed to the decision I have made to step away from my career." She glances over her shoulder at James, standing stoically behind her. "My husband almost single-handedly raised our family, and I can never thank him enough. Certain things I've done have hurt him, and I'd like to publicly apologize to him for that. My beautiful sons have become targets lately, and that is the price I have paid for being in the public eye. They have never asked for that, and I want to apologize to them too and let them know that I am going to be there for them every day from this day forth. Finally, I would like to appeal for privacy. We have lived our lives under a spotlight and now we would like to retreat to the shadows. Please give my family that peace and let us resolve our problems in private. Thank you."

She leaves the stage amid a flurry of questions. Keaton mutes the TV. "Mom did good."

Kent snorts, and we all raise our eyes to the ceiling. "What?" he yells, scowling.

"Let's hear it," Kal says. "Whatever derogatory bullshit you have to say. Get it out of your system before Mom and Dad get back."

Kent flips him the bird. "You're an ass."

"No, *you're* an ass," Keanu ventures. "Do you not get how big of a deal this is?"

Kent harrumphs. "I'm not buying this bull. I'll believe it when I see it. And I'm not buying the whole "I did it for my family" crap either." He puts on a pretend whiny voice. "She did it for herself so that slut Courtney wouldn't get the business or Dad. That's what she really cares about."

"You're wrong," Ky speaks up. "I believe in what she said earlier, and trust me when I say she still has a long way to go with me, but if I can give her the benefit of the doubt, then I think you should too."

"Bro," Keaton says, twisting to face Kent. "Mom barely ever takes a day off work. Now she's given it all up for us. She'll be here every day. It's going to be awesome."

I grin at Keaton. God, I wish I could bottle his enthusiasm.

"Hundred bucks says you'll be sick of her fussing over you after a month," Kent retorts.

"Never," Keaton loyally replies. "I will never say that."

Ky stands up at the sound of an approaching car. He pulls Keaton into an improvised headlock, mussing up his hair. "Brother, I'm proud of you even if you do act like a pussy most of the time. Don't ever change."

Kent emits an amused laugh. "Hell, this family is screwed. I blame you," he says, pointing his finger at me.

"Me?" My voice betrays my surprise.

"Yeah, you. You have everyone acting all emotional and touchy-feely. It's gross." He grimaces, and I laugh.

"I know you don't really mean that, and one day you're going to eat your words."

"Hell will freeze before that day comes."

I roll my eyes as Brad steps into the space. A chill of unease flitters across my skin.

"Hey, you ready to head out?" he asks Ky.

"Yeah. Just let me grab my bag." He turns to face me. "We're going to the track. You wanna come with?"

"Nah. You two go. Have fun." We all know that would be outside the realm of possibility if I went too. I stand up and peck him on the cheek. "I have some stuff I want to do, and I need to call Rose back."

"'Kay. I won't be late." He kisses me on the lips.

"Man, you are so whipped," Kent sneers.

"Whipped and proud," Ky replies, winking at me. It's ridiculous how much his admission thrills me.

After they have left, I pull Keven aside. "Do you have some time to spare before you leave for Harvard?"

"What for?"

"Come with me and I'll show you."

I bring him to my bedroom and power up my laptop. Then I show him some of my research. "You've been busy," he says.

"I've had plenty of time on my hands this week. What do you think?" I touch the screen, running a finger under the list of names I found on Memorial's alumni website. It was easy to find Peyton and Addison's mom from previous student records on the site, and I used that to dig up some old photos. The same group of girls appears in several pictures so I'm guessing they were friends. "Can you trace any of these people?" I ask.

"Watch and learn, little girl," he says, pulling up some cryptic-looking login page. "Watch and learn."

"Less of the little girl if you don't mind. I'm almost eighteen." I pout.

In a directly transparent move, he stares at my boobs. "Oh, believe me, I've noticed."

I elbow him in the ribs. "Oh em gee, I didn't have you pinned for a sleaze. Now I know where Kal and Kent get it. You are lucky Ky isn't here, and you'd better deliver the goods or I'll have to set him on you."

"Puh-lease, as if I couldn't take him." He flexes his biceps, before bumping my shoulder. "Besides, you know I did that on purpose. I'm only joking. And, for the record, I haven't been checking you out, not that it'd be wrong." He sends me a saucy wink. "I'm not your blood relative either."

"You did *not* just say that."

He laughs heartily. "You are way too easy to wind up."

"Shut it, jerk face, and just work your magic. Time is a-wasting."

Twenty minutes later and Keven has discovered that one of Wendy's old school friends is a waitress at a diner on the outskirts of town. "What do you say? You up for paying her a little visit?"

Keven checks his watch. "I'm not sure I have time. Rain check?"

I stand up, fishing my phone out of my back pocket. "No can do. Ky has this murder charge hanging over him like a storm cloud, and I want to get to the bottom of things sooner rather than later. It's cool, though. Don't worry. I'll call Rose and see if she can borrow her mum's car."

He puts his hand on my wrist. "Hold up. I don't like the thought of you going there by yourself. That place is a little rough. Ky would kick the shit out of me if he discovered I let you go there by yourself. How about I go with you and you arrange for Rose to pick you up? I think I can still make my date on time if I don't have to drive you back."

"Ooh, a date," I tease as if I'm ten again. "Anyone special?"

He snorts. "Hardly, unless you'd call a regular fuck buddy special?"

"Jeez, do you have to be such a pig?"

"Would you rather I lie?"

"No. Definitely not." I give him a push toward the door. "Come on. Let's get out of here. I'll message Rose from the car."

Chapter Twenty-Eight

Faye

The sky is painted an eerie purple-gray color by the time we pull up in front of the diner where Wendy Moore's high school friend works. I had phoned before we left the house to check she was working tonight, and someone up there must be looking out for us, because she is. While she was a little hesitant when I first suggested coming here to talk about an article I'm writing for the online school magazine, I managed to convince her when I mentioned it'd be a paid interview—that had been Keven's suggestion.

A bell tinkles as we push open the door. An older lady with dark hair approaches us with a forced smile. "Table or booth?" she asks.

"Booth, please," I reply, following her to an empty one at the rear of the diner. She hands us a couple of menus. "Could you let Stacy know that Faye is here. I spoke to her earlier on the phone." Mercifully, it's not too busy, so we should have time for a decent conversation.

A few minutes later, the waitress returns with a skinny blonde in tow. "I'm Stacy. You're Faye?" the blonde asks, and I nod, extending my hand.

"Thank you for agreeing to speak with me."

Her handshake is limp and damp, and I resist the urge to wipe my hand over the front of my jeans. Makeup is caked on her face, and hollow crevices line her forehead. Her eyes and lips are wrinkled at the corners, and she smells like smoke and cheap perfume. "And who are you sweetheart?" she asks Keven, thrusting her enhanced chest forward. Her uniform is short and tight, and if she strains any farther, I reckon her top will split right open. From the way she's devouring Keven with her eyes, I get the sense she really wouldn't mind all that much.

"I'm her cousin," is all Keven offers up.

"Nice tats." She licks her lips while focusing on the ink creeping up his arm. Sliding into the seat beside him, she flicks her stringy bleached-blonde hair over her shoulder and gives him an eye fuck. Mascara has clumped her lashes together, and the thick layer of jet-black liner rimming her eyes has smudged, giving her a panda-eye effect. I know from the pictures I found online that Stacy was quite the looker in her day, and I feel a pang of sympathy. There's no ring on her finger, and if her appearance is any indication, life has taken its toll. She's not actually that old, and it's pretty sad.

The other waitress smirks at Stacy's feeble attempts at flirting. "We'll take two coffees and two muffins," Keven says, ignoring Stacy's intense gaze. "Would you like anything, Stacy?"

"How about you?" she answers, giving him a saucy wink.

"Afraid I'm not on the menu." Keven's mouth pulls into a grim line, while I attempt to smother my snigger of amusement.

She pouts. "I'll take a coffee, Shell."

I pull out my folder and remove my pen and pad. "As I explained on the phone, I'm writing an article for the school magazine on the class of 1989. We'd like to find out what life was like in Memorial High back then, what kind of plans you had after graduating, and whether you have achieved your goals, etcetera." I deliberately don't look up. I doubt working in a sleazy diner was top of her list of ambitions.

Stacy is remarkably chatty, and I only have to ask a few questions every now and then to keep the conversation flowing. Shell brings our coffees and muffins as I try to steer the conversation in the direction I need it to go.

"Wow, that's great, Stacy," I say, when I finally get a word in edgeways. "You've given me tons of great material here. I was hoping you might be able to give me some information on a few of the girls you were friends with at the time, and perhaps some of them might be willing to talk to me as well."

She takes a slurp of her now-cold coffee. "Wendy Moore is the only one I still talk to, and our contact is sporadic at best."

Jackpot.

I try to temper my excitement at the fact that Peyton and Addison's mum is the only one she's still in contact with.

"Oh, I think I know her. She's Peyton's mom, right?"

Her brow puckers. "That's the dark-haired daughter? I always get mixed up. That woman has had more kids than I've had hot dinners." She throws back her head, cackling to herself.

I fake ignorance. "I thought Peyton was an only child?"

"Hell, no." She laughs, looking briefly over her shoulder before leaning in to the edge of the table. "I probably shouldn't say this, but you're looking for real life stories, right?"

I nod eagerly.

"In town, Wendy was known as a four-by-four for years," she chuckles. "On account of her having four kids by four different dads," she adds by way of explanation.

I allow my eyes to pop wide and prop my elbows up on the table, so I'm angled toward her. "That sounds interesting."

"It was a big scandal in school when she got pregnant at fifteen."

"Gosh, that was young," I say, playing along, while I compute calculations in my head. There's no way she could be talking about Addison because the dates don't stack up.

"Yeah. Her mom made her give the baby up for adoption, and Wendy wouldn't tell a soul who the father was because he would've been put away for knocking up a minor."

I decide to take a risk. The diner is starting to fill up, and I'm sensing our time is drawing to a close. "Can I tell you a secret?" I whisper conspiratorially. Her head bobs. "I heard Peyton's cousin is really her sister. Do you think that's true?"

Keven sends me a warning look, but I pretend not to notice.

She casts another quick glance around. "Oh, it's true all right. That was the other big scandal around town. Brittany, Wendy's other daughter, was only three years old, and Peyton was barely out of the womb when she got pregnant with her sister's husband's child. Now, very few know that's the truth. There was gossip to that effect all over town, but they neither confirmed nor denied it, and they managed to bury it. Nicole, that's Addison's *official Mom*"—she makes little air quotes with her fingers—"pretended to be pregnant at the same time so when she returned home with her daughter no one thought it was strange. Wendy said she couldn't cope with another baby and she'd given it up for adoption. She just never mentioned that her sister and her husband adopted the baby. Nicole couldn't have children, so I guess that's why she was happy to take on her husband's bastard as her own."

"Wow. That's quite a story. I can't believe Wendy would do that to her own sister."

Stacy rubs her hands, and her eyes glisten in delight. I bite back my distaste, retracting my earlier sympathy. Anyone that relishes spreading gossip so maliciously isn't deserving of my pity. Not that I'm overly complaining. This is gold, and I've barely had to work to get it.

"Wendy was always jealous of Nicole, and she hated the fact that she'd married up when she was stuck in a trailer park as a single mom. She deliberately seduced her husband, and although she hasn't admitted it, I'm convinced she got pregnant on purpose."

"No way!" I gasp, giving an Oscar-worthy performance. Keven looks out the window, fighting a smile.

"Nicole and her husband paid Wendy handsomely for Addison and to keep her mouth shut, and it worked until Wendy wanted more cash. When Nicole wouldn't cough up, she went to Addison and told her the truth. That's actually when we fell out. I thought it was really mean to do that to the kid, but Wendy is a cold-hearted bitch these days."

"Oh, so you aren't really on speaking terms with her anymore. You won't be able to set me up with an interview?" I continue playing my role although I'm delighted this isn't going to get back.

"We talk if we bump into each other in town but that's it. She's given me the cold shoulder because I had the nerve to stick up for Nicole and Addison. And, honestly, honey"—she leans over, patting my hand—"you really don't want to go here." She shivers, as if something nasty just crawled over her skin.

"That's too bad," I lie. "But thanks so much. You've been great, and I've got lots to go on." I slide an envelope with a hundred dollars across the table.

"Glad to help." She pockets the envelope, giving Keven some side eye. "And thanks for bringing the eye candy, much appreciated." She cackles again, squeezing his knee before she steps out. "I better get back to work before my ass is canned. Nice talking to you, hun."

"I think I need a body scrub and a lobotomy after that experience," Keven jokes once we step outside the diner. I have a ready-made retort lying idle on my tongue. One that involves the shady characters I found him hanging with before, but I say nothing. I can't afford to fall out with Keven or piss him off right now. Ky needs me to sort all this out, and I'm not going to turn away my best chance of help.

I nudge him in the ribs. "Aw, she wasn't that bad." I slouch against the side of his truck. "That was interesting, huh?"

"Very. I thought our family was hiding some skeletons, but that makes us sound like freaking angels. No wonder Addison is such a conniving cow. It runs in her blood."

"It still doesn't explain why Addison is going all gung-ho for our family. What about this other baby Wendy gave up for adoption when she was young—could you dig around?"

Keven opens the truck door, as Rose drives into the car park. "You think it's connected?"

"I don't know, but we should check every lead, right?"

He chuckles. "We might make a detective of you yet. You played it perfectly back there, by the way. I didn't have to say a word."

"I barely had to either." I snort. "Motor mouth didn't need much encouragement."

"Who needs enemies when you've got friends like that."

"I know."

"I feel ill at the thought of her hands and her eyes on me." He shudders, and I laugh harder.

"What's so funny?" Rose asks, swinging her legs out the side of her mum's car.

"Keven was being hit on by this cougar. She was only short of hitching up her skirt and straddling him right then and there."

"Now you're being unnecessarily cruel. I'll have nightmares for weeks." Keven's face contorts bitterly.

"Did you learn anything?" Rose asks.

I loop my arm in hers. "Let's hit the road and I'll fill you in."

Keven insists on waiting until we've driven off before he heads away in the opposite direction. I update Rose as she drives. When I've finished speaking, she throws back her head and laughs hysterically.

"You okay?" I ask when she eventually composes herself.

"Hells yeah. Better than ever. That has cheered me up no end." I look inquisitively at her. "When I first moved here, Addison looked down her nose at me. She was always outwardly pleasant, but I could tell she thought I was beneath her. It gives me immense pleasure to know she's beneath me. Can you imagine what it would do to her rep if it got out that she's actually trailer trash? She'd be ruined. No wonder she didn't want that secret getting out."

"Is it enough to threaten her with, though?" I ask, a bit skeptical. Apart from Stacy's word and Addison's real birth certificate, we don't have much else to go on.

"I think so. You tell her you'll leak her birth cert and tell everyone what you know unless she admits she framed Ky."

I twist in my seat. "Do you think she did it? Killed that man?"

Rose drags her lip between her teeth. "Honestly, I think that girl is capable of pretty much anything, but murder, and to do it for a boy ... it seems a bit farfetched."

I exhale noisily. "That's what I think, too."

"What are you going to do?"

"I don't know. Keep digging, I suppose, and see what happens next week. If the cops move to charge Ky, then I'll have no choice but to confront Addison and try to force her hand, but I want to plan my approach carefully. I want to find more dirt and only confront her when I have all my ducks in a row. This is my boyfriend's future at stake. I don't want to mess up the only chance I might have of making her go away."

"That sounds like a solid plan." She drums her fingers off the steering wheel. "Hey, I've got some good news to share."

I prop my sneakered feet up on the dash. "Please do. I could sorely use some of that."

"The diner is reopening under new ownership and new management."

I sit bolt upright, dropping my feet on the ground. "For real?" A wide smile spreads across my mouth.

"Yup. My dad knows someone on the town committee, and he said they just transferred the license and the new owner confirmed all the jobs are safe. Apparently, we're going to get contacted this weekend."

"That is brilliant news. I'm so happy."

My phone rings, and Adam's face appears on the screen. I hesitate for a fraction before answering.

"Hi, Faye."

"Hey, Adam." I cringe at my slightly hesitant tone, sure he's picked up on it.

"I'm just ringing to see that everything's okay?"

"Everything's great. I just heard that the diner is being reopened and that my job is safe."

"That's fantastic news."

"I know. I've really missed work."

He chuckles.

"What?"

"Can you try and brainwash my kids, please?"

"They don't work?"

"The twins are too young, and Whitney is far too spoiled and lazy to work. I am constantly at odds with her mother over the subject. She could learn a thing or two from you."

Hell. No. "Do me a favor, Adam, and don't say anything of the sort to Whitney this weekend. I want to try and get off on the right footing, and that would so not help."

"Don't worry, I'm not an idiot. Are you sure this weekend is still okay? I've been watching the news and—"

"He didn't do it," I blurt out, interrupting him mid-flow. "Kyler isn't that kind of guy. He's being framed."

"I'm sorry to hear that."

I can tell he's dubious. "Our original deal still stands. I'm not leaving the Kennedys, especially not when Ky needs me so much. I know him. He's a good person. He didn't murder anyone."

There's an exaggerated pause before he replies. "Okay. I trust you, and, look, it's fine if we need to reschedule Sunday. Just let me know as soon as you can."

"I already asked my aunt and uncle, and they said they are happy to go ahead as planned. Our house at two on Sunday, if that suits?"

"Great. We'll be there."

"There will be reporters at the gate, but James has hired a security detail, and they'll ensure you are guided safely onto the grounds."

"Thanks for the heads-up, Faye. I'll see you Sunday. Take care."

I say goodbye and hang up.

"How are things going with Adam?" Rose asks. I finally came clean and told her everything.

"Good, actually. He's not putting me under any pressure, and we're taking our time to get to know one another. It isn't as difficult as I thought it'd be."

"That's good."

"I still feel guilty though."

"That's natural. What about meeting your new brothers and sister. How are you feeling about that?"

"Quite nervous to be honest. What if they don't like me? Or they resent me? Think I'm going to take their dad away from them or something?" I chew on the corner of a nail.

"I bet they're every bit as nervous as you are, and they are bound to be a little suspicious at first." She reaches out and pats my knee. "Don't worry. They'll love you."

I hope she's right, because my quota for heartache and grief is pretty much maxed out, and my tolerance level is at an all-time low.

Chapter Twenty-Nine

Faye

I wake up late the next morning, surprised to find Ky still draped around me, fast asleep. Usually, he's up and out to the track early on Saturday morning. Maneuvering position, I curl into him, planting tiny little kisses all over his naked chest. I can't believe James and Alex haven't put a stop to this yet. Ky doesn't disguise the fact that he's sleeping in my room every night, but so far neither one of his parents has made any move to separate us. Not that I'm complaining. You'll never hear me complaining about that.

Ky's arms snake around my waist, and he kisses the top of my head. "Morning, gorgeous," he murmurs sleepily, and I melt on in the inside.

I want a lifetime of this.

Waking up in his arms, listening to endearments roll off his tongue, inhaling the masculine scent that is all him, feeling his skin against mine. I snuggle in closer. "Morning, babe. You sleep it out?"

He runs his fingers down my spine, curving his hands around my ass. "Nope. Don't feel like going to the track today."

Ignoring his wandering hands—with great difficulty I might add—I lift my head up. "Is everything okay?" I brush strands of his hair back off his forehead.

He shrugs.

I stick him with a serious look. "Talk to me. Tell me what's going through that beautiful head of yours."

He sighs, flopping down flat on his back. "I'm just not in a good mood today. You know why."

I lean over, pressing a kiss to his forehead. "Yeah." My tongue darts out, moistening my dry lips. "If you like, I could phone that therapist and see if she could fit us in today?"

He stares up at the ceiling, and I watch his chest heave up and down. "Okay," he whispers.

"Yeah?" My eyes search his face.

He angles his head so he's looking me straight in the eyes. "Yeah."

Three hours later, we are sitting in the therapist's swanky office on the fifth floor of a modern building occupying prime position in Beacon Hill. Boston Common is visible in the distance through the floor-to-ceiling window. Ky's knee jerks anxiously as we wait on the plush leather couch in the reception area. We are only here thanks to a last-minute cancellation.

The door to the room next door opens, and a small, well-dressed lady with a warm smile steps out to greet us. We both rise. "You must be Faye?" She shakes my hand, and I nod.

"Hello, Kyler." She extends her hand in his direction. "Would you like to come this way?" She steps aside, motioning him forward.

I give him a quick hug, hating how his body trembles underneath me. "I'm proud of you." I peck him briefly on the lips. "I'll be right here, waiting."

He gulps, making no attempt to mask his absolute terror. I squeeze his hand. "You can do this."

"We can take this at your own speed, Kyler. I can assure you this is a safe environment, and you can talk to me about anything or nothing." She smiles again, and his shoulders relax a little.

My heart is in my mouth as he steps into her room, and she shuts the door behind them.

I'm a bundle of nerves the entire time he's in there. Because it's Saturday, and we secured the last appointment, there's no one here. After pacing back and forth across the room, I drop to the carpeted floor beside the window, pulling my knees into my chest. I idly watch pedestrians on the street outside as I blow on the window, clouding the glass, and drawing a love heart with our initials inside. I snicker to myself, remembering how I used to doodle similarly when Luke and I first got together. But I was only fourteen then. I'm almost eighteen now. Too old for this juvenile carry on. Yet I can't bring myself to rub it away. As I stare at my jagged, hastily drawn love heart and our initials contained inside, I think of how accurate a representation it is. Ky's name *is* carved in my heart, as I hope mine is in his. The longer I stare at the crude drawing, the more my heart swells.

Growing up, the only measure of romantic love I had was my parents; however, I couldn't have had a better example. Their love story may not have been conventional, but it was true love, a real partnership, a genuine meeting of minds. They didn't *always* agree on things, but they respected one another. Respected their differences. Appreciated them. I never doubted how profoundly they loved one another, and I can remember wishing that I'd find a great love like that one day.

Now, I hover on the cusp of something great, and it's equally wonderful and terrifying. *Is it foolish at almost eighteen to believe that I've met my soul mate? The one person who is destined for me? To feel so much for a boy I've only known a few months?*

Memories flood my mind, and I lean my head back and close my eyes. I confided in Mum when I first struggled to deal with my changing feelings for Luke. He was my first steady boyfriend. The guy I'd given my virginity to. The one I'd thought I'd love forever.

Hence, all the love heart doodling.

I felt guilty when everything he did started to irk me. When I'd snap at him for no reason whatsoever. When I started making excuses to not want to spend time with him. I knew deep down what it meant, but I was afraid to confront that reality, so I asked Mum how she knew Dad was the only one for her.

I can still picture her in my mind's eye. She was wearing her favorite mauve knitted dress, and her hair was in a messy bun on top of her head. She had taken my hands in hers and stared earnestly into my eyes. "There are many reasons why I love your father so completely," she had said. "Far too many to mention, but if you want to know if he's the one, just imagine your life without him. What if he died? How would you feel? If you can answer that question, you will know what's truly in your heart."

Honesty and simplicity.

That's how you know.

How I knew I had to let Luke go.

How I know I can never let Ky go.

Because even the thought of him not being in this world sends my body into shock. A sharp, twisty pain pummels my heart; a physical pain so intense it causes my chest to throb excruciatingly. I rub a hand over the sore spot. My throat locks up, and my mouth is suddenly dry. Tears prick my eyes, overflowing, rolling down my face. I feverishly rub the aching spot over my heart, reminding myself that it's not real.

He's here. He's alive. He's mine.

He's all I'll ever want.

All I'll ever need.

My heart and my mind are in no doubt.

The door opens, and I quickly wipe away my tears. Ky steps into the room, and I scramble to my feet. I operate as if on auto-pilot, racing to his side and throwing my arms around him. As his scent invades my senses and I feel his solidity against me, my panic subsides. He envelops me in his arms, and we cling to one another. Burying his head in my shoulder, he emits a shuddering breath, and my protective instincts kick in. I hug him tighter, and if I could mold myself to his form, I would. He means everything. Everything. God, I would do anything for this boy.

The therapist clears her throat, and we reluctantly break apart. She smiles expansively. "Same time next week, Kyler."

"Thank you." His voice is raw, and his emotions are undoubtedly veering all over the place. I know how that feels.

Silently, we walk back to his car, holding hands.

"You want to hang around?" he asks.

"Sure. I've nothing planned." I received a text this morning confirming the diner is reopening in two weeks after a makeover so I'm free as a bird until then.

Ky drives us downtown, and once we've deposited the car in the biggest car park I've ever seen, we set out to explore the city on foot. We wander casually in and out of shops, and Ky is always touching me. Either his hand is on my lower back or his arm is around my shoulder or my waist, his lips kissing the top of my head, or our hands are entwined as we navigate the busy weekend crowd. But we are always touching, and I don't think I've ever felt this happy before. Which says a lot given everything we've got going on.

Ky brings me to that little Chinese place he spoke about before and orders about a million things from the menu.

"My feet ache so bad," I moan, leaning into his side in the booth. "We must've walked for hours."

He rubs his hands up and down my arms, pressing a tender kiss to my cheek. "I know, and I needed that. Needed to lose myself in the crowd. Thank you. For coming with me. For letting me drag you all over the city."

"You can thank me properly later," I say with a cheeky grin.

His chest shakes with laughter. "I think I've created a monster."

"I think so too." No point denying it. I have sex, and Ky, on the brain pretty much twenty-four-seven. I actually think I'm worse than a guy. My grin expands as my hand coasts up his impressive chest. "But I'm *your* monster."

He kisses the tip of my nose. "You'll only ever be my monster."

My heart thrills at his words. "Do you mean that? Like, really mean it?"

"I forever you," he whispers, kissing the tip of my nose, and I think my heart might fly out of my chest.

"I forever you, too." I tip my head up and give him a searing kiss. I don't care if it's inappropriate.

"I love you so much, Ky. Don't ever leave me."

He circles his arms around me, pulling me flush to his chest. "I'll never leave you. Never."

"Is it messed up that I'm deliriously happy right now?"

"That's the only thing that isn't messed up, Faye. You make me unbelievably happy. I've traded in my man card and I couldn't give two shits. I am yours to do with as you please."

"Now he tells me," I gripe, pretending to be upset. "When we're in public and I can't do all the wicked, naughty things running through my head right now."

Throwing back his head, he laughs. "You are like my own personal angel on Earth."

He looks adoringly at me, and my heart rejoices. I'll never tire of the way he looks at me. When the mask is down and he's just my guy. My Ky.

"Seriously, I don't know what I would've done without you these last couple of weeks. You're my hero, Faye."

"And you're mine. I know that things haven't been easy, but you haven't shied away from them. That takes balls."

"Well," he grins smugly, "we both know I'm not lacking in that department." He lobs a prawn cracker in his mouth as he pins me with a suggestive look. I snort, just as the waiter arrives at the table, and we're forced to behave.

"I think I just ate a baby," I groan, a half hour later, palming my swollen stomach. "I feel sick."

"I have something that'll make you feel better." I perk up at that. Ky removes a rectangular blue box adorned with a tied white ribbon from his inside jacket pocket, and my heart starts skipping again. He hands it to me, looking remarkably nervous which only adds to his appeal.

"What is it?" I fumble over my words, my eyes bugging out of my head as I read the Tiffany & Co. label. No boy has ever bought me jewelry before, let alone something from such a renowned jeweler.

He opens the box and my mouth hangs open. Nestled inside is a double heart pendant and matching bracelet. Warmth cascades over my body, and my lower lip trembles as emotion gets the better of me.

"Don't you like it?" he whispers, and I hear the anxiety behind his tone.

"I love it." Tears threaten to spill, but I bite the inside of my lip, hard, and tell myself to get a grip.

"I bought it when we were in Cleveland, and I intended to give it to you the next morning, but then the cops showed up, and everything turned to shit," he explains, removing the pendant from the box. "I've been waiting for the perfect moment to give it to you." He slides the two hearts aside to reveal a pink enamel finish.

Our initials are engraved, and I'm quickly losing the battle of the tears. It's like a classier, more sophisticated depiction of my window drawing. "Oh my God, Ky. It's beautiful. It's too much. You shouldn't have."

He pushes my hair to one side and fixes the pendant around my neck. "You're worth it. And I wanted you to have something real, something solid to remind you of my promise. I wanted to put "forever" on it, but they couldn't fit it in."

I trace my fingers over the silver, adoring how it looks resting against that dip in my collarbone. He fixes the bracelet around my wrist and I tilt my chin up, wrapping my arms around his neck. "I love them, I truly do, and I'm not ever going to take them off, but you know I don't need any physical proof of your love. I have you. That's enough."

His smile falters a little, and I get it instantly. I cup his face fiercely. "You listen here, and you listen good. You are *not* going down for something you didn't do. And if you only bought me this because you think you won't be around to promise me forever, then I'm giving it back."

I move to unclasp the pendant, but he grasps my wrist. "Don't take it off, please. I love how it looks on you. And that's not the only reason I bought it. I wanted to buy something precious for the person who's most precious to me." He chuckles. "Fuck. I sound like a pansy-ass." He laughs again, and then his expression turns solemn. "I'm scared, Faye. Scared that there's more going on with Addison than I know. Scared she's not going to be happy until I'm rotting in a jail cell."

I grip his shoulders firmly. It's oh so tempting to tell him what I've gleaned, but I can't breathe a word because he'll only insist that I back off, and there's no way I'm doing that.

Ky has hurt himself time and time again to protect the ones he loves.

To protect me.

Now it's my turn to do the same for him.

"That's not going to happen. I'm not going to let it happen." I kiss him quickly. "And that's my promise to you."

Chapter Thirty

Faye

It pains me to leave the warmth of my bed and Ky behind the next morning, but I need to get up early if I'm to bake some stuff for later today. I want to do something for Adam, something for my new brothers and sister, as a gesture. Adam mentioned he hoped I'd get to cook for him sometime, so I figure there's no better opportunity.

Alex has caterers coming in later to prepare an indoor buffet-slash-barbeque, so now is the only time I'll have the kitchen to myself.

I have my signature chocolate orange cheesecake chilling in the fridge, and I've only just removed a batch of scones from the oven when Keaton and Kal mosey into the kitchen. They gravitate toward the scones like moths to a flame. While Keaton is doing his best puppy dog impression, imploring me with his eyes, Kal has no such manners, snatching a scone and biting off a corner before I can protest. It's just as well I know my cousins by now and that I've already stashed the second batch in the press. Kal moans at the base of his throat. "Damn, that's good." His arm snakes around my waist, and he drops his chin on my shoulder. "Ditch my brother, and marry me."

"You only want me slaving away in the kitchen," I tease.

"I'm happy for you to be my plaything in the bedroom, too," he throws back.

"What the what?" Ky asks, walking into the kitchen at the wrong moment.

"You're dumped, dude," Kal says, slapping his brother on the back. "I'm marrying the goddess."

I roll my eyes, swatting the back of his head. "Don't wind him up. Be nice."

"Morning, babe." I wrap myself around Ky. He presses a kiss to my forehead, closing his eyes and holding me tight.

"For real?" Kent says, sauntering into the kitchen with a disgusted look on his face. "Because you two feeling each other up is exactly what I want to see first thing in the morning."

"I made scones." I shuck out of Ky's arms, dangling the plate under Kent's nose like a peace offering.

"I'll take one," he says, snapping one up. "But only 'cause I'd hate to see them go to waste."

Around here? As if. If there's any left in the next twenty minutes, it'll be a miracle.

"And it in no way compensates for the nonstop slobbering and groping you're subjecting us to. Enough already."

My cheeks flush. I've been floating around in my love bubble, oblivious to how it must look on the outside, and I'm embarrassed at the thought we've been overdoing the PDAs around the house. Kent is right—for once—and I vow to tone things down.

At least outside of my bedroom.

"Do you have to be such an ass all the time?" Ky inquires. "In case you hadn't noticed, I've got a potential murder charge hanging over my head, and Faye is the only one keeping me sane." He smacks the back of Kent's head. "And now you've embarrassed my girl, and I'm not having that."

Kent looks down at the ground, and I count the seconds waiting for the snarky retort that never comes. "I'm sorry," he mutters. "Thanks for the scone." He jerks his head in my direction, before hightailing it out of the room. Kal moves to the window, staring outside.

"What?" I ask with a puzzled frown.

"Just looking for the flying pig, or maybe I need my ears checked." He tosses a smirk my way. "Wonders will never cease." He grabs another scone, stuffing half of it in his mouth before I can snatch it back. He starts backing out of the room, grinning like a right idiot.

"I hope you get fat," I yell out after him.

"Bite me," he replies in a muffled tone.

I sigh, secretly loving it. "Never a dull moment."

It's five minutes to two, and my nerve is quickly failing me. I've changed into a dress that Alex suggested. It's a green-and-black-patterned skater-style dress that is more than casual but not quite formal.

A bit of an in between.

A lot like myself.

My hair is freshly washed and dried and hanging in soft waves down my back. I kept my makeup light, as usual. Much to Alex's disgust, I'm wearing my wedge platform shoe boots instead of the stilettos she preferred.

Really, I couldn't give a monkey's what I'm wearing or what I look like. Nerves have twisted my stomach into knots, and I must have looked at my watch like about a million times in the last hour. I clasp my pendant, distractedly rubbing my fingers over the cool silver.

"Don't worry," Ky says, for the umpteenth time. "It's going to be fine."

Through the glass panel beside the front door, I spot Adam's car pulling up outside. "Oh, God. I think I'm going to be sick."

Ky bundles me up in his arms from behind. "Relax, babe. I got you." I visibly tremble before forcing myself to get a grip. Reluctantly, I ease out of his embrace. Finding my boyfriend draped around me would no doubt only rile Adam up from the get-go. Ky places his hand against my lower back as Alex and James step into the lobby and open the door. Adam walks up to us, flanked by two cute boys who are impeccably dressed in designer clothing from head to toe. "Thank you for inviting us," Adam says, handing Alex a massive bouquet of flowers and an expensive-looking bottle of red wine.

"Thank you so much for coming, and thank you for these," Alex says, nuzzling her nose in the fragrant flowers. "I can't remember the last time someone bought me flowers."

Oh, for fuck's sake.

Even though I can tell it's an off-the-cuff remark, she might as well have driven a stake right through James's heart. James purses his lips as he thrusts out his hand. "Adam." He nods curtly, and Adam gives him a grim smile as he shakes his hand. A new layer of tension settles over me.

"And who are these handsome boys?" Alex asks, quickly sending apologetic eyes my way.

"I'm Jake," the slightly taller boy says, speaking assuredly. "And this is my twin, Josh."

Alex holds out her hand. "It's very nice to meet you," she says. "How old are you?" she asks Josh, turning her attention to him.

"We're eight," Jake confirms on his behalf. Josh edges closer to his dad, averting his vibrant blue eyes and hanging his head. Jake stares at me unashamedly. "Are you my new sister?"

I swallow my nerves and step forward. "Yes. I'm Faye. I've been looking forward to meeting you." He thrusts out his hand, startling me. I accept his handshake, surprised at how confident he is.

"Dad said your mom is dead. Does that mean you want my mom to be yours now, too?"

"Jacob!" Adam gasps, clearly mortified.

"It's okay," I tell him, trying to ignore the ache in my gut. It still hurts so much to hear it said out loud. I switch my attention to Jake. "My mum will always be my mum, and no one could ever replace her, but it would be really nice to meet your mom one day."

"I don't know if she'd like that," he replies truthfully.

"Oh my God, Jacob." Adam pulls him aside. "Go and tell Whitney to get out of the car." Jake runs back to the car without complaint. "I'm very sorry, Faye. He didn't mean to be rude."

"It's fine. I used to babysit the neighbor's kids back home, and they were about the same age." I shrug. "Kids speak their mind. It's actually pretty refreshing."

"Tell him to screw off," a shrill female voice rings out from the vicinity of the car.

Jake comes back empty-handed. "She says she's staying in the car and you can screw off," he repeats verbatim.

Adam looks like he wishes he was anywhere but here. I can't help wondering if he rushed this through for my benefit, before his children were ready. "We can do this another time," I rush to reassure him. "We shouldn't force her if she isn't ready."

"I'm really sorry about this. Maybe I was too eager for today to happen, but the boys were excited to meet you." He looks down at the boy clinging to his side. "Josh is a little shy when he first meets someone new, but he hasn't stopped asking about you all week." He toys with Josh's hair, and his voice turns soft. "I've known about you for two months, Faye, and I just want you to be a part of my family. To know you're included. That you're not alone." Out of the corner of my eye, I spot James scowling, and I shoot him a quick warning look. "But I'm sorry if I rushed you after I promised I wouldn't. We'll leave if you want."

"No! Dad!" Jake cries out. "We only just got here." His face turns sulky.

"You don't have to leave on my account," I calmly reply, casting a surreptitious look at the stubborn girl refusing to get out of the car.

A tormented look crosses Adam's face, and he throws a quick glance over his shoulder. "I thought Whitney would come around once she got here." Worry lines furrow his forehead, and he rubs the back of his neck. "Look, can you just give me a few minutes. Let me try talking to her again."

"Why don't you let me?" Ky suggests stepping forward. Adam looks skeptical. "What harm can it do?"

Adam rubs his jaw. "Okay. Be my guest."

"Daddy," Josh says. "I need to use the bathroom."

"Why don't I show you where it is?" I propose, holding out my hand. His response is to cling to his dad's side. I hunch over so I'm more on his level. "Daddy can come too, if you like?"

"Why don't we all move inside," James suggests.

I take a quick look back. The passenger side car door is open now, and Ky is leaning one arm on the roof while he talks to Whitney. Her long hair is dyed a shocking pink color, and her gorgeous smile is seductive as she grins up at my boyfriend with obvious interest. All the tiny hairs on my arms lift, and a sour taste forms in my mouth. The extent of my jealousy surprises me. It's not like I've got anything to worry about so why do I feel like running over there and gouging her eyes out with toothpicks?

"Kyler has this handled," James reassures me, nudging me into the house behind the others.

I lead Adam and Josh to the nearest bathroom, and then I bring Jake down to the games room and show him around. His eyes are out on stilts when he spots the massive TV screen and the Xbox console. Keanu and Keaton are in the middle of a game, but I don't care. They're being rude. Standing in front of the screen, ignoring their screams and protests, I introduce Jake.

"Is that NBA 2017?" Jake asks.

Keanu nods. "You want a game?" He holds out his controller, and Jake practically combusts on the spot.

"Yeah! But you have to promise you won't tell my mom. We're only allowed one hour of Xbox a day, and I already played before we left."

Keanu makes a zipping motion with his finger. "My lips are sealed. Sit down, little man. Let's see what you're made of."

Now that Jake's happy out, I head back to the lobby, following the sound of voices. Ky and Whitney are just ahead of me, walking into the living area together, and I have a full view of her sliding her hand down over his back, down to his butt, and squeezing.

"Get your hands off him." The words have flown out of my mouth before I've had time to even think them. My bitch-o-meter is cranked to the max, and I don't give a crap that she's my sister. She can keep her grabby hands away from my man.

She spins around on her knee-high boots, popping gum in and out of her mouth as her gaze rakes over me. She is wearing the tightest, shortest, black leather mini and a cropped, off-the-shoulder sweater that displays a strip of smooth, flat stomach, and the strap of her bra is visible. Her wide, blue eyes are a carbon copy of mine as she levels a loaded look my way.

"Nice dress." She snorts. "Did you borrow it from grandma?"

I could kill Alex for making me wear this. "At least I don't look like a cheap tart," I retort without thinking, instantly feeling a little guilty. This girl is my sister, and I don't want to get off on the wrong foot. This has got to be difficult for her too.

She pops her gum, slowly, and it irritates the fuck out of me. "No, you just act like one." She sends me a sly look. "Because there's no way a plain Jane like you could hold onto a hottie like him any other way."

What a horrible thing to say. She's pissed. I get it. *But why the hell is she taking it out on me?* I'm so not in the mood for this crap. "I'm not doing this with you, so just drop it." I'm determined to keep to a certain minimum level of maturity.

That clearly wasn't the type of response she was after, so she tries a different approach. Looking sideways at Ky, she licks her lips, demolishing him with her gaze. "How about you and me go to your room and I'll show you a good time." She opens her mouth wide and makes a disgusting gesture with her hand. "I give great head, or so I've been told."

"Oh my God. You are certifiable." My claws are coming out, and my inner beast is waking from its slumber. So much for keeping a level head. Coming to loggerheads with my new sister is not how I saw this day panning out. I have to remind myself she's at that awkward age and it's up to me to rise above this. I start counting to ten in my head.

"Faye." Ky walks toward me, subtly shaking his head. "Let it go," he mouths, and that only infuriates me further, even if he is probably right. Whitney has me wound up tight in less than five minutes in her company.

"Yes, *Faye*," she snickers. "Be a good little girl and do what you're told."

Every muscle in Ky's body locks up as he turns around and steps back toward Whitney, his eyes narrowing to slits. His lips curl into a sneer, and he pins her with a cold, stark gaze. The temp drops a few degrees as he stands there staring at her, waiting to pounce. His eyes drill into hers and she gulps nervously. He takes another step toward her and she instinctively rears back. His hands are curled into tight fists at his side as he puts himself right up in her face. She jerks back, undeniably petrified. I almost feel sorry for her. I've been on the receiving end of one of those looks before, and it ain't pleasant. No one does dark and dangerous quite like Ky.

When he starts speaking, his voice is guttural and low. "I thought I explained myself outside." He glares at her, and she visibly shivers. "Faye is the love of my life, and her happiness is my sole mission in life. If you fuck with her, you fuck with me." He tilts his head to the side. "I'm not very happy with you right now, Whitney. No one speaks to Faye like that and gets away with it. No. One."

He palms his hand against the wall overhead, and his impressive body hovers over her, caging her in on one side. She gulps, and her eyes dart around the room in a panic. "I didn't mean it," she whimpers.

"Then you'll have no problem apologizing," Ky replies coolly.

She ducks out from under his raised arm and levels a look at me. "Sorry," she says, not looking or sounding overly apologetic. "My bad."

Ky's gaze locks on mine as he opens his mouth to intervene again, but I silence him with a look. One I hope conveys my gratitude but suggests I can deal with this from here on out. While it warms my heart to know he will always jump to my defense, I am more than capable of standing up for myself, and I know full well how to handle this spoilt brat.

"I don't know what your problem is, but I'm telling you how it's going to go down today." I walk up to her, and she juts her chin up defiantly. Even in her hooker boots, she only reaches my chin. I talk calmly and quietly. "You clearly have some issue with me, which disappoints me, but I'm not going to lose sleep over it. However, you are not going to ruin today for your father or your brothers, and you won't disrespect my aunt and uncle when they have so graciously invited you here. So, do everyone a favor and at least *pretend* to be nice for a couple of hours."

She flips her middle finger up at me, and some of my control evaporates. "And while you're at it, keep your hands off my boyfriend, because if I catch you even looking funny at him, I will rip your hair out, one obnoxious pink strand at a time." Okay, that was probably going a tad too far.

She sends me an amused grin, almost like she approves, and I genuinely can't figure her out.

"Is everything okay out here?" Adam asks, poking his head through the door.

I give him my best smile. "Peachy. Whitney and I were just having a little chat. Coming to an understanding."

She harrumphs, brushing past and deliberately nudging me in the side.

Adam frowns, and his eyes scan my face. "Are you sure?"

"Yes." I smile sweetly.

"Have you seen Jake?"

"Yep. He's playing Xbox with my cousins, and they'll join us when they have finished their game." I loop my arm in Ky's, continuing the pretense. "We should eat. The food will go cold." Adam nods, walking back into the living area as we trail behind him.

Ky presses his mouth to his ear. "Will I get in trouble if I admit that you warning her off was the hottest damn thing I've ever seen?" I smirk. "And how I'm hard as a rock now and wishing you would take me to my room and—"

"Don't finish that sentence," I whisper, cutting him off as my knees turn weak and a surge of longing so intense ripples through me. "We can't escape now, and you're only teasing me. Save it for later." I slide my hand down his back and squeeze his butt in my own version of payback.

"And thank you for sticking up for me," I add, giving him another playful squeeze.

"I know you had it under control, but I wasn't going to stand by and let her spout all that sleazy shit. Let her act so disrespectfully toward you."

"I appreciate that, but you could've removed her hand from your ass a little quicker." I send him a knowing look.

He pulls me aside, and I try to ignore the inquisitive looks leveled our way. "Are you for real?" An angry spark flashes in his eyes. "You got there first, and her hand was on my ass for, like, three seconds, tops."

"That's three seconds too long." I pout, deciding to downplay it before it turns argumentative.

His shoulders relax, and he laughs. I release the breath I'd been holding. "I didn't think you could get any hotter, but you are so hot when you're jealous." He pulls me into his chest, all hint of anger vanished.

"Not funny." I push against his chest, attempting to resist his allure. "How about I call Brad over here and let him feel my ass for three seconds?"

I instantly know it's the wrong thing to say. Regret rears up and bites me. He releases me like I'm an infectious disease. "It's not the same thing and you know it. That was fucking low, Faye." He walks off into the kitchen, dragging his hands through his hair.

Shit. He's right. That was way out of order, and I don't even know why I said it. It's like my brain took a temporary vacation.

Out of the corner of my eye, I spot Whitney grinning in my direction, and I glower at her. I've imagined today going many different ways but not like this. Foolishly, I'd thought I might be able to strike up a friendship with my sister. Might be able to form the type of relationship I have with Jill and Rach with Whitney. That idea is shot to hell now. She wants nothing to do with me. Maybe, when she's had time to get used to the idea, she'll come around, but I'm not going to hold my breath. I'm a pretty good judge of character, and ...

My thoughts meander as I pick up on something outside the window. I squint as my feet take on a life of their own. I walk over to the window like there's a rocket up my ass.

No fucking way.

I blink excessively, wondering if it's possible I'm seeing things—but nope. Pointing out the window, I ask, "Is that ... Courtney?"

Chapter Thirty-One

Kyler

We all turn at Faye's words, and I'm beside her in a heartbeat, staring out the window with my mouth hanging open. Courtney is racing across the back lawn, in her bare feet, holding her shoes in her hand as she's chased by two of Dad's security guards. Her hair is flapping behind her, and the wild look in her eyes is kinda freaky. The guards are speaking hurriedly into their mouthpieces, no doubt requesting backup.

Dad curses low under his breath. "I'll handle this."

He turns to walk away, but Mom takes hold of his elbow, shaking her head. "I'll fix this. Can you call Kaden and see what their ETA is, please?" She's in professional mode as she smiles apologetically at Adam. "I'm very sorry about this intrusion. Please just ignore her."

Easier said than done. Although the guards are closing the distance on Courtney, she's making good use of those long legs of hers, and she's almost to the edge of the lawn, at the corner of the house. She stops for a minute, pivots around, and strategically flings her stilettos at the guards. The both duck down, narrowly avoiding a heel in the eyeball. Ouch.

She's closer now and there's no missing the venomous look on her face. Faye jumps as Courtney slams into the window, mashing her face up to the glass. The glass panes rattle. "I can see you, James," she yells. "Get out here and confront me like a man! If you think this is the end of it, you can think again. I've still got cards to play, and you are both going to be sorry you did this to me! No. One. Does. This. To. Me!"

One of the guards reaches the house, grasping her waist from behind. "It's not too late to negotiate!" Her shrill plea is borderline hysterical. The guard tries to pry her from the window, but she's stronger than she looks, and she grips the wooden window frame like she's clinging on for dear life. Her sharp, green eyes fix on me as her body is jostled about from behind. She still doesn't let go.

"Call Officer Hanks, please," Mom says, appearing outside. Her words filter in through the open window. "Tell him we want this woman arrested for trespassing and breaking an official court order."

Courtney pounds the glass with one clenched fist, reclaiming my attention. She points her finger at me, and her eyes bore into mine, sending prickles of alarm washing all over me. Icy chills rip up and down my spine. "Say goodbye to your nice life." She cackles, enjoying my obvious discomfort. Her eyes dart wildly around the room. "You're all going down! All of you!"

Faye's hand threads in mine and hauls me away from the window. "Okay, that was super creepy."

I allow Faye pull me away in a bit of a daze. Something about the way she looked at me has unnerved me.

Outside, Courtney has been removed from the window, but she's thrashing about uncontrollably, and the guards are struggling to restrain her. Her arms and legs are flailing about as she screams like a wild animal. Mom is trying to talk to her, her face a mask of calm composure, but they're too far away now to hear what's being said. A few minutes later, a cruiser pulls up in front of the house just in front of Kade's Jeep.

"The boys are here," Dad says, as if we haven't just witnessed the crazy woman making threats outside. "Let's sit down at the table."

Whitney cranks out a laugh, and Adam sends a warning glare in her direction. "I'm really glad I came now, Dad. You were right." She sends him a smug look as she flies off the arm of the couch. "This *is* fun."

Kent strolls into the dining room with Keaton, Keanu, and one of the twins. Jake, I think it is. Hard to tell, they are so alike. Except for the fact that the other boy, Josh, has barely left his father's side.

I wait for it. Knowing it's as predictable as the Patriots making the playoffs.

Ten, nine, eight ...

And there it is.

The moment Kent spots Whitney.

I saw this coming from the minute she opened her mouth outside. From the second her mischievous eyes roamed me unashamedly. From the instant the dirty proposition left her filthy mouth. The sense of déjà vu was almost overwhelming. It was like looking at a miniature female Kent in the making. She already has the derogatory look down pat, and the way she went at Faye proves the same arrogant, cocky immaturity flows through her veins.

My little warning outside apparently fell on deaf ears. I told her how important today was to Faye and that I wouldn't hesitate to crush her if she fucked things up for my girl.

Clearly went in one ear and out the next.

I'm losing my touch.

Kent stops, his eyes narrowing as he zones in on her like a predator marking his prey. He's across the room in a flash. Bowing dramatically at the waist, he extends his hand toward her. "Kent Kennedy at your service, oh gorgeous one." He straightens up, grinning as he takes her hand and plants a kiss on it. "Who are you and where the hell have you been all my life?"

I groan, recognizing the line. He borrowed it straight from Brad's mouth. *Could he be any more cliché?*

She eyes him like he's scum at the bottom of her fuck-me boots, but I see the flicker of interest, the sheen of excitement in her eye. She's not experienced enough to hide it. "Don't tell me that line actually works on girls? It's so 1990s."

I need to shut this down.

I stalk toward them. "Enough flirting, dipshit. Go get the door for your brother."

"Get lost, Ky, and get the fucking door yourself."

My fists twitch at my side. I'd love to knock some sense into the little shit, but I don't think Mom would approve of that type of discipline.

"Behave, or I'll make you." I send him a warning as I go out to greet my brothers.

Courtney is screaming like a banshee as I step outside. Kicking and screaming and cursing like the skank she is. Officer Hanks and his colleague push her into the back of the cruiser, and my ears give silent thanks.

Kade and Kev are looking on in amusement. A pretty girl with bouncy red curls is glued to Kaden's side. She's wearing a fitted black mini dress that is molded to her body, leaving little to the imagination. Her killer cleavage is on full display, and I mean, *full display*—if the neckline were any lower, I'd be able to see her nipples. She is perched on extremely high heels, looking like she could topple over at any time.

I fail to hide my smirk as Keven looks in my direction, grinning back at me in obvious understanding. He strolls over to my side as Mom talks urgently to the officer.

"Who the fuck is she and what's she doing here?"

"Tiffani," he drawls, "with an I, not a Y. She's his latest fuck buddy. No idea in hell why he's brought her here. Mom's going to blow a gasket."

I chuckle. "Perhaps, that's the intent."

Kev grimaces. "You could be right, but I think there's more to it, but, you know Kade; he doesn't say jack shit."

That surprises me.

The two of them are usually very tight. It always used to piss me off, but since I found out we are legit blood brothers, it's actually grated on my nerves a little more than usual. "How come? You two live together."

"Bro, I hardly ever see him anymore. And he's so secretive. Won't tell me a Goddamned thing. I haven't a clue what's going on with him these days." He slaps me on the back. "How are you?"

I shrug casually, as if having a death sentence hanging over my head is no biggie. "Fine."

"Yeah." He snorts. "That's what I thought."

Before I can retaliate, Mom is rushing us into the house. The moment she spots Tiffani is priceless. The look of pure horror on her face is impossible to miss, but she composes herself quickly, welcoming the girl. Only Kev and I see her wiping her palm down the front of her dress after they shake hands. "This should be fun," Kev jokes.

"You have no idea." Wait until Faye versus Whitney round two kicks off.

After all the introductions are made, we serve ourselves from the buffet and sit down. I pull Faye's chair out for her, conspicuously avoiding the heated stare Whitney is leveling my way from across the table. Kent sits down beside her—of course—proceeding to flirt up a storm the whole way through dinner. A couple of times, I have to kick him under the table to shut up. Adam appears to have shrewd instincts, and he's watching the pair of them like a hawk. Unfortunately, I think that only spurs Whitney on. I should be glad that she's stopped sending fuck-me eyes my way, and stopped glaring at Faye, but now she's fawning all over Kent, and I'm afraid things are about to head south. It's not like he needs much encouragement.

Faye's new sister is one hell of a spoiled bitch. No matter what Mom offers her, she refuses. The response is either she's "allergic" or "red meat clogs your arteries" or "dairy gives me, like, really insane migraines." There's no denying she's hard work, but that only appears to add to her appeal for Kent. His eyes have glossed over, and he's staring at her as if he's never seen a girl before in his life.

Conversation is strained at the table, although things are cool with me and Faye now that she's apologized for her earlier comment. I know she didn't mean it, but that didn't make it hurt any less at the time.

Dad and Adam aren't fooling anyone with their barbed comments and hate-filled looks. Faye has barely swallowed a thing, and I know the tension is eating away at her. She was already so worried about today without all this unnecessary drama. Every so often, I squeeze her knee or sneak a sly kiss when I think no one's looking. Whatever I can do to ease the stress.

Mom suggests we eat dessert in the conservatory overlooking the lawn so we head outside. My younger brothers return to the games room with Josh and Jake in tow.

Tiffani is laughing at something Kaden is saying in her ear, and the piercing sound is like a hyena with a sore throat. I can already feel a headache coming on. Faye nudges me in the side, not so subtly rolling her eyes. Tiffani's contributions at dinner were less than illuminating, and I'm struggling to understand how she managed to get into Harvard and how she's managed to worm her way into my brother's affections.

She must be one hell of a lay.

Perhaps she intentionally hides her brain under that bimbo exterior, but one thing's certain; if she intends to hold on to my brother—and all the indications are pointing to her being a clinger—she'll need to up her game.

Her current game face sucks butt. Big style.

"Whitney's been in the bathroom for ages," Faye whispers in my ear. I had noticed. Her direct look tells me she's thinking what I'm thinking.

Taking her hand, I pull her to her feet. "Let's go. It's best we find them before your dad does." Her step falters a little. "What?"

"You called him my ... dad." A flustered expression crosses over her beautiful face. "That's still difficult to wrap my head around."

I haul her into my side, kissing the top of her head. "Sorry. I didn't think."

"No." She shakes her head, her hair cascading in soft waves down her back. "I've got to face facts. And it's not really such a bad thing. Apart from Whitney, that is."

"She'll come around."

"Yeah, right." Faye snorts.

Inappropriate sounds accost us the instant we step into the lobby. Faye bites out a curse. "You've got to be kidding me." She's fuming as she stomps toward the guest bathroom, tucked in at the back of the mezzanine stairs. Yanking the door open, she curses again.

Kent is leaning back against the sink with his jeans and boxers pooled around his feet. His head is thrown back, and his eyes are closed as he moans in ecstasy. Whitney is crouched over him, eagerly sucking him off. I lounge against the doorframe, trying not to laugh at the disgusted look on Faye's face. She's like two seconds away from exploding.

Kent is a little asshole, but I've got to begrudgingly give him credit. Despite his cheesy one-liners, and his love-'em-and-leave-'em attitude, he still has girls crawling all over him. He's getting way more action than I did at his age, although, to be fair, I had a steady girlfriend. Kent opens one eye, spots us, grins, and then palms the back of Whitney's head, urging her to continue. What a cocky little bastard. I chuckle, earning a death glare from Faye in the process. Whitney looks up but she doesn't stop her feverish sucking, eyeballing me with a naughty glint in her eye.

A faint noise outside spurs me into action. Gently moving Faye aside, I grip Whitney by the shoulders and pull her off Kent. Faye averts her eyes. Whitney is bitching me out over it and wrestling in my grip. Kent is scowling at me like I just killed his firstborn. "Someone is coming!" I hiss through gritted teeth.

"That someone would've been me!" he snarls. "In like less than two seconds. You fucking asshole."

"Pull your pants up, you idiot!" I snap, rapidly losing patience.

Faye dangles a leopard-print bra from one finger. "And you better put this back on before your dad spots your bare nipples poking out through your shirt."

"I would if I could use my arms," Whitney huffs, slapping my arm to prove her point. I let her go, taking a step toward Faye. Brazen as all hell, Whitney pulls the sweater up over her head and turns to face us, bare chested, with a devilish smirk on her face. Kent groans, and I can tell what his next move is going to be. Pinning him with a deadly serious look, I shake my head. "Don't even think about it."

The footsteps are getting closer, and I make a knee-jerk decision. Grabbing the bra, I fling it at Whitney. "Get dressed, both of you, and stay quiet. We'll handle this, but I'm warning you, no continuation of what just happened, or we'll rat you out to both dads." Kent flips me the bird, as I lift Faye at the waist and pull her out of the bathroom. We shut the door and race out into the lobby in the nick of time.

Adam wanders into the lobby, looking lost. "Oh, Faye, there you are. I was just looking for Whitney. Have you seen her?"

"Yeah, she's fine. We were just with her. She's with Keaton. He's, ah, showing her his ... stamp collection."

I manage to disguise my snort of hilarity as a cough.

Adam frowns, looking skeptical.

I step in. "I'll send her out to you if you like?"

"Please." He looks at me a little sheepishly. "I mean no offense, Kyler, but I'd like to keep her as far away from your brothers as possible. Especially Kent. I didn't miss what was going on back at the table. Whitney is boy crazy, and she's rather fond of getting herself into situations a fourteen-year-old girl shouldn't be in."

"Don't worry, sir," I say in my most sincere tone. "We'll make sure nothing happens. We'll send her right out."

"Thank you." He tilts his head at Faye. "I'm sorry for the way she's behaving. Don't take it personally. I'm the one she's angry at, and she's at a difficult age. Everything and everyone frustrates her."

"It's okay, Adam. You don't need to explain," Faye says, in a louder tone of voice. "I understand. She's fourteen, she's pretty, and she thinks she knows it all, but once she grows up, she'll realize how selfishly she's acting."

I chuckle under my breath. My girl's got claws and then some. I'll bet Kent is struggling to restrain Whitney in the bathroom.

"Somehow, I don't think you're speaking from personal experience," he replies.

"Oh," Faye laughs, tossing her hair back, "I wouldn't quite agree with that. You'd be surprised at some of the things I've gotten up to."

His face pales a little. "Maybe there are some things I'd rather not hear about."

"Perhaps." She grins wickedly.

Adam retreats outside and Faye sags against me. "That was cutting it close."

I take her hand, pulling her back to the bathroom. "Come on. They're probably already on round two."

This time when we open the door, they are indulging in a hardcore make-out session, but at least they are fully clothed and there are no bodily parts on show.

"Playtime's over, kiddies," Faye drolls, and I snicker.

Whitney rips her lips from Kent, glaring at Faye. "You think you're so funny." She prods her in the chest. "And we heard every word, and I know you did it on purpose."

Faye removes her finger. "*Thanks* will suffice."

Whitney shoves her upturned middle finger in Faye's face. "This is as much thanks as you'll ever get from me, and don't go thinking I owe you or anything." Planting her hands on her slim hips, she smirks at Faye. "Stamp collection?! Is that the best you could do?"

"Don't be so ungrateful. It worked didn't it?" Faye snaps back.

"Speaking of," I say, "you best get your ass outside before Adam becomes suspicious."

Leaning in, she claims Kent's mouth in a hard kiss, her tongue visible as she thrusts it between his lips. Kent grips her ass, and Faye just rolls her eyes. Whitney breaks away, panting. "Rain check, pretty boy?"

"You betcha." He pinches her tit through her sweater, and Faye's about ten seconds away from tearing him a new one when the doorbell chimes.

"Saved by the bell," Whitney giggles, palming Kent's crotch one last time. "Later, baby." She saunters outside, swishing her hips deliberately, and Kent can't take his eyes off her.

Faye scowls as she notices the growing bulge in his jeans. "Oh, God," she mutters, rubbing her eyes. "Please let this day be over already."

The bell rings again, more insistently this time, and I walk toward the door. The second I open it, I'm pushed back as the detective from Bayfield barges into the house surrounded by four uniformed cops. Slamming my face up against the wall, he secures cuffs around my wrists. In the background, I hear Faye ordering Kent to fetch Dad.

Getting arrested three times in the space of two weeks has got to be some kind of record.

The detective eyeballs me. "Things aren't looking so good for you, son."

Tell me something I don't know.

Chapter Thirty-Two

Faye

I throw my phone on the bed, screaming in frustration. *Where the hell is Brad when I need him? When Ky needs him? Needs us?* It's ten p.m. and he should be back from his aunt's by now. He had left early this morning for the two-hour trip out of state, but he should be home already. I don't want to confront Addison by myself, but it's looking like I won't have much choice. It's been four hours since the cops hauled Ky out of here. Alex and James went with him, but they insisted I stay here. Keven went back to Harvard promising to stay up all night searching for anything that might help.

But I'm all out of patience.

I tried talking Kal into coming to Addison's with me, but he's siding with Keven, and they both made me promise profusely that I wouldn't do anything stupid.

Thing is, we have different interpretations of the word, and I'm not opposed to breaking my promise if the situation demands it or taking whatever actions are necessary to protect someone I love.

Rose is out on a date with Theo, and Brad was my only hope. But I've phoned him a million times. Left a trillion messages. And he's still a no show. Perhaps he's avoiding me on purpose. Not that I'd blame him—Ky did warn him to keep his distance.

I hop up, bristling with restless energy. I refuse to hang around my room moping when my boyfriend is actually being charged with a murder he didn't commit.

Someone has to do something practical to help him.

That gun could only have been planted by one of two people—either Addison or Courtney. Considering Courtney was fixated on Alex and James and Kennedy Apparel, my money's on Addison. Besides, Courtney is safely behind bars right now, leaving Addison as prime suspect.

I strip off my clothes, pulling jeans and a black hoodie out of my wardrobe and throwing them on in record time. Shoving my feet into my sneakers, I lace them up quickly. Time is running out for Ky, and if I'm going to intervene, it has to be now.

I leave a hastily scribbled note for Kal and Brad, knowing one of them will check in on me at some point. At least if Addison does away with me, they'll know exactly who to point the finger at.

Before I leave the house, I grab one of the smaller chopping knives from the kitchen. Using some medi-tape from the first aid kit, I strap it around my ankle, covering the evidence with my jeans. Between that and my self-defense techniques, I'm confident I can fend off anything Addison throws my way. I'm hoping she only had access to the one gun. The one that's now evidence in police lockup.

The alternative doesn't bear thinking about.

The taxi is waiting for me on the road outside the old entrance at the rear of the woods. I give him directions and sink back in the seat, trying to quell my nerves. I fiddle with my phone, ensuring I have the record button all set up. This will only work if I can get Addison to confess to something on tape.

I ask the taxi driver to pull over in almost the exact same spot Rose parked in the last time we were here. I hand him a wad of notes and tell him I'll double it if he's still here when I get back. Sliding out the door, I head across the fields and out to the wooded area that borders the back of Addison's house. Then I push the send button on the message I'd already constructed.

"I know who your real mother is, and I know what you've done. Unless you want me to share the deets all over the net, meet me in the woods at the back of your house right now. Faye."

Short and to the point.

Her reply is almost instantaneous. *"On my way."*

I stick close to the small wooded area, making sure to keep out of visible light. Every sound from behind has me jittery. Perhaps coming here on my own wasn't such a good idea after all but there's no backing out now.

It seems like I've been waiting an eternity before I detect a shadowy figure vaulting over the fence and heading in my direction. As she draws closer, I have to smother my grunt of surprise. I have never seen Addison looking anything but immaculately turned out. Right now, she's paying homage to her trailer trash roots. She's wearing gray, tatty old sweats tucked into beige Ugg boots and a black windbreaker that I wouldn't be seen dead wearing, and I'm fairly casual when it comes to clothing. Her long blonde hair is pulled into a severe ponytail, and her face is wiped clean of makeup. If I didn't know she's on her way to meet me, I actually wouldn't believe it was the same girl.

"Are you crazy?" she demands in a hiss as she approaches.

"Of the two of us, I'm pretty sure I'm the least crazy one," I reply coolly, shoving my hand in my pocket and activating the record button on my phone.

"What do you want?" she snaps.

"I want to know why you planted that gun on Ky, and I'm not leaving until you tell me."

"I don't know what you're talking about."

"Nice try. We know it was you. That day in the lobby, that's what you were up to when you faked an asthma attack."

"I didn't fake anything," she growls, her eyes narrowing to slits. "I did have an asthma attack. I might've just exaggerated it a little." She looks around me. "If Ky's so concerned, why isn't he here?" She plants her hands on her hips. "Or does he send you to do all his dirty work now?"

"Ky can't come." My nostrils flare. "He's in the police station being charged with a murder he didn't commit." My eyes glimmer with indignation and rage.

She stumbles a little. "What?" If I hadn't witnessed her acting skills up close and personal before, I might actually believe the shock splashed across her face is genuine. "But they let him go?!" Her voice rises a notch. "I don't understand."

"They re-arrested him earlier tonight. I'm not sure why, but he's been there for hours, so it's not looking good. Did you plant more fake evidence for them to find?" She rests her hands on her knees, and her breath is snaking out in panicked spurts. I take a step toward her, wishing I'd thought to remove the knife from my ankle before she got here. "I know it was you. Just admit it, Addison. You say you love him?" I tilt her chin up and stare earnestly into her eyes. "Then prove it. Tell the police the truth. Let him go free."

She straightens up, and the look on her face transforms to one of absolute terror. "You don't understand." She grips my arm. "I would if I could." Her grip tightens and the look in her eyes is starting to scare me. "It wasn't supposed to happen like this! You've got to believe me. I just wanted to make him dependent on me. I didn't sign up for any of the other stuff."

"You know I don't know what you're talking about."

She lets go of my arm. "It's better you don't know." She massages her temples. "Look, I know you hate me as much as I hate, you but you've got to believe me. I *do* love him, and I would never do this to him."

I snort. "Puh-lease. After all you've done, you expect me to believe that?"

"I know it's hard to believe, but it's the truth."

"Well, excuse me if your word means fuck all. Haven't you ever heard the phrase 'actions speak louder than words'?" My eyes drill into her skull. "Now would be a great time for you to show you mean what you say. Time is running out for Ky! If you love him, you'll make it right. I know you're involved in this, Addison. You can stand here and deny it 'til the cows come home and I still won't believe you. Just admit what you've done and turn yourself in. Please." I'd get on my knees and beg if I thought it'd do any good. "I'm not asking you to do it for me. I'm asking you to do it for him."

A sharp snapping sound has both of us spinning around, squinting into the black depths of the woodland.

Addison tugs on my arm, attempting to drag me forward. "You shouldn't be here. You need to leave."

I'm taller and I've definitely got a few pounds of muscle on her, so shoving her off takes minimal effort. "I'm not leaving until you admit it."

So far I have nothing that I can bring to the cops. If I can get her to confess to something, even if it's only a small thing, that should be enough to cast doubt on Ky's conviction.

"Faye, please. You have to go." She gulps, and a spark of terror burns bright in her eyes. "I know you have no reason to believe me, but you have to get out of here. Now!"

She attempts to grab my arm again, but I side step her, grabbing her arm instead. "Quit with the act, Addison. You can't fool me. Tell me what you did. Better yet, come to the cop station with me and tell them in person."

"Okay." The word flies out of her mouth without hesitation, and she nods her head vigorously. "I'll come to the station with you." I narrow my eyes suspiciously. *What's she up to now?* She starts dragging me away as I try to decipher the confusion in my head. Addison wouldn't capitulate that easily.

What is going on here?

I resist her pull, digging my boots into the ground. "Hang on here a sec."

She turns around, and her eyes stretch so wide I'm afraid they're going to explode right out of their socket. "No!" she screeches, and I lift my hands to cover my ears.

The almost indecipherable sound of approaching footsteps accosts me a split second too late. My heart starts jackhammering in my chest and adrenaline floods my system as I slowly turn around.

Pain explodes in my skull, and black dots mar my vision before an ominous dark blanket of doom creeps slowly across my retinas. My body slithers to the ground just before I lose complete consciousness.

Chapter Thirty-Three

Faye

I don't know how long I've been out of it when I finally regain consciousness. Judging by the faint streams of daylight trickling through the small window in front of me, it's got to be at least six or seven hours since I was last awake. The pounding pain in my skull has me moaning as I come to. My eyes blink open and shut, refusing to cooperate. Try as I might, I can't keep them open for more than a couple seconds at a time. My head lolls forward as I lick my dry lips. The metallic taste in my mouth combined with a pulsing ache in my arms is like a shot of liquid reality straight to my veins.

The memory surges to the forefront of my mind, and my eyes blink wide open. Blood rushes to my head, and if I wasn't already tied to the chair I'm sitting in I think I would've fallen off with the sudden burst of dizziness.

My breath gushes out in panicked spurts, and my heart is slamming wildly against my ribcage. I look down at the rope tied firmly around my midriff and the second layer of binding around my calves. My hands are tightly pinned behind the back of the chair, and every muscle in my arms throbs with the strain.

"About damn time," a familiar bored voice says.

My breath hitches in my throat, and bile coats the inside of my mouth.

"I know you're awake, Faye. Look at me."

I keep my head down, racking my brain for some kind of escape plan. But I come up empty-handed.

I'm so screwed this time.

Something blunt hits my temple, and I scream as intense pain rattles through my already sore skull.

Warm liquid trickles down the side of my face.

"Was that really necessary?" Addison asks in her usual nasally tone of voice.

A hand fists in my hair, and my head is yanked back. My neck strains at the awkward angle.

"Hello, precious Faye," Courtney says. "You have no idea how happy I am to have you here." She makes it sound like she's invited me over for dinner.

"Wish I could say the feeling's mutual, but that'd be a lie." My voice sounds remarkably calm considering the epic panic party detonating fireworks inside me.

Courtney twists my hair tighter, and I feel the sharp tug all the way to the base of my ribcage. "What do you want with me?"

She laughs. "I always knew you weren't that smart despite how much *Alexandra* gushed about you. Haven't you figured it out already?"

She releases her hold on my head, but my relief is short-lived. Walking around in front of me, she crouches down and slaps my face from side to side. "Wakey, wakey, you dumb Irish bitch."

"Court." Addison sounds almost bored. "What is this?"

"Don't interrupt me!" she snaps. "You are only here at my invitation, and I can change that any time I like."

Panic is like a vise-grip around my heart as Courtney whips a gun out from the waistband of her pants, brandishing it in Addison's direction. Addison is wearing the same clothes she had on when I last saw her and pretty much wearing the exact same terrified expression, although she is doing her best to disguise it.

That act last night wasn't an act. Addison was genuinely scared and trying to warn me off. And I didn't trust in it, or her.

Some of the puzzle pieces start slotting into place. My eyes scan my surroundings as my mind churns the connotations. Lighting is dim, courtesy of four candles, flickering softly behind glass covers. We appear to be in a small log cabin of sorts. Rustic, thick timber log walls rise to meet a tongue-and-groove triangular-shaped roof. The wooden floor under my feet is scuffed and dirty and littered with withered old leaves and other natural debris. A discolored, patterned rug lines the floor directly in front of the door. To my left is an open stone fireplace. Cold, blackened cinders fill the hearth. A stack of logs is piled up to one side, facing a lumpy looking red and gray colored couch. Over the other side of the cabin is a small kitchen area. I count eight presses, four on the bottom and four on the top, fronting a small, rectangular wooden table and chairs.

"Like what you see?" Courtney asks, dragging a chair over. She sits down facing me, tipping my chin up with the barrel of her gun.

I gulp. "Where am I?"

She laughs. "One stupid question after another." She shakes her head. "Do you really expect me to answer that?" Her eyes shimmer with excitement as Addison yawns, pretending to be bored.

My eyes flick to Addison, and she subtly shakes her head. I focus solely on Courtney, trying to ignore the growing trembling taking hold of my body. I've got to keep her talking. "I know it was you," I tell her. "You killed Doug Grant and framed Ky."

She leans back in her chair with a smug grin on her face. "Finally! Maybe there is hope for you yet."

"You two were working together," I add, jerking my chin at Addison.

Addison looks glum, while Courtney purses her lips. "I wouldn't quite call it that. I'm in charge of this show, and Addison does what I tell her to do."

Addison harrumphs. "Oh, come on, Court, you know you never would've gotten this far if it wasn't for me. Don't you dare downplay my role. I was the one who got you the evidence you needed to blackmail James and Alex. You wouldn't have gotten anywhere without that."

Courtney purses her lips unhappily. "It was still my plan, and I sent you up to his office that night with the safe code to retrieve it."

Alarm bells ping in my head. "That night we caught you in James's study, when you said you were looking for the tape of you and Ky? That's really what you were doing?"

Addison nods, looking pleased as punch, and I can't tell if she's genuinely proud of herself or if this performance is for Courtney's benefit. "Yeah. I had it stuffed up my shirt if any of you had even thought to search me." She snickers. "But you were too busy trying to get me away from Ky to care."

"And what about all the recordings? Screwing Brad and sending the evidence to Ky. Screwing Kal and showing the evidence to Lana. What was that about?"

"That was all part of my plan to get him to commit to me for life. I wasn't lying when I told you I love him. I've always loved him. He was meant to be mine!"

If I wasn't already forcibly sitting down, I'm sure I would've just fallen off my chair. "How the hell do you figure that one out?"

She pushes off the door and walks over to the fireplace, supporting her butt on the edge of the ledge. "It was Court's idea." She glares at Courtney. "She said I had to break him. To separate him from everyone he loved, and then I'd be there to build him back up. He'd see that I was the only one he could count on, and I'd get him back. Get that ring on my finger that I've dreamed of for years. That's why I did all that stuff. I was doing it for Ky. He belongs with me."

I'm not sure who is the more delusional of the two. Courtney for even suggesting such a crackpot scheme or Addison for believing in it. And how did Addison and Courtney even join forces? What could ha—

I gasp out loud as it comes to me.

"You're half-sisters." I stare at Courtney as it all starts to come together. "Wendy is your mum, too. You're the baby she gave up when she was in high school."

Courtney claps loudly. "Okay, maybe you're not as dumb as you look. And I see you've been doing some homework of your own." Her eyes narrow, and she shunts forward in her seat, pinching my knee. "How do you know that?"

She can't know about Keven or that anyone else knows about this. I decide to share some of the truth. "I wanted to get Addison away from Ky, so I snuck over to her house one night, and I heard a conversation between her adopted mum and her birth mum, and it didn't take much to figure it out."

Addison gets up. "You spied on me?" she shrieks. Courtney sends a warning look her way.

"You can hardly get mad at me considering all you did. And you expect me to believe you did it as part of some warped plan to get Ky back? To make him reliant on you? I'm calling bullshit on that."

Courtney grins. "I think she just challenged you." She winks at Addison.

Addison's mouth twists into an ugly grimace. "That *was* the main reason, but I also wanted financial independence. I want away from my family. They have tried their best to ruin my life, and I wanted to take back control. Wendy only told me she was my mother because she was hoping to get more cash from my dad. The woman I thought was my mother has lied to my face for seventeen years, and my dad is a cheating skeeze who fucked his wife's sister and got her pregnant."

She flaps her hands about, pacing in front of the fireplace. "I'm irrelevant in the midst of all that. I'm just some possession they enjoy arguing over. My life is completely fucked up, and I just wanted to take something for myself. Court understands that, and if her plan had succeeded, she would have married James, controlled Kennedy Apparel, and we both would've had more money than we knew what to do with. And I would have Ky by my side which is all I've ever wanted. No one else I've been with comes even close to him."

Well, on that we can agree. Not that I'm admitting that out loud.

She stabs Courtney with a heavy hostile look. "But I've lost him now, thanks to you!"

Courtney's eyes narrow to slits, and a new layer of tension filters through the air. Her eyes focus on my chest, and a conniving look slips over her face. Reaching out, she yanks the pendant from my neck with one sharp tug. Pain rips across the back of my neck, and I bite on the inside of my cheek to avoid crying out.

I won't give her the satisfaction.

She turns it over in her hand, inspecting the engraving with a growing smile. Her head whips around, and she fixes her evil eye on Addison. She holds up the pendant, letting it dangle from the tips of her fingers. "He never gave you anything like this, did he?" She separates the hearts and points at the inscription. "He loves her in a way he obviously never loved you." Her eyes narrow as she moves in for the kill. "Him not loving you anymore has nothing to do with me. You lost him all on your own."

Addison's eyes narrow, and a red flush sweeps up her neck and over her cheeks. Her chest heaves as she stands there fuming. Ignoring her sister, she turns a scathing look on me. "That's the truth. Happy now?" she screams at me, although I sense she's more furious at herself.

Courtney jumps up, racing toward Addison and smacking her hard across the face. "Keep your fucking voice down."

Addison pushes her sister away. "Fuck you, Court. And no one can hear us here. You made sure of that."

Courtney puts her face right up in Addison's. "I don't much like the way you're talking to me. And I don't much like what you were trying to do last night."

"What?" Addison frowns, looking surreptitiously at me out of the corner of her eye. Her gaze is pleading.

"You went out to meet with her without telling me." She points at me. "If I wasn't tapping your cell phone, I would never have known. And the way it looked to me, you were trying to warn her off. Do you need a little reminder of what's at stake here, sister darling?" She runs the tip of the gun down Addison's body in a deliberately slow fashion.

Addison pales, and her limbs start visibly trembling. "No." Her voice is shaky.

"You sure about that?" Courtney circles her body, trailing the gun up and down her torso with intent. Addison swings clear but panicked eyes on me. As our gazes connect, an unspoken communication passes between us. I discreetly nod my head.

"Why?" I shout out, attempting to reclaim Courtney's attention. "That's what I don't understand, Courtney. Why the Kennedys? There are tons of rich people in Wellesley, so why did you target my family? Is this something to do with Alex?"

The mere mention of my aunt has Courtney's blood boiling. She stalks over to me and grips my shoulders painfully. "That bitch will pay." Her voice lowers, and she talks in a chilled manner that sends shivers up my spine. "She thinks she's seen the last of me, but this isn't over until she is."

"You hate her that much?"

"Yes," she roars, losing some of her composure.

I quirk an amused brow. I can't help it. Courtney slams the butt of her gun into my other temple, and I yelp in pain. Black stars blur my vision, and my head starts slanting. She grips my chin firmly, slapping me a few times across the cheeks. "No, you don't. You are going to stay conscious for this. I want you to feel everything I'm going to do to you."

"Do your worst, bitch," I spit out, and she punches me in the face with the back end of the gun. Blood spurts out of my nose and mouth.

"Jesus, Court."

"Stay out of this, Addison. What did you think was going to happen here?"

Fighting my dizziness, I try to focus on the two fuzzy figures in front of me.

"What do you mean?" Addison's voice is barely above a whisper.

"You know she can't live. Not now she knows the truth."

"I didn't sign up for murder!" Addison shrills. "I didn't sign up for this." She waves her hands around in a panic, and I silently urge her to stick with the program. Courtney needs to believe she's still on the team.

I blink my eyes repeatedly, willing my body to fight the slumber. A sharp slapping sound resonates in the room.

"Stop hitting ME!" Addison yells. "Or so help me God, I'll leave you to handle this on your own."

"Don't you dare threaten me. I can bury you, Addison. And don't think I haven't taken precautions because I have. If anything happens to me, a file will be sent to the police commissioner with evidence linking you to all the stuff you've done."

I hear Addison's sharp intake of breath as I shake the last vestiges of sleep off. I lift my head up and look over at the warring sisters. Blood is dripping down my chin, and onto my jeans, and a mad wave of déjà vu comes over me. I shutter my eyes as images of David pinning me down, his hands wrapped around my neck, threaten to overwhelm me. In my head, I count to ten and try to regulate my breathing. My survival depends on me staying alert and not panicking. I'm not sure what the chances are of surviving two life-threatening situations in one lifetime, but I'm determined to buck the odds.

I open my eyes, finding keen green eyes examining me.

"I may have misjudged you, Faye. You're smarter than I gave you credit for, so, I'm going to level with you. You're not getting out of here alive." She pokes the barrel of the gun in the fleshy skin on my cheek. "You know too much. Besides, your death will devastate them all, and it will send a direct warning. They'll hear about the cops I shot dead in the cruiser after we left your house, and when your mangled corpse is discovered, they'll know I'm responsible for your death too. They'll be living in fear, and they are right to be afraid. I won't stop until I've taken everything and everyone she loves from her."

From my peripheral vision, I watch Addison edge quietly and carefully toward the stack of piled logs. "If I'm going to die, then you might as well tell me why. What did Alex ever do to you?"

"She stole my whole life!" Courtney roars. "She has the life I should have, and she's going to pay."

Addison chooses that moment—when Courtney is distracted by her rage—to strike. Accosting her from behind, she brings the log down on top of Courtney's head with force. Courtney didn't even see her coming. Addison swings the log a second time for good measure, and I watch as Courtney's eyes fade in and out. She falls off the chair, collapsing on the floor, unconscious.

"Hurry, Addison. Get me untied before she wakes."

Addison races to the kitchen, yanking drawers open. "Fuck!" she screams. "They're all empty."

"Here!" I yell, trying to lift my leg. "I have a knife strapped to my ankle. I can still feel it there." It's a miracle Courtney didn't find it when she was tying me up.

Addison sinks to her knees in front of me, pushing my jeans up and unstrapping the knife. She quickly sets about removing my restraints while I keep my eyes trained on the inert body on the floor. "Hurry the fuck up, Addison." My entire body is pumped full of adrenaline and I'm shaking all over. Her hands are shaking too as she fumbles with the bindings.

"For the record," she says, not looking up at me as she works to cut the last few ropes. "I'm not doing this for you. I still loathe you, and I want him back, but I can't fight for him if I'm languishing in a cell jail as an accessory to murder." She looks up, her gaze full of determination. "This is self-preservation, pure and simple. I draw the line at murder, and I sure as hell didn't want to see Ky framed for something he didn't do. She did all that on her own." She pierces me with a worried look. "She's totally flipped. Like psycho crazy, and after you came to me last night, I was going to go to the cops and confess everything. I swear. I know you love him, but I love him too, and I would never have let him go to prison."

The last bind snaps, and I'm free. I push off the chair with my hands, swaying as I struggle to my feet. My head pounds and my vision is unfocused again. Every part of my body throbs. Addison slides her arm around my waist and starts hauling me toward the door.

"For the record," I say, "I believe you." We share a look.

"Aw, you two have bonded. How cute," Courtney drawls, and I shriek when I hear the click of the gun.

Addison's eyes contort in panic as a wild, fluttery sensation kicks off in my chest. "Run!!" I yell the same time Addison screams.

Fireworks explode in my eardrums as the gun goes off.

Chapter Thirty-Four

Kyler

"Oh, fuck. That was a gunshot!" I turn panicked eyes on Brad. "Hurry the fuck up, man." I check the app on my cell, and our destination should be around the next bend. Brad does his best to floor the engine, but it's difficult on this narrow dirt track. If we'd had time, we could've taken Kade's truck, but I didn't want to waste a single second when I got back to the house and Brad told me Faye was missing. He showed me her note, and we'd headed straight to the Sinclair house. We had woken Addison's parents up and made them go up to her room. Predictably, she was missing too.

Now I know she has my baby, and I swear to God, I'll kill Addy if she has harmed a hair on Faye's head.

This is exactly what I was afraid of.

It's why I told the cops their little proposed setup was too much of a gamble. I won't ever willingly place Faye in harm's way.

Kev called when we were on the highway here, confirming the news that Courtney was the baby Addison's birth mom gave up when she was still in high school. Everything clicked into place then except I don't know who the ringleader is. Whether it's Addison or Courtney calling the shots.

Keven implored us to pull over. To wait for help. He thinks it's too dangerous to head in there on our own, but he doesn't get it. He's never loved any girl the way I love Faye. I'll die before I'll let anything happen to her again. I wasn't there for her when David almost took her life, and I'm fucked if I'm going to walk away now. I've seen enough crime shows to know that things can quickly get out of hand when the authorities are notified and that the hostage doesn't always make it out alive. I'm not prepared to risk Faye's life by notifying the authorities.

I'm going in there myself to save my baby, no matter what.

I'm pretty sure he's called Mom and Dad and the cops by now, but there's no way they'll get here before us. This place is too far off the beaten track, and the nearest cop station is miles away.

A second gunshot goes off as we round the bend, and a small decrepit wooden cabin comes into view. I curse. So much for stealth mode. We should've parked back there and made the rest of the trip on foot. The cabin is nestled on top of this godforsaken mountain, surrounded by a dense forest, and we would never have discovered it if Faye's cell had been discarded. Although we've been driving most of the night, and neither of us has had a lick of sleep, I'm wired tight and ready to pound someone into oblivion.

"Shit!" Brad exclaims. "How do you want to play this?"

"We're out of time, and there's no other option now but to bust our way in the front door. There's no way they didn't see us pull up." I remove Dad's gun from my pocket and unlock the safety. "Let's go."

I jump out of Brad's car the same time he does. He grips a baseball bat firmly between both hands as we race toward the cabin. I keep the gun in front of me as we approach the wooden structure. I bang on the door, and the wooden walls rattle. "We know you're in there, Addison and Courtney. And we know you have Faye. We're coming in, and I have a gun, so don't try anything or I'll shoot."

I lift my leg, ready to kick the door down when it swings open.

I point the gun at Courtney's forehead, desperately trying to conceal my fear. She has Faye in a vise-grip in front of her body. One arm is locked tight under Faye's neck, and the other holds the gun shoved into her temple. Faye is clawing at Courtney's arm, struggling to breathe. Her face is a bloody mess, and my protective instincts kick into overdrive. Rage is pummeling my insides, and in my head I'm screaming blue murder. If I get a hold of Courtney, nothing or no one will stop me from killing her. I'll rip her from limb to limb with my bare hands, and still it won't be enough. "Let her go or I'll shoot you," I demand.

Courtney laughs, and a maniacal glint illuminates her eyes. She's totally insane. "Come now, darling brother of mine. Don't even pretend like you have any power in this situation. You will do as I say or I'll kill her right now." She moves her finger on the trigger, and panic floods my veins.

"Don't!" I push the barrel of my gun in Courtney's forehead. "Let her go and take me. I'm the one Addison wants after all."

"That ship has sailed," Courtney smirks, flicking her eyes to the floor.

My heart almost arrests at the sight of Addison, face down on the ground, with blood pooling underneath her from an obvious bullet wound in her back. "You shot your own sister?"

Courtney shrugs, as if it's commonplace to murder your own flesh and blood. "She failed me. She was trying to help this little bitch escape." She tightens the hand around Faye's neck, and a strangled plea rips from Faye's mouth. Blood lust thrums through my veins, and it's taking considerable willpower not to lunge for Courtney and throw my girl free. But I can't risk it. The gun is prodding Faye's skull, and I can't risk Courtney pulling the trigger. Dammit.

Brad growls beside me in shared frustration. Faye's terror-filled eyes meet mine, and the truth of Courtney's statement rings true in her gaze.

"Here's how this is going to go down," Courtney says. "You will both drop your weapons on the floor and move into the middle of the room."

Brad and I exchange impassive expressions, but we know each other well enough to read the meaning behind the cool exterior. We have no choice but to do as she says and wait for an opportunity to gain the upper hand.

The click of the gun is like a knife straight through my heart. I whip my gaze to Faye's, watching her visibly gulp as alarm skitters over her face.

"I wasn't asking," Courtney snaps. "Do it. Now." I place my gun on the ground as Brad drops the baseball bat. It hits the floor with a loud thud. Courtney kicks both weapons off to the side, maneuvering herself and Faye to the left of the door and ushering us forward. Stepping over the inert body of my ex wasn't on my list of things to do to Addison. No matter what she did, she didn't deserve to die like this.

Courtney backs us up against two chairs occupying the middle of the floor. She drags them beside one another and shoves me down into one. "Tie his hands behind his back," she commands Brad. "The rope is on the table." She forces Faye to her knees in front of me, prodding the gun into the back of her head. "Don't try anything. Either of you. Or I'll put a bullet through her skull."

Faye pants, sucking in fretful breaths.

"It's okay, baby." I try to keep my voice and my expression calm. She needs to believe we have this under control, even though that's the opposite of the truth.

"Did I say you could fucking speak?!" Courtney shrills, narrowing her eyes at me. "*It's okay, baby*." Her voice mimics mine, but I refuse to rise to the bait, locking eyes with Faye instead of looking at the psycho lording it over all of us.

She grips Faye's chin with force, keeping the gun at the back of her head. Her nails dig into Faye's skin, drawing blood.

"Leave her alone." The threat bubbles out of my mouth in a low, dark tone of voice. "I'm going to fucking kill you, Courtney. And I'm going to enjoy every second of it."

She chuckles, and I surge to my feet, ready to pounce, but Brad steps in between us, cautioning me with his eyes.

"Agghh," Faye cries out and blood turns to ice in my veins. Brad is blocking my view so I don't know what's happened. He steps aside, and my chest tightens. It goes against all my instincts not to rush to Faye's side, but I can't push Courtney too far, or it could end in disaster. Faye is hunched over on the ground, clutching her stomach and whimpering. Courtney is hovering over her, pointing the gun at her body.

"Try anything like that again, and I'll kill her stone dead. I'm only keeping her alive at this point to torture you into submission. So, please, be my guest, keep pulling shit like that so I can take it out on her."

I slump back in the seat, utterly dejected. All I'm doing is making things worse for Faye. I move my hands behind the back of the chair as Brad loosely ties the rope around my wrists.

"Not so fast, Brad," Courtney demands, dragging Faye up by the hair. Tears are rolling down Faye's face, but she doesn't cry out or say anything.

Courtney pulls her around behind my chair, and laughs. "Yeah, thought you might try that. Tie that rope tight. Until I see his flesh turning red with the strain."

Brad reluctantly complies, and there's no way I'm getting out of this chair anytime soon. I'm starting to get really worried, and I'm struggling to see how we're all going to get out of this alive. I can only hope that whoever Kev called is on their way and they get here in time.

"I do hope Mommy and Daddy are on their way here, Kyler. I'd hate them to miss the grand finale," Courtney says, nudging Brad into the chair beside me.

"I hate to disappoint you, but no one knows we're here," I lie, wanting to lull her into a false sense of security.

"Nice try, Kyler, but I'm not buying it. Besides, by now they will know something is wrong even if you didn't tell them. Why do you think I kept Faye's cell on?"

Shit. Of course, Courtney would know that all our cells have tracking apps. I should've known. I was the one who called Courtney after Faye's cell broke her first day here. I was the one who asked Courtney to get a new one for her. I feel sick as realization dawns. "This was a trap."

"Now you're getting it." She pushes Faye on the ground behind Brad's chair. "Tie him up." She throws back her head, cackling like the Wicked Witch of the West, laughing at some joke we're not privy to. "I'll bet under different circumstances you'd love the sound of that, Brad, or have you gotten over your little crush?"

"Fuck you, Courtney."

Keeping the gun pointed at Faye, she kneels down beside him and smooths a hand over the front of his jeans. I puke a little in my mouth. "You know I'd be so down for that. I've always thought you were hot, and when I saw the tape Addy made of you two, I must admit I was jealous." She moans, and my gag reflex kicks in. "Who knew committing murder could be such a turn on?" Licking her lips, she continues to stroke him, noticing the growing tent situation the same time I do. "I do believe you're turned on too," she whispers, her eyes filling with lust and I'm wondering if we might use this new development to our advantage.

"I'd rather fuck a dead dog. This is a pure physiological reaction, that's all," Brad responds automatically. "You gross me out."

Faye is fumbling with the binds on his hands, and I shoot her a knowing look over my shoulder. But Courtney isn't as oblivious as she'd like us to think. Yanking her hand from Brad's crotch, she grips Faye by the shoulder. "Tie it tighter, bitch."

"Don't fucking talk to her like that," I grit out, thrashing about on the chair. I shoot her my most venomous look.

"Pipe down, little bro. I was beginning to doubt the same DNA flowed through our veins, but you're just like him, aren't you? I've seen the same anger, the same aggression, the same disregard for women in you."

Her earlier comments return to me now, and I think I'm going to be sick as I join the last few dots. It's obvious Courtney was calling the shots, which means she killed my dad. Ignoring the bait, I focus on the other reality. "Doug was your father too? That's why you killed him?"

She drags Faye around so they're both facing us. Forcing Faye to her knees again, she wraps her hand around her neck at the front, and sticks the gun in the back of her skull again. "Please," she laughs. "That man was on borrowed time, and just because he was there when I was created gives him no right to call himself my father. I did us all a favor." An evil glint appears in her eye. "I followed you all the way from Wellesley, and I waited outside while you were in his house. After you left, I knocked on Doug's door. I hadn't intended to kill him. I was hoping to blackmail him into helping with my plan, but before I could tell him that, before I could tell him who I was, do you know what he did?"

Anger blazes in her eyes.

"He put his hand up my skirt! He felt up his own daughter! Told me I was beautiful and he would fuck me so hard I wouldn't be able to sit down for a week. I knew right then that pig had to die. The idea to plant the gun in your room came later. It was genius."

She sends me a gloating look, pausing momentarily as if she's expecting a pat on the back or a gold medal.

"If I didn't hate your mother, I might actually feel sorry for her. Framing you for his murder was the cherry on top of my revenge pie." She glances briefly over her shoulder. "I can't wait until Alex gets here. Until she understands that she's lost. That I win. That I *always* win."

Brad urges me to keep her talking with his eyes. I sense the subtle movement behind me as he quietly works to free his hands. Diverting Courtney with talk of Doug Grant worked. She was too distracted to notice Faye hadn't tied the binds as tight as she instructed. "Why exactly do you hate my mom so much?"

"She ruined my life, and I've made it my life's mission to make her pay for that."

"I don't understand," I say, although I have an inkling where this is going.

She kneels on the ground behind Faye, keeping her hand secured firmly around her neck. I want to rip her insides out with a pitchfork. "Doug Grant got my mother pregnant when she was fifteen. He swore faithfully that he loved her and that he would stand by her if she promised never to reveal who fathered her child. His motocross career was only starting to take off, and a scandal like that would have finished him. He would've gone to jail for sleeping with a minor. My grandmother intervened, forcing Wendy to give me up for adoption when she refused to put the father's name on my birth cert. By then, Doug was making a name for himself on the motocross circuit and he was away a lot. They grieved for me and made plans to get me back."

She shakes her head, and unadulterated anger flickers across her face. "He filled her head with a load of crap that she fell for. When she was twenty, he set her up in the trailer park and promised her he'd make an honest woman of her. Promised he would find me and we would be a family. He strung her along for a few more years, making empty promises he had no intention of keeping. He was also sleeping with Alex for some of that time, and when she got pregnant with Kaden, he decided he wanted to settle down with her. That she was a much better prospect. He broke things off with Wendy, shattering her heart and her dreams."

She turns hatred-fueled eyes on me. "If your mother hadn't come along, my life would've been so different. Instead, I was bounced from foster home to foster home. Had all manner of horrific things done to me in care. It's Alex's fault that I grew up without my family. When I turned nineteen, I tracked Wendy down, and she explained it all to me, and I set about exacting my revenge. I took my time, planned it all out. I only went to college so I could get a degree and use that to get a job in your mother's office."

I glare at Courtney. "My mom isn't at fault for that man's actions. It's hardly Alex's fault if Wendy couldn't hold onto her man." That earns me a slap to the face. As my head whips around, I cast a quick glance at Brad's hands. The rope is loosening and it should only take another couple minutes before his hands are free.

"It *is* all your mother's fault!" Courtney screams, and the hand around Faye's neck loosens a bit. Faye looks at me intently. Her eyes casually drift to Courtney's hand and she gnashes her teeth in a subtle communication. I nod once, quickly, confirming my understanding.

This is risky, but it's all we've got. We may not get another opportunity. I sense Courtney is coming to the end of her story, and I fear what that means for us.

Brad and I share a quick look, and I detect the understanding in his gaze. "And I won't stop until I've taken her life from her in the same way she took mine from me." Courtney continues ranting. "I was so close! I had James where I wanted him, and I was only five days away from gaining control of the company, and she had to go and ruin everything for me. Now, she'll be sorry." She glowers at me. "Now she will watch as I kill you. As I kill James. Then I'll take her with me and make her watch as I kill the rest of her precious sons." She makes a popping sound with her tongue and the side of her mouth. "Pop, pop, pop. And they all fall down." She roars laughing, and Brad coughs. Faye's surprisingly alert eyes latch on mine and I nod.

It's now or never.

Faye sinks her teeth into Courtney's hand, biting down really hard, giving it everything she's got. Courtney howls out in pain, dropping the gun involuntarily. It skids across the floor, coming to rest close to Addison's prostrate form. Brad lunges out of his chair, sliding across the floor with his hand outstretched. But Courtney recovers quickly, digging her elbow sharply into Faye's back, and Faye yells out, crumpling to the floor in a ball. Jumping up, Courtney makes a grab for the gun the same time Brad does. They wrestle on the floor, as I shunt forward in my chair toward Faye. "Baby, can you move? Can you untie me?"

Using her hands, she pushes off the floor until she's on all fours. Slowly, she starts crawling around my chair. Brad yells, and I look over, aghast as he curls up, clutching his groin and rolling in agony. The bitch must have kneed him in the balls. My eyes widen in pure dread as Courtney staggers to her feet, swaying a little, but her grip on the gun is firm. "Oh, you really shouldn't have done that." She stalks toward Faye with her arm extended and her finger curling around the trigger on the gun.

Mad panic seizes control of me, and I stagger to my feet, still strapped to the chair, and charge at Courtney.

The noise of the gun going off reverberates in the room, dulling my senses. A burst of pain hits my upper body, and I fall awkwardly to the ground as unconsciousness overwhelms me.

Chapter Thirty-Five

Faye

The gunshot goes off, and the ringing in my ears intensifies. A scream erupts from my mouth of its own volition. Ky's chair clangs noisily, the wooden slats splintering the second it impacts the floor. Terror grips my heart as I watch his head whack against the floor. I scream again, sliding toward him on my belly. The force of the gunshot sent Courtney flying to the ground on her butt, but that woman is like a cat with nine lives. She is climbing to her feet as the door of the cabin slams open and a swarm of heavily armed men dressed in black fatigues with yellow FBI lettering across their chests burst into the room.

I've never felt so relieved or so grateful to see anyone in my life. When Adam showed up to save me in the diner, I was too badly injured to feel emotion of any kind, but now relief swathes me in a blanket of gratitude. I can hardly hear over the shouting and the ringing in my ears, and my eyes dart wide as I scramble to take everything in. My eyes land on Ky, and my gratitude dissolves as renewed panic emerges. Sobbing, I drag myself over to him as my heart aches in my chest. Blood is gushing out of a wound in his shoulder, and he's completely unconscious. I reach his side and touch my finger to his neck, almost collapsing in relief when I feel the weak thud of his pulse. He's still alive. Crying hysterically, I place my hand over the wound and press down firmly in a desperate attempt to stem the flow of blood. "Baby, I'm here. It's over. We're safe. Please wake up. Please don't leave me,

Ky. Don't you dare die." Tears plop down my cheeks and onto his face. I lower my mouth to his, and the warmth of his lips goes some way toward reassuring me.

Steady arms lift me up from behind, and I thrash about, adrenaline surging through my veins, giving me a new burst of energy. "Let me go," I half-yell, half-cry. "He needs me!"

"It's okay, Faye. I'm Agent Cooper and you're safe." His voice is muffled, and it's as if I'm hearing him from far away.

I wriggle about as he lifts me into his arms. "Put me down! I need to stay with him!"

"Listen to me, Faye. You're injured and you need medical attention."

"I'm fine. Ky needs help! Get the medics in here. Please. He's been shot." I burst out crying as the words leave my mouth. She shot him. That bitch shot him. I hope she rots in jail for the rest of her life. I hope they lock her skanky, crazy ass in the worst prison and she gets pounded on every day for the rest of her miserable life.

"We are taking care of your friends. Look." Very gently, he turns my head in Ky's direction. A team of medics surround him, lifting him carefully onto a gurney.

"I love him," I cry. "He can't die. Promise me you won't let him die." I grip his shoulders with more strength than I thought I possessed. "Promise me or I'm not leaving."

"Here," he says, handing me off to another agent. "Hold her for a minute." He goes over to one of the medics, talking quietly in his ear. When he returns, he takes me back into his arms and walks outside. "Your boyfriend is going to be fine. He took a bullet to the clavicle, but it doesn't look like it hit an artery. He's lost some blood, but he should be fine. They are going to airlift you both to hospital. We're just waiting for the chopper to land."

The early morning sun assaults my eyes, and I lean my head on his shoulder, blocking out the blinding light.

"Faye!" Brad's urgent tone reverberates around the forest, and I lift my head, squinting to see what direction the sound came from. "Faye, are you okay?" he asks, running toward me with some difficulty. A myriad of blacked-out SUVs, three ambulances, and one fire crew with flashing lights are parked in front of the cabin. Various men and women in official uniforms float around me, some talking into cells and others conversing among themselves.

Brad grabs me out of Agent Cooper's arms, hugging me close. "Thank God, you're okay. Is Ky ...?"

"He got shot in the shoulder, and the agent said he should be okay, but I'm scared, Brad." I gulp. "What if he's not?" Fresh tears prick my eyes, and I start quaking in his arms.

Brad brushes tangled strands of my hair back off my face. "He's one of the most stubborn people I know, and he's also madly in love with you. He's not going anywhere, beautiful. He won't leave you. I'd stake my life on it."

I cling to Brad, sobbing profusely as a buzzing, whopping sound grows more insistent in the background.

"Faye. It's time to go," Agent Cooper says, landing a gentle hand on my shoulder. "The chopper is here." He reaches out for me.

"I'll carry her," Brad says, holding me tight to his chest.

"Son, you look beat."

"I'm fine." Brad shakes off his concern. "I've got her."

Agent Cooper nods, walking silently alongside us as Brad limps toward the chopper. I lift my head up, wiping my tears with the sleeve of my hoodie. A mix of blood and grime streaks across the cotton, and I shudder to think of the state of my face. My body aches like a bitch, but it doesn't feel like anything's broken. Up ahead, Ky is being loaded into the chopper. As we approach, I urge Brad to let me down. "Can he come with us?" I implore Agent Cooper.

"Afraid not. There isn't room, and his injuries are minor. The ambulance will take him to the hospital, and he'll only be a couple of hours behind you."

"Where are we?" I ask, as a kind woman with soft hazel eyes helps me into the chopper.

"We're in Philadelphia," Brad confirms. "This land belongs to Addison's father's family, but it's mostly abandoned."

Before the medic straps me into my chair, I lean out and kiss Brad on the cheek. "Thanks for coming to rescue me."

"There was no way we weren't coming," he replies, pressing a kiss to my forehead. "I'm so glad you're okay. We were both absolutely terrified the whole trip here."

"Miss. We need to take off now." The medic nods at me.

"I'll see you in the hospital, Brad."

He blows me a kiss, as Agent Cooper hauls ass into the helicopter. The medic helps strap me into my harness, and I reach out, resting my hand on top of Ky's. They have cut off his shirt, and a makeshift bandage covers the place where the bullet entered his body. Dried blood is caked over his chest and he looks deathly pale. A tube flows into a vein in his hand, pumping intravenous fluids into his body. I squeeze his hand, hating how cool his touch is. The female medic places a blanket over his body just as the chopper starts to elevate off the ground. Keeping my hand securely fixed in Ky's, I lean my head back against the headrest and pray like I've never prayed before.

Despite my protests, we are separated the minute we arrive at the hospital. I'm taken to an examination room, while Ky is brought straight through to surgery. A couple of hours later, I'm back in a hospital bed, wearing a yucky hospital gown, with a thick beige dressing around my torso. At least this time most of my injuries are superficial except for the two cracked ribs I have courtesy of the swift kick Courtney delivered earlier.

Every doctor or nurse who walks through the door is subjected to my volley of questions, but the answer is always the same. "Mr. Kennedy is still in surgery, and his condition is described as stable."

My head jerks up when the door to my room swings open again. I breathe a sigh of relief as Alex, James, and all my cousins pile into the room, crowding the small space. Kal is on top of me instantly, cradling my head gently as he kisses my temple. "You're getting way too fond of this place," he teases.

"Kalvin!" Alex chastises. "This is no laughing matter." She rounds the bed on the other side, leaning down to kiss my cheek. "Sweetheart, you scared the life out of us. The three of you did."

One by one, my cousins come to my side, hugging and kissing me. Even Kent. And there's no smartarse remark out of his mouth either. Wonders will never cease.

"How is Ky?" I ask in a rush. "They won't tell me anything."

"They haven't told us much either," James admits from the foot of my bed. "All we know is that his injury isn't life threatening and he should make a full recovery."

I practically sink into the bed. "Thank God." I clutch a hand to my chest. "That's what Agent Cooper told me, but I couldn't be sure he was telling me the truth."

The door creaks open, and Brad enters the room. My face lights up. He strides to my bed, bending down to kiss my cheek. "How are you feeling?"

"I'm a bit sore, but it's not as bad as ..."

I trail off as Adam appears in the doorway, breathless and red-cheeked as if he's just run a marathon. He eats up the gap between us, reaching my side in a second. Brad moves aside, allowing him to get closer. Tears shine in his eyes as he scans me from head to toe.

"I'm alive!" I joke, my voice warbling as I put on a funny accent and wiggle my fingers in the air.

He looks like he wants to tear strips off me but thinks better of it. "I thought we agreed you weren't going to do this to me again?" He is deliberately keeping his tone lighthearted, and I know that's purely for my benefit.

"Sorry," I whisper. "It wasn't intentional. I was just trying to get Addison to admit to setting Ky up. I didn't want him arrested for something he didn't do."

"Sweetheart." James sighs. "You should have waited like your cousins told you." He gestures toward Keven and Kal. "Ky wasn't arrested."

I frown. "He wasn't?"

James shakes his head. "No. The police wanted it to look like that so it would get back to Courtney and Addison. When we were at the station, they explained how they had been tracking the girls' movements and they knew one or both of them were involved in Doug Grant's murder. They wanted Ky to wear a wire and arrange to meet Addison. He was going to try and trick her into confessing."

"What?" I shout. "Why didn't anyone tell me that?" I flop my head down on the pillow, frustrated that I put all our lives in danger for nothing.

"We were going to when we got back home, but you'd already left."

"Did you know?" I ask Brad, and he shakes his head.

"I was late coming back from my aunt's and cell coverage was patchy. I only got your messages when I arrived in Wellesley. When you weren't picking up, I went straight to your room and found your note. Then Ky came back, and I showed it to him, and we just took off. When we reached Addison's house and neither of you were there, we knew you were in trouble. On the way Kev called and told us Courtney was Addison's half-sister, and we figured it out. Then he tracked your cell, and we headed straight for you."

"And none of you thought to inform an adult?" That's from Adam. His furious expression bounces from Keven to Kal to Brad.

"As soon as I discovered the Courtney connection, and I realized the danger they were in, I called my parents," Keven admits. "And for the record," he adds, crossing his arms over his chest, "*I'm* an adult."

"That's how the FBI came to be there?" I ask.

Brad clears his throat. "Not quite. Turns out the FBI have been following me."

"That was who was in the black SUV all this time?" I ask, arriving at the obvious conclusion.

He nods. "Turns out they had bugged the house, my car, and my cell too. They were hoping Dad would reach out to me and they'd get some lock on his location. They were listening in as Ky and I headed to the cabin, and they sent out a team. I had my cell set to record while Courtney was spilling her guts, and they have her whole confession on tape."

"She's never going to see the light of day again," James confirms.

"What about Addison?" I ask, feeling slightly guilty for only thinking of her now. "Is she dead?"

"We don't know," Alex replies.

"She tried to save me," I tell them. "And I believed her when she said she didn't know Courtney had escalated to murder. She seemed genuinely afraid of her."

"Pity she didn't have an attack of conscience at an earlier stage," James supplies. "Then all of this could've been avoided."

The door opens and a nurse sticks her head in. “Mr. and Mrs. Kennedy?” James and Alex whip around, sharing equally terrified expressions. The nurse smiles warmly. “I just wanted to let you know that your son is out of surgery. He’s awake and he’s fine.” She turns her focus my way. “He’s asking for you, Faye.” She comes into the room, pulling a wheelchair behind her. “If you’re up for a quick visit?”

The covers are off and I have my legs halfway out of the bed before she even reaches me. “Are you kidding? Nothing would keep me from him. Take me to his room, please.”

Chapter Thirty-Six

Kyler

A moan slips out of my mouth as I come to. Mom's worried green eyes stare softly into my face. "Honey? How are you feeling?"

My shoulder throbs and I ache pretty much everywhere, but I don't care. We made it out alive. The first word out of my mouth when I woke earlier was "Faye." The nurse reassured me she's fine, and that hard knot in my gut loosened a little. I whip my head to the other side, and Dad smiles at me. The knot tightens again, and the monitor beside my bed starts beeping. "Where is she?" I ask. "Where's Faye?"

"Sweetheart, calm down, she's fine." Mom pats my hand. "She was here earlier, but you were asleep. We'll send for her now."

"I need to see her." I turn pleading eyes on Dad. "Please, Dad."

He squeezes my hand. "I'll get her, son. She's been worried about you as well." He stands up.

"Thank you."

He exits the room, and I turn toward Mom. Her eyes are bloodshot and swollen. "You gave us one hell of a scare, Kyler. I was terrified we'd lost you." Tears stream down her face. "And all I could think was how your last memories of me were horrible ones. I don't know if you can ever forgive me for the past, but I swear to you that I will never stop trying to make things right between us. I love you, Kyler. I love you so much, and if anything had happened to you today, a part of me would've died too."

A soulful pang hits me in the chest as thoughts of the last twenty-four hours invade my mind. It brings a sense of clarity, a form of peace. I thread my fingers through hers. "Mom, I love you too. It's okay, you're forgiven."

She can barely see over her tears. "Really, sweetheart?" I try to lift her hand to my lips, but the searing hot pain in my shoulder stops me in my tracks. I wince, gritting my teeth and forcing back the tears that automatically well in my eyes. "Honey, don't try to move on that side. You're going to be out of action for a few weeks, I'm afraid." She leans in and kisses my forehead. "You're still my baby. You'll always be my baby. These last few months have been difficult for all of us, but it's over now. I think this is the fresh start we all need."

"I like the sound of that." I smile.

She beams at me. "You've changed, Kyler. Grown up."

I contemplate her words. "Not really, Mom. I've just kept this side of me hidden. I was angry over what happened, and then with everything that transpired with Addison and Brad, I felt like I couldn't trust anyone."

"Until Faye." She smiles knowingly.

"I love her, Mom." I stare earnestly into her eyes. "This is not just some teenage crush, some fleeting relationship. When I'm with her, I feel like I'm free. Free to be myself without fear. Free to open up and tell her the things I've been hiding in my heart. Free to love with the whole of my heart. I feel like I'm breathing for the first time in years. Like I've found where I belong. She makes me feel alive, and so unbelievably happy. I know I'll never feel this with anyone else. I'm going to marry her someday, Mom."

A loud cough from the doorway startles me. Dad grins as I jerk my head up. "You might want to keep that sentiment to yourself around Adam. At least for a little while."

Faye is sitting in a wheelchair in front of Dad, dressed in a hospital gown and sporting a multitude of bruises and cuts across her face. She is still the most stunningly beautiful creature I've ever seen. A smattering of tears glistens in her eyes. "That was beautiful," she whispers. "And I feel the same. I want to share my life with you." Mom and Dad exchange a wistful look.

"Dad." He chuckles at my impatient tone, wheeling Faye over to my side. I peel back the covers on my uninjured side.

Dad opens his mouth to protest, but Mom jumps in there first. "Let them be. They're in love. I can still remember what that feels like." She walks around the bed and helps Faye get in beside me. "No sudden movements, either of you." She pins us with a cautionary look. "You both need to let your injuries heal."

I crank out a laugh. "I don't know what you and Dad got up to when you first got together, but banging Faye in this hospital bed is not part of my agenda. I've way more respect for her than that."

"Wow. Delicately put, Kyler." Dad smirks. "I notice you didn't refer to your injuries."

I snort. "I'm injured, Dad. Not dead. Where there's a will, there's a way." Now it's my turn to smirk. Faye nestles into my side, giggling.

Mom exhales loudly. "Well, on that note, I think we'll leave you two to *talk*."

"Dad?"

"Yes, Kyler."

"I want to say something. It's something I should've said sooner." I kiss the tip of Faye's nose. Then I look at him and unburden my heart. "I love you, Dad. I know we fight and stuff, but it doesn't mean I don't love you. It doesn't matter that you weren't the one to conceive me because anyone can do that. But it takes someone special to be a dad—someone like you. You're the only dad I'll ever want."

Dad approaches the other side of my bed. When he leans down to rest his forehead on mine, his eyes are wet. "You have no idea how much it means to hear that, and it works both ways, kiddo. It doesn't matter that my blood doesn't flow in your veins. You are a part of me, and I'm a part of you, and that's the natural order of things. You have always been *my* son. You will always be *my* son. I'm very proud of the man you're becoming, Kyler. Never forget that."

A choked sob erupts from Faye, breaking the heaviness in the air. We all laugh. "I'm feeling so emotional. I think my heart could burst with joy." She lands her hand delicately on my chest. "Isn't he great?" Her gaze flits between Mom and Dad.

"You're both great," Dad says, leaning over to kiss her on the forehead. "I'm so glad you came into our lives, Faye, and I'm very happy you have found each other. Treasure one another, and never forget that what you share is so special few people ever get to experience it." Sadness creeps into his face, and I know he's recalling happier times with Mom.

"Come on." Mom tugs on Dad's elbow. "Let's give them some space."

The door closes with a small snick, and I angle my face so I'm staring down into her eyes. "How much do you hurt?" My fingers sweep across her face, examining all the cuts and grazes and the bruising rising to the surface on her skin.

"I've two broken ribs, and I'm achy all over, but it's not so bad."

I press my lips into her hair. "Always so brave," I murmur.

"I was so scared, Ky," she whispers, and her warm breath leaks over my neck. I shiver and my body temp elevates. "When you threw yourself at Courtney and the gun went off, I was so terrified I could barely look. I thought you were dead!" Her voice trembles, and I wrap my good arm around her, holding her tight to my side.

"Ssh, babe. I'm okay. We're okay." I press my lips to her forehead. "Although I do have a bone to pick with you. What were you thinking of? Running off to meet Addison on your own like that? It was far too dangerous!"

Her features soften. "You are always protecting everyone, and I wanted to be that person for you this time. I wasn't going to let you go down for this. Not without a fight." She wets her lips, and I covet the motion. "No one protected you when you were ten, and I'm not going to let that happen ever again. I'll always have your back, Ky."

Tears prick my eyes, but I blink them away. "You have no idea how incredible it feels to hear that, and how grateful I am that you want to be there for me, but you have to promise you won't put yourself in harm's way again. I can't bear the thought of losing you." I crush her to my chest, feeling instantly relaxed. She cannot fathom how much she means to me. "We're lucky we got out of there alive," I whisper a few minutes later.

"Not all of us," she mumbles. "Addison ..."

"Addison is alive, Faye." I run my hand up and down her back.

"What?" She blinks up at me.

I nod. "Her parents stopped by to see me when I first woke up. She's still in surgery, and they don't know if she's going to make it, but technically, she's alive. The bullet hit her spine though, so if she survives, the likelihood is she'll be paralyzed."

"How do you feel about that?"

"She's gone out of her way to hurt me and those I love, so it's hard to find any compassion in my heart for her, but ... she tried to help you escape, and I'd like to think she'd seen the error of her ways. She still deserves to be punished but not like that."

"I agree, and she does actually love you in her own warped way. I think if Courtney hadn't gotten into her head, she wouldn't have done any of the stuff she did."

"Guess we'll never know." My hand wanders lower. "But enough talking about her. I want to talk about us. You know what this means?"

"What?"

I smooth the grooves in her forehead with my thumb. "All the shit is out in the open now, and we can finally move forward with our lives. Plan for college. Plan for our future. Date and be a normal couple for a change."

She sighs contentedly. "God, I love the sound of that."

"Me, too, and I can't wait to start all that with you."

She uncurls her fist, holding her palm up to me. "Agent Cooper found it on the floor of the cabin, and he returned it to me." The double heart pendant I gave her rests in her palm. "The chain is broken, but the hearts are intact. Just like us."

I close my hand over hers, curling both our hands around the pendant. "We're not broken, Faye." She pins me with one of those looks, and I know she's seconds away from arguing. "Okay, maybe on the outside, but inside? In here"—I touch my chest and then hers, right in the place where our hearts beat in sync—"we're whole. I wasn't always, but you fixed me. Just by breathing the same airspace. Just by staying by my side through all the crap. Just by loving me. I meant what I said to Mom. I *am* going to marry you one day, if you'll have me. And until then, ensuring your happiness is my number one goal. I'm going to prove that I'm worthy of you."

"Oh, Ky." She tips her chin up and kisses me softly. "You big romantic, you." She grins, kissing me again. "Don't you know you already have?"

Epilogue

Seven Months Later

Kyler

"Faye?" I holler, cupping my hands around my face. "Babe, come on! We're going to miss our flight." Not that I'd mind—then I'd have an excuse for commissioning the private jet to take us to Ireland, but Faye is determined that we're going to be a normal couple in every sense of the word. And we've been following that motto, dating up a storm and doing all the usual stuff couples our age do. I can honestly say the last seven months of my life have been some of the happiest I've ever known.

Faye means the world to me, and I'd trek to the moon and back to give her everything she wants and needs.

And that's how I've ended up here—trying to psych myself up for my first charter flight.

She opens her bedroom door and pops her head out, looking up the corridor. I lean against the doorframe from my position in the lobby. "Baby, I'm almost ready. Promise." She holds up a palm. "Just gimme five."

I glance at my watch, tapping one finger off it. "I'm timing you," I shout as her head retreats back into her room.

"I am so looking forward to seeing the back of you two," Kent pipes up behind me.

"Excuse me?" I spin around to face him.

"*Baby. Babe.*" He mimics our voices, slapping a hand against his forehead. "I swear all your mushy talk has actually irreparably damaged my brain."

"Hell no. You're not pinning that one on us. Blame the bimbos and the booze."

"Now, now, bro." He slants a smug look my way. "Lose the jealous streak. You chose to tie yourself to one pussy at eighteen, so don't take it out on the rest of us."

"Once a douche, always a douche," I joke, grabbing him into a headlock. He doesn't get it. None of my brothers do. Everything comes back to Faye. I have the girl of my dreams, and she loves me as much as I love her. That's all that matters to me.

"Screw off, asshole," Kent yells, trying to elbow me in the ribs.

I muss up his hair, knowing how much he hates it, and then shove him away. "Miss you already, you little shit."

Keaton and Keanu amble into the lobby then. "Cutting it a bit close?" Keanu suggests, looking at the clock on the wall.

"Try telling that to your cousin," I deadpan. "I'm all packed." I gesture at the large black duffel bag by my feet.

"Girls need more stuff," Keaton unhelpfully supplies. "And it's their prerogative to keep their men waiting."

"Dude," Kent says, pinning Keaton with a strange look. "That's some weird shit coming out of your mouth right there."

"Thanks for your blinding observation," I retort. "But it's not exactly helpful."

"I'll see if I can help," Keaton says, taking a step into the corridor.

"No need." Faye is nearly breathless as she runs up the corridor, hauling two massive bags on wheels behind her. "I'm ready," she pants out.

"About damned time." I reel her into my arms, and I'm instantly hard. The measure of time hasn't eroded the strength of my feelings for her. Or my lust. When it comes to Faye, I'm primed and ready twenty-four-seven. The scent of vanilla and lavender tickles my nostrils, and I bury my head in her hair.

"Dude. Did you just sniff her hair?" Kent asks, with a look of absolute disgust on his face.

"I did." I smirk, uncaring. I traded in my man card a long time ago. "I love how my girl smells. Shoot me if it's a crime."

"Bro," Keanu says, gesturing at my crotch. "Mom'll be here any second. You'd better disguise the boner."

Faye's head tips down, and I watch her eyes darkening with lust. "Fancy joining the mile high club?" I suggest with a wink.

Her eyes sparkle and then dull. "You haven't seen the size of the toilets on a commercial flight. I think that'll be a no." She looks disappointed.

"It wouldn't be an issue if we were taking the jet." I ravish her with one very suggestive look. "There's still time to change our minds."

She shakes her head. "No way, mister." She prods me in the chest. "You are not going to manipulate me with your amazing dick." A few splutters of laughter echo around us, reminding me we're not alone. "Besides, it's hardly a hardship. We're traveling first class when really we should be going economy for the full experience."

Hell to the no. I can still remember the argument we had when she first suggested that. I draw the line at economy. A guy has to have some standards. I hold up a hand in defeat. "Fine, but your ass is mine the minute we land on solid ground."

A mischievous glint appears in her eye. "Deal."

"Get your horny asses in the car," Kal commands, appearing at the front door. "Unless you actually want to miss your flight?"

"Wait!" Mom screeches, careening into the lobby. "You can't leave without a hug." She flings herself at me, holding me tight. Easing back, she pinches my cheeks. "Have a great time, honey, and we'll see you in three weeks."

Faye and I wanted to spend some time in Ireland on our own before the rest of the family descend, so everyone else is flying out later, and we're going to do the whole tourist vacation thingie then. I'm looking forward to seeing where Faye grew up.

Mom envelops Faye in a hug. "Mind yourself, and look after my boy." I roll my eyes. I'm eighteen now. In a committed relationship and attending Harvard in the fall. I'm hardly a *boy*.

"Of course," Faye responds. "I'll look after him *really well*. You have nothing to worry about." She says this is a sweet tone of voice with that fake, saintly grin on her face, and I have to smother my snort of amusement at the hidden meaning behind her words. My mind goes into overdrive mapping out the many ways I intend on having her once we get to her house in Ireland. With no one to disturb us, I plan on rocking my girl's world until she aches in places she didn't know existed.

But Mom's no fool. "You have that bag I gave you?" she asks, with an equally innocent smile. Faye gulps, nodding as her cheeks flush red. "Excellent." Mom smiles again before spinning around and thumping me in the upper arm.

I eye her suspiciously. "What the hell?"

"Do not get Faye pregnant!" My brothers dissolve into laughter. "I'm far too young to be a grandma."

It's on the tip of my tongue to call her out for hypocrisy, but I stop myself in time. We had been led to believe she got pregnant with Kade in Ireland when she first met Dad, but that's not how it went down at all. She already had two toddlers and me in her womb by the time she reached Irish shores. Our relationship with Mom has definitely improved since she sold Kennedy Apparel. While she is still consulting for them in an unofficial capacity, it's only a few hours a week, and she does most of it from home.

Having her around all the time was been wonderful but weird.

Dad moved out after Christmas, but he bought a house three miles away, so we see him all the time. While we still call here home, we tend to split our time fairly evenly between both parents. It's not ideal, but it could've been a lot worse. Surprisingly, their split was remarkably drama free. Even though both of them appear to be coping well, neither one of them is dating; I can't help feeling sad that it came to this. However, there's been no mention of divorce in months, and technically they are separated but still officially married. I know we're all hoping that somehow they'll find a way to reconcile.

My therapist is helping me process my feelings on everything that went down, but I'm making progress, and my bad days are few and far between now. Having Faye in my corner helps enormously. I honestly cannot imagine what my life was like before her. She illuminates my world in so many ways.

Courtney's case came to trial last month—a few weeks before we graduated—and reliving everything under the glare of so much publicity was pretty harrowing, but we got through it. They threw the book at her, and she'll spend the rest of her life behind bars. Addison was also dealt a life sentence of sorts. Paralyzed from the waist down, she's facing a much different future than the one she had planned. All charges against her were dropped, considering the circumstances. It helped that she didn't play any part in the murders Courtney committed, and Faye spoke out in her favor, testifying that she tried to save her.

David's trial has yet to pass. He's still hiding behind the insanity shield, but he'll get his day in court, too, and we'll be ready to face it, face *him*, when the time comes.

"Kyler." Mom clutches my arm, dragging me out of my head. "Did you hear me? No knocking that beautiful girl up. Not for a few years, at least. Then you'll have my full permission." She smiles dreamily. "I can just picture your cute kids."

"Mom!" *What the hell has gotten into her?* One minute she's telling me not to impregnate Faye and the next she's swooning over our imaginary children? My family is seriously insane.

Faye splutters, and I take that as my cue. Seizing her luggage, she starts hauling ass out the door, reaching out to grab me as she passes. "Bye, everyone!" she shouts. "We don't want to miss our flight." I chuckle at the sudden rush of urgency that was lacking a few minutes ago.

Faye

Oh em gee. I can't believe Alex just said that in front of everyone. Ground: open up and swallow me, please. I should be used to it by now. Ky's brothers tease us relentlessly over our relationship and privacy is a virtual impossibility around here. Which is part of the reason why I'm so excited to be going back home. For the first three weeks of our stay, we'll be living in my old family home. I have mixed feelings about being back there, but at least Ky will be with me this time, and I plan on making lots of new memories in that house. I'll need to decide what I'm going to do with it while I'm home, and I'm still in two minds. While a part of me can't bear to let go of the house that meant so much to my parents, another part of me believes selling it will release me from that last sliver of heartache.

I have moved on with my life, and my future is looking bright. I know that's what my parents would want, and I like to think they are looking down on me from heaven and approving of the choices I've made.

Keaton and Keanu swoop in, snatching my cases up and bringing them out to the car. Kal sweeps me up into his arms, twirling me around as he carries me outside.

"You're going to make her sick," Ky chastises him.

"Pussy," Kal retorts over his shoulder, before turning his smirking grin on me. "I should hate you for turning my brother into such a boring pansy-ass, but you're too adorable to hate."

"Gee, thanks." I slap him about the head. "And your brother is not a boring pansy-ass. Take it from me, he is anything but." I snigger, recalling in vivid Technicolor what we did last night. My cheeks heat at the memory.

"God," Kal groans, putting me down on my feet when we reach his car. "You two are disgustingly horny. It's abnormal. Mom's right—you are *so* going to come home pregnant."

"No, we're not." Ky wraps his arms around me from behind. "But we are going to have lots and lots of hot, dirty, sweaty sex." He grins at me, before leveling a smug look at his brother. "Jealous?"

Kal looks highly offended. "Who? Me? Not likely. I'm reformed, remember." Before we can respond, he's hopped into the driver's seat and shut the door.

We share a knowing look. Out of all of us, Kal has probably changed the most this last year. While he can't claim sainthood, he's definitely put his party-boy-player days behind him. He clams up if the subject of Lana ever crops up, but I know he isn't over her. Not by a longshot. But if the way he's gotten his act together is any indication, at least something positive came out of that whole sorry mess. Kal built up enough credits to skip senior year, and he just graduated with us. We're all going to Harvard together, and I couldn't be any more excited if I tried.

Ky opens the back door for me as Brad pulls up on his bike. I hate that Ky has decided to put his motocross ambition on hold, because I remember how much he loved it, but he hasn't been able to summon the same enthusiasm for it since all that stuff went down with Doug Grant.

I'm hopeful in time the spark will ignite in him again, and for now, I'm going to revel in the fact that we're going to college together and I'll get to see him every day.

Brad parks his bike and dismounts quickly, tugging the helmet off his head. "I thought for sure that I'd missed you." He runs a hand through his matted blond hair.

"We're running late because I left packing to the last minute."

He smirks. "Why doesn't that surprise me?"

I mock pout, punching him in the arm. "That's not true. I'm usually way more organized, but with graduating and sorting out some stuff back home before the trip and then visiting Adam at the weekend, I ran out of time."

"You know I'm only kidding."

Kal pokes his head out the window. "Seriously, guys, we need to leave. Now."

Casting a nervous glance in Ky's direction, Brad leans in and gives me the briefest of hugs. "Have a great time back home." He straightens up, flicking his head in Ky's direction. "And make sure he doesn't get into any trouble."

Ky groans. "Not you, too."

Brad arches a brow. "What did I say?"

Ky slaps him on the back. "Nothing, forget it. You sure you'll be okay here by yourself?" We really wanted Brad to come with the others on the second leg of our trip, but he bailed, citing commitments at the track and some extra classes he's taking to build up more college credits over the summer.

But we all know it's just an excuse.

Things are still strained between the three of us, although you wouldn't guess it looking from the outside in. I hate that there's still lingering tension between us, but it's the proverbial elephant in the room that none of us want to tackle head-on. I'd hoped it would be resolved before we move to Harvard, but that's looking unlikely at this point. I keep praying he'll meet someone special. Someone who'll help him forget all about me and then things will settle into a normal pattern, but Brad seems determined to avoid any and all potential relationships. *A constant revolving door of hook-ups and one-night stands?* No issue. *But the prospect of an actual relationship?* He's sworn off.

"Yeah, and I'm sure you'll get on just fine without me," Brad replies with a smile. To anyone else that would look on the level, but it's exactly this kind of talk that starting's to wear me down. Maybe when I'm home, I'll offer up a novena for his soul.

I hop into the back seat, lowering the window down. "Take care, Brad, and we'll see you when we're home." Ky slides into the passenger seat, tipping his head at Brad. Kal cranks the engine, and we wave at the others as the car glides down the driveway.

"Well, that was awkward," Kal deadpans.

I sigh. "Please, don't. I don't want anything putting a dampener on this trip." I sit forward in my seat, circling my arms around Ky's shoulders from behind.

Angling his head, he leans back and kisses me. "That's not going to happen, babe. We have. Three. Whole. Weeks. All. To. Ourselves."

My grin is almost electric, and I'm practically bouncing on the back seat. Ky holds my hands, and I lace my fingers in his. The prospect of all that alone time, showing him all my old hangouts, and getting to chill with Rach and Jill again has me giddy as a goat on steroids.

"Kent's right for once. You two are positively dripping in smug happiness and it's nauseating." The engine slows down. "Actually, I think I'm gonna puke." The car slows to a snail's pace, and he starts gagging.

"What?" I level an incredulous look his way.

"Ha! Gotcha going, didn't I?"

I roll my eyes, though I'm secretly pleased. Sometimes, I really miss Kal's juvenile humor and tactless jokes.

Ky slaps the back of his head. "Get a move on, slow poke. We've a plane to catch."

"What are you going to do about Dad and Adam?" Ky asks when we're out on the highway. Adam is going to join us for the last week of our trip. He wants me to meet his parents—my grandparents—while we're in Ireland even though the thought breaks me out in giant hives. Worse though is the prospect of James and Adam spending any length of time together. They still can't stand one another; they try their best to hide it, but they ain't fooling any of us.

"Probably the same thing you're going to do about your mom and dad sharing the same air for that length of time. Keep my head down, and steer clear of the fireworks." While everything has been very amicable with Alex and James, this will be the first time they are in each other's company as separated spouses while on vacation. I'd be lying if I said I wasn't a teensy bit worried about the atmosphere on the second leg of our holiday; however, I'm planning on being totes relaxed by the time the rest of the fam arrive, and I'm praying that'll help offset the incoming stress.

"Please tell me Whitney isn't coming?" Kal asks, glancing at me through the mirror. "I can't stand that kid."

I snort, although it doesn't stop the dull ache spreading in my chest. I've tried reaching out to my sister on several occasions, but she won't give me the time of day. I used to think my stubbornness was legendary, but it isn't a patch on Whitney Ryan's. "For real? She hasn't spent one second with me since the disastrous meet and greet in the house that day. She goes out of her way to avoid me, so I'd say it's safe to assume my sister won't be accompanying Dad and my brothers to Ireland."

Ky and Kal both jerk their heads around, staring at me with slack jaws.

I raise a hand to my face, wondering if I've some food remnants on my skin or if my lip gloss is smeared or something. "What?"

Ky's expression softens. "You just called Adam Dad."

My heart stutters in my chest. "I did?" I gulp over the sudden wedge of emotion in my throat. He nods, and I slump back in my seat. "Huh."

I stare out the window, quietly analyzing the implications of my slip of the tongue. I've enjoyed getting to know him and my half-brothers these last few months, and I can honestly say Adam has gone out of his way to take things easy with me. I've grown really fond of them, and it's as if they've always been a part of my life, but I've held back from calling him Dad because it still feels like such a dishonor to the man who raised me, and the only man I've ever called Dad.

I've been seeing a new therapist these last couple of months, and she's helping me deal with the aftermath of my near-death experiences and the family revelations that threatened to unhinge me. Gradually, I'm learning to let the past stay in the past, to live in the moment, and plan for my future.

Dad.

I roll it around on my tongue, envisioning how happy Adam would be if I called him that.

I owe him a lot. When I discovered he had secretly bought the diner—purely so I would continue to have a job—I'd never felt so conflicted in my life. As grand gestures go, it was right up there with the best of them, but it seemed so excessive and over the top, and I was actually really embarrassed about it for a good while. Once I got over the initial shock, and it turned into a sound business investment—the diner is a little gold mine—I was able to come to terms with it. Sorta. I don't think I'll ever feel one hundred percent comfortable with my American family's flippant attitude toward money, but I've learned to accept that's just how they are.

Considering everything Adam's doing for me, how patient and supportive he's been, even paying my tuition in Harvard and lining up a part-time job in the city, would it be that difficult if I called him that? Dad. I roll it around my tongue again, trying to get used to it.

"I can almost see the wheels churning," Ky says, twisting around to face me. "What's going through that beautiful head of yours? Talk to me, baby."

"If they're dirty, I don't want to hear them," Kal cuts in before I've had a chance to reply. "I haven't been laid since the Ice Age, so one naughty word and I'm primed to explode in my pants."

I scrunch my face up. "Ugh. Yuck visual. Thanks a bunch."

"I aim to please." He grins at me through the mirror, and I grin back.

Ky's earnest gaze hasn't faltered, and I know he won't give up until I tell him the truth. That's how we roll now. "I'm thinking about calling him Dad in public. I think he'd like that."

"Babe," Ky says, crawling in the back seat beside me. "Adam would *love* that, but you should only say it if it's what you feel in your heart."

I tap a finger idly off my lower lip as Ky drapes his arm around my shoulders. "You know what?" I look up at him. "I think I'm ready to embrace it."

He kisses me sweetly on the lips. "That's awesome."

"Almost as awesome as your amazing dick?" Kal asks, chuckling.

I stick my middle finger up at him. "I forgot you were listening." Ky always has that effect on me. It's as if the outside world ceases to exist and we're locked in our own private love bubble. "Besides, I thought you couldn't even think of naughty words without creaming your pants?"

He squirms in his seat. "Low blow, cuz. Real low blow."

"Kal." Ky applies his authoritative voice, the one he usually reserves for Kent. "Can you please just concentrate on the road. I'd really like to make it to Logan International with all my body parts intact."

The flight is delayed when we reach the airport, so we have a bit of time to kill. Kal comes in with us, and we grab a coffee. James phones, wishing us a safe trip. I know he's super excited about returning to Ireland, and we've already made tons of plans, including a visit to my parent's graves. My heart does a funny little twist. I can think of them now and not fall to complete pieces. It still hurts; I've no doubt it always will, but it doesn't cleave me wide open like it used to. My parents were the grounding force in my life, and I've so much to thank them for, including this new life they've given me. In requesting James as my guardian, they have set my life on a new path. All the hurt and anger at their betrayal has dissipated. I can focus on the positives and not dwell on the secrets and lies that threatened to drag me down.

Kal coughs, interrupting my thoughts. "Eh, guys." He scrubs a hand over his jaw. "I have something I need to tell you." We both fix our gazes on him. "I'm going to tell Mom and Pops this weekend so they'll have gotten over their hissy fit by the time we reach Ireland."

Oh, oh. That sounds ominous.

"Let's hear it," Ky says.

Kal's Adam's apple bobs in his throat, and he rubs his hands down the front of his pants. I haven't seen him this nervous since his trial. My sixth sense tingles as I wonder if this has anything to do with Lana.

"I'm not going to Harvard with you."

Ky and I exchange puzzled expressions. "What do you mean?" I ask. "I thought it was all sorted?"

"I need to branch out on my own." He levels solemn eyes on us. "And I want to major in architecture, and the University of Florida has a great program."

Ky's eyes pop wide, mirroring my own, although I think it's for different reasons. "Shit, bro." Ky sits bolt upright. "I'm all for following your own path but Florida? For real?"

Kal shrugs, and my eyes narrow suspiciously. "I've already been accepted and everything's set up. That's where I'm going. Besides, they have some off-site learning opportunities in Nantucket so I will get to spend some time closer to home."

I lean over and hug him. "I'll miss you, but I think it's great that you know your own mind and you're following your heart's desire." His cheeks flush a little, and I wonder if my suspicions are correct.

They call our flight and we all stand. Kal and Ky slap each other on the back, and I hug my cousin so tight he can hardly breathe. "Try and stay out of trouble," he tells us with a final cheeky wave as we make our way to the boarding area.

I'm still mulling it over in my head as we settle in our plush, first class seats. Ky nuzzles his head into my shoulder as we lock our harnesses in place. "What has put that little worry line on your forehead?" he muses.

Gosh, he doesn't miss a thing.

"Can I ask you something?"

He kisses me. "You know you can. Shoot." He sits back, entwining our fingers.

"Did Kal and Lana ever discuss going to college together back in the day?"

Ky jerks up and stares at me with a wary expression. "Okay. That's right up there on the randomness scale." His eyes narrow, and his mouth pulls into a tight line. "Does this have something to do with what Kal just told us?"

I nod.

He cups my face, rubbing his thumbs along my cheeks. "What is it, babe? What do you know?"

I stare deep into his eyes, and little bubbles of hope rise to the surface. Kal deserves to be happy, and I want that for him so badly. "Either destiny is fucking with our family again or Kal hasn't quite given up on Lana yet."

Ky looks perplexed. "Meaning?"

I lean in and kiss him slow and long as I contemplate the implications of what I'm about to say next. When I pull back, we are both flushed and devouring one another with our eyes. Unspoken promises fill the empty air between us, and I smile. Good. I need him in a relaxed mood when I tell him this.

I clear my throat, clasping his hands firmly in mine as I speak. "Meaning ... I happen to know for a *fact* that Lana is also attending the University of Florida this fall."

This concludes Faye and Kyler's love story although we most definitely haven't seen the last of them yet! Both will feature in later stories, most prominently in *Saving Brad*, book five in the Kennedy Boys series coming fall 2017. Meanwhile, the saga continues in *Loving Kalvin*, available to pre-order now. *Loving Kalvin* is Lana and Kalvin's love story, and it can be read as a standalone story in the series with an HEA and NO cliffhanger ending.

Subscribe to The Kennedy Boys newsletter to read exclusive bonus content, advance samples of future books, be the first to hear of discounts and freebies, and enter giveaways to win tons of cool stuff. Paste this link into your browser: http://smarturl.it/KennedyBoysList

Kennedy Boys Series - Future Books

This is the current list of provisional titles in this series. Please note release dates are subject to change and dependent upon continued demand. Subscribe to my newsletter and/or follow me on Facebook to get the most up to date information in relation to the series.

Loving Kalvin
*Saving Brad**
*Seducing Kaden^*
*Forgiving Keven^*
*Adoring Keaton^*
*Releasing Keanu^^*
*Reforming Kent^^*

*Releasing 2017
^Releasing 2018
^^Releasing 2019

Loving Kalvin

(The Kennedy Boys #4)

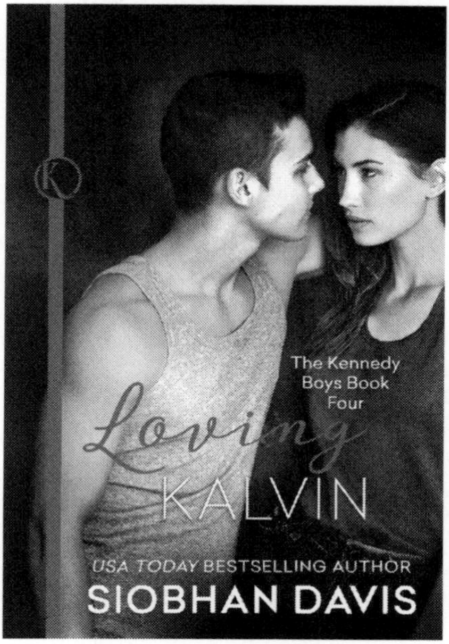

A second-chance romance from *USA Today* bestseller Siobhan Davis. Standalone with HEA and no cliffhanger.

Lana

I knew it would end in disaster, but I didn't listen to reason. I didn't care. Because I loved him so much.

Kalvin Kennedy ruled my heart.

Until he destroyed it.

Shattered it so completely that I became someone else. Someone I loathed. Someone who repeatedly lied to her loved ones.

So, I ran.

From him. From myself. Desperate to hide my new reality.

But I could only run so far.

When he reappears in my life, I'm terrified. Unbelievably scared of facing the consequences of my actions.

Never mind that I still love him and want him so badly—there's too much at stake now.

How can I trust him with the biggest secret of all when he's likely to rip my world apart again?

Kalvin

Lana was always far too good for me. Everyone knew it but her.

I tried to stay away, but I was weak.

And I hurt her.

Crushed her until she barely resembled herself. Forced her to follow a path she would never have willingly chosen.

And then she was gone.

And my world has never felt as empty, as lonely.

She begged me to stay away. Not to find her. To forget she ever existed.

But that's like asking me to slice my heart in two and toss half aside.

I've never believed in fate, but when I rock up to the University of Florida, I'm ready to eat my words.

Because she's here. Like I hoped she would be. And I'm determined to prove I deserve a second chance.

About The Author

USA Today bestselling author **Siobhan Davis** writes emotionally intense young adult and new adult fiction with swoon-worthy romance, complex characters, and tons of unexpected plot twists and turns that will have you flipping the pages beyond bedtime! She is the author of the international bestselling *True Calling*, *Saven*, and *Kennedy Boys* series.

Siobhan's family will tell you she's a little bit obsessive when it comes to reading and writing, and they aren't wrong. She can rarely be found without her trusty Kindle, a paperback book, or her laptop somewhere close at hand.

Prior to becoming a full-time writer, Siobhan forged a successful corporate career in human resource management.

She resides in the Garden County of Ireland with her husband and two sons.

You can connect with Siobhan in the following ways:

Author Website: www.siobhandavis.com
Author Blog: My YA NA Book Obsession
Facebook: AuthorSiobhanDavis
Twitter: @siobhandavis
Google+: SiobhanDavisAuthor
Email: siobhan@siobhandavis.com

Acknowledgments

I'm going to keep this short and sweet this time—thank you so much to everyone who worked with me on this project. I couldn't have done it without you!

I would also like to thank my street and ARC teams and bloggers the world over for supporting my work.

Thanks to family and friends, especially my husband and sons, for facilitating me to live my dream.

Most importantly, massive thanks to all the readers who have embraced my Kennedy Boys and empowered me to continue this series. I have a special surprise release announcement coming soon along with Kalvin's book in July/August. *Saving Brad* will be the fifth book in the series which I'm aiming to release before the year's end followed by *Seducing Kaden* in early 2018. The other boy's books will follow thereafter, provided there is continued demand for the series. I'm also releasing a standalone new adult contemporary romance before the end of 2017 (provisionally entitled *Inseparable*) that I am super excited about. Subscribe to my newsletter, check out my website, or follow me on Facebook for full series information including expected release dates.

Glossary of Irish Words and Phrases

The explanation listed is taken in the context of this book.

Bedside locker » Nightstand
Bill » Check
Bloody » Damn
Boot » Trunk
Car park » Parking lot
Chuffed » Pleased
Cling Film » Saran Wrap
Come the heavy » Act strict
Cooker » Stove
Dressing gown» Robe
Duvet » Comforter
Euromillions » The EU state lottery
Fecked » Fucked
(Well) Fit » (Very) Hot
Footpath » Sidewalk
Guts me » Upsets me
Gutted » Heartbroken
Happy out » Happy
Hob » Stove
Jelly » Jello
Kitted out » Equipped, dressed
Knickers » Panties

Knocked (him) for six » Knocked for a loop
Lethal » Awesome/Incredible
Lift » Elevator
Mobile/Mobile phone » Cell
Mum » Mom
Not a patch on » Not (nearly) as good as
Press » Cupboard/Cabinet
Piggy in the middle » A person caught in an awkward situation between two people
Puncture » Flat tire
Ride » Hottie
Spoofing » Lying
Sucking the face off » Making out
Tarmac » Asphalt
Trinity » Trinity College Dublin (TCD)

Books By Siobhan Davis

TRUE CALLING SERIES

Young Adult Science Fiction/Dystopian Romance

True Calling
Lovestruck
Beyond Reach
Light of a Thousand Stars
Destiny Rising
Short Story Collection
True Calling Series Collection

SAVEN SERIES

Young Adult Science Fiction/Paranormal Romance

Saven Deception
The Logan Collection
Saven Disclosure
Saven Denial
Saven Defiance
The Heir and the Human
Saven Deliverance
*The Princess and the Guard^*
*The Royal Guard^*
*The Assassin^*

KENNEDY BOYS SERIES

Upper Young Adult Contemporary Romance

Finding Kyler
Losing Kyler
Keeping Kyler
Loving Kalvin
*Saving Brad**
*Seducing Kaden^*
*Forgiving Keven^*
*Adoring Keaton^*
*Releasing Keanu^^*
*Reforming Kent^^*

STANDALONES

New Adult Contemporary Romance

*Inseparable**

MORTAL KINGDOM SERIES

Young Adult Urban Fantasy/Paranormal Romance

*Curse of Gods and Angels^*
*Infernal Prophecy^^*
*Mortal Ascendance^^*

SKYEE SIBLINGS SERIES (TRUE CALLING SPIN-OFF)

New Adult Contemporary Romance

*Lily's Redemption^*
*Deacon's Salvation^^*

*Coming 2017
^Coming 2018
^^Coming 2019

Check www.siobhandavis.com for updates in relation to new releases and publication dates.

28298996R00195

Printed in Great Britain
by Amazon